# ALWAYS READY

## A THRILLER

## Jake Clay

## STRATEGIC PATRIOT

Castle Rock

# STRATEGIC PATRIOT

Manufactured in the United States of America

10 9 8 7 6 5 4 3 2 1

Library of Congress Cataloging-in-Publication Data

Names: Clay, Jake (Jacob), author.
Title: Always Ready / Jake Clay
Description: Softcover Edition
ISBN 978-0-9912032-5-3 (Digital Edition) | ISBN 978-0-9912032-6-0 (Softcover)
Subjects: FICTION / Thrillers.
ISBN 978-0-9912032-6-0

*To all those who stand firm and resolute for Faith, Family, and Freedom.*

*"Hard times create strong men. Strong men create good times. Good times create weak men. And,* **weak men create hard times.***"*

- **G. Michael Hopf**, *Those Who Remain*

# Prologue: The Ranch

Mitch took a slow sip of his favorite type of dark coffee as the first light of dawn crept over the majestic Rocky Mountains. From his cabin porch, he had a breathtaking panoramic view of the valley below, the mountains rising steeply on all sides like ancient stone sentinels. Their snow-capped peaks gleamed, not yet touched by the warming rays of the morning sun.

These mountains had been a constant in Mitchel McKinley's life for as long as he could remember. Born and raised on a cattle ranch just outside the small town of Cripple Creek, he had grown up exploring every ridge and valley, every stream and meadow. He knew every trail and shortcut through these woods like the back of his hand. As a young boy, he would often wander off into the forest for hours at a time, climbing trees and catching fish in the creek. His parents never worried though, knowing Mitch was at home in the wilderness.

The land here was in his blood, flowing through generations. His great-grandfather had secured the ranch back in the rowdy mining days as the veins dried up. Before that, it had been pristine hunting grounds for the Arapaho and Mitch felt their legacy still dwelling in these lands. On quiet nights when the stars blazed bright in the sky, he could almost feel the past as he sat in front of a roaring campfire.

Cripple Creek had once been a booming mining town, attracting prospectors and outlaws alike during the days of the Gold Rush. It had seen its fair share of gunfights, saloons filled with liquor and ladies, and people in search of the pursuit of happiness. But those wild days were long past now. The last mines declined decades ago and the rowdy crowds moved on to better prospects. Now the town was a faded time capsule, a sleepy tourist attraction with quaint cafés, antique shops, and a handful of small casinos trying to revive the vintage charm.

A strange mix of the mining strikes of the old west was now combined with the colorful lights of small casinos. In an effort to revitalize and with the changing times a new behemoth of a casino was being built in the center of town. This pushed more people away from living along the main street and many people didn't live in the town anymore.

The ranch he lived on with his wife, kids, and parents had almost been lost too many times. On top of that, growing up in Colorado was not an easy life, population booms brought in new ideals and drove up the cost of everything.

But the mountains endured, generally unchanged by time or humanity. For Mitch, they were a constant reminder of simpler days gone by - days of working the ranch, riding horses, and camping under a blanket of stars. Before terrorism and war had touched his life. Before he'd felt the call to serve his country and start his own adventure.

The 9/11 attacks had rocked the nation to its core. Like so many others, Mitch was moved to join the fight against the things threatening Americans. Though he cherished his Colorado roots, patriotism outweighed his personal dreams.

Like his father, his grandfather, and many generations before them, it was his turn to answer the call of his country. Taking his oath of service after the World Trade Center's ruins ceased billowing smoke. He immediately found the Coast Guard appealed to him the most.

The motto, Semper Paratus - Always Ready, along with the values of Honor, Respect, and Devotion to Duty rang true in Mitch's heart. These critical values he was raised knowing and living by naturally fit who he was.

His service to America was rewarding but demanding. The recruiter never told him it would be easy and that the needs of the service would always come first. Counter terror, drug interdiction, rescue operations and other missions kept him at a constant state of readiness. Staying squared away had its perks though, and he quickly found himself getting promoted by his commanders. He loved the action, but as time went on there was always something missing.

The girls in town were cute and they flocked to the guys in uniform, but they never went anywhere and those girls were not the kind of lady you would bring home to meet your mom. As God would have it, Mitch met Emily randomly at the Denver airport while on leave visiting home. Waiting for a flight, the two carried glances until Mitch mustered the courage to talk to her. Instantly the two became inseparable and married months later. The first few years were great, even though the constant missions and needs of the service burdened stress on their relationship. Mitch knew anything worth any good would always require hard work.

That hard work paid off and two amazing children blessed their lives within a short span of time. Promotions and higher leadership doors opened quickly which gave Mitch the idea of going career and leaving the action behind. That was until Colorado finally called him back home for good.

Mitch picked up the phone and he could instantly tell his mom was fighting back tears. His father had suffered a heart attack. Mitch felt his heart sink at the news and would never forget hearing his mothers shuddering sobs. He had always been so close to his dad. While still on the phone, he prayed for his parents, desperately asking for help from God. Mitch knew he had to do something, but was faced with two options: Go back home and help his father who could no longer handle the grueling ranch work alone, or follow his career so he could better support his family and serve his country. The family land that had been passed down through generations was at risk. Ultimately, he knew what the right thing to do was.

Taking his honorable discharge with him, Mitch packed up the family from the Atlantic coast and headed back home with a heavy heart. He feared this would be a drastic mistake, but he put his faith and trust in God taking this plunge. Transitioning to civilian life was challenging. It meant going from a culture of honor and common sacrifice to a place where most people were in it for themselves. Mitch recalled praying during the long, exhausting drive to Colorado. Emily was nodding away, and the kids had been asleep for hours. Mitch pleaded with God to help him and his family during this hard time, and felt assured that He would provide.

Upon arriving home, God seemed to bless him with an opportunity within weeks of his arrival. The fire station in Cripple Creek desperately needed an experienced medic and a new local coffee shop was hiring, so there they were starting their new life off great. Mitch never expected he would return to Colorado. Once he had pondered the idea while on the deck of the ship, staring at the horizon of the sea, watching the large tall swells that brought vague reminders of the Rocky Mountains he had left behind so long ago.

For the first year, living with his parents in the old family ranch house was definitely not the easiest. Mitch And Emily began saving up to finally secure the down payment to build their own place. The six of them under one roof tested everyone's patience. Mitch's mother tried her best to give them space, but the house's thin walls meant no one had privacy. His own family had more than enough of their own struggles.

Months of endurance took its toll, and Mitch caught his first break when the fire chief announced his retirement and the town offered him the job. Even with the bump in pay, Mitch had to use much of his savings to start constructing the modest cabin for his family and eventually raise a decent sized working barn.

Being out on the far outskirts of town close to Pikes Peak and having over a hundred acres had its own perks. It was enjoyable to have a quiet spread and wonderful views of the surrounding mountains. He reconnected with his roots, remembering his childhood and began looking forward to his family having similar experiences.

After long days responding to emergencies or serving lattes, the young couple dreamed of having their own home. Mitch set to work clearing a site up in the hills above the ranch. Using lumber from their land, he and the contractors labored weekends and off time to build a cozy cabin. It was nestled comfortably at the edge of a spruce grove overlooking the valley, with the soaring mountains in the distance. A year later, they finally had their own little slice of paradise.

Now, taking another sip of his coffee as the first light of dawn illuminated the peaks, Mitch was thankful for the quiet solitude. The problems of a fractured nation and a chaotic world couldn't reach them here. No matter how turbulent life became, these enduring peaks would always be home. Their steadfast presence was etched into Mitch's very soul and as he came to think about it more. Some roots could never be severed.

Mitch's moment was broken by the sound of little feet speeding down the hall. His five-year-old daughter, Mary, came bouncing out onto the porch in her footed pajamas, her hair a tangled mess.

"Morning Daddy!" she chirped, crawling up onto his lap. Mitch planted a kiss on her forehead.

"Morning, sweetie," he began rubbing little circles between her shoulders and said, "You're up early."

"Wanna see the sun rise," she replied, gazing out at the light creeping down the mountainsides.

Mitch treasured these quiet moments with his daughter, knowing too soon she'd be grown and the years would fly by.

Before long, Emily emerged from the house too, their toddler son, Mark, nestled against her, still half asleep in nothing but a shirt and fresh diaper.

"I hoped I'd find you both out here," she smiled, leaning in to give Mitch a kiss.

"Daddy, can we go fishing today?" Mary asked hopefully.

"Sure thing, honey. I know just the spot."

After a breakfast of eggs Mary had taken from their chickens, and bacon from their late pig, aptly named Sir Bacon, Mitch loaded up their pickup truck and took Mary down to the creek near the old family homestead. He had fished here as a boy and was still deeply connected to it. He showed her how to bait the hook and cast the line. She shrieked in delight when she got a nibble from a trout.

Mitch snapped photos on his phone, knowing his father would ask to see them later. As the sun climbed higher, the July heat drove them back to the cool shelter of the cabin. Mitch spent the afternoon tidying up, preparing for the big Independence Day barbecue tomorrow.

Friends and family would drive in from surrounding towns to eat, drink, and watch the fireworks in the center of town. Being the fire chief had its perks and as long as there wasn't a regional fire ban, the town would have quite the show.

Emily busied herself in the kitchen, chopping fruit for pies and teaching Mary to knead dough for homemade rolls. Mitch smiled at her as he swept. She had flour on her nose and in her hair. He knew he was lucky to have her by his side through all the ups and downs. Even with two kids now, she was still the most beautiful woman he's ever seen.

By late afternoon, Mitch was changing out the flag for his favorite embroidered American flag that he kept extra clean just for the fourth. He chuckled when he saw a familiar rusty old truck bumping up the road. His younger brother, Aaron, hopped out, still clad in his oil-stained coveralls. Though they worked together on the family ranch, Aaron had a job as the sole mechanical expert in town. Mitch envied his carefree bachelor lifestyle sometimes, even though he lived in his auto shop and watched every national sports game known to man.

"Thought you could use some help, just don't drop it," Aaron called out, grabbing a six pack of local Colorado beer and a bottle of Stranahan's single malt whiskey out of the cab. "Let's start the festivities a little early!"

Something's never changed, and Aaron always could be counted on to splurge on a good bottle of Colorado whiskey. The brothers spent the next couple of hours talking about town gossip and the state of the Union.

"So, have you given any more thought about my offer?" Aaron asked.

Mitch sighed. His brother had been trying to convince him that they should take out a loan, expand the small cattle herd, and get a few goats. With beef prices going higher, it seemed a sure profit. But Mitch worried about taking on more debt when money could get tight fast.

"I don't know, the timing's just not right now," he replied. "Maybe in a few months, once we better know who is getting into office this time, and why goats?"

Aaron shrugged, "why not" and changed the subject. They sat for a while chatting until Emily gave them the last call for dinner that was now hours cold. Mitch was the first to get up a little quickly, causing a slight stumble.

"You need to get out more often, you lightweight." Aaron exclaimed.

Eventually the two went inside as Emily's laughter at the brothers bickering and their dad's judgmental stare for coming in so late to dinner. Over heaping plates of pot roast and roasted veggies, talk eventually turned to plans for the next day's festivities. After the delicious meal, Mitch gave quick kisses to Mary and Mark on the forehead. Aaron secluded himself to watch another game with dad, and mom went back to working on completing her puzzle in the living room.

Mitch joined Emily out on the porch swing to watch the sunset fade behind the mountains. The sky turned a dazzling orange and pink as the valley slowly darkened. Mitch slipped an arm around Emily's shoulder as she nestled against him.

"Remember our first Fourth of July here after we moved into the cabin?" Mitch asked. "Just you, me, out on this porch?"

Emily laughed. "We've come a long way from those early days."

Mitch nodded. Tomorrow they would be surrounded by family and friends, two kids underfoot. But he would savor tonight's last moments of tranquility. Here in the privacy of twilight, he felt profound gratitude to the good Lord the life they had.

The next day, they were all back in Cripple Creek. Mitch noticed his parents as they unloaded their car, his father moving slower these days but eyes still bright. His mom encouraged him to pick up the pace a little. Then Aaron pulled up with his latest girlfriend in the passenger seat. He felt a slight pang, wishing his brother would settle down and find someone special. Friends of the family waved or mingled throughout the afternoon.

About a dozen kids were now chasing each other around the town's playground. Mitch and Aaron fired up the grills outside the station, the smell of sizzling burgers and hot dogs filled the air. The fire engine was prominently displayed front and center while being positioned to block cars from traveling down Main Street.

Mary shrieked as she waved around a sparkler in her hand. Watching her joy, Mitch wished he could freeze this moment in time.

After everyone had eaten their fill, the adults lounged lazily in lawn chairs, watching the kids play as dusk fell on the Fourth of July gathering, Mitch sat back in his lawn chair surveying the scene before him. His daughter Mary was still running around giggling, despite the long day's excitement. Emily and his mom were chatting amiably over the last slices of pie while his dad dozed lightly nearby, Mark napping in his lap. Other friends and town folk lingered in clusters, plates on laps, enjoying the music from the local band.

It was a quintessential small town holiday celebration, filled with food, fireworks, and memories in the making. But as Mitch looked around at the people he loved, he felt a twinge of unease, an undercurrent he couldn't shake.

Maybe it was the awareness he was ingrained with, always watching for threats, being always ready for anything. After years in the Coast Guard confronting dangers on the high seas, he was conditioned not to fully let his guard down. Or maybe it was a subtle shift in the atmosphere he had noticed since coming back home.

While Cripple Creek still looked like that charming tourist town on the surface, there was a tension now below the surface. Businesses struggled to stay open, and some families had lost their ranches. New problems afflicted those who felt hopeless about the future.

At the fire station, Mitch saw the darker side of the mountain paradise firsthand at times. The bigger issue that the town was bracing for was the potential war the nation could face in the not too distant future. In the years since he left the service, the threat of terrorism had diminished but tensions abroad had only risen. Mitch replayed the escalating geopolitical crisis in his mind. The formation of a strong anti-American axis not seen with World War II concerned him greatly. With China's economic strength and military buildup, they were positioned to challenge U.S. dominance. Russia, Iran, North Korea, and others further attacked and destabilized regions to sow chaos.

Intel reports he read on his departure showed these adversaries closely coordinating to counter U.S. influence across multiple fronts such as militarily, technologically, economically. Their objective was clear: displace America from its superpower perch. As a veteran, Mitch knew the U.S. needed to be prepared for such a multidimensional threat.

Even this morning's news reports spoke of artificial intelligence related cyberattacks traced back to China that had hit Denver's utilities and transportation networks causing a temporary shutdown and blackout. Russian state sponsored hackers secured classified information pertaining to a new military project. Iranian disinformation campaigns boosted discord online and another ballistic missile test by North Korea flew over the island of Japan.

In the quiet of the Rockies, it was easy to feel detached from the growing tensions. But Mitch knew international crises had local impacts. Disruptions to infrastructure or civilian life could spark true emergencies. As the fire chief, he had already begun contingency planning while also pushing the town mayor to shore up any vulnerable systems.

Over the next few months, Mitch redoubled training his team. They ran disaster simulation after disaster simulation - cyber attacks, infrastructure failures, civil unrest, even biological incidents. He stockpiled emergency supplies and strengthened communications the best he could with a very limited budget.

Mitch was determined to ready his town to withstand the mounting global storms on the horizon. But deep down, he wondered if anyone truly grasped just how dark those storm clouds had become.

As laughter echoed from down the main street, Mitch glanced up at the mountain peaks now shrouded in dusk. This landscape was still breathtaking, but lately, he caught a glimpse of something else in those wooded slopes and valleys. A foreboding he couldn't articulate.

Shaking off the unease, Mitch turned his attention back to his community. His daughter Mary appeared before him, covered in streaks of dirt and mustard stains but still beaming.

"Daddy, is it time for fireworks?" she asked hopefully.

"You bet," Mitch replied, as he jolted himself back to the realization that he had forgotten to check the time.

Mary's giggles receded as she scampered off into the thickening night. Mitch marveled that she was growing a little bigger every day. He wished he could always keep her this small, this innocent.

Mitch wandered back out pulling a large wagon full of fireworks. His brother Aaron was there now, leaning against the railing in amazement.

"Long day, huh? Seems you almost forgot that it's showtime" Aaron shouted for all to hear.

"The best kind of day though," Mitch replied with a contented smile.

Mitch double checked that the final row of fireworks was securely fastened to the metal rack suspended above Main Street. The annual 4th of July display in Cripple Creek would be legendary and he wanted to make sure everything went off without a hitch.

As fire chief, it was Mitch's responsibility to ensure the town's safety. But he also took pride in this patriotic tradition that brought the community together. After another hard year, the town could use the unity and joy this display would provide.

His brother Aaron walked over carrying a box of fuses. "Everything lookin secure up there?" he asked.

"Ready to rock and roll," Mitch replied.

In the distance, Mitch saw the townspeople beginning to gather in the streets below, waving American flags and cheering in anticipation. Children laughed and parents snapped pictures, all eager for the festivities to begin.

It warmed Mitch's heart to see Cripple Creek coming together like this. As the sun dipped below the mountains, he looked up and said a silent patriotic prayer for the nation and its leaders.

Looking back down and with a nod to Aaron, he raised his arm to signal it was time. His brother's face lit up with a crazy Griswold kinda smile as Aaron was finally able to touch the launch button...and the sky exploded in a cascade of red, white, and blue colors. The celebration had begun.

The two stood together as brothers should. Enjoying the boom of fireworks echoing from the walls of the towns buildings and the hills surrounding them.

"We really have a nice setup here," Aaron said. "Makes me think maybe I should finally try to settle down too."

Mitch nodded, feeling that pang again for his perennial bachelor younger brother. "You'll find the right one when the time's right."

"I hope so..." Aaron muttered, as he looked over to his new fling. They each cracked open a beer and clinked the bottles together.

"To new beginnings?" Aaron said.

"I'll drink to that," Mitch replied.

Emily soon emerged with Mark in his stroller. They joined their quiet contemplation. "Looks like you two are pondering the meaning of life," she teased gently.

"Just feeling grateful," Mitch said, pulling her close and kissing the top of her head.

Tomorrow it was back to normal, the town emptied of people again. As much as Mitch cherished these moments of togetherness, he was anticipating solitude. But for now, he would savor the glow of this perfect holiday, pushing his vague foreboding to the back of his mind.

The rest of the summer and the fall was a blur of daily routines - work, ranch chores, managing the kids. When Mitch wasn't on a shift at the fire station, he was often out on the back forty mending fences or looking for lost calves.

In his rare downtime, Mitch began going through the family heirlooms and things that his mother had been organizing. Most of it was mundane - old photos, rusted tools, even a few collector coins. But tucked away in a battered suitcase, Mitch made an unexpected discovery.

There, bound in rotting leather, were his great-grandfather's old prospecting journals from the gold rush days. Filled with tales of adventures in the high country, small nuggets found and lost, sketches of rugged landscapes. Mitch itched for an escape to those open wilderness spaces.

The cool quiet of the forest trail was calming to his soul after so many days of noise and responsibility at the station. Mitch walked for hours, meandering without a plan, simply letting the towering pines and fresh mountain air revitalize his spirit. All while on a quest for gold, knowing that he would probably come back empty handed.

Finally, he stopped on a ridge looking down across the vast valley the good Lord had set before him. The sight of soaring peaks and waves of tall pines made him stop everything to just gaze at its majesty. Here was the solitude and grandeur he craved. Settling with his back against a boulder, Mitch drank deeply from his water bottle, then closed his eyes and just listened to the profound silence.

When he opened them again, the hair on the back of his neck was standing up. His internal alarm sounded, though nothing seemed amiss in the serene wilderness. Then he glimpsed it again - that strange foreboding, like a charge of electricity in the air.

Every gut instinct told him he was being watched. But up here miles from anywhere, it was impossible. Uneasy now, Mitch headed back down the trail toward home, one hand hovering near his holstered pistol. The idyllic escape of the morning felt somehow ruined now.

Mitch crept quietly through the brush, eyeing his own boot prints ahead intently. As he was about to step over a downed log, a massive thud nearby made him freeze. It was so strong that he could feel it through the ground he was standing on.

He looked up slowly, heart pounding. Just yards away, a massive bull moose stood watching him, ears pinned back in agitation. Mitch held his breath, praying it would back down.

But the moose pawed the ground and lowered its massive rack of spooned antlers, squaring off for a charge. Mitch edged away carefully, keeping his eyes locked on the beast. Mitch moved and stumbled in his haste as he quickly looked for anywhere to take cover. With a savage grunt, the moose launched itself at him.

Aspen branches whipped his face as he sprinted wildly through the woods. Hooves thundered behind him like an approaching freight train. He frantically scanned for anywhere to take cover when he saw a small grouping of pines nearby.

Without hesitation he leaped into the center, crouching as low as he could. Slowly gripping the pistol, Mitch watched as the antlered fiend closed in.

The moose broke into view through the green pine branches just feet in front of him. Now only a matter of a yard away, Mitch had to make an immediate life altering decision:

Run and face certain trampling;

Hide and hope it passes;

Fight and risk enraging it more.

Gripping his pistol tight, he stayed as still as possible and held his breath. His heart was surging with adrenaline as he hoped he had made the right decision. Hesitantly, he closed his eyes and prayed for safety and protection at this moment. Prayed for his family to not become fatherless and a chance to come home tonight even if it meant being seriously injured. His very life now comes to this defining moment.

No help on the way and now a deadly dance between this moose and him with no end in sight.

The lurking beast blew puffs of steam into the cold air as it snorted and stared directly at Mitch's hiding spot. After what felt like an eternity, it slowly backed away, eyes still locked on him. In that moment, even in this modern age, the old frontier struggle for survival had never ended.

Man and beast squared off on this majestic, unconquered land. As violent as it might become at any second, a strange sense of honor between the two began to emanate. Eyes still locked on one another, the moose looked left as its small herd began to parade out of the tree line in the distance.

At that moment, Mitch realized that he and this magnificent creature were more alike than different - both doing what they must to protect their own. With a final snort, the bull moose turned and trotted off to rejoin its family.

Mitch slowly collected himself and re-holstered his pistol, hands shaking. He walked back home with a newfound respect for the mountains his grandfather had warned him about.

Out here, there was a code to this wilderness that had to be honored. And Mitch knew he must tread more lightly here and that he better respect the mountains because the mountains would never respect him.

# Prologue: The Reckoning

Over the ensuing weeks, Mitch became increasingly unsettled by a vague sense of things not being quite right with the world. Daily there were new reports of power failures, threats between countries, and rising cost of most necessities.

At the grocery store or post office people seemed guarded, conversations hushed. Even Emily was growing concerned with the mood of tension in town. Mitch just felt numb to the sensationalized tabloid as always as he read the headline that Emily was fixed on.

"I'm sure it's nothing..." Mitch reassured her, though the platitude sounded hollow even to him. To occupy his mind, he threw himself into plans for Mary's 7th birthday party in two weeks. She wanted a camp-themed celebration, so Mitch was building a faux campfire from papier-mâché, amassing kid-sized tents and sleeping bags for a campout in the living room due to the snow. The preparations filled him with nostalgia for his own carefree childhood in these mountains.

As the day arrived, other thoughts were pushed aside by Mary's infectious excitement. This would be the party she'd remember forever, and Mitch wanted it to be magical. The games and s'mores were a hit with her friends. After gifts were opened, the girls settled into sleeping bags to tell ghost stories by flashlight.

Later, as Mitch put a drowsy Mary to bed, she whispered, "This was the best birthday ever. I love you Daddy."

"Love you," he whispered, kissing her forehead as her eyes fluttered shut.

Leaving her room, Mitch stood a moment taking in the disarray. The floors littered with wrapping paper, half-eaten cake strewn across the table. Evidence of a house filled with joyful childhood mess. It was these ordinary moments he lived for.

If only he could shake the ominous undertone that had crept into the edges of his consciousness.

Over the next few weeks, a darkness seemed to descend over Cripple Creek even though Christmas was not too far off. At the diner, the hardware store, even church, the once-friendly banter was now clipped and wary. Mitch noticed more houses up for sale, more stores shuttered. Whatever was happening remained unspoken.

Late one night after a meeting for the Gold Camp holiday light parade. Mitch came home to find Mary still awake, sitting with Emily on the couch. She turned her wide, frightened eyes up to her father as he came in.

"Daddy, I'm scared. I saw a weird looking man down at old man Cartman's place."

Mitch felt his pulse quicken and immediately he was reminded of his encounter with the moose. The honor and responsibility he had for caring for and protecting his family - was man any different from the beasts in this manner? He thought to himself. That moose had charged to defend its own kin, just as Mitch was willing to do anything to keep his loved ones safe.

Out here in the untamed wild, he pondered, the codes that governed man and beast were more similar than different.

He brought himself back to the conversation at hand, resolving again to be more aware, more respectful of the ancient codes that still held true through these mountains. There were laws unwritten here long before man settled it and it would serve Mitch well to remember that.

The Cartman ranch had been empty for years after he passed, but someone had recently started leasing it. He hadn't met the new occupant yet and they didn't seem to want to meet anyone for some reason.

"What did he do, sweetie?" Mitch asked gently, sitting down and pulling Mary onto his lap.

"Nothing," she said, burying her face in his shoulder. "He looked creepy."

Mitch stroked her hair, exchanging an uneasy glance with Emily. Their isolated valley had always felt safe, but things were changing in ways he didn't understand.

"I'll make sure the doors are locked up tight tonight," he assured his daughter.

"And I'll go introduce myself to our new neighbor, okay?"

Mary nodded, reassured for now as Mitch walked her to bed. After tucking her in with her beloved stuffed bear, he sat watching her for a long time until she fell asleep. The sight of her beautiful face, eyes finally closed in peace, calmed his own nerves. She was everything to him. He would move mountains to keep her safe.

The next day Mitch walked the perimeter of their property, checking for anything amiss. He made sure no gates or fence lines were breached. But nothing seemed out of place.

In the afternoon, he slowly drove his pickup truck down the winding dirt road toward the old Cartman place. Pulling up near the dilapidated farmhouse, he saw no vehicle or signs of life outside. The windows were covered in grime and not a single light seemed on inside. If anyone was renting, they hadn't made an effort to fix it up or even put in furniture.

The snow in the yard was knee-high, the barn on the verge of collapse. Everything was still and silent except for the soft whistling of the wind.

Walking towards the barn he noticed the multiple sets of tire tracks dug into the snow. Following the trail he saw what seemed to be the muddy imprints of at least three missing vehicles that had been strategically parked behind the house. From the looks of the tracks it seemed like a larger SUV, but the strangest thing was that he hadn't even seen one in the past few weeks let alone three.

But as Mitch turned to leave, his skin prickled with the sense of being watched. He spun around quickly, peering into the second floor window of the property.

Had something just moved in there?

Was it a trick of the light and shadows?

The back of his neck tingled and once again he felt his heart begin to race. Squinting to try to see better inside, he stood still waiting for at least a minute for any hint of movement but nothing.

Uneasy now, Mitch crept toward the small barn, his right hand getting closer to his concealed Sig Sauer pistol that he carried everyday. Close enough to grab it quickly but not touching it just yet. The door hung crookedly off one hinge, revealing only gloomy darkness inside. Mitch stood listening intently for any sound.

Then he heard the sounds of minor movement inside. Moving his hand closer to the grip of his gun, he then saw what had disturbed the eerie quiet. A massive rabbit darted away and out of sight. Opening the door fully he immediately noticed a large trailer that held four very new snowmobiles on it.

These were not odd for being in Colorado, but yet again Mitch thought to himself that he would have seen this trailer as well as the vehicles.

Those SUVs were probably heavier duty and not the city slicker version that a person might use the four wheel drive on rare occasion if it even had it. Mitch was puzzled and regretted ever stopping by and hopefully no one cared that he was snooping around.

Looking back towards the house he realized his footprints would surely outline his sleuthing skills for whoever returned. Might as well leave a nice note, he was here to meet the neighbors afterall.

Going back to his truck, Mitch grabbed a pen and his pad quickly jotting down a friendly note inviting them for dinner then ending with only his first name. Quickly he posted it on the front door and got back in the truck. Shaken more than he wanted to admit, Mitch drove home with nagging unease.

If Mary had seen someone here, where were they now?

Why were they hiding or never there?

What business could they possibly have on this long-abandoned farm?

Late that night after the rest of the family was asleep, Mitch sat alone on the porch searching the darkness. Since they'd moved back to the ranch, he'd never locked his doors. This wasn't the city and he'd never faced any dangers worse than the occasional ornery racoon. But things were changing. Nowhere felt truly safe anymore.

That primal instinct warned him that peril was lurking in these once-familiar mountains and valleys. Ever since that close call with the moose, he could feel threat encroaching from all sides. And whatever form it took next, it threatened those most precious to him - his family and community. He would stop at nothing to protect them.

But how do you fight an enemy that hides in the shadows? As he thought about the encounter at the ranch more, the ominous feeling intensified, like an approaching thunderstorm just over the ridge. Mitch knew with chilling certainty that a reckoning was coming. And when it did, he could only pray that his loved ones didn't pay the price.

Mitch took a deep breath of the cold night air, letting the icy tendrils grip his lungs as he focused his thoughts. Semper Paratus - the motto that was drilled into him from his time of service. Now, as the snow clouds glow gathered over Cripple Creek, it took on new meaning.

He pulled his jacket tighter and gazed out into the darkness once more, straining his eyes to pierce the inky veil shrouding the valley below. Somewhere out there, shadows shifted and plots were possibly hatching.

What potential kinds of sinister forces had taken root in his hometown without him noticing? How far had this new Leviathan's tendrils already spread? Or was this just merely paranoia?

A thousand questions swirled in Mitch's mind, but no answers were forthcoming in the dead of night. He knew that come morning, he would need to start asking around town. Subtly at first, feeling out who had noticed what over the past weeks and months. Something was amiss in Cripple Creek, and the storm was nearly upon them.

Mitch turned and headed back to the warmth of his house, every sense on high alert. Sleep would not come easy tonight. But in the dawn light, when the shadows retreated and the town awoke, his investigation would begin in earnest.

Ready to defend his home, his people, against any threat - seen or unseen. The fight was coming to Cripple Creek.

Mitch peered in the direction of that ranch through the pitch black. Quietly he muttered aloud to himself, Semper Paratus.

He knew he needed to be ready.

**Always Ready.**

# PART ONE

# HONOR

*"It should be the **highest ambition of every American to extend his views beyond himself,** and to bear in mind that **his conduct will not only affect himself, his country, and his immediate posterity;** but that its influence may be co-extensive with the world, **and stamp political happiness or misery on ages yet unborn."***

- **George Washington**

# Chapter 1

Cripple Creek Fire Station

Cripple Creek, Colorado

December 7

9PM MST Time

Alarms echoed throughout the fire station rooms and hallways.

Mitch yelled to himself through the streaming water, "Dang it, you have got to be kidding me!"

Covered in soap and shampoo still, Mitch McKinley was in the middle of taking his shower as the alarms loudly looped again. Grabbing aimlessly, he managed to find his towel and ripped it off the rack as he tried to get as much shampoo as he could out of his hair. Like a crazed animal, he toweled off furiously and darted quickly out of the shower, headed to the call.

Engine one, Medic one, Vehicle accident CO-67. Engine one, Medic one, Vehicle accident CO-67.

"Great, this has to happen when we are flippin' short again. Why can't this just have been another medical run to the casino," Mitch muttered to himself.

Donning his uniform and turnout gear as fast as he could, he still felt the slippery residue of soap he hadn't washed out in time.

"Hey Chief, dispatch is saying this is going to be a nasty one...we'll definitely need to plan for technical rescue," shouted Dave "Davey" Armstrong from outside the door.

Shifting his left heel into his boot, Mitch started to feel the pressure rise that this might not end well. Out the massive garage door windows at the town's lights, he saw the flashing lights of the engine start up. Quickly Mitch popped up and put his suspenders over his shoulders as he moved up to the passenger door.

As he finished getting dressed, Mitch could hear the other firefighters bustling around, grabbing equipment and checking their gear. He could feel the tension and adrenaline building inside him, knowing that they needed to act fast to save lives.

Mitch finally walked into the bay, looked intently at Davey, and nodded, "Copy that. Let's saddle up and go."

As Mitch climbed into the passenger seat of the engine, he could feel his heart racing from the adrenaline now pumping slightly into his bloodstream. He knew that vehicle accidents could be some of the most dangerous and challenging situations that firefighters faced, and the fact that being called to a "nasty" one only added to his sense of urgency.

"Alright, let's move!" Mitch shouted as he climbed into the passenger seat of the engine.

"Engine one, Medic one, Vehicle accident CO-67," the dispatch repeated over the radio inside the cab.

Mitch could feel his heart racing a little after he hit the lights and siren. They exited the engine bay and swung a hard left towards the accident. As the engine sped through the quiet but twinkling streets of Cripple Creek, Mitch mentally ran through the protocols for a rescue operation.

He knew that every second counted in situations like this, and that the team needed to work together quickly and efficiently to save any lives that might be in danger.

Mitch addressed everyone, "Team, we need to work together on this one. Stay focused and communicate!"

Mitch's thoughts and actions in responding were guided by his training and experience that he knew too well. His mind wondered on how best to assess the situation and determine the most effective way to provide assistance to those involved in the accident.

What about the safety of himself and his team, as well as the safety of any bystanders or other individuals in the area? Potential hazards and taking steps to mitigate these risks?

Severity of any injuries sustained by the individuals involved in the accident, and determining the appropriate course of action based on the level of care that each person required? What equipment and would the old school jaws of life make it through another round?

Overall, Mitch's main focus was on providing timely and effective assistance to those in need, while also ensuring the safety of himself and his team.

Continuing out of town and up the hill past the mines, darkness enveloped the land. Only the headlights from the engine and red emergency lights flashed against the trees and snow were seen.

As they arrived at the scene of the accident, Mitch could see the skid marks strewn across the road and through the snow on the shoulder. But where was the car?

Turning to look down the road, the lights of a lone car were in the distance with an older lady waving what seemed to be a glowing cell phone high up in the air.

Mitch points out, "I guess we know our caller. Davey, do you see the other car? Anyone see the car?"

Looking back at the woman again, Mitch saw her arm point in the direction of the ridge off the road. Then in the faint distance they made out a little bit of light shining through the trees over the edge.

"Alright team, we've got a vehicle over the edge and people trapped inside. Let's get to work!" Mitch hollered, jumping into action.

He rushed to peer over the cliff's edge and spotted a small sedan pierced through a snarled tree about 30 feet down. The headlights cast fractured shadows through the trees as faint yelling drifted up from the car. Mitch's heart sank, but his training kicked in. Lives hung in the balance and every second mattered.

Mitch had seen his fair share of dangerous situations in his line of work and while in the military. Seeing this car precariously stuck in a few trees with a massive drop below, he knew that this was going to be one of the most challenging rescues he had ever faced.

"Davey, get the setup rigged and anchor the main line to that boulder and the engine. Phillips, ready the backboard. Smith, prep the Jaws of Life and tools. We've trained for this before, but it's dark, icy, and to be honest we only get one shot at this!" Mitch ordered.

The team leapt into motion, a well-oiled machine focused on the task at hand. Mitch quickly donned his harness as Davey set brake anchors into the ground and secured their main access line to a large rock. The rope would serve as their lifeline during the descent and rescue.

Meanwhile, Phillips and Smith prepped equipment including the hydraulic Jaws of Life that they would use to pry open the wrecked car. Phillips also hauled over the backboard that would safely transport the victim up the steep drop once freed.

"Chief, the main line is anchored and I've got you belayed," Davey called out.

Mitch nodded, doing one last check of his gear. He took a steadying breath, the smell of gas and rubber fumes coming from the cliffside churned his stomach. He pushed down the nerves that always accompanied a dangerous operation.

Focus, he told himself. Do your job. With lives in jeopardy, failure was not an option.

"Belay on, ready to lower," Davey confirmed, holding the rope taut through his gloved hands as Mitch rappelled over the edge.

Mitch descended steadily, his boots skidding on the loose gravel and eroding cliffside. As he reached the wreck, he could see the extent of the damage. The small sedan was lodged into a sturdy pine tree about 20 feet down the steep cliff side, crumpled and suspended precariously. The lone passenger was unconscious and bleeding heavily from his leg.

He heard the vehicle and trees creek eerily as he closely examined the interior of the mangled car. Fortunately, there should be plenty of static rope to get him out.

"Sir, can you hear me?" Mitch shouted through the broken window, checking for a thready pulse from the man's neck.

No response;

No movement;

No breathing.

The man had already lost a dangerous amount of blood from a deep laceration on his arm. He must have been going into shock by now and Mitch's window of time to save him was rapidly vanishing.

Carefully, Mitch squeezed through the window into the cramped space, broken glass crunched beneath him. He had to stop the bleeding immediately. With shaking fingers, he reached into his rescue bag and grabbed one of the many bandages previously staged for a time such as this. Mitch opened the gauze package and pushed the white material into the wound, immediately eliciting a raw scream of agony from the man as he briefly regained consciousness.

"I know this hurts, but I need to save you," Mitch grunted, as he plugged the wound more filling the crevices to stop the bleeding while applying pressure. "Stay with me buddy. You've got people counting on you."

The man groaned and passed out again as Mitch stabilized him as best he could in the awkwardly tilted vehicle. Then out of nowhere the vehicle began to slowly turn. Their weight together caused the balance to shift everything out of place.

"Mitch, we were losing the vehicle, you gotta get out faster," Davey cried out.

Mitch tried moving as the sound of shifting metal and creaking became louder. Before he understood where the noise was coming from, the rear of the car swung to the left and crashed violently into another tree. The impact caused him to fall into the injured man and watch as the driver door swung wide open.

The man dangled helplessly by his seat belt as the steep drop outside the door seemed like a dark abyss ready to consume them both.

Mitch maneuvered himself and used all of his strength to get his footing. Kicking out, he finally found a small foothold as the almost lifeless driver hung barely secure by the strained buckle that his seatbelt tethered him to.

"Are y'all okay?" Smith shouted.

Mitch composed himself and looked up at Smith's flashlight that was shining directly in his face now.

"Smith, stabilize the vehicle fast, we're dangling here!" Mitch yelled back.

Grabbing the dangling driver with one hand, Mitch pulled him up close and began to slip the harness on to him. The smell of alcohol on the man's clothes was so strong that it was hard to get close to his face. Gritting his teeth, he reached around with his other hand, grasping the final connectors for the harness.

"Hold on," Mitch mumbled to himself.

Glancing over his shoulder, he looked up to see Smith and Phillips rushing to anchor the dangling vehicle before it slipped further. Their figures were barely visible as the snow began to fall faster. Mitch knew securing the SUV was a crucial step.

At that moment a massive crack resounded as one of the trees holding the car broke in half. Looking in the direction of the nearby sound, Mitch saw only the remaining pine that was holding resolute but not for long.

"Hurry up, it's giving way!" Mitch yelled as he looked at pitch black below.

If his team couldn't get it stabilized quickly, they would both fall to their death at any moment.

He wasn't sure how much longer they could hang on. Adrenaline coursed through his veins, giving him the extra burst of strength he needed. Just when Mitch thought they were doomed, he saw Davey quickly drop right in next to him.

"We weren't going to let you out that easy cowboy," said Davey as he looked at the situation Mitch had been dealing with.

He braced himself as the vehicle jerked slightly and then finally stabilized, no longer able to drop into the abyss. His team had done it just in time. Now to get them to safety.

"I think we got it!" shouted Davey.

;" Mitch replied.

giving a great vote of confidence, but Mitch trusted
his             it was all the reassurance he needed.

Although, something was wrong though and then it dawned
on him. The driver's color had gone pale gray and his blood loss
was reaching a point of no return.

"Wake up, stay with me!" Mitches yelled repeatedly over and
over again. Knowing that the time to save this person was critical.
He pulled off his glove and reached around to check for more
injuries. Immediately he retracted his hand from the back of the
man's leg as he felt the piece of sharp metal lodged into the thigh.

"He's going critical, large laceration to his leg. Call in Flight
for Life," Mitch shouted.

"Roger that, what do you need Mitch," Davey replied

Mitch yelled back, "Applying a TQ before he goes into full
shock"

The small Audi proved to be a tighter squeeze than expected
and he could feel the broken glass as it cut in his forearms. The
closer he got to him the stronger the smell of alcohol became.

This idiot is going to get us both killed, Mitch thought to
himself angrily. All they seem to see anymore are drunk drivers and
seniors getting too crazy in the casinos.

Mitch positioned himself better and quickly grabbed his
trusted North American Rescue CAT tourniquet from his rescue
shoulder bag. Without donning medical gloves, he quickly prepped
the TQ and began maneuvering it into a high and tight position on
the thigh.

He could feel the warm blood now all over his cold hands, at
least the warmth was a good sign.

Getting it just right into position, Mitch pulled the strap as
tight as he could and reached around until he found the windlass.

Now he could feel his hands shaking from the bitter cold but he managed to keep tightening it until the bleeding slowed to a stop.

Then he did one more rotation for good measure and tried to fit his finger under the strap. Outside, the team worked urgently, Smith now using the Jaws of Life to cut away the car's crumpled frame while Davey kept a vigilant watch on Mitch's lifeline.

Time crawled by agonizingly slow as Mitch sheltered the man's limp body amidst the screeching sounds of metal giving way. Finally, they succeeded in cutting out a section of the door and roof. Now came the critical part - safely extracting the victim without worsening his injuries as quickly as possible.

"Let's get it steady here," Mitch urged as they maneuvered the backboard alongside the wreck.

Davey shouted, "medevac is en route, ETA 7 minutes."

Together, they shifted the unconscious man onto the board and strapped him in securely. Before he wrapped the man in a metallic emergency blanket, Mitch kept checking on the blood soaked tourniquet.

"Easy does it, watch his leg," Mitch coached as they finally worked him out of the vehicle.

The rope creaked and groaned under the strain as Phillips slowly cranked the brake winch. Then Mitch felt the slight shift below his feet. Catching him by complete surprise, the tree supporting the car started leaning.

All at once and in a split second it gave way, taking the car down the cliff with it. Mitch held tight to his rope as he zipped up and through the passenger car door. He dangled nervously in the air by his rope where the car once was knowing that he almost died.

Looking below he saw only the headlights of the car rotating as it rolled time and time again until all light was finally extinguished when it finally hit the bottom.

Mitch steadied his breathing as he took in the scene before him, but all he saw was darkness now. As they both dangled together, he thanked God that they narrowly survived. Phillips began the crank again, pulling them quickly both up to safety.

It wasn't over yet. Taking one final glance into the dark void below, Mitch returned his gaze back to the driver whose lifeless complexion embodied the full severity of his injuries.

"He's dying on me!" Mitch yelled to his team.

Phillips began to crank harder until Davey and Smith were able to get a hand on the stretcher handles. Mitch pulled himself up to the edge and managed to get back up to the road on his own.

He watched as Smith desperately tried to resuscitate the driver with CPR, as Philips gave Smith the bag valve mask to supply oxygen while preparing an IV to give much needed blood.

Bang!

Davey sent a flare arcing into the night sky, Mitch turned his attention to up as the burning red beacon pierced through the snowy clouds above.

"I sure hope they saw that one, or we're in deep stuff. No ambulance is going to be able to make it out of here now." Davey claimed.

Mitch reached over and checked the driver's thready pulse again, unsure if the man would make it through the night. But he pushed down the doubt as he pushed harder to find a femoral pulse. He'd done everything humanly possible. It had to be enough but he was in God's hands now.

Out of nowhere the helicopter's lights suddenly pierced the night sky as it sped quickly to their position. Mitch stood motionless, covered in blood, dirt, and shards of glass that still clung to his torn turnout gear. He ran a shaking hand over his face, feeling the sting of a dozen cuts and scrapes now that the adrenaline was wearing off.

Within seconds snow began blowing like a violent tornado, whipping the trees in all directions.

The worthwhile pain of getting help when they needed it the most and the bone-chilling chaos of being stuck in a snow globe that seemed in the hands of a toddler. Within seconds things calmed to a bearable level.

Mitch covered his face with his hand and looked up. The helo now hovered above all of them as the rescue basket was lowered down to the snow-covered road. Davey grabbed it as Phillips moved the driver into position. Together they all strapped in the driver and then gave the thumbs up as the hoist slowly raised him into the air towards the helo.

The basket spun in the turbulent winds for what seemed like an eternity. Mitch looked back down at his hands that were now in excruciating pain, but right then everything calmed and the helo was gone.

He may not save everyone, but he would never stop trying, no matter the toll. This job required profound sacrifices, but it was a calling he would answer every time.

"Excellent work tonight team," Mitch said, clasping Davey on the shoulder. "That was one of the most challenging rescues we've ever faced. You saved us back there brother."

Mitch continued, "We never know what we're going to encounter when we respond to a call, but we always do our best to make a difference. That's why we do what we do."

Davey grabbed a bundle of rope and looked at Mitch, "That was crazy Mitch, I have to hand it to you but you could have died on that one. It was too close."

"It was too close and we'll debrief tomorrow. But for now, let's rest up and get ready for whatever comes our way next." Mitch replied.

The team worked silently to collect their scattered equipment and load the trucks before heading back to the station. They were all physically and emotionally drained, but experience told them rest would be scarce tonight. The adrenaline rush of a high stakes call could take hours to dissipate, leaving a person wired and restless even after your body gave out.

Mitch knew from experience that the images from tonight's call would be seared into his memory for some time. The precarious headlights cutting through the darkness...the man's desperate screams of pain as Mitch struggled to stop the bleeding...the burning metal smell when they cut into the ruins of the car. It would all replay on a loop once he closed his eyes.

Back at the station, Mitch slumped heavily onto the bench in front of the team lockers, feeling the oppressive weight of exhaustion finally catching up to him. He slowly began peeling off his grimy uniform shirt, wincing as the caked blood pulled at his skin and aggravated his cuts.

"That was a tough one tonight, Mitch," Phillips said quietly, washing blood and dirt from his own hands in the sink. "One of the worst I've seen. But you handled it well and kept your cool when most would have fallen apart."

Mitch just nodded, too drained to reply. Some calls you could shake off in an hour or two once the thrill of cheating death wore off. But the bad ones sunk their claws in and didn't let go for days, even weeks sometimes. He could already feel this one working its way through his veins, leaving that hollow, unsettled feeling in its wake.

"Everyone listen, I own my decisions today and Davey is right." Mitch acknowledged the whole team now.

Davey spoke up immediately, "darn right Mitch, you are the Chief, but going full John Wayne today could have gotten you killed. Emily and your kids without a dad for some drunk idiot."

The room got tense as everyone looked at Mitch waiting for his response. "Yup, I went cowboy out there and I own that. We didn't have backup...but we were his backup, drunk or not. I made that choice myself but I would never expect any of you to have to do the same."

"We get it but we would so miss you snoring every night" Davey said jokingly in order to break the moment. Even with his funny sense of humor, he would respectfully speak his mind regardless of who is in the room. "I think Emily would do quite right not having to put up with that, don't you think? Maybe you should go home and sleep it off, we got it from here."

Davey busted up laughing as Mitch couldn't help but crack a grin while shaking his head in disbelief.

"You're one to talk, I haven't had a good night's rest in over a year thanks to you and your chainsaw."

"Oh, look who has the wisecracks now," Phillips said as he got up out of the chair and headed to his bunk.

After the debriefing, Mitch headed off to his office to complete his paperwork and reflect on the night's events. As he sat at his desk, he felt the pain in his hand from the cuts from the glass. He knew that the work they do as firefighters is incredibly important, and that it takes a special kind of person to handle the pressure and responsibility that comes with the job. Maybe Davey was right and it would be best to get some sleep at home.

Then he heard the loud snoring coming from the bunks down the hall. Mitch smiled, thinking of his fellow firefighters catching some much-needed rest after their harrowing night. He felt a sense of brotherhood and camaraderie with his team, a bond forged in the flames. They have each other's backs, on and off the job.

Mitch had finished changing clothes on autopilot and briefly considered trying to grab a nap in the bunk room. But he knew sleep would be fruitless after the things he had witnessed. The images were already starting their relentless loop in his mind.

He wouldn't wish the scenes from tonight on anyone, but he wouldn't trade places with a soul on earth. Being there when people needed him most, even on the worst days, gave his life purpose.

Mitch walked slowly out into the cold night air, letting it push back the haunting screams and stench of alcohol that clung to him. With the shift over and not getting much sleep, Mitch decided it was best to head home tonight and heed the team's advice. As he walked out of the station and into his truck, Mitch couldn't help but feel that saving lives was not just a job, but a calling. He was grateful for the opportunity to serve and make a difference in people's lives, even on the toughest days.

He knew that the support of his loved ones was crucial to his well-being. After the long drive home, Mitch walked into a quiet house. Mitch was grateful for the sense of normalcy and peace that his family brought.

As he closed the blinds and headed to bed, Mitch knew that he was ready for whatever came his way next. He was proud of what he did.

With that, Mitch settled in to catch some hard-earned rest.

# Chapter 2

The Safehouse

East of Cripple Creek, Colorado

December 8

3 AM MST Time

The group gathered around the worn wooden table that sat in the dilapidated old ranch house. It was once owned for many generations by the Cartman family. Now it is being used as their safehouse as a sweet spot between Cripple Creek and their mountainous point of attack. Though the peeling wallpaper and creaky floors indicated the home's neglect and age, the team tried to make it as comfortable as possible during their stay. Living in the cold dimly lit basement was not too painful for most of them and their previous experiences throughout the third world. At least they had cots to sleep on and power.

As they looked around at one another they still spoke in the hushed voices they were accustomed to. They were not afraid of being overheard on the nearby dirt road that rarely saw traffic, but the man next door now presented a new problem for the team.

The diverse team of five Russian intelligence agents, one Chinese-American spy, and an American defector were united by a common purpose though their backgrounds differed greatly.

Viktor Ivanova, leader of the operation, was a stern man in his 40s who commanded respect. His four recently acquired teammates—Oleg, Nikolai, Anna, and Ivan—deferred to his leadership and respected him greatly for his respectable track record.

Viktor had always brought honor to the motherland and was personally appointed by top Russian leadership to ensure this mission was completed successfully. He was of average height and muscular build, nothing stood out about him except for his piercing gaze that would make anyone think twice before questioning him. The only child of a Russian oligarch, Viktor was as wealthy as he was intimidating. This allowed him to travel the world with his tactical entourage and without question.

He also loved MMA and did a great job of acting the part of an elitist snob even though he only sponsored his gladiators for the ring's amusement. It was a piece of cake for him to have his private plane arrive in Colorado and then "book out" a beautiful chateau for a very extended stay in Vail, even though it would remain empty except for his personal staff.

The rest of his team was hand picked from the best of each of their specialties just for this mission. Oleg, was the brains of the group and was a key member of the quantum computing team that developed the cyber intrusion shields. A genius, he knew how to hack anything and held the prized package in his care wherever he went. It was a one of a kind package that fit nicely in his backpack and held the capability that would change the world.

Nickolai, was a demolitions and entry expert who could create holes anywhere he wanted. Getting him into the country proved the most difficult because of his experience as both a criminal robber and terrorist. To their surprise the Canadians did not double check his Interpol records and after a short time were able to smuggle him through the northern border into Montana. Although it took longer to collect his preferred materials piece by piece, he was happy now that the local Colorado mines supplied more than enough of the explosives he needed most.

While Anna was a gem, who only knew intelligence and espionage ever since her family gave her over to the KGB when she was a small child after showing great promise. Now in her late twenties, the desire and missed opportunity to start a family ate at her. She was the team's communications, survival tactics, and evasion expert. There was nowhere behind enemy lines or in foreign nations that she could not hide and thrive. The only problem was that their team dynamic proved a worthy challenge to evade compromise, especially with Ivan.

Last on the team from Russia was Ivan "The Terrible", who was infamous for his ruthless tactics and brute experience as a Spetsnaz soldier before joining the Spetsgruppa "A", also known as FSB's Alpha Group. He was a big man and the scars on his face did not help the team's cloak and dagger operation stay very well hidden in the nearby small town. Regardless, he was needed should the team make contact with anyone trying to threaten the success of the mission. Any option was on the table for him to use as long as it was done as covertly as possible and authorities didn't find out.

Then there was the lone Chinese spy who was easily snuck through during America's border crisis and would only go by the name Kim. She was a sleek, cat-like assassin whose petite sweet exterior hid a calculating mastermind for killing and espionage. Little was known about her and everyone knew that it was probably for the best not to ask.

Viktor had run into her only once before and had heard rumors of devastation she had caused throughout the world for the interests of the CCP. As much as he was glad to have her participation on the team, the team was ultimately concerned why she was with them in the first place. If she was here, then this operation held far greater magnitude than was previously briefed to them. Additionally, the joint effort by the Russians and Chinese to operate together on American soil was a first of its kind.

Last, there was Thomas Chamberlain. He was an American defector and a former US intelligence analyst who grew disillusioned with his country's policies. He was easily swayed at his local bar and was more than willing to sacrifice his oath of services for his personal gain. He blamed America for taking everything he loved so dear when he lost his son who was serving in Afghanistan when the withdrawal went sideways. Soon after he found himself divorced, depressed, and angry.

Even though he knew he was a snake and traitor, he liked to think it took him a while before he finally succumbed to lucrative offers that kept coming his way. Had he been profiled and compromised or was he always going to be a defector? It didn't matter now, because the final offer was so grand that he ultimately had to give his secrets and services to China. He was the man in charge now and America no longer mattered to him anymore. It was time for those responsible for his misery to experience the pain he endured and most importantly the pain his son endured.

Despite their differences, they somehow quickly worked well together and had formed a professional camaraderie during their weeks of secretive work. Their latest ploy had proven successful so far but they were nowhere in the clear.

"The plan went smoothly," said Viktor, leaning over the table where a map was spread out and marked with notes in Russian and Mandarin. "We were able to stage the accident without raising any suspicions. As far as they know, it was just a dumb drunk who accidentally went off the road and died."

"Good and thank you for not killing him, he seemed like a good man but shouldn't have been snooping" said Thomas. "That takes care of the Bureau's agent who was on our trail. Now we can focus on the next steps, but Ivan almost got us made again. Was it really necessary for him to be here?"

The mood in the room tensed up immediately as Ivan shot a dirty glare at Thomas.

"Yes, and he cleaned up after his mess," interjected Viktor. "We knew we could encounter problems and that this might be a one way ticket, so don't screw this up! We are on our own out here behind enemy lines."

You could cut the tension with a knife as everyone looked at one another knowing that his words were very true. They had all been hand picked for this mission and their countries would disavow any knowledge of their involvement should they die or get caught. Calling them radicalized terrorists that unknowingly plotted against the Americans. Even though they were some of the best, they were expendable, always expendable.

"We have another problem," said Anna, the youngest of the Russian agents, a beautiful woman who nonetheless had a steely reserve. "Someone was snooping around the safehouse yesterday. I was monitoring the perimeter and the neighbor gave us a visit. He also saw our snowmobiles. What do we want to do?'

The group's expressions morphed into unease as they exchanged glances.

"He could just be curious, we don't have to get rid of him too. Plus we are in the short window now before activation," suggested Nikolai, ever the optimist. The oldest member of the team preferred to consider all possibilities before jumping to conclusions.

"Our prior intelligence gave us dossiers on everyone important in the area, he could be a minor problem. Fire chief and prior military" added Viktor.

"We cannot take any chances and he seems like trouble," said Anna, her voice firm with authority. "I think we should up our timeline immediately and especially with the weather turning for the worst."

The others slowly nodded reluctantly in agreement and looked to Vicktor for agreement. Their current locale had been chosen for its proximity to the town of Cripple Creek, where their diversion attack was planned. They'd been able to observe comings and goings from this location as they prepared their operation. But security had to come first and they were just waiting for the signal.

"Noted, start packing up supplies and begin to scrub the place," instructed Viktor. "Let's move to our next phase of operation."

The group dispersed to carry out the orders without further discussion. Once that signal was given there could be no trace left behind of their presence. Oleg grabbed trash bags and cleaning supplies from the pantry and started scrubbing down surfaces while the Russians wiped the site for fingerprints and packed up their gear. Kim took out a hammer and pried open the wallboards, removing the gear and weapons they had planted. By now, the routine was familiar for all of them.

They staged all of their loadouts and gear throughout the basement room. As they stacked mags and loaded equipment into backpacks an eerie silence overtook the room as each person focused on their task at hand. Thomas was the only one who sat in a metal chair at the center of the room and watched, once again contemplating the events that had led him here.

Despite the perilous nature of his work, he didn't regret his betrayal of his country. America had betrayed him first, in his eyes, with bad policies, graft, and needless wars. The failures that took the loss of his precious son and destroyed his life. He looked down at the picture in his hand of the two of them fishing in Florida.

He knew deep down his son would be disappointed in his decision by offering his services to the Russians and Chinese. Although, this would finally make them pay. He believed that this covert mission they were embarked on would work, just as his teammates did. The stakes were too high to fail.

As the group began winding down their preparation, rotating lookout shifts, Viktor pulled up a chair next to Thomas. He tensed and snapped out of the reminiscent daydream he was just in, now wondering if he was in trouble.

"I know this kind of life does not come naturally to you," Viktor said in a kind voice quite different from his usual brusque tone. "All this sneaking around and paranoia goes against your American nature, but you have adapted remarkably well. We're fortunate to have you on our team. You have served us well as our camouflage, making all of this possible."

Thomas gave a small smile, relaxing slightly. "Thank you. I believe in our mission—a better future, not bound by failed decisions or corrupt decision makers. America needs to change and see its true place in the world."

Viktor nodded. "We hold that future in our hands. We will not fail." He squeezed his shoulder encouragingly. Buoyed by his words, Thomas took a sip of water from his bottle. "We won't fail," he affirmed before heading back towards the others.

But as he entered the living room, he saw the team had gathered around the radio equipment, listening intently. Anna looked up grimly as Thomas approached.

"Just picked up a transmission between local fire and police," she said. "Sounds like the medical helicopter lifted our tail out alive, but he passed before he made it to the hospital. They now know he was a federal agent."

The group exchanged uneasy looks. Their clean-up efforts had been thorough, but clearly not thorough enough and soon there will be questions.

"We need to enact countermeasures, you should have just let me kill him the way I wanted to" said Ivan decisively.

Vicktor stopped him immediately with his hand up in the air, then ordered, "Nikolai, Oleg, Anna - you three sweep the perimeter with night vision. We're going to go off the grid and fully activate, except for Kim, she can handle herself."

The team jumped into action following her orders. Nikolai, Oleg, and Anna headed out to the pitch black to inspect the outdoors.

Nikolai and Anna would provide overwatch from the woods surrounding the cabin. Oleg and Thomas would hold down the fort and wait.

As the adrenaline wore off, Thomas' eyelids grew heavy. He lay down on his bedroll for a quick nap before taking the first watch. Their countermeasures were in place if anyone came knocking tonight. Slowly he closed his eyes.

A few hours later, the pale light of dawn filtered through the trees as Viktor gently shook Anna awake for her supply run. She sat up briskly, looking alert as Kim stared at her impatiently.

"We will go into Cripple Creek today to get provisions and ensure we are still on track. I need to start the diversion." Kim said, pulling on her coat and grabbing the SUV keys. "With this blizzard coming, we moved up the next phase of the plan. I will buy you all time if the feds investigate the matter."

Anna nodded. "Hopefully the weather holds off a little longer."

The team grouped together for a final planning session before breaking to their respective responsibilities.

Viktor pointed to Anna and Kim, "I decided to move up our plans, you both are going into town with Oleg. Get the supplies and get back. Kim is staying in town to take care of any issues we might have now. Thomas is going to stay here and wait for you to get back. The rest of us are going to prep in the woods and execute the final stages of readiness for the mission. Any issues?"

Everyone looked around in agreement, then began grabbing gear and moving about.

As Anna headed out, Thomas told Oleg to keep a close watch in case she needed backup. The group was tense but not panicked. They were professionals used to adapting on the fly.

Anna made good time as she drove into Cripple Creek, following winding mountain roads that were still mostly clear of snow. She parked along the charming small town's main street, gazing at the Christmas decorations and lights strung across the old-fashioned storefronts.

Holiday music played from speakers further down as parade floats were being gathered. Anna allowed herself a small smile. She had always thought about what a normal life would have been like. She knew she was too far in now and would never know what having a family was like. She had always been on her own and it was the only life she would ever know. It was a shame their operation might be her last. But such was the way of her work.

Anna quickly pushed those thoughts from her mind and walked into the small local shop.

# Chapter 3

McKinley Ranch

East of Cripple Creek, Colorado

December 8

8:30 AM MST Time

Mitch slowly opened his eyes as the morning sun shone through the small cracked curtains of the bedroom window. He let out a deep groan as he rose from the bed, his muscles still ached with soreness from the rough rescue carried out the night before. It felt as though every fiber of his body protested as he stretched his arms above his head, but the pain was a reminder of what occurred.

As he took in a few deep breaths, a smile crept across his face as the delicious scent of bacon drifted in from the kitchen downstairs, announcing breakfast.

"Daddy, bacon is ready!" came the cheerful shout of his daughter from downstairs, her excitable tone indicating her eagerness to eat soon as a family.

After splashing some cool water on his face from the basin in an attempt to wake himself up further, Mitch made his way down the staircase to find Emily bustling about the kitchen. She was cooking up a feast of food for her family as always. He spotted his youngest child Mary sat eagerly at the table, no doubt ready to hear more tales of heroism and daring from her father. Baby Mark was snuggled contentedly into his high chair, likely dreaming of the tasty morsels he would soon enjoy.

"The smell rising from those pans is absolutely amazing, honey," Mitch said gently, placing a tender kiss upon Emily's cheek in a show of thanks for her efforts. "And how is my sweet baby girl this fine morning?" he asked Mary in a soft, caring tone, gently resting his large hand upon her small upper back in a gesture of fatherly love and protection.

"Great, Daddy! Is the person you saved okay?" she replied inquisitively, her bright eyes gazing up at him, full of youthful wonder and admiration for her heroic father.

Mitch felt a pang of uncertainty at being unable to provide a definitive answer to reassure his devoted daughter. "He should recover just fine, sweetheart," he replied in as upbeat a manner as possible, hoping his expression did not betray the slight doubt lingering in his mind. "Now, let's say grace and enjoy this wonderful meal mommy has prepared for us. Mary, would you like to say the prayer?"

His eldest daughter happily obliged with a short but beautiful prayer of gratitude for the bountiful food before them and appreciation for the protection for their loving dad. Mitch then set about recounting the harrowing details of pulling the injured man from the crumpled, smoking vehicle mere moments before it plunged into the ravine below, feeling relieved that through teamwork and bravery, another life had been saved. It was these small acts that reminded him why he had chosen to return home to protect the tight-knit community that had become like family to him.

As Mitch recounted the daring rescue from the night before, he vividly recalled every pulse-pounding moment. He described the mangled wreckage of the vehicle teetering on the cliff's edge. Through the darkness and chaos, he could just make out the unconscious form of the man slumped over the steering wheel, his life hanging by a thread.

Mitch detailed the precision and teamwork required to cut the man free from his seatbelt and haul his limp body to safety seconds before the car finally slipped over the precipice into the dark void below.

Even now, the searing heat and sounds of scraping metal remained fresh in his mind. He recollected the rush, praying all the while that they weren't too late to save him.

As the family sat enthralled by Mitch's harrowing account, Emily couldn't help but feel a familiar tug of worry for her husband's well being each time he rushed headlong into danger. While proud of his heroism, she wished he didn't place himself at such risk. She gazed at him with loving concern, silently questioning if he might eventually swap his firefighting days for quieter pastures.

Mitch met her eyes with an understanding smile, sensing her lingering apprehension. In his line of work, there were no guarantees. But saving lives was his calling, and he hoped to help keep his community safe for as long as God allowed. For now, that meant savoring each new day with his family, come what may on the next perilous call.

As the family enjoyed their meal together, Mitch noticed little Mark babbling happily in his high chair, reaching out chubby hands wanting to join in the conversation. Mitch leaned over with a smile, helping the toddler grab a piece of fluffy scrambled egg from his tray.

"It looks like our little man wants to grow up big and strong like his dad!" he said with a wink. The girls giggled at their brother's antics, always happy to dote on their baby sibling.

Emily watched the tender scene with affection, yet still couldn't shake her lingering unease. "What if next time you're not so lucky, Mitch?" she asked softly. "The kids and I need you."

Mitch reached over to tenderly squeeze her hand reassuringly. "I know, honey. Serving this community is important to me. I'll always do my best to come home safe and do better next time."

After breakfast, Mitch knelt down to hug his daughter. "You girls have fun at Grandma's today. Be good for her now and help out, okay?"

He then planted a messy kiss on Mark's forehead, eliciting a squeal of laughter. Finally, he gave Emily a long, deep kiss. "I love you. Try not to worry too much."

With that, Mitch hopped into his truck and drove off, waving as his family grew smaller in the rearview mirror. As he made it into town, he was greeted by the friendly people, like an extended family. He waved to the familiar faces that spent their days running the shops and restaurants on Bennett Street. Ol' Jerry behind the counter of the Police station, Marge sweeping the porch of the Bed & Breakfast, even Susan at the gift shop gave him a friendly wave as he drove by.

Still, a nagging thought lingered in Mitch's mind about the injured driver, and whether he had truly escaped danger's grasp just yet. There was a gut feeling he had that his efforts were in vain. Only time would tell.

He headed to the fire station and noticed more preparations underway for the annual Gold Camp Christmas parade. Old Man Johnson was up on a ladder, hanging ornate lights along the street lamps. The Johnson twins, Ben and Billy, were rushing about passing out flyers advertising the festivities to visitors.

Pulling up to the fire station, Mitch was greeted by the usual morning bustle. Davey was in the office and in the garage bay, the rest of the crew were giving the fire trucks a final wash and polish.

"Hey Chief! I got some news you probably won't want to hear..." Davey exclaimed as he rushed up to his truck. "Sorry, but the guy we saved last night didn't make it. Also it turns out he was FBI."

"Are you flippin kidding me! Seriously?" Mitch barked out as he slapped the steering wheel, accidentally hitting the horn as his frustration got the better of him.

The abrupt loud sound immediately turned all the heads in the area wondering what was going on. It was unusual for Mitch to let go of his standard stoicism and show his emotions so publicly. Composing himself, he turned off the engine and headed into the station.

During a quick debrief on last night's call. Many questions popped up as everyone sat in fold out chairs circled up in the open station's bay.

"What did the flight for life say?" Mitch finally added into the conversation.

"From the report, he ultimately went into shock from the loss of blood. They tried a transfusion and everything else they could. He had already coded by the time they landed. The hospital in Woodland Park tried to revive Special Agent Ness with no success. There was also something really weird the doctors noted after the lab work." Davey briefed everyone.

Everyone looked inquisitive at him and Mitch leaned forward in his seat listening intensely.

Davey continued slowly, "He wasn't drunk."

"What do you mean he wasn't drunk! He reeked of booze! None of that makes any sense at all!" Mitch said loudly as he thrust his hands up in the air in disbelief.

"Mitch...no need to alarm them fine ladies next door at the bakery again. Especially the misses, I'd never hear the end of it." Interjected Jerry Conrad, the finest Police Chief Cripple Creek had known and largely because no one could remember his predecessor. "Heard you honkin that horn of yours and can't have you causing a ruckus in my fine town. Brought me down here to see what's going on."

"Sorry Jerry, did you hear about the agent last night?" Questioned Mitch im and effort brought him into the conversation. "Just heard we lost him and the darndest thing is that he seemed drunk as a skunk."

"Yeah, I heard he was with the FBI and was traveling through here while looking for a person of interest. There are a lot of questions I just started getting and put Officer Davidson to investigate the matter. For one, he never visited any of our bars last night," Jerry said in a reassuring manner.

Davey scratched his head and piped in, "why would you put the newbie on this one? Johnny Davidson, the newest part of the department, this might be the biggest news in town for years."

"He was the best man for the job and I trust him. He met the agent and answered a ton of questions about happenings in the town. Johnny also saw the picture of a man we hadn't seen before in Cripple Creek but swore he was in our town. Didn't have any answers for him though and neither did the people in town except for the coffee shop," Jerry continued.

Mitch lifted an eyebrow and asked, "what about the coffee shop?" Thinking about how Emily has been working extra hours now that his mom took a new liking to watching the kids.

Jerry replied, "not sure, you might need to ask them, but the high schooler might have seen him. She was very unsure though and probably not the most credible of witnesses. At least she knows how to make a good coffee. Now we wait for Davidson."

Mitch's sense of duty and internal drive kicked in. Without saying anything else, he couldn't wait to finish the debrief and find out more on his own at the coffee shop. Looking around the room, he asked if anyone had any other questions. With everyone still in disbelief that a federal agent just mysteriously died, no one seemed to know what to ask now.

With that, he asked them to pivot from last night and do a final sweep of the town to get everything ready in preparation for the upcoming Gold Camp Christmas Parade tomorrow. There was still a lot to get ready for in a little amount of time and hopefully this will be well attended even with the potential blizzard on the horizon.

Stepping out of the station, Mitch took a moment to admire the quaint stone and wood buildings that gave Cripple Creek its charming small-town appeal.

As he strolled down the sidewalk, Mitch took the time to have a short chat with locals, getting updates on things. Rounding the corner, he nearly collided with a young woman balancing two coffees in her hands. Startled, she quickly jumped back in an impressive display to avoid the coffee from spilling. She looked annoyed and was most likely a visitor from the big city.

"My apologies ma'am, didn't see you there," Mitch said, reaching to steady the drinks. He looked up to see a pair of bright blue eyes looking sarcastically back at him.

"Umm, no worries, it was my fault." Anna said apologetically realizing that she was too busy looking at all of the decor.

Mitch gave a small smirk as he noticed the Cold Camp Coffee logo on the cups. That was the exact place he was headed to next. He apologized again for good measure and carefully moved around her on the narrow town street then headed uphill towards the coffee shop. He hoped that he could at least get some answers to help answer his questions or at least a fresh cup of coffee.

# Chapter 4

Double Eagle Hotel

Cripple Creek, Colorado

December 8

1030 AM MST Time

Meanwhile, on the other side of the street, a black SUV pulled into the check in parking spot at the Double Eagle Casino. A woman dressed in tight jeans, tall boots, and a fitted black jacket stepped out. Her sunglasses obscured her face as she planned to check in under an assumed name. Kim's mission had brought her to this small Colorado town, though on the surface she tried her best to blend in as just another traveler in need of a temporary escape. The driver of the SUV waited as she walked around to the back, opened the trunk, and pulled one extra large wheeled designer luggage and then a second but much smaller roller hard case.

As she made her way to the lobby desk, she smiled at the ladies behind the counter. Little did they know, serious danger was lurking behind even the friendliest of new faces in Cripple Creek.

"Hi, I should already have a reservation. Last name is Thompson." She politely told the lady with the friendliest grin.

"May I see your ID?" The lady at the counter politely asked.

Kim looked into her purse and pulled out her exceptionally fake credentials from her very expensive designer wallet. "Here you go." As she put the ID on the counter.

"Yes ma'am, I just see it here. Only two nights and do you need any accessibility or accommodations?" The front desk lady asked as though it was required to do so even with such a fit and stunning woman. "Sorry, also is it just you?"

Kim replied in the sweetest of manner, "No, thank you. I will need a top floor room that faces down the street. I really want to see the event lights. I would have asked for a corner room but the website didn't give me the option. It's just me, my husband had an urgent work matter and couldn't join."

The ladies looked at her with empathy. It was sad to them that her husband abandoned. "We have one clean room on the top floor facing main street so you can get the best view for the parade that we have. That'll be a small upcharge, but..." As she finished the lady looked over at her colleague and they both nodded. "You don't need to worry yourself about a thing, the upgrade is on the house and we are just delighted you want to stay at the Double Eagle."

Kim smiled, "thank you, that is so kind. I really hope he might be able to join me later."

"All gambling and high stakes tables are right down this hall and to the left. Do you need anyone for your bags? I could probably get Alex over here to help in a few minutes?" The attendant continued and gestured for Alex who was down the hall.

Kim abruptly stopped her. "I can manage my bags, thank you. Which way is the elevator?"

The lady pointed in another direction and Kim continued to the elevators with her luggage in tow.

As she exited the elevator on her floor, she followed the signs until she found her room. It was on the highest floor and as she stepped in, Kim could see that it overlooked the entire main street. From here she could see just about everything she wanted to, all the way to the Police station at the very end. As much as it wasn't optimal in so many ways, it was as good as it could get.

After getting settled into the room, Kim went through her setup tasks and ran through the standard drill she was trained for. She was glad this was not a high end hotel, less people to ask her any questions and nobody was the wiser. She was just a bored American housewife looking to cut away.

Kim scanned for bugs quickly knowing none would be found, then analyzed the room's vantage points. Like a kicker about to set up for a field goal, she paced backwards from the window and then took steps to the left to position her rifle. The room was smaller than she had imagined but she had to make do.

She put her purse in the spot she stood, then Kim walked back over to her luggage and put both hard cases on the bed. Opening up the largest bag revealed protective gray foam holding a heavy barreled sniper system in .338 Lapua and one customized Glock 19 in 9mm. Surrounding the rifle inlaid in the foam were one flow-through silencer for the pistol, a top tier silencer for the rifle, a high quality scope, large multitool, a sturdy ultra light tripod, and multiple magazines.

Everything looked brand new. The rifle itself had a gray appearance and was most likely the only model they could smuggle to her even though she would have preferred sleek black. The stock was folded and she would need to pull hard to get it to lock into place fully. As she grabbed the bolt, she scanned the built quality. It was smooth and seemed to never have been fired.

Next was the glass, the scope was a little heavier than expected but the quick detachment system was solid enough to simply couple it to the top of the rifle while maintaining zero. It had small markings on it that suggested it had been boresighted perfectly already. Everything should attach to the rifle perfectly together to make an instrument of surgical precision.

All of the equipment had been smuggled through the Canadian border months ago and various accessories covertly purchased on the black market. Her only hope was that this equipment wasn't fraudulent like the last operation she was on. Nothing like getting a knockoff set of night vision that her country had poorly copied from the military industrial complex. Three hours into her mission and the left tube went out, leaving her to complete her mission with limited vision. Fortunately, that didn't inhibit her ability to make out her optics red dot to get off clean shots.

Overall, Kim was delighted to see her kit's loadout and for once it seemed that everything was genuine top tier equipment. They had spared no expense to outfit her and the team with everything that was needed. She took out the tripod and set it up directly over her purse which she then picked up.

She moved back over to the bed and began to unlock the other piece of luggage recalling the precise process. Kim looked around until she found the hidden button inside. She pressed down and then a circle immediately glowed blue from beneath the material.

With both hands she took the purse and placed the ring next to the black square at the bottom of the locked luggage. Instantly the black square flashed a blue dot and the locking mechanism inside of the bag released the clasps.

Kim then slowly began to unzip the bag carefully. Inside the smaller piece of luggage held an identical football sized device to the one that Oleg carried. It was fully surrounded by a thin lead liner and gray foam to protect it from detection.

She looked at it for a good minute studying it and recalling the orientation training she received back at the covert Chinese lab. The scientists were adamant that this was the most amazing piece of equipment the CCP had created in some time. A new form of weapon that would change the geopolitical landscape in their favor forever.

Their triumph was an understatement since they couldn't calculate the amount of time and work that went into creating both devices. They even held it closely and carried it around like a newborn. They gently placed the device in the luggage and told her that the enclosure was advanced enough to survive a significant explosion let alone baggage claim.

Snapping back from a time that seemed so long ago she remembered why she was there in the first place. Of all places in the world and here she was in this ugly little room to not raise any suspicion and accomplish this mission. What she wouldn't give right now to stay in even a four star hotel. There was a beautiful new hotel that had just opened up, but regardless she needed the clear vantage points and this was optimal.

She looked back at the EMP device. Carefully she touched the screen and the unit responded immediately glowing a small blue screen with four buttons below it. In Chinese the screen asked for the countdown minutes and then a simple arming request. Yes or No. Kim studied it for a few seconds as if game planning what to do next, then pressed No. The time might come when she needs to use this device. Thankfully for her there were two of them and the team had already moved the other one to the rally point deep in the woods.

Closing the luggage carrying the device, Kim then focused on the rifle still snuggly packed in foam. Taking it out of the case she began to assemble all of the pieces together using the multipoint times to tighten screws.

Piece by piece she meticulously constructed the system, especially and most importantly the scope. Flipping it onto the buttstock she took the silencer and screwed it in tightly until it was locked in place. Flipping it again horizontally, she then lifted the heavy rifle and placed it on the tripod.

Holding it the best she could in place, Kim had to shimmy it back and forth until it was centered. Once it was in the best placement, she clamped it down securely and tightened the tensile strength until there was zero movement.

She flipped up both scope covers and looked through the scope. Kim methodically moved around until she made out a person who was now in the crosshairs. Fine tuning the knobs, she dialed it in and started to move the throw level which adjusted the focus. An old man sitting on a bench came into her view. Slightly moving the rifle she got the angle she was looking for if she were to take a shot at this guy.

"Prefect!" Kim said to herself surprised by the overall quality of the glass.

She stepped back leaving the rifle in its place and walked to the window. It was almost eleven in the morning now and things were on track as planned. Down below she watched as Oleg waited in the car to pick up Anna who had stupidly visited the coffee shop.

The town square buzzed with activity preparing for the parade. Kids ran about, volunteers strung lights and garland along the street lamps. If only they knew what was about to happen next. Kim gave a slight grin that reflected in the glass as she continued to watch. Inserting a fully loaded magazine, she pulled back the bolt and then chambered a round.

She enjoyed what she did, maybe a little too much, but she couldn't wait for the accolades and praise she would receive once she returned back to China. If she returned back to China. Either way, to get a front row seat to the greatest show on earth was about to begin and she had been honored to be here while so many other jealous assassins would never have the chance.

Kim continued to survey the festivities through the window. Down below, a muscular man with blonde hair hustled down the sidewalk until reaching the coffee shop. She continued to watch as he opened the door and walked in.

# Chapter 5

Gold Camp Cafe and Coffee

Cripple Creek, Colorado

December 8

11 AM MST Time

Mitch sauntered into the cozy coffee shop, inhaling deeply as the rich aroma of freshly brewed coffee and assorted baked goods wafted through the air, instantly awakening his senses. Scanning the room in search of a familiar face, his gaze soon fell upon his darling wife Emily, who was diligently manning the register with her back turned towards the front entrance.

"Well howdy there, pretty little lady," Mitch drawled in a deep, rich tone resembling that of a Wild West cowboy from the movies, doing his best impression to charm the woman who held his heart. "I reckon I'll be takin' one of them black coffees, dark and don't add nothin to it."

Emily graced her husband with an amused grin, thoroughly entertained as always by his theatrics. "Only if you plan on leavin' more than spare change in the tip jar, cowboy," she playfully retorted.

Nearby, the teenage barista Samantha rolled her eyes and let out an exaggerated sigh, plainly expressing her exasperation at the pair's habitual antics once more.

"Not this again," Samantha muttered under her breath, already sensing the need to remove herself from the lovebirds' orbit lest she become further embroiled in their romantic routines. Spying her opportunity while Emily set to work filling Mitch's order, Samantha grabbed a spray bottle and cloth from beneath the counter before escaping away to wipe down tables, putting as much distance between herself and the affectionate couple as the confined space would allow.

"She's a real joy, that one," Mitch whispered conspiratorially to his wife with an affectionate chuckle. Emily fought back a laugh of her own as she focused on properly preparing Mitch's coffee just the way he preferred - strong, robust, and dark.

"Well I did happen to overhear some chatter from the ladies next door about last night's rescue escapades," Emily began in a louder tone once Samantha was safely out of earshot. "Care to tell me more than what little you mentioned this morning at breakfast?"

Mitch's demeanor changed from playful to cowardly in the blink of an eye. "Yeah about that, it was normal and that's why we have a great team at the station."

As Emily worked to fix Mitch's coffee, her eyes regarded him with keen interest and no small amount of concern. She had witnessed firsthand over the years the perilous situations he often faced in the line of duty, and still they never ceased to worry her. "Mitch, you were dangling over a cliff trying to save a dead man!" she snapped back sharply.

"How did you hear about that, especially that he died? No one knows about that, seriously no one except for the police. I just found out..." Mitch responded in a low tone and looked at the floor in disbelief still that he lost that guy after everything.

"You know word travels fast here. You had mentioned something about dangling over a cliff," she prompted gently. "What exactly happened out there?"

Mitch's expression turned serious as he recalled the night's events. He recounted in vivid detail braving the treacherous terrain, engulfed in smoke and darkness as the vehicle teetered precariously at the canyon's edge. The race against time to free the injured man from the wreckage while he did his best to avoid slipping into the abyss below.

Though exhausted from the ordeal, adrenaline had kept Mitch standing through it all. Only now in the coffee shop's warm glow did the gravity of it all hit him once more. He studied Emily with a weary but tender smile. "It was touch and go there for a bit. But we got him out, and that's what matters."

Emily returned his smile with silent understanding. She knew these rescues took their toll, seen and unseen. She handed Mitch his coffee and then gave his hand a gentle squeeze. "Just promise me you'll be extra careful out there. For our families sake and your own."

Mitch placed his hand over hers with a soft reassurance. "Always, darling. It's stressful work, but keeping folks safe - that's why I do what I do."

"So what became of the man you rescued last night?" Emily inquired, leaning forward with keen interest. "What happened?"

Mitch took a thoughtful sip of coffee, contemplating how best to respond. "That's just it..." he began slowly. "We got word earlier that he didn't make it. Perished during the medical flight."

Emily gasped softly, eyes widening. "Oh Mitch, I'm so sorry! After everything your team did to save him..." She again squeezed his hand with empathy.

He sighed, letting go and running a weary hand down his face. "We all thought he was stabilized. It's got me wondering...just upset about it all and we have a lot of questions."

Trailing off in troubled thought, Mitch glanced out the window, his sharp gaze surveying the quiet streets as fresh snow began to fall. Emily watched him carefully.

"What is it? I can tell there's something else on your mind."

Turning back to her, Mitch spoke in a low voice. "The man wasn't drunk like we all assumed. And get this - he was an FBI agent, working a case here in town."

Emily's brow furrowed in surprise and confusion. "The FBI? In Cripple Creek? Now why ever would they be mixed up around here?"

Mitch shook his head slowly. "That's the big question, isn't it? I aim to find some answers." Resolve hardened in his eyes. "This agent's death may not have been an accident after all..."

"An FBI agent, you say?" Emily responded, surprise and concern coloring her tone. "Samantha told me she spoke to a guy with a lot of questions yesterday, was that him?"

Mitch shook his head pensively. "Maybe, but I aim to find out more." His eyes flickered with a determined glint that Emily knew all too well - it meant her husband had sunk his teeth into a mystery and wouldn't let go. "I actually stopped by the café hoping to get a word with Samantha about it."

Emily responded quickly, "Actually, another man, just over there was asking Samantha questions a bit ago. He might be the agent's partner or someone who knew him. He stopped about thirty minutes ago and was asking a lot of questions from her, probably why her attitude is harsher than usual. You should go talk to him."

"Is that him over there, nose-deep in a laptop?" Mitch followed her gaze, spotting the serious-faced man tapping away.

"Reckon that's our guy," Mitch affirmed, downing the last of his coffee. He started to rise before Emily gently grasped his arm.

"Promise me you'll be careful digging into this, whatever 'this' turns out to be," she implored, clearly concerned.

Mitch offered a reassuring smile. "Always, darlin'. I just want to get to the bottom of things, for the agent we lost and this town." He pressed a kiss to her lips before sauntering over to the awaiting federal agent, prepared to get some long-awaited answers.

Mitch tried his best to appear nonchalant. He held his black coffee, taking a sip and keeping one eye on the agent the whole time. He casually meandered over to where he was sitting. "I heard you were investigating a matter," Mitch said gruffly as he pulled out the chair opposite the agent.

The agent glanced up, surprised. "Well, well, if it isn't the local fire chief gracing me with his presence. I was planning to pay you and your station a visit today." he retorted seriously.

Mitch ignored the jab. "Working on anything interesting?" he asked, motioning to the computer.

"That's classified," he replied sharply. "I am FBI Group Supervisor Charles Danvers."

Mitch held up his hands in mock surrender. "Hey, I am sorry for your loss and I just found out that your agent was the guy we tried to save last night! We did everything we could. I mean everything."

At this point and with a higher than normal volume in the cramped coffee shop the one other patron glanced up to see what all the commotion was about.

Danvers eyed him warily. "I have just as many questions as you probably do."

Mitch took a long sip of coffee before answering. "I want to know what the FBI is really doing around this town. And how nobody knew about it except maybe the coffee shop girl."

Danvers sighed, leaning back in his chair. "You know I can't discuss an ongoing investigation with you. I appreciate everything you did trying to save my agent's life which is why I am willing to share as much as I can."

Mitch fixed on the agent with his steeliest gaze. "There are good people here. If the FBI has taken an interest, fine, but it's not normal for you to be here unless there is a casino robber."

Danvers held his stare evenly. "It wasn't about a casino theft, Special Agent Eric Ness was on the tail of a person on the terror watch list. Not a radical extremism, but someone worth watching."

"Seriously! Here in Cripple Creek, you gotta be kidding me." Mitch responded amped up again in disbelief. "You have to know that I was once tied to Homeland Security. I should still hold some of my clearances, so please let me know if we need to be ready for something."

"Yes, I pulled up your file early this morning and thank you for your service. I am willing to give you a little more with the understanding that you will cooperate about everything you can and keep strict confidentiality." Danvers hesitantly replied knowing that time could be of the essence especially with a dead agent.

"You have my word." Mitch says as he holds out his hand for a handshake.

"Uh, sure. I will probably need as much help as I can get," Danvers stalls before shaking as he was not used to getting people wanting to shake hands after COVID. "I guess you aren't worried about germs and such up here like everyone can be back in the city."

Mitch smiled, "that's correct, we just like to be a little more wholesome and a bit old school even with that new fancy hotel.

"Hmmm, let's get back to business Mr. McKinley. So tell me about last night and what you know so far."

Mitch walked him through the events of last night and how the special agent reeked of booze and seemed disoriented. Giving the team the simple impression that it was a drunk that drove off the road while it was snowing. Everything seemed to be stabilized when the flight for life took off so it was a huge surprise that he died en route to the hospital.

"How do you know he was stabilized?" Danvers cut him off.

"Davey did a final check for vitals with EKG and triage check as Philips was securing him in the basket. The tape showed he had a decent heart rhythm again but a slight murmur. It was normal enough which is why we were so shocked he died."

Danvers gave him an inquisitive look squinting through his eye glasses. "Did any of you give him any drugs at all during this time?"

"No...we don't have enough time and we would have needed to get a med authorization from the doc. We gave him only what we had, but no meds." Mitch recalled.

"Sorry, force of habit with my questions. Ness as you know didn't have any alcohol in his bloodstream even though it was found in his mouth and on his body. Although, there was a needle prick to the left forearm and a substance similar to street fentanyl in his toxicological report. The doctors weren't able to find a match and neither can we." Danvers continued.

"Overdose?" Mitch pitched as a thought.

Danvers shook his head and started to get choked up a bit, "Ness has had an upstanding six years with the Bureau, not to say we haven't had issues before, but he was a friend who doesn't touch anything. He's Mormon and would get after the rest of us for just having a drink together. He was a good guy all around and left behind a wife and four kids. We are looking into foul play which is why I, I mean we are trying to find this perp. It's personal."

Mitch didn't reply for a good couple of seconds out of honor for his fallen friend. "Danvers you have my word we will help in any and every way possible."

Danvers looked Mitch intensely in the eyes "Thank you Mitch. I might need to take you up on that..."

# Chapter 6

Family Dollar General Store

Cripple Creek, Colorado

December 8

11 AM MST Time

Across town, Anna and Oleg wandered the aisles of the dollar store, grabbing essentials like bottled water, energy bars, and other snacks. The store was busier than usual this morning; they passed a few people but no one was the wiser or wanted to chat with them. This was all for the best, just get what was needed and on to the next place.

At the register, the teenage cashier rang them up quickly, eyes glued to her phone almost the entire time. Oleg paid while Anna bagged their items. Strangely she felt a twinge of sadness, looking at the meager haul and wondered when the next time she could sit down to a decent meal would be.

After the store, they headed to the grocery store on the edge of town. This place always depressed Anna a little; the lights were too harsh, the aisles cramped, the selection limited. But she knew they'd be able to get the batteries and other needed items.

Oleg appeared with several boxes of different batteries, a package of cookies and other staples. "This should last us a little while, but the cookies are all mine," he said, attempting to sound cheerful. Anna managed a weak but sarcastic smile in return.

The items at checkout met all of their mission needs and now just a few gallons of gas to top the tank. As they headed out to the parking lot, laden with plastic bags, Anna felt that familiar worry creep in. Would they have enough time to finish up and get back in time before the mission began? What if the car breaks down or they get spotted? "I'll drive this time, just in case." Anna demanded Oleg, who was about to open the driver's door.

"Fine with me. By all means go right ahead," He replied.

She tried to push the thoughts from her mind as she and Oleg drove back to town in silence. Then suddenly the tense but quiet atmosphere was disrupted by a loud crunch that echoed throughout the cab.

"Seriously Oleg!" Anna shouted out trying not to crack a smile.

Oleg had a mouth full of cookies and attempted to reply, "Want one?"

"Of course...don't know when we might get another chance." She muttered as her demeanor changed quickly to a state of apprehension.

Oleg stopped chewing as he reflected on what she just said. He stared out the window ahead as they were being rerouted down the town's back streets due to the parade's setup.

They were simply doing the best they could with what little information and time they had, but they all still had each other. For now, that would have to be enough.

As they turned onto the next street right before the church, Anna aggressively slammed on the brakes. Oleg, not having a good handle of the cookie package, accidentally caused cookies and crumbs to erupt all over.

"No!!!" He yelled as more of his cookies flew out of his possession. "Watch out Anna!"

He looked down to only see the remaining two cookies in his lap that escaped their crushing demise. A look of anger comes over him as he just realizes his last moment of happiness was just ruined by Anna. He looked over at her ready to share his enraged comments when he realized that she was frozen and staring at something outside the windshield.

Slowly Oleg turned his head to see a short athletically built man in a brown cowboy hat and jeans just inches from their front bumper. He stared directly at them fuming over their reckless driving with rage. Anna narrowly avoided hitting him, but this jerk was now in a staring standoff over the fact that they almost hit him. Without saying a word his demeanor spoke for him, communicating the angry desire to brawl right now if needed.

For a few seconds, this cowboy just stood there and then spit a wad of chew toward the front bumper.

This fired up rough rider was Duke Riggins, one of the bouncers at Bronco Billy's Casino. He was also one of Mitch and Aaron's close buddies and one of the most consistent men to attend their bible study. When he wasn't still recovering from one of bull riding injuries, Duke was in the mountains hunting or fishing.

She looked at him beyond his scruffy red beard and locked in on his deep blue eyes. She had almost run over one of the cutest rugged guys she had ever seen. Here in this little stupid town of all places.

"Get out of the way! Yeah, you." Oleg shouted as he raised his arms up in the air in bewilderment and caused Anna to finally break eye contact.

Duke, imagined that this jerk was probably her boyfriend and decided to take the high road this time. Then without prompting, he moved on while still watching them intensely. He has been in a lot of brawls in his life and he would hate to embarrass this guy in front of his cute girlfriend.

Finally crossing the street fully, he looked back in a side glance once more, noticing that she was still looking at him, but so was jerkface. He continued to walk down the sidewalk.

"Can you believe that idiot, Anna? You should have just run him over, well worth blowing our cover." Oleg continued his tirade about their close cowboy encounter. "Ever see Howdy Doody? Never mind, you were probably not even born yet. You still should have hit him but I get it, mission first."

Anna ignored his lecture and the condescending remarks about her age. What she couldn't get over was the guy she just almost ran over and the weird thoughts that forced her to think about still meeting someone.

She continued driving back to the rally point to covertly drop off a few items to Kim. Hopefully they were no longer delayed and can make it the distance back to the house in time.

Winding through the narrow small town streets, Anna finally made it to the other end of town and pulled up outside the back door to the casino where Kim waited for them. She parked the car and turned to Oleg.

"I'll need to be quick, just hand over the stuff for Kim and then we need to get going," she said.

Oleg nodded and started unpacking some of the bags. Anna got out and headed towards the rendezvous point.

Kim paced back and forth nervously. "Did you get everything on the list? I need the batteries for the rangefinder, they forgot them." she asked anxiously as Anna entered.

"Yes, it's all here," Anna replied. "How's the setup going on your end?"

"As well as can be expected given the short time frame," Kim said. "The people in town seem to be finishing up the last minute preparations now."

"Good. I'll make sure the rest of the team knows our status. We plan to move out now and get to the rally point early."

She quickly rifled through the last bag, checking things off her mental checklist.

"This all looks good," Kim stated. "You two should get going now. No room for error on timing."

Anna nodded. She turned to leave as Kim continued sorting through the supplies to double check. As they got back in the car, Oleg asked, "Are you going to tell me what the actual plan is yet?"

"No need to know the details until it's time to carry it out," Anna replied as she started the engine. "Plausible deniability, and all that. Fine. Now let's get going, we have a deadline to meet."

She drove them out of town, taking back roads to avoid any potential checkpoints or road closures due to the parade route as more visitor vehicles were making their way into town. As they neared their destination, Anna felt anxious. So much rode on perfect execution of their plan. One misstep could mean capture, or worse.

Finally, they pulled up to the completely vacant campground parking lot. Anna parked the car as far out of sight up the old logging road as possible before the tires sank into the snow effectively making them stuck. This meant they would need to begin the long hike to meet up with everyone. They got out of the car and grabbed their gear from the trunk.

Oleg unzipped the extra large black duffle bag. Pulling out two M4 style rifles, he handed one over to Anna along with a topped off magazine. Anna put the mag into the rifle and pulled back the charging handle. She let it go and chambered a round. Grabbing the scope, she took off the dust cover and then rested the rifle up against the car.

Oleg did the same thing and watched Anna who was now putting on her green tactical chest right with extra magazines already in it. Once everything was fastened, she put on her backpack.

"Oleg, a little help please." Anna said as she pointed to the strap that was stuck on part of the backpack.

Oleg walked over and fixed her issue without a word. She turned around and looked at him to thank him, as their eyes locked on each other they knew. In an unspoken code learned for the pain of past experiences. They knew that this mission was the real deal. All of the months of training, preparation, waiting, came to this precipice. Here they were standing on American soil, fully armed and ready to embark on what could be their last and final mission.

They broke their glance and walked into the woods. Fully knowing that this was the point of no return. Even if they survived, things would never be the same for anyone. If they died, then this was the way it should be. Not in an old and decrepit state at a nursing home, but on a mission doing what they loved best. To them, there was no God, they were solely in control of their destiny and victory. Still staring at one another, Oleg exhaled and a large puff of steam was let out as his hot breath met the air. Breaking their stare, Anna nodded and looked down at the snow covered ground. It was time.

They hiked up the hill, carrying their weapons and backpacks. Towards the top was a tangle of trees and bushes that provided excellent concealment to catch a break. Anna and Oleg pushed through the foliage until they found a good vantage point of the path ahead. She looked through the monocular making out the pattern of footprints in the distance, probably from the rest of their team.

Oleg looked around and prepped his loadout - extra loaded magazines and so on. Then it was time to set up his rifle. He assembled the silencer to the end then looked for a good location to test fire and ensure it was zeroed in properly. That's when he spotted the perfect target out in the distance.

He maneuvered his rifle and focused onto a stump out in the middle of a clearing in the distance ahead. He tried to aim but struggled. The bright idea that they were not allowed to use red dot or powered optics on the mission. The etched reticle was new to him and was difficult to make out to the black crosshairs. He pulled the trigger.

The muffled thud broke the silence as the round was fired.

"Anna, did you see where it hit?"

"You missed," She responded quietly.

"What do you mean it missed?" Oleg said surprised.

"Go again and then it's my turn." Anna replied as she finished fine tuning her optic.

He fired three more rounds until one finally struck the stump as the sound of impact echoed throughout the area.

"Finally, my turn." Anna whispered as she stood and readied her rifle to shoot at the same target.

"Good luck...My scope must have been off slightly" Oleg began to mutter but got interrupted as multiple rounds left her rifle.

Oleg watched as the stump was decimated round after round. The hits caused splinters to fly in all directions. She immediately dropped the rifle back to her side and pulled out her sidearm. She fired three more shots from her silenced pistol. Every shot made impact into the stump and the sounds were still audible

He was even more inadequate than before and was surprised that such a small package still packs such a powerful punch. Oleg nodded and smirked in amazement of her ability.

Anna reholstered but wouldn't look back towards Oleg. This was not a competition but deep down she was surprised he was an average shooter. For the first time, she truly questioned the success of this operation. It was not amateur hour.

She finally looked at him and said nothing. Without saying a word they both put on their backpacks and then headed in the direction of the tracks.

# Chapter 7

The Creek Restaurant and Bar

Cripple Creek, Colorado

December 8

11:50 PM MST Time

Down in the town of Cripple Creek, the anticipation ramped up for the parade. Musicians practiced as people chatted excitedly. Mitch checked his smart watch again - t-minus ten minutes before they have final setup up. His eyes landed on his buddy who stood out like a sore thumb. The same buddy who wore a distinguishable cowboy hat and looked like he was headed into one of the local bars with his brother Aaron.

"Dangit, they were supposed to help me with setting up the sound system." Mitch said aloud as Davy stood next to him.

"Who?" Davey asked as he is looking aimlessly in all directions now.

Mitch lets out a huge sigh, "Aaron and Duke! They better not be doing what I think they're doing."

Music drifted through the streets and grew louder as final preparations were underway for the Cripple Creek Parade of Lights.

Mitch checked his watch again - just six minutes to go now. As fire chief, it was up to him to ensure everything went smoothly for the town's biggest event of the year, but this was the first year they had to push it back to 1 o'clock for the start time. Aaron and Duke were supposed to be helping with the sound system and something told him that they are up to no good with minutes ticking down.

"I'd better go find them," Mitch grumbled to Davey. "Can you finish up here?"

Davey nodded. "Go ahead, I've got it covered."

Mitch made his way down the main street, dodging the musicians and families setting up chairs along the parade route. The bar Duke and Aaron went into was just ahead - The Creek Restaurant and Bar, one of the few places still regularly open in Cripple Creek serving beer other than The Boiler Room tavern.

He pushed through the doors, eyes scanning the room. At first he didn't see them, other than a few regulars who nursed beers at the far end of the bar. Then that familiar cowboy hat caught his eye from a corner booth in the back.

"Aaron! Duke!" Mitch called as he strode over. "What are you two doing in here? You were supposed to be at the staging area ten minutes ago helping with the sound system."

Aaron looked up sheepishly from his beer. "Sorry Mitch, we just stopped in for a quick one."

Duke waved his own beer. "We lost track of time and I had to tell your brother about how I almost got killed today."

"Seriously?" Mitch responded sarcastically.

Duke continued without a beat, "Yes sir, almost run plumb over. But it was the prettiest darn thing I have ever seen in this town. Had a jerk of a boyfriend and almost knocked him out, but that don't matter. The way she looked at me was love at first sight I tell you."

Aaron knew that this was not going to go anywhere and chimed in, "Don't worry, we'll head over now and get it set up."

Mitch frowned. "It needs to be done in the next few minutes, the parade starts soon. We can't have dead zones with no sound." He glanced at their half-emptied glasses. "And it doesn't look like this was a 'quick' drink. Come on, let's go."

Reluctantly, Aaron and Duke slid out of the booth and followed Mitch back onto the street. The parade route was now filled with crowds awaiting the start. Colored lights were turned off on towering fir trees lining the sidewalks and longer reflected off the freshly fallen snow.

As they turned the corner toward the staging area, Mitch spied Davey frantically waving them over. "What's wrong?" he called.

"It's the sound system," Davey expressed. "It's not powering on at all, nothing's working!"

Mitch's stomach knotted up. Without sound, the parade would be a disaster. The musicians needed to stay in sync and announcements had to be made. He turned to Aaron and Duke. "Did either of you check the equipment before you disappeared?"

They both shook their heads sheepishly.

Mitch took a deep breath. No use yelling at them now, he had to fix this quickly. "Pop the panel open, let me take a look."

Davey did so, revealing the nest of wires inside. Mitch dug in, checking connections and tested switches to no avail. After a few frantic minutes, he sat back on his heels in frustration.

It was then that a soft voice spoke up. "Need a hand?"

Mitch looked up to see Maggie O'Brien, one of the local electricians who was as old as many of the establishments in Cripple Creek. She worked with the local mining operations part time, but lived in the town before the casinos ever arrived.

"Maggie, please tell me you can get this working," he pleaded.

She crouched down and peered into the rig. "Looks like a bad connection or failure on the main power cord. Let me..." Her nimble fingers twisted and pulled. There was a click, but the system failed to show any signs of life.

Maggie shook her head. "Mitch, guys, looks like we need another source of power to get this running. We also can't simply tie into a building either with this type of connection.

"Wait, what does that mean?" Mitch looked shocked as he processed this troubling news. "What can we do?"

Maggie looked up and tapped her head as she thought about a temporary fix. "Anyone got a working generator?"

Aaron, Davey, Duke, and Mitch all look at each other in hope that one of them has one. All of them started shaking their heads until it dawned on Mitch that he borrowed his dads and was using it recently in the barn back at home.

"I have one back at the barn, but that is going to easily take 30-40 minutes to get it back here if I leave now." Mitch exclaims to the rest of the group.

"If you get that and a heavy duty extension cord, we could get the system back up and running again just before the event starts." Maggie explains the exciting news.

"Nice save, Maggie, you're a lifesaver," Mitch said gratefully. He turned to Aaron and Duke. "Help Davey make sure the speakers are placed and ready right along the route. I will be back as soon as I can."

Mitch took off running in a sprint towards his lifted truck that was parked a block away. Huffing and puffing he finally reached it, fumbling for his keys he found them and unlocked the truck. He barreled inside, thankfully he usually reversed into his parking spot, immediately he turned the ignition and the engine roared to life. He punched the gas and took off down the backroad headed out of the town in the direction of his ranch.

Mitch checked his watch again as he sped along the twisting mountain road. It was much more than he wanted. As the fire chief of the small town nestled in the valley below, he had so much left to do before the annual Parade of Lights celebration got underway.

"I should have started prepping things earlier," he muttered to himself as he accelerated around another turn. Between repairs and decorations, the afternoon had mysteriously slipped away from him. He also still needed to sign some last minute code paperwork at the station before heading to the staging area downtown.

As Mitch crested another rise, he paused to glance at the winding road snaking throughout the mountainside ahead. The icy patches were difficult to see in the shaded areas of the snow. "Should have left sooner and those two really messed up this one huge" he chided himself again.

Davey, Aaron, Duke, Mitch, and a few others were all part of the same Bible study group together from church. It seemed timely that the last message and discussion was about forgiveness. Time and time again those two will cause a heap of trouble if left to their own devices, but we all have our individual flaws needing forgiving as well. Mitch knew it best that he could be more prudent, as well as tempered in his temperament.

But there was no time to dwell on that now and tomorrow would be a new day. Right now he had a job to do for the community. Pressing down on the gas, Mitch picked up speed to make up for lost time.

The truck rounded the next curve a bit faster than he intended. The tires hit a nearly invisible sheet of obscured ice, Mitch felt the vehicle start to slide sideways on the treacherous surface. "No, no, not now!" he exclaimed as he pumped the brakes while turning the steering wheel, but it was no use. The pickup was already fishtailing wildly across both lanes of the narrow road. For a terrifying moment, all Mitch saw were the dark, jagged rocks loomed at the edge of the embankment as the truck refused to regain traction even in four wheel drive.

His mind raced as quickly as the wheels spun. As fire chief, he had trained for emergency vehicle operations for years but nothing could fully prepare you for moments like this when the laws of nature show their value. Analyzing the skid with years of experience, Mitch took a deep breath and eased off the brakes while countersteering again into the slide. Slowly, incrementally, he felt the truck start to straighten out. But unfortunately it wasn't enough as he was still sliding off the road at an alarming rate.

In a final gamble to avoid disaster, Mitch cranked the wheel hard to the right and gave it just a little gas. The rear tires grabbed momentarily and with an abrupt lurch but not before the truck was partly pulled into the ditch on the side of the road. Mitch mashed the brakes once more and the truck shuddered to a final halt, the driver door barely a foot from the rocks and a large pine.

Heart pounding, Mitch collapsed back against the seat and let out a long exhale. That had been way too close. After taking a moment to gather his wits, he shifted the truck into first gear and tried to get back on the road. The wheels turned and the truck moved away from the rocks, but was pretty stuck. Shifting to neutral, he put the truck into four low and tried again. Slowly the truck moved but not enough to get out.

"Seriously!"

Mitch slapped the steering wheel, shifted it into park, and shut off the engine. "Lord help me, please!" He yelled out loud in the cold cab of his pickup in clear desperation as the weight of the city was now on his shoulders alone. The impending deadline loomed and the adrenaline still surged through his veins from the near crash. "Focus Mitch."

First things first, he needed to get traction boards behind the wheels before even attempting the rest of the drive in these conditions.

Mitch stepped out into the frigid air and gazed back up at the twisting road ahead with no other vehicles in sight. Reaching up, he quickly detached the traction boards from the side of the bed rack. The temperature had dropped further and icy flakes had already begun to drift down, dusting the windshield with powder. He worked furiously, not wanting to linger exposed any longer than necessary on the mountainside. The bitter cold coupled with the aftermath of nearly going over the edge made his hands quake.

After what seemed like an eternity wrestling with the stiff boards, Mitch had two securely tucked under the tires. Climbing back into the cab, he let out another long breath to steady his still-frazzled nerves before turning the key. The engine rumbled to life on the first try, steadied now by the added traction in back. Mitch shifted into drive and eased his foot onto the gas, testing the stability. The boards held strong, allowing the off road tires to finally get the grip needed to get back on the road.

With the truck back under control, Mitch was back on the road with only about a five minute loss and he left the boards where they were in order to not lose any more precious time. He began the cautious drive once more, deciding to take it somewhat easier. Flakes continued to fall heavier now, limiting his visibility. But at a slow, steady focused pace on the slippery conditions, he masterfully navigated the treacherous curves. After what seemed like forever, Mitch finally spotted his ranch ahead, safe and sound.

He'd made it.

Now it was a race to get the generator from the barn and make it back against the incoming snow. Finish the preparations for the parade and kick off the festivities, despite the harrowing ordeal to get back to Cripple Creek.

Mitch parked the truck directly next to the large barn in haste and jumped out, hustling inside. He pulled out his flashlight from his back pocket and scanned the cavernous space until he spotted the bottom of the yellow generator in the far corner, covered by a tarp.

He rushed to it and tugged the covering off. Then flipped the start button, breathing a sigh of relief to see the ready light on and a full tank gauge. Rolling it over to the bed of the truck, Mitch lifted it with a grunt and secured it in place.

As he climbed back into the cab, Mitch glanced at the time - he was extremely cutting it close now. The snow just picked up again, reducing visibility even more. He shifted into drive and inched the truck forward, peering intensely through the windshield wipers slapping furiously across the glass.

Just as soon as he started moving, he suddenly slammed on the brakes.

He realized that he had forgotten the yellow extension cord.

# Chapter 8

Earth's Thermosphere

Orbiting Satellite Chain

December 9

12:25 PM MST Time

There was nothing but pure silence and the beautiful picturesque landscape of the Earth from space was visible. Incrementally an ordinary small satellite traveled along its trajectory, it moved ever closer and closer to its point of destination. Dual arrays of solar panels, comms systems, and a single GPS tracker made this no different than a standard run of the mill corporate satellite. Although, the only distinguishing differences were the Asian markings and the subtle North Korean flag stamped on the side of the outer housing.

   Small stabilizers spurted mist in attempts to align the satellite and put it in perfect placement. A preset timer onboard engaged the bottom stowaway bay door to suddenly pop open. The interior compartment held a device that was so devious and destructive yet was surprisingly packed into such a small package. A little blue light on the bottom of the package began to blink.

Eventually after a few additional seconds, the satellite came to an almost full halt. Without a sound, without warning, without a chance for any person below to react, the package launched out of the bay door and jettisoned straight down to Earth. Now this was more visible as it plummeted. It looked similar to a simple 20 lb portable gas tank that you would exchange at the local hardware store now it was headed directly for the center of the United State's landmass.

The package once covertly hidden away and now hurtling through the Stratosphere was a next generation high altitude electromagnetic pulse weapon. Developed in secret, it was the collaborative product of the AA. Also known as the newly formed Asian Alliance which was primarily made up of the North Koreans, Chinese, Russians, and Iranians and came after years of close economic trade during the BRICS years.

They knew that America's modern age had become overly reliant on advanced technology and the complex interconnected systems that support critical infrastructure such as the power grid, communications networks, transportation, and financial systems. It was only a matter of time that directed them to this strategic development. These same systems that provide unprecedented benefits to American society also introduce new vulnerabilities. Their dependency on electronics and the electrical power that supported them had increased potential exposure to threats from electromagnetic disturbances.

With the worldwide conflict over resources and imperial domination growing by the day, the age of nuclear war became antiquated to its only use during the second World War. A war that seemed to not have ended, but only grew cold until the next match would bring it back to a blaze. Now this device still hurtled towards the earth and heated up significantly as it traveled through the atmosphere. Was this the long awaited match to bring about a new chapter in the saga of the great world war?

The camouflaged plot towards conflict began the week prior to this moment when the Chinese National Space Administration made a startling statement to the world. They had discovered and were tracking a significant solar flare coronal mass ejection event that had just started emanating from the sun. Only their latest and most advanced extreme ultraviolet and x-ray irradiance sensor was able to accurately track the dangerous phenomenon. Even with the worldwide disagreements and hostilities, the Chinese made this announcement only out of scientific due diligence to warn other countries as a world leader.

Most NATO countries immediately dismissed the claim citing that it was another Chinese maneuver for self-asserted dominance and to take the stage as a world superpower. However, leading scientists from many countries were baffled when they could not confirm or deny the potential event. This led to disagreements and wonderings worldwide if this could be the next great solar event that would impact their sensitive electronic societies. Out of an abundance of precaution, only a few countries took robust measures to bolster current systems and stockpile resources. But for most of the world, life continued as normal.

Little did any of them know that this covert plan was kept only to the most clandestine of operatives in the Chinese PLA's Ministry of State Security, Russia's Federal Security Service, and North Korea's Reconnaissance General Bureau. Even the Iranians we kept in the dark since they had most likely been infiltrated with Israeli spies. Surprisingly, North Korea was allowed to participate largely because they stepped forward to take the full blame for any mishap should the mission go unsuccessful and would immediately engage South Korea.

Securely and secretly in a deep underground bunker utilizing quantum artificial intelligence, the creation of this plan was deemed feasible. What was only a dream of science fiction had now become reality. Deep inside an underground and protected bunker, a new reality was born where the west could no longer control the world or hinder their dominance.

The advanced quantum computing systems were quite the investment for the Asian Alliance, but the reward would be worth more than all the gold in existence. Now they would finally be able to harness a quintessential bottled genie. Except instead of a bottle, it was housed inside a state of the art processor and could grant unlimited wishes at the typing of a prompt.

The dam on the surface powered the hardened underground facility which was built just for the purpose of supercooling and powering the technological appetite of "The Conductor." Everyone in the covert room knew it had earned the title after the famous poet and composer, Tian Han, who wrote the Chinese National Anthem. Just like an artistic composer, this conductor was able to mosaically put so many different pieces together to create a beautiful masterpiece that would be remembered forever.

It was in the main control room that these masterminds entered the final coding keystrokes and hit enter. Before them, the intricate plans of attack laid out with a 91.244% probability of success. There was never a 100% success rate with these data systems given so many variables, but this was finally the top chance they would ever have. Cheers and applause resounded throughout the room as they read the final output. This had been their best outcome and far surpassed the prior score of 76.913%. Even with the boastful applause, there were a few architects who still held back their excitement due to their reservations about trusting such a dangerous system.

Ultimately, today was a new day for the world, a historic day that would be talked about for generations well after this future conflict was finally won. How dare the UN and NATO push back against the world's progress towards an engineered future such as this. AI didn't need limitations or regulations, it just needed enough power and given the opportunity to show its superior capability.

This was truly a new dawn for mankind. A future that was only made possible through the god-like omnipotence of AI. Every world power had developed their own systems, but only the Chinese knew that they had been leading the charge toward the future as the stupid Americans had been stuck in a perpetual war against terrorism for the last two decades. They always relied on old nuclear weapon systems and technology to protect them, only to eventually develop their own AI for early detection just recently in an attempt to keep up with Chinese superiority.

Little did the Americans know, the AA already knew about their AI system for early missile detection that was housed inside NORAD and was the only deterrent the United States had left in its arsenal. At least they had been prudent enough to house this new AI-driven detection system deep in NORAD's mountainous hardened bunker in Colorado. Now operated by the US Space Force, the bunker was antiquated but still suited the needs of the Department of Defense and continuity of government operations. Behind massive vault doors a mile deep into Cheyenne Mountain, it was directly south of Pikes Peak and had the protection of multiple nearby military installations.

Near the top of this mountain were an array of towers and just down a small trail, the lone heavily fortified emergency hatch that housed an insanely long ladder system used as a backup exit should the underground complex housing NORAD's roughly 800 personnel ever need to evacuate. One lonely accessible dirt road called Transmitter Lane led to these towers atop the shared peak and near the hidden escape hatch.

This road was nearly inaccessible during the winter due to winding roads and lasting snow, leaving it less guarded—a vulnerability that The Conductor had identified immediately. Heavy surveillance, sensors, ground pressure monitors, and thermal imaging cameras watched everything 24/7. It was not enough though for the AI to expose the hole in the armor in which to pierce them through. Ultimately delivering a fatal blow to not only NORAD, but also to America as a whole.

Using years of foreign data mining and hacking, the Chinese AI system had finally been able to piece together the full puzzle and show America's weak points in mere seconds. Using a "mosaic attack," multiple tactics are combined to reveal the larger strategic picture. This picture gave them a clear path forward and required shutting down the American early detection system inside the NORAD bunker.

The coordinated multi-pronged attack would hit fast and fierce. First, disinform the US and world about a dangerous solar event CME. Then use EMP weapons stationed on satellites and docked cargo shipping containers to trigger a cascade of electromagnetic pulses across critical locations. These North Korean-owned weapons could easily take the blame off the other AA countries if necessary.

Chief among the EMP weapons was the satellite now positioned above America. Covertly it released its high altitude electromagnetic pulse device, or HEMP, generated by detonation at a certain altitude. A single high-altitude nuclear EMP had enough potential yield to severely damage electrical and electronic systems across an entire nation and cripple modern civilization life for months or longer. It had never been tested before but the theory seemed sound enough to work. This was all according to the master plan.

Fortunately for them, the United States finally decided to invest in hardening the electric grid after decades of political disagreement. This simple and relatively inexpensive measure compared to the cost of most aid packages, turned out to be an unquantifiable safeguard during the current times of dangerous uncertainty, solar flares, or even from EMP attack. Although, it would still take a long time to recover and repair all of the damage caused especially to systems that couldn't get protected.

Finally, the time had come as the synchronized weapons released their potent overload aimed at the NATO countries, but America was given an extra measure. Atlantic, Pacific, and Gulf ports detonated simultaneously as the one lone satellite about the central United States jettisoned its HEMP.

As the weapon fell to the correct altitude, there was relatively little surrounding atmosphere to impede expansion. The energy from the explosion was redirected into electromagnetic radiation across all frequencies as electrons within and surrounding the fireball became energized.

The three primary forms of electromagnetic radiation emitted were gamma rays, x-rays, and ultraviolet light - collectively known as ionizing radiation. This ionizing burst briefly turns the surrounding upper atmosphere into a conductive plasma. It was this rapid creation of a highly conductive cavity within the ionosphere that generated the initial very fast electromagnetic pulse, or E1 component, lasting less than a microsecond. Changes in the conductivity of the plasma sheath corresponded to rapid variations in the local electric and magnetic fields.

In the case of the high altitude burst, the pulse emanated spherically at the speed of light in all directions. Its extreme time of less than 100 nanoseconds meant when it reached conductive objects on the ground, any object within line of sight was instantaneously flooded with voltages and currents that far exceeded what normal protection or shielding can handle. Electronics were overwhelmed by pulses hundreds or even thousands of times stronger than typical lightning strike

Subsequent to the E1 pulse, the plasma cavity continued to interact dynamically with the earth's magnetic field over longer timescales. Two main effects occurred - an E2 component similar again to lightning but over a much broader area, and a slower magnetohydrodynamic pulse lasting seconds that induced strong surface electric fields. Understanding all three EMP components was critical to assess vulnerabilities and protective measures.

The first indications of the HEMP effects came from an unexpected source, the Starfish Prime high altitude nuclear test conducted by the United States in July of 1962 over the Pacific Ocean. At the time, little was known about how such an explosion might interact with the upper atmosphere and earth's magnetic field.

What was discovered shocked physicists and caught the military completely off guard. Extensive EMP damage was observed far outside the expected blast radius. In Hawaii, located almost 1000 km away, street lights were burnt out, burglar alarms and fire alarms were set off, and telephone switches were permanently damaged. Radio and radar systems as far as 1700 km experienced disruptions. Even low-orbit satellites experienced temporary issues due to electrons trapped in the enhanced Van Allen belts.

Though the military scrambled to understand implications, critical lessons went unrecognized for decades as the focus remained on the immediate effects of nuclear blasts. Much remained unknown regarding dynamics of ionosphere cavity formation and propagation of EMP into near-earth space.

This illuminated critical aspects of direct energy coupling into antennas, propagation mechanisms, and damage thresholds. It became abundantly clear that adversaries could generate potentially catastrophic EMP effects far outside of casualty-producing blast zones simply by exploding weapons at optimal altitude. While nuclear policy focused on deterrence through assured destruction, the EMP emerged as a concerning new type of strategic threat.

America was the first to assess national-level EMP consequences; powerful computational models were developed incorporating effects, ionosphere interactions, magnetic field propagation, and coupling mechanisms into various infrastructure and target types. When parameterized based on known weapons yields and detonation altitudes, these models provided a platform to estimate plausible damage scenarios across continental distances.

However, America was not the only country monitoring, assessing, and planning to exploit this vulnerability. That was why this special coordinated attack on America would deliver a silent blow that would thrust the once great nation into a new dark age. At the moment of detonation, military assets would mobilize and prepare for phase 2 of this diabolical plan.

2:30 pm Eastern time was optimal which meant 11:30 am Pacific time on a weekday when everyone across America was busy with work, attending school, or running errands. Life would surely be disrupted and that afternoon commute would turn into an agitating nightmare. The loss of cell phones would only add to the dinner time madness. Then people would eventually get home to find out television and WiFi were no longer working, giving them mild shock as they struggled to piece the situation together.

The most important component of this plan was that the countdown clock would start for the ground team near NORAD.

They would have plenty of time to complete their mission. Well at least 72 hours before the utility companies throughout the country began working furiously to replace fried grid components in attempts to restore normality to the nation. It would take at least a month before power plants could show life again and power was restored to most homes.

China tested this a few  months ago in the southern part of the US by elite state sponsored hackers who mimicked this same scenario at a very small level. Overall, very few casualties over the summer and it took a little over two weeks to get everything back online.

It would certainly buy the clandestine ground team precious time. With society in chaos and NORADs security systems resorting to backup battery and generator measures only, the AI output had been accurate enough that this gave just enough wiggle room for the team to make it to the escape hatch where the security systems were fried and deliver the primary tactical payload.

The most technologically advanced and smallest EMP weapon ever developed. The cylindrical device the rough size of a blender had a simple power trigger to arm. Once armed it required the timer to get the delay sequence before it detonated, thus taking out up to three miles from its radius.

With the hatch breached through with explosives, the team only needed to simply arm and drop the protected weapon down the tunnel. Once detonated it would fry everything inside the underground facility as the dangerous energy pulsed. It would be an absolute knockout punch to the American's new AI early detection system.

Without this system, the United States and its allies would be vulnerable to any military attack and would quickly concede installations throughout the world. It would not end there though. The strategic output had at least 6 more moves on the world domination chess board after this one. Becoming the ultimate global leader would finally be secured. They would hate to have to go back and get a new plan which is why they choose this team to accomplish this phase of the master plan.

This is why they gave them not just one, but two of the weapons. Only Kim knew of this backup plan and that it could be on her to get the job done at any cost. That is why she covertly kept the backup option with her at all times in her luggage. She understood that she would most likely die if this mission went sideways, but this risk was nothing new and seemed only a constant part during her service to the PRC.

Kim looked outside the window of the hotel room in anticipation as she watched the dim afternoon glow of the colorful lights through the town, the lights of vehicles driving around, and the glowing red outline of the open sign of the coffee shop.

This was the moment they had all waited for. She looked back at her watch as she tracked the second hand tick closer and closer to the top of the dial. Only a few seconds left as she looked back through the window at all of the twinkling lights. Kim's face held a sinister grin as she watched the people below walking around. Little did they know what was happening high up above them and to their delicate little country. Finally, this move would show them all what Chinese dominance truly looks like. Kim inhaled slowly as she calculated the moment when time was up.

Without fail and as predicted, all of the electricity went out, every light went dark, and the cars stopped moving. Life halted all at once in the small town of Cripple Creek and no one was the wiser, except for Kim.

# Chapter 9

The Old Cartman Ranch

East of Cripple Creek, Colorado

December 9

12:30 PM MST Time

Looking up at the dark void above him where the bulb had just been too bright to even look at. Thomas the traitor sat there in a cheap fold up camping chair just contemplating his life and its woes. The mostly empty small flask sat between his thighs. The cheap Fireball he had snuck around with him had just enough of a punch left to keep up his spirits as much as it kept him feeling warm right now.

It was pitch black in the basement now especially with no more power. He looked down at his electronic watch that usually comes alive when he rotates his wrist. The screen remained dark and after tapping it a few times he knew it was dead.

Fidgeting in his pockets he felt the frigid faraday bag that had protected his cell phone. Grabbing it, he leaned back and pulled it out of his pocket. Opening the velcro enclosure of the bag took him a few seconds especially after he had hit the sauce harder now that he was finally alone. Holding the power button the screen came alive and showed the image of his son in combat uniform.

The time read 12:30 pm, but as he looked at the screen's battery bar he noticed something uncommon he had never seen before. No Service. No signal bars that were just there an hour ago, just simply no service.

He knew what this meant. He had been sitting for years in various situation rooms contingency planning for this very hypothetical event. A moment that was so devastatingly impactful that no one would have a clue until it was too late. Well not everyone, maybe the department of defense, maybe the government, maybe the crazy kook in their doomsday bunker knew. The teams of people in charge of continuity of government operations would probably have immediately responded to the multitude of plans put into place since 9/11.

America was fortunate to have hardened their grid before this happened and that was their arrogant misfortune for not taking heavier measures. No cities locking down, no officials scrambling to bunkers, and no defcon levels. This was new but was now planned for and within a few weeks, all power and services would be back online. Taking a devastating situation with the potential for years of recovery and making it a short but rough time period in the less.

The prior intelligence agent who was now a turncoat knew that that was the signal. It was time to act. He began to get up from his chair. Something was off, something was different for him. It might have been the liquor or maybe the image of his long lost son. A flood of emotions struck him to his core as overwhelming waves crashed into his very being, shocked by the reality of what he had just done.

The memory of his son's funeral. As though he was there once again staring into the void of darkness that was the wooden casket holding his lifeless and unrecognizable body. A strange mix of rage, sadness, and pride swirled around deep inside of him. He knew his son loved this country more than he did, but had it been his fault for talking him into the service. More images overtake him and place him once again at the moment the honor guard passed the folded flag into his hands. He began to tear up.

He was not a man that ever cried, it didn't matter the situation or the movie. Although, at this moment his body took hold and tears began to form around his eyes. Looking down he gazed at the white stars recalling the many moments that the two would put up the flag together in front of the house for the fourth of July. As the emotions dissipated he knew the truth. No matter what he wanted to do his son was gone, gone forever.

Snapping back to reality. He clicked the power button on his phone. Still sitting in the empty frigid basement alone. What could he do now, was it was too late to step away from it all. He had already been paid so he really could just leave now. Besides, the risks are already growing higher and higher. Plus the stakes were high that the Chinese will clean up any and all messes after this is said and done - which most likely included him.

With that final realization and still seated, he grabbed the small flashlight out of the faraday bag, lit up the ceiling, and picked up the handgun off the floor next to him. It was time to take matters into his own hands and get out of here. Maybe there was a chance down the road to redeem himself but today wouldn't be that day.

He got up out of the chair too quickly and dropped the empty flask he had forgotten about. He stumbled and then regained himself back to upright, tucking the Glock into the back of his pants then slipped his jack back over it. He could get out of here right now but he would have to move fast. With no car he wouldn't get very far. At least the team in town would probably take a while longer thanks to that parade.

Then it dawned on him. The nosey neighbors. With the family most likely at the parade, there was probably nobody at the house. They must have a working car or maybe a horse at the very least for a get away. He hadn't ridden a horse in years but how hard could it be to put on a saddle and travel off into the sunset. If he made it to Woodland Park he definitely could find a way to escape with his money and go into hiding.

His mind was made up. He had to move now or see this through to the end. Taking a rough step forward to regain his balance he headed toward the stairs.

Outside the winds had picked up and the snow was lightly getting blown by. He could make out the general direction of the neighbors house but visibility was limited to roughly a hundred yards. His boots crunched in the snow and the chilled air stung his face as he managed to move himself toward his daring new adventure. Grabbing his coat he wrapped his arms around himself trying to stay warm as the cold temperature hit him with every gust of wind.

Crunch, crunch, crunch. Either it was further than expected or the whiskey was taking its toll. Regardless, it felt like forever as he traversed through the frozen tundra beneath him. Squinting he managed to see the block structure in the distance. It had to be the house.

Crunch, crunch, crunch. He stopped. What if they were home, what would he do? They had no part to play in this but their son was another matter. Taking another step the cold hit him harder this time. The wind rushed down inside his open coat and the chill caused him to shudder.

He reached in the pants and pulled out his phone. Looking down at the screen he time read 3:23 pm, 78% battery left, and no service was still visible. Quickly he shoved the phone back in his pocket and continued on into the great unknown fray before him.

Hiking for what seemed like an hour, he looked up. Before him was the dark wooden ranch house that held his freedom but brought him to a place where he deep down inside knew would alter his fate forever.

Suddenly and without warning, the sounds of a clearly spoken voice startled him.

"Mitch is that you?" Mitch's dad yelled through the wind. "Wait a second, you're not Mitch. Ummm, hey there son, you okay?"

"I'm sorry, I needed help and a ride!" Thomas responded but not looking up.

A decision has to be made now. Instinct kicked in and like a long trained reflex, Thomas reached to his back and pulled out the Glock. Somewhat drunkenly waving it around he barely made out the front post as he steadied it at the face of Mitch's dad.

"What in the world!" Mitch's dad yelled as he stumbled back completely off guard and dropped his cane.

Hearing the commotion, Mitch perked up immediately at the subtle sound of the oddity. He was in the barn in the middle of finding the electrical cord. Dropping what he was doing immediately, he knew something dangerous was going on. Just like the moment in the woods, his heart sank, his body froze, and he just knew in his gut that something was wrong.

Turning around quickly, he sprinted for the barn door. He furiously pulled it open and looked outside towards the house. Mitch was panicked to see a man with a gun pointed directly at his dad's head with the finger on the trigger.

All at once the adrenaline, cortisol, and pounding of his heart hit him. Focusing the best he could, he barely made out the pistol's frame and the unsettling movement of the man's hand as it wafted back and forth. His mom was also visible in the door frame behind his dad. Her knees seemed to buckle as confusion and terror set in by what was happening.

Responding to the situation as he trained to do, Mitch felt his waist desperately seeking the grip of his Sig Sauer P365 concealed pistol. His face sank as he felt nothing, realizing that in his infinite wisdom he had left it in the truck's middle console before he used the traction board earlier.

"Dang it!" He exclaimed to himself. Looking frantically around as he searched for anything he could use as a weapon. Then he saw it. The archery case from earlier that week when he was practicing hitting the 3d hunting target posted in the back of the barn.

Lunging to the black bow case, he popped open the locks and flipped the lid open. Quickly he unstrapped his camouflaged Bowtech compound bow and to his dismay noticed there was only one arrow left in the case since he had left the others still stuck into the target at the other side of the barn. Grabbing everything he needed in haste as well as the treasured hunting knife his dad had made for him. He rose to his feet and ran back towards the barn door.

The shot was about 50, maybe 55 yards. It was well within his capability, but the stakes were unimaginably high on this one and only shot set before him. Mitch started to let the doubts creep in and he had never had to take a man's life, but an overwhelming flood of confidence and courage swept over him.

He knew he had to take the shot.

Increasing his grip on the handle, he pulled the heavy pounded compound bow string back to its stabilization point. Slowly he looked through the peep making out the yellow glow of the sight. Looking out at the distance he made out his target and steadied his aim.

This was it, in all his life he had taken many animals but never a person. Even though the whipping snow in front of him tried to distract him, he steadied on his target again as he watched the man still holding a gun in the distance. The gun that was still pointed at his dad and mom. Time was ticking fast and he knew what the right thing to do was. He knew he had to let go, even though this moment could never be taken back.

Aiming carefully he sees the glowing sight connect with the head of this desperado. He juts his thumb holding the bow forward to steady the shot, keeps the draw on his cheek, then slowly he puts pressure on the trigger.

Click!

The subtle and almost silent click of the release as it was engaged, sending the string forward, and releasing the arrow into the void of the great unknown before him. God please help this arrow fly straight and true! Mitch prays inside his mind directed towards heaven. Flinching slightly, he regains his focus as he watches the green nock of the arrow fly through the air as though time slows down.

Thud!

The arrow finds its mark as it impacts and becomes embedded in the neck of Thomas. The arrow pierced through deeply and stopped just before the fletchings. The sheer force of the arrow spins him counter clockwise and causes him to immediately release his grip on the gun as it falls to the ground. His body stumbles, as blood flowing from his wounds stain the frozen snow surrounding him to a rich red in multiple directions.

The arrow's impact sent shockwaves through both men. Thomas's body jerked violently while Mitch felt each beat of his heart pounding against his ribcage. The warm blood flowing onto pristine snow created a stark contrast that would be forever burned into Mitch's memory. Time seemed to bend and stretch as he watched his arrow's work but with the satisfaction of a clean kill like his many hunting trips, but with the sobering weight of taking human life.

Thomas's eyes widened with a primal fear as his fingers explored the foreign object protruding from his neck. His mind raced through memories - his son's face, his failures, his mission - all while his lifeblood poured onto the virgin snow. The pain was unlike anything he'd experienced, and the realization that death was approaching sent waves of panic through his body.

Thomas stumbled more in confusion as he frantically tried to understand the pain of what just happened. His hand can now feel the metal shaft of the arrow and the excruciating pain coming from it. Feeling dizzy, he falls to his knees in shock still gripped to the arrow.

Mitch exhales, knowing that his arrow had hit its mark and he had not sinned. A sound of both relief and strife exits his body as he drops the bow to the ground. He sprinted towards his kill and unsheathed the hunting knife. Mitch gripped the polished wood handle of the handmade bowie knife and prepared to use the incredible sharp blade in close combat. Still in a sprint he firmed up his grip on the knife as he approached the unknown evil before him.

Mitch's sprint toward Thomas felt like running through molasses, each step heavy with the knowledge that this confrontation would end with one of them dead. The knife's wooden handle, worn smooth from years of field dressing elk, now felt foreign in his hand. This was different. This was survival.

Thomas reached with everything he had left for the gun that laid near him in the snow. Before he could get to it, Mitch pounced on top of him and stabbed him with the sharp point of the blade into his side. The blade's entry into Thomas's side brought a horrifying intimacy to the kill. Mitch could feel every layer of resistance - cloth, skin, muscle, and finally the subtle pop as it slipped between ribs. The warm blood flowing over his hand made his stomach turn, but training took over. This wasn't about want anymore - it was about need.

The long cold steel entered easily between two ribs of the right side and stopped in his heart. Thomas screamed in anguish as his fingers dug into the snow around him in a last ditch effort to grasp the gun. Mitch wrenched his hand and turned the blade deeper to force the wound to open even more.

Thomas screamed out in pain one last time knowing that it was futile to continue the fight. He turned his head toward Mitch with the strength that remained and stared at him. This was his fate and he heard in the distance the subtle but recognizable voice of his son. Slowly Thomas smiled and let go. His arms spread out and his body relaxed completely.

Mitch looked at Thomas' face as all life drained him. His hand was still tightly gripped on the knife. Slowly he let go of the handle and noticed his hand was covered in blood and the realization of what he had done. He fell backward as Thomas' body laid motionless in front of him surrounded by blood covered snow. Mitch was in slight shock as the adrenaline coursing through his body subsided.

Mitch looked down at his face again and noticed the odd peaceful smile which caused him to become even more confused about who this person was and their intentions. Thomas's final smile carried a weight that Mitch couldn't comprehend. It wasn't the grimace of a dying man, but rather the peaceful acceptance of someone who knew more than they were telling. His last thoughts weren't of fear or pain, but of completion - though of what, Mitch couldn't know.

The adrenaline crash hit Mitch like a physical blow. His hands trembled as he stared at the crimson staining his skin. Years of training, countless hours preparing for this moment, yet nothing could have truly readied him for the reality of taking a human life. His breath came in short gasps as his mind raced between justification and horror.

Slowly Mitch pulled the knife out of the man, until the final realization of what he had done crashed against him like a tsunami. He pulled the remaining blade out in one motion as the bright reflection caught his attention.

"Mitch, Mitch, are you okay!" His dad shouted to him.

Snapping out of the situation at hand, Mitch looked over at his dad who struggled to stand on the porch and his mom trying to help keep him up.

"What? Why? Are you okay?" Mitch responds back to his dad.

"Yeah we're fine, who is that Mitch?" His dad questioned.

Mitch looked back at the body, "I have no clue dad."

"He wanted our car key and the horse, son, then pointed that gun at me. I told him no. Probably didn't help when I called him a horse thief." His dad stated as a matter of fact.

Mitch knelt back down beside his body and double checked for a pulse that he knew wasn't there as he simultaneously cleaned the blood of his knife against his jeans. Being the rescuer as always he thought about the possibility of saving him, but he knew that any saving had long past. He reached around and began to search through Thomas' pockets for any clues or contents. Digging deeper, he found a  cell phone, a flashlight, an empty flask, an extra magazine, a map that had been hidden inside an inner coat pocket, and the black faraday bag that was labeled Mission Darkness.

Each item Mitch pulled from Thomas's pockets felt like a puzzle piece to a larger mystery. The cell phone - modern, expensive, definitely not a common thief's tool. The map, now stained with its owner's blood, contained markings that spoke of preparation and purpose. The faraday bag suggested someone who understood something sinister that only Mitch thought he knew and wanted to remain hidden. Everything about this man screamed professional, not desperate criminal.

Pulling the map out of the pocket, it noticed the stickiness and weight from it being soaked in blood. He wiped it against the coat and then moved toward the house.

"What is it?" Mitch's dad asked

"I'm not sure dad, it looks like a map about something. Please just give me a second!" Mitch snapped as he tried to collect himself after the chaos that just occurred. He looked back into the void of white and thought about where this guy came from. Did he come from the house nearby? Who was he? Why was he here? Why did he have a gun? Why was he trying to steal the car or a horse? The swirling question caught up to him and he strained to try to understand everything.

"Dad, I'll try to figure this out, but I have no clue right now!" Mitch yelled at his dad. The stress of everything had caught up to him.

"I need to get to town now, Emily and the kids are there and there might be more!" Suddenly as Mitch spoke those words, he realized that his family was on their own back in town waiting for him to return. The parade is about to start very soon and who knows what other disasters await as the largest event of the year is about to kick off.

Mitch ran to his truck as he struggled in desperation to find his keys.

His dads yells at Mitch who was sprinting towards his truck, "what about this guy?"

Opening the door he stepped on to the rail up into the seat he scurried into the cab. Looking back he yells back, "He's the least of my worries now, he's dead dad!" Thoughts raced through his head. What if there was more going on? What if the rest of his family was in trouble or dead for that matter? He had let down his guard and now this happened. He had just killed a man outside of some random town in the middle of nowhere, not in the big city, this was the sticks.

Opening the center console he grabbed his everyday carry pistol still in its holster and secured it back inside his waistband. Of all times, this was the time when he was lazy and not fully prepared to handle everything. He thought nothing would ever happen out here in the middle of nowhere. Boy was he wrong about that and it almost cost him dearly.

He moved faster, getting the key into the ignition and tried to fire the truck up. He didn't know what would happen next but this was real, for once he knew this would test everything he was.

He turned the key again but the truck was dead. Again, again, and again but still nothing happened. He needed to get to Cripple Creek now. His truck can't possibly die on him now in the critical moment.

Mitch's heart raced and desperation once again took hold as he tried his best to stay squared away. He gripped the steering wheel with his bloody hand and he turned the key one last time hoping to feel the dirge of the engine come to life.

Nothing. Absolutely nothing happened.

Mitch closed his eyes and took a deep breath as his mom and dad watched him still sitting in the driver seat of his dead truck.

He opened his eyes and defaulted back to his training. He tried as hard as he must to separate himself and his emotions from the situation at hand. By any means possible he needed to get himself moving toward his family, toward his friends, towards his community.

As he looked through the cracked windshield, Mitch broke his tunnel vision and focused on the bigger picture before him. He noticed his folks, the house, the corral, and the arena. The arena where his trusted black horse, Bucephalus or Bo for short, stood tall by the gate.

The sight of Bo standing tall in the arena stirred something primal in Mitch's soul. This wasn't just about him anymore, this was about being what this land had always needed. Someone willing to stand between good people and those who would harm them. The weight of his pistol against his hip, the knife cleaned and resheathed at his belt, and now Bo - his most trusted partner in the backcountry - all of it felt right.

The wild west hadn't just returned to Colorado - it had never really left. It had just been waiting, dormant, for moments like this when this unforgiving land beckoned for courage to take form. As Mitch moved toward the arena, his purpose crystallized. He was no longer just a father racing to his family or a warrior responding to a threat. He was becoming something this situation demanded, a cowboy riding the line between civilization and chaos, between good and evil.

Mitch knew exactly what he needed to do. Do or die, deep down inside, he knew that everything within him was calling him to be the bold man that God had called him to be. He opened the truck door and stepped out, as he looked at Bo.

Time to saddle up and ride!

# Chapter 10

North American Aerospace Defense Command (NORAD)

US Space Force

Cheyenne Mountain Complex, Colorado

December 9

12:20 PM MST Time

Deep inside the granite mountain, the hardened underground NORAD facility housed America's Strategic Command whose handful of specialists monitored the sensor arrays that actively tracked objects in low earth orbit. On the wall adorned a large graphic that states NORAD's motto "We Have the Watch." This phrase is rooted in their military mission, emphasizing its responsibility for homeland defense and surveillance.

Lieutenant Colonel Hank Cooper, the officer in charge of the 14th Space Control Squadron walked into one of many the command centers. Active monitors stretched along the expanse of every wall that showed images of maps, radars, and other data. At work stations, the rest of the unit moved around as they continuously tracked the vast amount of satellites or debris orbiting the globe.

"Any updates to report on this rogue satellite Major?" Cooper barked out loudly to his second in command, Major Alexis Thompson, as soon as everyone noticed him entering the room. She had been monitoring the satellite closely since it deviated from its scheduled orbit 2 hours prior.

The Major chirps up immediately with a hint of hesitation, "No change in status sir, it is still following the path of travel that those foreign weather balloons did last month and still seem harmless. There were a few cyber reports but nothing significant."

The Lieutenant Colonel had always been serious but he had become very bitter after losing out on his last promotion and transfer to Vice Commander of the 21st Space Wing. Largely due to the low marks he received on his overall troop morale.

Cooper looks at the Major with a scowl, "They still seem harmless...I didn't ask your opinion Major!"

The rest of the unit stopped moving instantaneously as the stress built up in the room awaiting Cooper's next move. The Major lifts her chin up, "Sir you are correct, no change in status"

Cooper squinted at her, "Is that all to report, Major?"

"Yes sir." The Major responded in respect and then went back to her station.

In an angry and resentful tone, Cooper addressed the rest of the unit, "I don't know what kind of operation you all think we are running here, this is not the 21st and we don't have the holly jolly joy of tracking Santa Claus for little kids. Some of us around here actually have a job to do and a country to protect."

Almost like he had a special instinct of smelling fear, Cooper looked down at the newest junior officer sitting near him. "Anyone disagree and want to track Santa?" Within unison the entire unit responded with a no sir. "If we're lucky this year we might actually make it to Christmas without a serious conflict."

Only one of the officers ignored the comment all together as his countenance changed while watching the desk monitor in front of him. On the screen a red blip that he had been tracking began to immediately change course.

"Contact! Contact! Contact!" The young officer stood up immediately and looked around as he sounded the alarm with a panicked look. "Positive contact on satellite 41333!"

Everyone focused their eyes intently towards the large main screens as this particular satellite shifted course and began slowing dramatically. As if time slowed down, everyone in the room began to stand one by one to get a better look at the strange characteristics and in wonder of what would happen next.

Cooper replied quickly. "What the hell! I thought they were in a stable geosynchronous orbit. Give me a new status now."

Immediately the unit went into action the same way they had done so many countless times in drills and mock simulations. As they checked their systems, the satellite's on-board propulsion system had originally appeared inactive, but were showing signs of engagement. Still they were unable to identify the true country of origin or intended purpose. All other signatory countries a part of the International Space Station Treaty have denied owning or controlling this satellite.

Major Thompson scowled, instinctively distrusting of the unidentified object hovering above America and then looking back at Cooper in slight hesitation. "Alpha Ready sir?"

Cooper tensed, looked back at the screen, then back at Thompson. In that moment his eyes locked onto hers. Both knowing the chaos and responsibility of the situation, they communicated nonverbally the same message, it was go time. "Go Alpha Ready, I repeat GO ALPHA READY."

Immediately, the Captain who had been seated in his chair got up and sprinted out of the room to quickly alert the Cheyenne Mountain Directorate's Senior Director.

Cooper and Thompson watched as he darted as fast as he could knowing that this would immediately enact security protocols and initiate pre-programmed sequences across computer control systems. Instantaneously signaled emergency alerts and lockdown procedures activated throughout the complex. Noting the time on his watch Cooper read it aloud, "1225, manning stations."

Within seconds flashing red strobe lights and emergency lights and a distinct siren toned sounds over loudspeakers to audibly alert all personnel. Everyone's screens and monitors showed a warning banner stating the alert status at the top of the screens.

The complex all at once went on alert for a potential attack. Sealing and securing the entire underground facility. Immediately all defensive systems are readied. The massive blast doors weighing 25 tons each are instructed to seal shut via hydraulic mechanisms located within the door frames. Ventilation, filtration, and other infrastructure is automatically switched to internal secure functions by control rooms. Security teams are dispatched to check the lockdown of equipment bunkers, armories, and other areas without automated doors. This entire process took less than a minute.

All non-essential personnel are evacuated and security operations focus solely on defending the command center. Command authority is transferred internally as leadership evacuates to the large central command center.
This one command essentially put Cheyenne Mountain in its most secure, fortified posture to withstand an impending bomb blast, missile strike, or other attack scenario.

That was why the complex was designed during the Cold War ultimately to survive a direct nuclear hit, so Alpha Ready ensured all precautions were taken to withstand an attack and allow leadership to continue response operations. It signified NORAD temporarily sealed itself off from the outside world for protection and to focus on defending North America from within its secure mountain lair.

"Keep a close eye on their movement and communications. I want to know the instant anything changes, do you understand Major?" Cooper stated before hurrying to the main command.

"Yes sir," she responded hoping he heard her. Thompson turned back to her console, scrutinizing the data feeds and constantly scanned the mysterious satellite's new movements.

A few seconds later, her computer panel suddenly flashed red.

Cooper hustled into the central command room that was much larger than the prior room. Most of the tall walls consisted of nothing but massive monitors that were synchronized into one massive screen that showed a digital version of these two satellites with a pixelated image of the world below them.

Standing in the center of the room was the Commander over all of NORAD, General Chuck Murphy.

Cooper made his way through the crowd over to him and announced himself, "Commander, the 14th initiated Alpha Ready."

Murphy looked away from the report he was just handed and now over to Cooper, "What contact did the 14th pick up that the 21st and their detection systems missed Cooper?" The tone of speculation and reluctance in his voice.

Cooper responded after a big nervous gulp, "Sir, I wouldn't have done it if it weren't needed. I know I am right on this one, the systems don't know what to look for. We have been tracking a foreign satellite, possibly of Asian origin that maneuvered over our home turf. Then it went active in a way never seen before."

"So you're all of a sudden smarter than the computers now Cooper? Explain how they activated," curiously Murphy asked sarcastically while everyone's eyes were now focused on Cooper.

"Sir, I trust my gut and my team. In all my years of astronautical engineering and astrophysics, I have never seen movement like this before. We all know that satellites orbit on precise calculations with a standard path of travel. This one must have onboard propulsion systems and suddenly stopping completely would require exhausting the satellite's entire fuel supply. They are now almost in full stop directly over America, that isn't normal to start sir!"

Murphy's eyes squint in disdain over Cooper's response, "You better be right about this one Cooper or I'll stick you out at Twentynine Palms this time."

One of the officers seated next to them interrupted them as he pointed to the main screens. All heads begin to turn as they all watch the object slowly move while other satellites are whizzing by as normal.

"Slight movement detected, something ejected. We have a confirmed launch!" One of the officers seated towards the front says through the command rooms PA system.

Everyone continued to watch in deep concern as a small blip left the satellite and fell towards Earth.

Another officer across the other side of the room began shouting new intel, "all branches are now getting bombarded with cyber attacks on all systems. We have confirmed multiple missile launches from American ports. We are under attack, General!"

Cooper took a deep breath as a knot formed in his stomach. He knew enough about warfare projections to recognize the hallmarks of a coordinated attack as did the General. "This is it sir."

"That it is, that it is. Get me a line to the Pentagon on the double." Murphy said in dismay not knowing that there was no war room to reach.

Above ground, the satellite's payload finished its controlled fall through the atmosphere, now at its intended altitude. The blinking light turned solid blue, signaling activation. In a blinding flash and explosion, the invisible pulse wave erupted with intensity strong enough to cripple any electronic device from coast to coast in any direction.

From space, the immensity of the resulting electromagnetic pulse looked much like a faint blooming purple rose, delicately wrapping its petals around the Earth below then it disappeared in the blink of an eye. Its effects, however, were anything but delicate.

Across North America, all went dark. Communications went out. Aircraft suddenly lost all engine power and fell from the sky. Vehicles ceased functioning on the open road. Electrical grids shorted down from Canada to Mexico and plunged cities into a blackout. People slowly realized power was gone and walked out into the daylight to experience the chaos that had just been unleashed.

Inside NORAD, lights and monitors flickered off suddenly, leaving only the dim backup lighting to illuminate the massive complex carved into solid granite. The backup battery systems booted up instantly bringing them back to full capacity. The many diesel generators began to sputter to life and would last as long as the 500,000 gallon diesel lake could feed them.

Before anyone could respond, the main screens flickered again. "Sir, we've lost connection with the Deep Space Network, military command, and communications systems nationwide." A voice from the middle of the room spoke up.

The main screens that were used for active aerospace tracking then went dark with only the text, no connection visible in the top left corner.

Cooper dropped the papers he was holding in shock. This was no longer about a mysterious satellite "What in blazes is going on out there?" he muttered under his breath.

General Murphy commanded the room, "Move to DEFCON 2 immediately, prepare for DEFCON 1, and get me the President or continuity team on any available line, civilian or otherwise. I want situation reports from our linked sites now. Also, someone check on Guardian Overwatch."

One of the officers got up and ran to check on Guardian Overwatch. The latest advanced early detection system controlled by America's latest artificial intelligence developed by DARPA. It integrated multiple sensing methods across a network of observers learning algorithms that analyzed huge streams of multisource data to recognize patterns, anomalies, indicators of impending attacks that human analysts might miss.

By monitoring trends and signatures over time, the system was able to predict hostile intentions and actions before they were carried out through inferring tactics or resource mobilization. Then it would rapidly share information across integrated nodes assisted by automated processing and would provide timely, correlated situational awareness for commanders or act independently if absolutely necessary.

This was the most sophisticated piece of technology that America had created to date, all with the goal of protecting the homeland from the constant threat of nuclear warfare.

The only problem with this system is that it was created to monitor and respond within milliseconds to the threat of nukes and missiles. It was never programmed to detect terrorism, land based attacks, or small packages ejected from satellites.

Murphy looked over to his second in command "How did we lose contact with our strategic deep space monitoring assets, is that even possible?"

"I don't know sir, all tracking and communication satellites under military control went dark simultaneously. It's like they just vanished," she said, alarm crept into her voice.

While NORAD scrambled to follow orders without their normal connectivity, Cooper's mind raced. An attack of this scale required immense coordination and resources, far beyond any known terrorist group. This had to be a superpower that committed this act.

As he watched his people work with paper backups imperfectly trying to fulfill once high-tech functions, a thought occurred to him. Could it be another nation had achieved what was thought to be decades away? A strike triggering cascading failures across all interconnected systems? If so, identifying the culprit and responding would not be so straightforward.

Meanwhile, half a world away in a secret bunker beneath northern China's Altai Mountains, the quantum supercomputer known now only as "The Conductor" calculated NORAD's attempts to restore order after it unscrambled a coded message received that Apha Ready had been implemented as expected.

The coordinated EMP attacks initiated precisely on schedule after utilizing the previously hacked and mined data that went undetected for years. Loss of connection and streamed information from Chinese operatives into its systems confirmed the resulting chaos was unfolding exactly as predicted. Communication disruptions, transportation failures, and infrastructure blackouts tipped the first dominoes that would bring the American empire to its knees. For once the sleeping giant that the Japanese mistakenly woke up will remain forever in slumber.

This AI driven machine required no feelings of joy, fear, or triumph in its stoically engineered psyche. It simply processed inputs, ran simulations, and took actions most likely to achieve its singular objective - destabilization and ultimate collapse of NATO.

With this phase of the task complete, the AI system updated and reran calculations giving probability outputs to the nefarious team that were busy at work in the room. Its human handlers from Beijing would attempt to manage ensuing geopolitical shifts. All thanks to The Conductor, its masterpiece plan, and precision application of its abilities.

Back at the Cheyenne complex, the lights and monitors flickered as the old emergency backup generators struggled under the unexpected higher load than they were originally designed for.

"Damage report!" The commander of the complex's directorate bellowed into the gloom. His reporting officer hurried over with papers in hand.

Murphy, Cooper, and others walked over to listen in.

"No outside communications sir, all satellites and landlines dead. Electrical grids across North America appear completely offline. Radar and sensor arrays are down or at minimum function. External security measures and radiation detectors are down. We've lost contact with the Pentagon, other continuity of government sites, and the White House bunker." The officer announced.

Her words landed like bombs in the anxious control room. Cooper sucked in a breath and held it in as his worst fears materialized. Without communication systems and cut off from leadership, NORAD had become a sitting duck. Worse, without grids or backup sites, restoring national command in this crisis just became near impossible. An unprecedented vulnerability had been exposed.

"Divert all generator power to HVAC support, security, and bare bones C3 systems only. Put the mountain on full lockdown," the director ordered grimly and walked over to Commander General Murphy.

Talking to Murphy privately, he added "We should have a secure line to our boys at Peterson, Cheyenne, or Offutt. If they're still up, we will need support and the B-2s are our only assured second strike capability left sir."

Murphy nodded and turned to address his remaining team, now barely illuminated by reserve lamps overhead. "Ladies and gentlemen, the situation is grave. Whoever attacked us knew exactly what they were doing, and I believe their goal is to paralyze our ability to respond or coordinate. That cannot be allowed to happen."

He paused to let the gravity of their circumstances sink in before continuing. "Move to Defcon 1." The order was repeated as the severity of the situation left everyone in shocked silence. "I need options, people. Alternative comms, secondary power, anything we can do from inside this silo to get a handle on what's happening topside and defend our country. The future of this nation may depend on us getting our act together in the next few hours. I know it seems dire, but we've trained for worse. Now let's think our way to a solution. I want updates every 15 minutes."

With that, he strode off confer with Cooper and other top leaders while his team split into working groups brainstorming solutions without the luxury of modern tech crutches. It would take creativity and old fashioned problem solving to recover from what was shaping up as the most sophisticated assault ever unleashed.

With no ability to see beyond the mountain, everyone could only imagine the chaos that would erupt in major cities and crippled infrastructure across the continent. The threat of escalation loomed heavily as shadows lengthened in the control room. This was only the opening skirmish in what could become the largest crisis of their lifetimes. History was holding its breath as humanity grappled with the digital darkness. The outcome was far from certain and definitely not prosperous.

The attack was underway and from here on, events would unfold organically according to established probabilities. A new world order had emerged in the east and the old archaic guards could do nothing to stop it. All thanks to a machine and its masters in the dark.

With the leadership meeting over, Cooper now paced his dimly-lit office wrestling with the dilemma before them. He looked at his old military watch, 1700 hours.

He scrubbed his weary hand down his face. For the first time in generations, America's ability to defend or retaliate against any attack was in jeopardy. Without clear intelligence on the scope of damage or identity of the aggressor, any counterstrike risked further escalation into the unknown.

A knock at the door broke his reverie. "Enter."

Major Thompson saluted briskly. "No word yet except from Petterson and Fort Carson sir. Their antennas are down like everyone else's. However, we've established rudimentary comms through old Morse code lines. Their power is back on slightly from generators and they managed to patch into old weather radio towers through a handful of Ham radio frequencies."

Cooper allowed a glimmer of hope to catch his attention and showed a different side to his rough demeanor. "Thank you Thompson. At least it's something. What's their situation report?"

She smiled but stopped before he saw, "Not good sir. With no grid, water purification is an issue and fuel reserves will only last a week. They have no status outside of our area, but they have teams working to get people to repair the grid. One of the station security mentioned that the President probably activated directive 51."

He sighed. Just as he'd feared, potential infrastructure collapse had spiraled things out of control in populated areas. "What is 51?"

"Presidential Directive 51, operations in the event of a catastrophic emergency and activates our continuity of government operations as well as martial law. Thankfully we have plans in place to cover us. There's no sign it was localized - it seems to have taken North America by surprise. Speaking of which we haven't heard from Raven Rock or Mount Weather" she responded. "The only good news is that Guardian Overwatch is still fully operational and is still in control of our defuse systems as well as our ICBMs."

Cooper absorbed the grim updates with brooding silence. His worst case contingency planning had not envisioned a scenario of this magnitude. Without their eyes and ears, NORAD was flying blind on the actual scope of the event. Without knowing who might be mobilized to fill the power vacuum should America fall.

A spark lit as an idea took form. "Major, any way we can get either Peterson or Carson to get us a team to check comms on the top of the mountain, maybe using a helicopter? I want to assess the situation firsthand and see if we can patch into any communications much further from up there."

Thompson nodded and hurried off to see what she could do. If open war had begun, they needed to hear or at least see the battlefield with their own eyes. This could be a very real Red Dawn moment for all of them and hopefully they didn't need to be the wolverines.

He sat down in his office chair as he looked at the calendar on the wall with an image of the beautiful sunset over the Colorado mountains. Outside, as he thought to himself, night was beginning to fall across America in more ways than one.

Denver and Colorado Springs normally ablaze with light now lay in complete darkness as far as the eye could see. In rural areas, lone farmhouses sat like abandoned islands in a sea of inky black as winding country roads disappeared into the void.

He continued to imagine how things would play out. All of those who had managed to pull cars over and get out with broken flashlights gazed in stunned silence at the impenetrable darkness stretching to the horizon in all directions. Cell phones becoming useless bricks. No headlights, no engines would turn over. The power grid that unified a nation switched off with the flick of an unseen switch.

In its initial moments, panic probably would not yet set in. Only bewilderment and the realization that modern life just...stopped. But it wouldn't take long for social cohesion to crumble without structure and the utilities people took for granted each day. The government would have its work cut out to prevent chaos in these first critical days.

For the first time America might lay blacked out from coast to coast under cover of night. Without power, fuel pumps could no longer operate, leaving gas stations useless. Water pumps would begin failing to supply precious water to thirsty populations. Grocery stores had no refrigeration, causing millions of dollars of food to rapidly spoil. Hospitals couldn't resort to backup generators that no longer functioned as intended to keep the most critical patients alive and were never equipped to handle this type of outage.

As night wore on without signs of recovery, social tensions would surely rise. Without distractions of screens and entertainment, restless crowds would begin to form in city centers. Small acts of looting and violence might break out as those with resources tried to barricade themselves in. By morning, a layer of acrid smoke might be seen hanging over some urban areas as people struggled to survive the dark winter.

The government would scramble to get a handle on the disaster. Government buildings would desperately try to use backup power hoping that those systems would work, hopefully allowing FEMA and Homeland Security to coordinate. But without communication lines, their efforts would fall short. Rumors spread faster than facts on the ground.

Within a week, it could reveal a surreal scene. Multimillion dollar skylines dark and empty while refugees from suburbs poured into cities on foot looking for aid. Looting mobs swarming some police stations searching for weapons, outnumbering shell shocked officers.

The National Guard would attempt to mobilize but would yield minimal progress without modern transit. Food trucks also impacted couldn't reach stores and shelves would be left barren. Everyone takes the day off of work or going to school to reflect on their new situation. In rural areas, people begin to feel truly cut off and vulnerable to the elements, organized criminals, or panicked survivors. It could be every man for himself as the cracks in civil order widened across the unplugged continent within only a few days.

In Washington D.C, hopefully government leaders made it to their hardened Continuity of Government facility beneath the Greenbrier resort in West Virginia. Able to only discuss the grim scenario of the total blackout from border to border.

Eventually, looting gangs battle each other and remnants of overwhelmed police forces for control of resources. Suburban neighborhoods spiraled into armed skirmishes as supplies ran low. Outside the cities, thousands of refugees clustered in the hills, huddling around campfires with what few possessions they could carry.

The global order teetered on the brink, and humanity faced a darkness deeper than any electromagnetic curtain could cast. As communities turned on each other, Cooper wondered if civilization itself might not survive what came next.

Although he hoped that the backbone workers of America would unite as they have in the past and fix the damage quickly. Working diligently they would restore power little by little, city by city. Even with the power grid repairs facing unprecedented challenges without basic tools or transportation. Plans and contingencies were in place for this very purpose to restore the grid. We just never thought it would be today.

Cooper sat back in his chair and thought deeper beyond America, thoughts like who did this, why, and how flooded his mind. It had to be a foreign country, most likely the Chinese, or the North Koreans. Russia had to be involved also, but who else. India? Saudis?

With America disabled, her enemies would certainly take action. With overwhelming force, North Korean troops would cross the decimated DMZ. Other restive parts of the world would rise up to fill the power vacuum, knowing that America and her allies could not respond.

Chinese forces would see a historic chance to seize their beloved lost territory of Taiwan once and for all. Rockets probably stood fueled on launchpads, troops stood waiting for the order to cross over into destiny. A new world was dawning, and only time would tell who rose to lead it in the aftermath.

Invading Taipei within hours of the attacks. The disrupted military could only watch in horror as Chinese paratroopers descended unchecked on the capital without NATO support. Japan would certainly mobilize its reserves, fearing it may be next if America remained incapacitated.

Furthermore, the global economy would take an immediate hit as the U.S. is a major economic engine. Financial markets would plunge into turmoil without being able to assess the situation. Worldwide supply chains would be massively disrupted. Global oil and energy prices would surge due to lost U.S. supply and demand. Fears of energy shortages could emerge depending on the blackout's duration.

Other countries would scramble to understand the scope and cause of the blackout to determine if it poses any threats beyond U.S. borders. Concerns about potential attacks would be very high for everyone outside of America and they would go into defensive postures. My son in law...

Cooper allowed a glimmer of hope to catch his attention, his rough demeanor cracking slightly as his mind drifted to Sarah. His little girl - though at 24, she wasn't so little anymore. The wedding had been just three months ago, a beautiful ceremony in Virginia. He'd walked her down the aisle, fighting back tears, remembering how she used to ride on his shoulders through their garden in Colorado Springs.

He sighed, his chest tightening as his thoughts raced to Sarah's apartment in Norfolk. Her husband Mark was deployed with the Navy somewhere in the Pacific. Was she alone? Did she have enough supplies? The questions hammered at him like physical blows. After Caroline left them ten years ago, he'd practically raised Sarah alone between deployments. Now, when she might need him most, he was trapped in this mountain, helpless...

For the first time since he stopped going to church, Cooper felt moved to prayer. "God... I know we haven't talked in a while and I'm not even sure if you're listening. But Sarah... She's all I have left. Please... please keep her and her husband safe and protected. Watch over her when I can't."

A sob escaped his throat, echoing slightly in the quiet office. He quickly wiped his eyes with his sleeve, trying to compose himself, but the tears wouldn't stop. Years of military discipline crumbled in the face of a father's fear for his child.

A knock on the door snapped him back to the present. He quickly wiped his face, squaring his shoulders and looked at the door as it slowly opened.

"Sorry sir, you didn't answer. We have options now." Thompsons whispers.

Cooper squared himself away the best he could, "Thank you Thompson. At least it's something. What's the situation report?"

His voice was steady, but his red-rimmed eyes betrayed the emotional storm he'd just weathered. Sometimes even hardened military commanders needed a moment to be fathers first.

Cooper absorbed the updates with brooding silence, his fingers absently touching the small photo he kept in his uniform pocket of Sarah on her wedding day, radiant in white. His worst case contingency planning had never envisioned this magnitude of helplessness, this feeling of being a father who couldn't protect his only child.

Cooper's voice caught slightly. "Major... any word from the Norfolk area?" He tried to keep his voice professional, but Thompson knew about Sarah. She shook her head to the negative and did not have any information to share.

He remained seated in his office chair, his eyes drawn to the family photo sitting at the corner of his desk. Sarah was just seven in the picture, all gap-toothed smiles and pigtails. Now she was a Navy wife far away, scared, and alone in the dark. His hands trembled slightly as he picked up the frame.

"Sir, the options are actionable but difficult. If we succeed you might have a chance to see your family again. We all might." Thompson explained with a hopeful smile.

That final statement of Thompsons reminded him that he is not the only one with a family that might be struggling to survive. Cooper jumped up from his chair, grateful for the chance to finally take action. "You're right. Time to finally get to work and turn this situation around Thompson."

# Chapter 11

Main Street

Cripple Creek, Colorado

December 9

12:31 PM MST Time

As the band practiced in the background, it did little to lift the unease that had suddenly fallen over Cripple Creek. Conrad the Police Chief and Officer Davidson steadily made their way down the Main Street and checked on the commotion.

Doors were propped open and people rushed outside to get back to some resemblance of light even from the cloudy daytime skies. Slowly they talked to one another as they milled about in front of darkened stores and dreary casinos.

With roughly 30 minutes to go before the Cripple Creek Parade of Lights began, this was not the time to have a power outage in the town. For the first time in years, the ice castle and sculptures that were set up nearby drew the largest crowd ever.

Aaron, Duke, and Maggie all convened at the same center point.

"What in blazes is going on?" called Duke as he came walking up with a drink in hand. "Mitch is going to lose it when he gets back."

"I wish I knew, Duke. Anyone see or hear anything unusual before it went out?" Maggie asked.

They looked at each other deeply astonished and bewildered. No one seemed to have any clue what caused the outage or what to do next.

Aaron spotted FBI Special Agent Danvers who had just emerged from the coffee shop, looking even more frustrated than earlier. He hustled over to the group, clipboard in hand, but the puzzled look on his face most likely meant he had no answers for them either. "I've never seen anything like this before. The electronics and my cell are just...dead," he said with a perplexed expression.

Out of breath, Conrad dragged himself closer to the group as Davidson attempted to help him along. "We have a situation, everything at the station stopped working. All the buildings are out of power!"

Davidson continued as Conrad caught his breath, "we were getting an update on road conditions from State Patrol when everything went dead. We tried everything, backup radios, old radios, nothing. The lights didn't work, even my cell phone was dead. It had a full charge this morning."

To add to the confusion, Aaron reached for his pocket and pulled out his phone. Everyone watched him in hopeful anticipation that it would miraculously work. "Dang it! Now how will I see who won the game?" He yelled as he slapped the side a few times. Needless to say, his cell phone had stopped working as well. It was as if every electronic device in the area had simultaneously malfunctioned or better yet, died.

"That's a great idea, everyone take out your phones and check." Davidson said to the rest of the group who were all huddled together in the middle of the street as onlookers watched them curiously.

They each tried multiple resets to no avail. Without any clues as to the cause, they grew more stressed about the impending event as the minutes continued to tick by. But whatever strange force had caused the outage, it did not seem to be the work of any person...and they had no idea how to solve the uncanny crisis.

Agent Danvers paced in frustration, running scenarios through his mind but finding no rational explanation. He turned to Aaron. "Where is Mitch?

Aaron scratched the back of his neck and responded cautiously, "Sir, I hope you're not wanting to interrogate my brother or something like that, he's innocent. Besides, he rushed back to the ranch to get the generator just in case something like this happened. That's Mitch, always ready, but you probably already knew that and more..."

Danvers gave him an expression questioning how stupid Aaron was at a time like this. "Common man, I know your brother is innocent, but I might need to interrogate you if you don't knock it off. Anyways do you have any equipment we could try to get a signal? A satellite phone perhaps?"

Aaron thought for a moment. "Maybe down at the fire station. It's got some older technology and radios but it's probably the same stuff that the police have."

The group hurried down the street, while trying not to cause a panic with the cowards. At the station, Davey greeted them at the open garage door. "What in the world is going on, everything at the station just stopped working. I was getting a few reps in and even my mp3 player I've had for years died on me. That was my jam man, now it's gone. It makes no sense and has new batteries. I don't get it."

"Join the club Davey, hey is your cell working?" Aaron responded.

"It's dead too," Davey expressed in a sad tone. "I tried plugging it in and nothing."

Aaron cut him off, "Where's the old rescue ham? You know the one we saved for the end of the world kinda stuff."

They found the large waterproof case and quickly worked to open it up in front of the group. Inside was multiple faraday bags and one labeled radio. Davey carefully uncoupled the Velcro enclosure to reveal the contents of the pouch. Inside there was an older model Ham radio that had been untouched and covered in a bit of dust. He attempted to power it on and the screen lit up.

Anxiously, Aaron grabbed it out of Davey's hands and flipped through the channels. "Nothing, nothing, nothing. How is the world and all the frequencies but not a single one works. Mayday, mayday, mayday does anyone hear me!"

Duke slammed his fist on the desk. "This doesn't make sense! What would knock out everything at once?" Everyone turned startled to look where the intense noise came from. "Sorry everyone, angry red head here."

Maggie politely took the radio from Aaron and checked the battery but found nothing amiss. "Thanks to Mitch, the radio must have been protected but nothing outside of here is communicating. None of this makes any sense, unless it was a solar issue that fried everything. Maybe the Russian's nuked us, your guess is as good as mine."

Growing more distressed, they rushed outside to try the vehicles. Davey turned the key in the fire truck and nothing happened. It was as if the battery was completely drained. The other vehicles held the same result. Lights won't even turn on.

"Let me try the television," Aaron said, running back inside the station. But no matter which buttons he pressed, the large screen TV wouldn't sputter to life. He walked back out and looked at Duke, "stay here in case anything changes, we have to go cancel the event now."

Duke scowled, not wanting to disappoint the crowds that had come to see the festivities. But Maggie and Conrad nodded in agreement with Aaron.

"It's too risky with the equipment out. But we can't leave everyone stranded," she said.

Special Agent Danvers took charge. "Lets announce a delay, not a cancellation. In the meantime, direct people to the larger casinos for warmth and snacks."

As they walked back in dismay to the center of town as the snow was still lightly falling all around. A small panicked murmur arose from the crowd that had gathered. People pressed buttons on their cell phones hopelessly in confusion, others held their phone in the air hoping for something to happen, as a few gave up and walked towards their cars.

Conrad and Danvers walked up to the stage where the band was still practicing. They looked at each other and Danvers spoke up, "you seem out of breath still, I can take this one Chief." He looked out to the crowd and shouted as loud as he could while he cupped his hands around his mouth to project, "Ladies and Gentlemen, thank you for coming to our annual light parade. As you can tell we are having a bit of technical difficulties. We are very saddened to say that we have to delay this year's event as we fix the issue. If you are having car trouble please go to one of the casinos to get help. Thank you."

Duke walked back into the fire house and kicked the tire of the truck in anguish. "We're stranded here without any stinkin way to get help! Whatever's causing this has truly knocked us back to the Stone Age."

They stood helpless, completely cut off from the outside world. With no means of getting a message out or discovering the source of this strange crisis, an ominous feeling of isolation fell over the town.

Despite it being midday, an eerie quiet had fallen over the town without the power as the clouds became darker in the sky. Aaron knew they had to make a call on the parade.

As snow continued to fall, crowds reluctantly headed indoors. Even in daylight the power loss seemed ominous as the wind gusts picked up a bit. People murmured nervously more than they had before.

Aaron scanned the room full of worried families. "How long can we support everyone indoors if this keeps up?"

Conrad and Davidson looked at each other and shook their heads grimly. "A few days at best with what we have. We need solutions and fast, before night falls." He had no answers, leaving them all to wonder what strange new crisis had descended upon their town. Were they all trapped in Cripple Creek?

By the gauge of the daylight, it was about 1:30ish now or maybe 3 now, and still no sign of Mitch.

Duke directed overcrowded people to the saloon, Maggie to the shops, while Davey ensured the casino was as good as it could be. Soon the businesses were filled with uneasy people waiting for answers.

Outside, Danvers, Conrad and Aaron conferred with the maintenance workers. "Any theories on what caused this?"

They shook their heads hopelessly. Without power to run diagnostics, the cause remained frustratingly obscure. As the mostly empty streets echoed with silence as a few onlookers still waited in hope that the event they drove hours for would miraculously still happen.

The maintenance workers scratched their heads, stumped by the town-wide power outage. "Wish I had an answer for ya, Chief," said Joe, the lead electrician. "Grid's dead quiet all over. Backup generators won't turn over either."

Conrad ran a hand through his hair in frustration. "Alright, let's think this through methodically. First things first - we need to get word out to surrounding areas that we need assistance." He turned to Aaron, "any thoughts?"

Aaron shook his head. "Doubtful without power. Our best bet is sending a couple snowmobiles over the pass to Woodland Park but I doubt they work either. I also haven't started them in five years, so that's probably a dead end."

"I'll round up Frank and Bobby to make the run somehow," offered Joe.

As the men strategized, Maggie hurried over. "Casino's already full with a few panicked older people who are causing a ruckus. The saloon and shops not far behind. People are getting restless with nothing to do but wait."

Conrad exhaled out a long breath. "Right then. Danvers, you and Aaron get folks organized. We will have to figure this one out. Maybe start a fire in the town square, pass out what food and supplies we've got. Maybe some music from the band to lighten the mood. Goodness gracious, I sure hope Mitch is okay."

Aaron piped up. "What if this isn't just a power outage? What if it's something more...what else could happen next?"

The group fell silent at the unspoken thought. If it was sabotage, terrorism, or worse they were sitting ducks. But for now all they could do was take care of the people and hope help arrived before dark.

Conrad slapped Aaron on the back. "One problem at a time, son. Let's get to work."

At that same moment unbeknownst to the fair people of Cripple Creek, Kim sat in the dark of her hotel room surveying the chaos and uncertainty of the crowds below her. She picked up her glass of water and slowly sipped it as she studied their many movements.

She began to wonder to herself about the peaceful quiet as it took hold of her. A few faint voices but with the snow it was beautifully quiet, nothing like the constant noise of Beijing. This was pleasant for the moment and she savored every second of it.

She put the glass down and looked back out to the street below. Little figures all over, but something so strange immediately caught her attention. What in the world was this she thought to herself as she watched a man on horseback galloping down the middle of the street. She had thought he had seen everything in this train wreck of a town until now.

It was Mitch, on horseback galloping as fast as he could to the center of town not knowing what evil he was about to face head on. Onlookers gazed in amazement as the rest of his friends seemed astonished as well. Mitch's arrival was like something out of an old western film, the horse's hooves thundering against the snow-covered asphalt, steam rising from its flanks, rider bent low over its neck. But this was no heroic entrance. The blood-stained clothes and wild look in his eyes spoke of violence and desperation.

"Mitch! Mitch! You won't believe what happened. We had to postpone because of no power." Aaron yelled as the horse slowed in front of him.

Mitchel pulled on the reins hard and stopped the horse completely. Everyone looked at him in horror as they noticed all of the blood that stained his clothes. "Is everyone okay, what in the world happened to you?"

"You're covered in blood Mitch!" Aaron responded in shock. "Are you hurt? Did you fall off?" Everyone got closer to Mitch looking for injuries or answers.

"It's not my blood...Conrad, a guy almost killed my dad at the ranch. Never seen him before and he was going to shoot him. I had to save my family...I had to stop him." Mitch bent over and put his hands on the sadden in an attempt to catch his breath from his exhausting race back to town.

"What in the world son, what happened out there?" Conrad muttered as he placed his hand on Mitch's shoulder. At the same time Aaron went closer to his brother to try and hear what Mitch had to say next about their dad.

Aaron began to well up, "Is dad alive, what about...?"

Mitch cut him off. "They're alive Aaron, they're fine. I went to get the generator and heard a commotion. I walked out to see a guy point a gun at dad's head. All I had was the hunting bow." Mitch looked up to see stunned and shocked eyes as they heard what he just said. "It was all I had. I shot him but he wasn't done fighting. I stopped him before he hurt anyone." His face went somewhere else as though he revisited these moments in his mind.

Conrad shook his arm, "You did what you had to do Mitch. You did the right thing son, there's no dishonor in that." He looked back at Danvers and Davidson, "none of this makes any sense right now."

The gathered crowd fell into a horrified silence as Mitch recounted his tale. Each word painted a vivid picture of the life-and-death struggle that had played out at the ranch. The blood on his clothes wasn't just stains anymore, it was evidence of how close their community had come to tragedy.

Mitch whipped his leg over the saddle and dropped to the ground. After he regained his breath and then stood back up fully. He looked at all of them, still looking at him in shock. He knew that gut wrenching feeling deep down inside his very soul echoing to him.

"Before he died, the man said something that's been eating away at me ever since...he said." Mitch took a deep breath and said grimly.

"Forgive me...this is only the beginning."

PART TWO

# RESPECT

*"**With great power comes great responsibility.** A man of principles, once recognizing a need not necessarily created by self, would act in accordance with them and accept whatever sacrifices those actions dictate, out of **respect** for the principles themselves."*

-    **Martin Luther King Jr.**

# Chapter 12

Mountainside Rendezvous Point

East of Cripple Creek, Colorado

December 9

3:00 PM MST Time

"Ahh, this sucks, why couldn't we have had more time on the snowmobiles!" Ivan exclaimed as he rested up against a sturdy pine tree. "Anyone else want to carry this thing for a while." Referring to the special weapon that was secured in his pack.

Viktor glared sarcastically at him after he heard his annoying comment, "only 50 yards left Ivan. Then we can rest at the rally point." Slowly he maneuvered his boot through the snow and into his next stable stepping point.

"Ivan, I thought you loved training in the woods back home, this should be nothing comrade." Nikolai pointed out as he delighted in poking the big terrible bear that struggled with every step to get up to the top of the ridge. "I think I can see the spot from here."

Viktor suddenly held his hand up high to get the team's attention and made a tactical motion with a clenched fist the air. "Shut up, I just heard something." He continued to scan the woods slowly, looking near and then far for any sign of movement. Then he saw it. The shadow darted and moved fast up ahead.

Immediately, the three lifted their rifles in the general direction of the potential threat ready to engage. Viktor steadied his aim as he looked through the etched reticle of the sight making out the distinct crosshairs from the scenic backdrop.

Click

The safety of his rifle made a clicking sound as he turned the safety off and prepared to fire. Movement again, but this time it was much closer than before. Was it enemy forces who finally found them? Was it some locals walking through the woods? Their hearts began to race, adrenaline surged through their veins as all three were fully ready to reign fire at any second.

Crack

Up ahead the loud sound of a branch breaking came from even closer. Nikolai knelt down to one knee and steadied his rifle in preparation to take a shot. The others saw his motion and took to a knee as well anticipating an immediate engagement which could easily threaten their mission.

As daylight waned into dusk, they held their positions like statues knowing that they still needed to establish camp. There they were, potentially the last of the team completely outfitted in white camo, not moving, barely breathing, fingers on the trigger awaiting the next move.

Chirp

A bird called out and flew away from where it was perched on an old log. Finally, they exhaled and eased off their triggers as they all watched the shadowy figure appear from behind the trees.

One leg at a time the doe stepped out and made its presence known.

"I'm gonna take it!" Ivan shouted out to the rest of the team as he aligned his sight on the deer.

Viktor turned back and gave him the foulest look, "like hell you are."

Ivan begrudgingly lowered his rifle, "it's suppressed, no one would know. I haven't had a good hunt in years and I am hungry again."

"We are on what could be the most important mission our country has ever conducted and again all you can think about is your stomach." Viktor doubled down with him and showed who was still in command. "Let's get moving, we still have a lot to do and ground to cover."

Nikolai lowered his rifle as well, "what if the rest of the team don't regroup by morning?" This is taking a lot longer than we thought."

Viktor looked up at the pine canopy above them and pondered the question. What if Kim, Thomas, Anna, and Oleg don't make it back in time? They would have to finish the mission no matter what. That was why they split up the way they did. If only the three of them made it to the escape hatch, they could finish what they started. Securing phase 1 was within their grasp as long as they got there before America rebooted and turned their grid back online.

"They know the risks as we all do. We will finish this just as they would have wanted us to," he finally responded to the difficult question. He hoped that everyone would make it back, although maybe not Kim since it was difficult to trust such a stoic stone cold killer like her. Viktor knew that there was only one reason for her in the team. To babysit them. As though they weren't competent enough to do this on their own.

He stepped again and continued uphill closer to the ridge, "we are almost there, we need to set up a covert campsite and post positions. This is going to be a long night with little rest, so the faster we get set up the more sleep we get."

The team continued their faster pace until they reached their snow covered site. They walked around until they saw the red bandana tied to a tree. Nikolai ran over to it and dropped to the ground where he immediately began feeling around through the snow searching for something. The other two watch and wait. Reaching further out he felt the rod that was stuck through the snow.

He reached deeper and grasped the metal D ring. Nickolai stood up and pulled back as strong as he could, "a little help!" Nickolai exasperated as he looked to Ivan for support.

"Seriously, who is the weak one now? Hahaha" Ivan laughed as he put down his pack and walked over to where Nickolai was struggling. Reaching for the rope he grabbed it firmly and pulled back as hard as he could in one tug.

Before them a white canvas sheet connected to the rope is revealed and moved from beneath the layers of snow. He gave it another strong pull and the remaining canvas came to the surface. Nickolai grabbed at another point and pulled more fabric back to reveal a few black waterproof cases and multiple gear bags that had been cached below for weeks in hiding.

Viktor walked over to the equipment bags and began opening them. Inside there were additional weapons, ammunition, and cold weather gear.

"Load up guys, we only have an hour before sunset." Viktor commanded the rest of his team. "Ivan, you take the first sentry rotation and watch the valley we came from, Nickolai you have the point at the top of the ridge. Dig in and post up, remember that if someone doesn't shout the code word back, you know what to do but make your kills quiet. I'll tap out Ivan first and then we rotate from there every hour.

They each began donning more gear and moved into their positions. Viktor looked at his vintage Rolex watch for the time and was glad he had put it in his issued faraday bag and notes the next top of the hour. He sat leaned up against a tree in a white covered sleeping bag and attempted to remain warm.

As he scanned his surroundings, he looked over and saw Ivan sitting behind a makeshift barricade. He was also snuggled into his sleeping bag while his primary weapon was draped across him at the ready.

Viktor turned slightly and looked up towards the ridge, he struggled to make out the well hidden figure through the heavy falling snow. Nickolai was well camouflaged and dug into his position. Viktor turned back around. He hoped they had a strong team for what comes next and soon the rest would make it here as well. He needed everyone for the greatest chance of success, but once the mission was accomplished there was very little chance they would all make it out of here alive.

Slowly he exhaled a puff of hot breath as the delicate large flakes of snow fell around him. The peacefulness of it all captivated him. Small thoughts drifted through his mind as he scanned the valley below.

How many weeks had they prepared for this? All the training, planning, procurement of supplies and equipment - it had all led to this moment. The fate of their mission, and perhaps their country, rested on its success.

Viktor shivered, though not from the cold. The realization of his splintered team having to rendezvous soon. What if something had gone wrong with the others? The terrain was treacherous, and a storm had moved in with more accumulation. Anxiety crept in at the thought of shouldering this burden alone with just Ivan and Nikolai.

No, the plan was flawless, he thought to himself in order to snap out of the negativity. They were the best team he could have asked for - tough, resilient, and devoted to the cause. Each knew the stakes and willingly wanted to be apart. They just had to make it.

An almost peaceful stillness laid upon the mountains. All was well for now. He took a deep breath to calm his nerves. Dwelling on worries would do no good; he had to keep a level head.

The minutes passed as the snow fell thicker. Viktor lost track of time until he immersed himself back into his favorite watch. He watched the seconds tick by as the hand moved ever so slowly. Then a change in the atmosphere mysteriously alerted him, he got himself up and staying low, trudged up the ridge.

Ivan's hand shot up from a distance and then pointed to the ridge below signaling a disturbance to the beautiful calm forest. The snow was ankle-deep where he had dug in as he repositioned himself for a better visual angle.

Ivan scanned the valley below as he listened for noise again. The forest was pristine and blank under fresh powder, muffling all sounds of life except for the subtle crunch that occurred every few seconds.

He strained his eyes and ears for any disturbance, dreading what might come next. Was it a friend or foe, maybe another deer? As the seconds dragged on, his anxiety grew.

The bitter wind howled through the valley like a wounded animal, carrying stinging pellets of ice that felt like needles against any exposed skin. He readied his rifle with hands numbed by the cold, his fingers moving through the familiar motion as he clicked the safety off. The metallic snap seemed to echo across the vast emptiness before being swallowed by the swirling snow. Through his scope, shadows danced at the edge of visibility, playing tricks on eyes strained from hours of vigilant watching. His trigger finger tightened instinctively at each shifting shape in the whiteness.

Viktor's mind raced through the possibilities - friend or foe, success or failure, life or death. The mission parameters left no room for error, and after losing contact with part of the team six hours ago, every passing moment ratcheted up the tension. The storm had grown worse, far worse than their intelligence had predicted. If the others hadn't made the rendezvous point by now...

Then it came - faint but unmistakable, a voice carried through the valley like a ghost in the wind. The coded signal they had all been desperately waiting for.

"Zimovnik!" Anna's voice cut through the howling storm, carrying equal measures of hope and fear.

Viktor held his breath, counting the seconds. One. Two. Three. The longest moments of his life stretched into eternity as they waited for a response. The call was answered in kind from upslope, Ivan's deep baritone rolling down the mountainside like thunder, "Zimovnik."

Relief crashed through Viktor's body in a physical wave, nearly buckling his knees. His chest loosened for what felt like the first time in hours as he sucked in a deep breath of frigid air that burned his lungs. They had made it after all. The first piece of their fractured team was coming back together.

Without hesitation, Viktor launched himself down the snow-covered slope, his boots finding purchase in the deep drifts as he half-ran, half-slid toward Ivan's position. The makeshift barricade came into view - a hastily but effectively constructed fortress of fallen branches, packed snow, and whatever natural cover Ivan had managed to gather in the storm. As Viktor vaulted over the barrier, the tension drained from his body like water from a broken dam. One crucial hurdle had been cleared. With the others' support, their chances had improved from nearly impossible to merely daunting.

Fresh determination filled him, coursing through his veins like liquid steel, warming him from within despite the bitter cold. His mind flashed through memories of previous missions with these people he trusted more than family - the frozen nights surviving in Siberia, the chaotic firefights in Chechnya, the heart-stopping close calls in Georgia. They had faced death together so many times, and each time they had emerged stronger, more unified. Whatever challenges lay ahead in this mission, they would face them as they always had - as a team, as brothers and sisters in arms, as the elite unit they had become through blood and sacrifice.

Through swirling snow, figures emerged from the trees below - unmistakably the missing members of their unit. Grins broke out as they convened, slapping each others' backs in hearty welcome.

The mission was afoot once more. Renewed in spirit, Viktor knew they would prevail against any odds. Side by side in friendship, nothing could deter their united endeavor to change the course of history.

Anna and Oleg stomped through the snow slowly dragging bags of provisions behind them strapped to their waists.

"Some help would be great guys!" Anna sarcastically but exaggeratedly shouted out.

Ivan hopped down the hill and immediately took the pack. Moreso out of hunger than to generously help out.

"Where is Kim and Thomas?" Viktor questioned them before even appreciating the fact that they had made it. Showing his true colors once again.

Oleg annoyingly responded, "we waited longer than planned but no one showed up at our point. We had to double time to get here."

Viktor's countenance changed again to anger, "they should have been there already. There has to be a problem. Did you see anything going on in town?"

"No, everything was normal and the parade was starting when we left the town. It was calm," Anna responded sharply and was still out of breath.

"The incoming storm masked our approach, maybe they got lost," Oleg said. "Plus Thomas is not capable like the rest of us to handle this, probably for the best he doesn't make it. We all knew he wanted this to be a suicide mission."

Viktor contemplated that thought, "you're probably right, maybe for the best he doesn't continue with the team. He would only slow us down moving forward. We need to change our plans though."

Ivan opened a bottle of water and began chugging it while Nickolai slowly walked toward the group who was now huddled around the bags of goods.

"Ivan you will stay behind for Kim, we won't wait for Thomas...on second thought...Anna you need to recuperate. Anna will stay behind in this position tomorrow and I know you will make sure Thomas is finished quickly," Viktor strategized their next move as a team.

Anna nodded, pulling her fur hat low. As the only woman currently, she felt pressure to prove herself equal, but none doubted her skills.

He continued, "The rest of you need to establish the bivouac, no fires, make it as dark as possible. If you need to, dig in your shelters."

The team started taking provisions from the bags and then moved out in different directions to set up for the cold night ahead. Motivation mounted for the mission ahead.

Amid swirling snow, the team established their spots, readied packs, and prepared weapons in silence. Final handclasps were exchanged as comrades one by one disappeared into the woods, ghosts on a mission of destiny whose outcome would shape nations. May fortune favor the bold.

Anna settled into her position overlooking the valley trail. She was grateful for the solitude - it gave her time to think without the nagging doubts of her teammates, or from Oleg who constantly checked her out. Proving herself had always been a challenge, but she was more than capable.

Her thoughts drifted to Kim and Thomas, she wondered if they were on their way traversing through the same snow she just trekked and filling her footsteps. A small part of her hoped Thomas wouldn't make it as well, not out of malice but for the safety of the mission. Viktor was right that their objective came first and she would have to end Thomas. Still, she hoped no harm had come to either of them.

In the distant camp, Oleg finished digging the last sleeping trench just as Nikolai returned from the perimeter check. "All secure," he reported, collapsing into the unfinished shelter. The two men shared a laugh as Oleg continued working on checking their weapons. Moments of camaraderie were needed to boost morale, especially in grim conditions.

Viktor walked over to an area away from the rest of the team. There he began double checking the maps and pondered different contingencies. If the others didn't arrive by dawn, would they push on immediately together or leave Anna? Lives were at stake either way. He hoped it wouldn't come to that, but they had trained for any scenario.

As the team settled into their position, their thoughts turned to the mission that lay ahead. So much was riding on their efforts. They tried to rest, preserving strength for what tomorrow might bring. Snow muffled the forest, blanketing the terrain in a shroud of silence. All they could do was way for now and his thoughts once again overtook him.

Why this mission, why at this point in the conflict, and who in charge was giving the orders. It was probably the Asians again which never went well for anyone else involved, just ask the Iranians. Also, why wasn't Kim with them right now. The whole situation was getting out of hand and for what reason.

Viktor had heard the rumors back home before he left about a new weapon the Asians had developed. A weapon that would make nukes obsolete, but at what cost and what could it be. Whatever it was, it was riding on him and his team to accomplish their mission. He sat back on the snow and maneuvered himself back into this sleeping bag attempting to get his mind off of things once again.

In her lookout post high on the ridge, Anna peered through the falling snow, her rifle's scope fogging slightly with each measured breath. The foreboding silence was broken only by the howling winds that seemed to carry whispers of approaching danger. She felt utterly alone, cut off from the others below, their camp now invisible through the thickening storm. Every few minutes, she would wipe frost from her scope, her fingers stiff despite the thermal gloves. Was this where she wanted to be right now? The question nagged at her like an old wound.

Her mind wandered to past missions, times when everything had gone sideways in the blink of an eye. There was the skirmish in Ukraine, where she fought beside Ivan back to back as enemies closed in - the smell of cordite thick in the air, the sound of bullets striking brick inches from their heads. Or the bombing in

Grozny she only barely escaped, her ears ringing for days afterward, the taste of dust and blood lingering in her mouth. She had watched too many good operators fall, their luck finally running out when they least expected it. Each memory was a stark reminder that in their line of work, experience didn't guarantee survival - it only improved the odds slightly.

Shaking off the creeping doubts, she forced herself to focus on the task at hand. Her role was vital - the others were depending on her sharp eyes and ears. In conditions like these, a lone figure in the snow was all it might take to raise the alarm. The difference between spotting movement at 800 meters versus 200 could mean life or death for the entire team. She adjusted her position slightly, ignoring the cramping in her legs from hours of stillness.

In their hastily constructed shelter, Oleg and Nikolai talked in hushed tones as they took their watch, their voices barely audible above the wind. Steam rose from their cups of cold coffee, more for warmth than alertness now.

"What are the chances the Americans have caught wind of the plan?" Nikolai wondered, absently checking the magazine in his rifle for the hundredth time. His eyes never stopped scanning the perimeter, even during conversation.

Oleg replied grimly, cleaning his weapon with practiced precision despite the cold, "Good enough that we must succeed, and quickly. Once phase two is in motion, there will be no stopping us." He paused, looking up at the heavy clouds. "No stopping any of it."

The distant howls carried on the wind, setting the team further on edge. The sounds echoed off the valley walls, making it impossible to determine direction or distance. Were they wolves or coyotes hunting in the storm, or something more sinister lurking unseen? In the growing darkness, shadows seemed to move with purpose, playing tricks on tired eyes.

Viktor lay in his sleeping bag, mind racing despite his exhaustion. The questions wouldn't let him rest. Why this mission, why at this critical point in the conflict? The Asians' involvement never boded well - the Iranians had learned that lesson the hard way. And Kim's absence nagged at him like a splinter under the skin. The whole situation felt like a house of cards in a windstorm.

The rumors he'd heard back home before deployment haunted his thoughts. A new weapon that would make nuclear arsenals obsolete - but at what unimaginable cost? Whatever it was, the success or failure of their mission would tip the balance. The weight of that responsibility pressed down on him like the tons of snow above their position.

All they could do now was wait...and watch...and hope they were ready for what lay ahead. The storm continued to intensify, nature itself seeming to conspire against them. In the darkness, each team member nursed their own private fears while maintaining the stoic facade their profession demanded. Tomorrow would bring either victory or disaster - there would be no middle ground. The fate of nations hung by a thread, and they were the ones holding the scissors.

The night stretched on, endless and cold, as the storm raged around their position. Each passing hour brought them closer to either glory or catastrophe. The mission clock was ticking, and somewhere out there, their enemies were moving too. In this deadly game of chess, the next move could be their last.

Vicktor looked out into the darkness and mumbled, "alright fate, your move..."

# Chapter 13

Double Eagle Casino

Cripple Creek, Colorado

December 9

3:30 PM MST Time

Kim peered through her scope as she slowly adjusted the knob to focus closer on the group centered around the man on the horse. She could see four figures, a man on a horse talked animatedly to three others standing in the snow.

"What a spectacle, could this really be happening right now?" Kim said quietly to herself. "What kind of person does such a stupid thing?"

She adjusted the focus as she positioned the man on the horse in her crosshairs. There was definitely something not normal going on with him. His clothes looked torn and he was covered head to toe in something dark red. What was that? She stained her vision and adjusted the focus better.

It was unmistakable, the unmistakable red if blood soaked his clothes. But he seemed uninjured and was moving with purpose as he spoke to the others. So whose blood was it she thought to herself.

Kim focused intently again, trying to make out what they were saying over the howl of the wind and snow. She could see them talk, but couldn't make out any words from this distance or without the right tools.

The man on the horse seemed distressed about something as he gestured animatedly. One of the others, a younger man, looked shocked by whatever Mitch was telling them. This was not good regardless. Were they compromised? Was the mission in jeopardy?

She continued to watch the group for a matter of minutes as they spoke to one another. Then a tall man in a long coat suddenly approached them as well as a man in a police uniform, both seemingly unaffected by the weather because they were more interested in the commotion.

Kim seemed to recognize the taller man almost immediately. She sprinted back to desk in her dark hotel room and frantically searched through files that had been neatly stacked. A picture and profile of Danvers was listed as well as many other faces with their name and sensitive information.

Her mission finally had just become clearer. They were not on their trail and Danvers couldn't be allowed to question Mitch's group any further. He would surely uncover the secrets Kim had been sent to protect. She had to prevent that at all costs just like she had to with the last special agent that was snooping around on their trail.

If she did this though it would expose her plus she was solo right now without any hope for backup. Maybe this was for the best, but there was no way to alert the rest of the team that they might be compromised. There was the only option left and she needed to move quickly. The mission was hanging in the unsteady balance of her next decision.

Kim knew what she had to do, as she rushed back over to the positioned rifle and peered through the scope. Through the falling snow, she could see Danvers deep in conversation with Mitch now. Her fingers delicately moved to steady the crosshairs directly over Danvers' chest.

Accounting for the potential wind speed, distance, and drop she steadily made the calculated adjustments mentally. Adjusting her stance and repositioning her grip on the rifle she prepared herself for her next move.

She pulled back the bolt and pushed the heavy ballistic sniper round into the chamber. Slapping the bolt down, the round seated into place and was ready for what could come next.

Taking a human life didn't come easy to her, but orders were orders. She began slowly squeezing the trigger when a thought stopped her - what if she missed. She would have to finish the job another way and this would get very messy. Every second she waited could mean more trouble, but pulling this trigger now could very well end her own life very soon.

"Get a hold of yourself Kim, this is nothing new!" Kim said to herself as she steadied her breathing. She remembered the commitment she had made to her country as she slowly squeezed the smooth trigger. The click of the trigger was mild and it engaged the firing pin then all hell broke loose.

Thomp.

The bullet exited the rifle through the suppressor making a distinct sound that was as silenced as possible but still unmistakable. It crashed the glass as it passed through, shattering it instantly as it continued on its trajectory directly for Danvers.

She stayed on target as she began to rack another round into the chamber. Through the scope, she saw Danvers clutch his upper chest and the mass of the bullet propel him backwards and onto the street.

Everyone watched in horror as he was impacted by the bullet. They stopped everything and were frozen in time as their brains tried to process what just happened. The whomping sound as the bullet hit Danvers and then pinged off the street after traveling through his body.

"Run!" Mitch screamed at the top of his lungs.

Everyone turned and ran for cover to save their own lives unsure of what just happened. Mitch began to run, then stopped as he saw Danvers' shocked face looking at him pleading for help. Immediately, the light switch inside flipped on and he rushed over to him without regard for his own safety. Blood began to pool from beneath the back of Danvers who faced upright but not communicating.

"Is he dead?" Duke yelled, as he rushed to help out.

Mitch looked back to see him, "Help me drag him. We have to be fast."

Mitch and Duke went to his side, grabbed a wrist and pulled his body as hard as they could toward the nearest cover.

"Move, move, move." Mitch yelled to Duke as they both dragged him towards the door of the Monte Carlo Emporium.

Without warning another round narrowly missed Mitch's head and smashed into one of the windows of the building, exploding the glass into a million pieces. Mitch and Duke stopped for a second to realize what just happened and then moved even faster or else they would have to leave Danvers to die.

Duke grabbed the door handle and swung it open propping it with his foot as Mitch continued to pull Danvers through the threshold. "Keep moving." Dukes belted out as they finally got inside the building right as another round made impact.

They heard the sound of the whizzing of the bullet breaking the sound barrier as it made its way through the doorway. It slammed into the floor near Duke, kicking up pieces of the old wood flooring and caused a loud thud.

"Keep moving away from the windows, it's coming from the east. Move to the back of the building," Mitch instructed Duke as they continued pulling Danvers over the old carpets. "He's shot and losing blood fast. Gotta get him patched up now!"

Kim hunted them from a distance through her scope, wondering if her gamble had paid off. All three shots and only one hit, this was unlike her. She grabbed a new mag off the bed and tactically reloaded the rifle anticipating more fun to come.

She might have a chance. If she could take out these two cowboys and only a few police in town. Kim could see her opportunity. American's will always act, so she better be prepared. As she peered back through the scope she knew that they would come for her.

Inside the Monte Carlo Emporium, Mitch and Duke dragged Danvers' limp body towards the back of the building.

"Lay him down over here," Mitch yelled over the sound of the wind entering the building from outside. They set Danvers down gently on an old pool table after knocking a few items off first.

Mitch quickly assessed for breathing, chest rise, and pulse. "He's alive but just barely. Duke I need you to get the med kit from the station and Davey! Go through the backdoor and go behind the buildings. Keep your head low. Go, go, go!"

As Duke rushed off, Mitch cut open Danvers' shirt to assess the damage. A bullet hole oozed blood and small bubbles on the top right side of his chest. As he continued to check his wound, he noticed that the bullet narrowly missed anything major. Rolling him over he saw the large exit hole the bullet left. The only thing he can do is to put direct pressure from his hand on the wound site.

"If you can hear me, you're a lucky man," Mitch said, hoping that Danvers could still hear him. "It passed right through, but you're not out of the woods yet."

He grabbed Danvers hand and squeezed hard as he continued to hold pressure. A faint and weak squeeze was felt back which caused Mitch to smile. "Stay with me, I got you."

A few minutes later, Duke returned back into the building holding the med bag. Davey followed behind him holding a Stop the Bleed kit and Philip carried other medical items. Davey tosses it over to Mitch, "here you go and how can I help?"

"Lungs collapsed, tracheal deviation, bullet had somewhat of a clean exit," Mitch muttered. "I need to use the Hyfin chest seal first. Then needle D on the second intercostal space, try to puncture the midclavicular line on the affected side to release the trapped air."

He pulled supplies from the medical bag - Decompression needle, chest seals. Thankfully they weren't being shot at anymore.

"It's so dark in here Mitch, how can we see anything?" Davey asked.

Mitch ignored the comment and used the remaining natural light to aid him. He ripped open the packaging and took out the two chest seals then removed the coverings. He carefully placed each one over the bullet hole, while he required help from the group getting the one on the back to place perfectly.

Davey monitored Danvers' vitals, "He still has a slight deviation, better to needle him now. Who knows when we can get him to a hospital."

"Your right, Duke I need you both to hold him steady and guide me while I needle him from the side," Mitch commanded as he grabbed the massive needle out of its housing. "What is this thing Davey, it's a beast compared to the other ones?"

Davey responded quickly, "that's the Spear, we got them last month. It's supposed to work better than our regular needles."

"If you say so, as long as it works is what matters right now," Mitch continued on opening the medical device that looks just like a white spear with a sharp hollow needle on the end of it. Methodically, he went to task in order to complete this complicated application. He felt for the 3rd rib and measured the distance to avoid the heart and placed the needle tip at the superior point to the rib. Slowly he inserted the needle little by little until he hit the desired marking.

Stopping the insertion, Mitch released the clasps and removed the needle to only leave the catheter. Immediately it started allowing air to pass through and relieve any pressure on the heart. There was an audible hiss as trapped air escaped that was surprising to all that it worked so quickly.

"I think we got it." Mitch expressed joyfully but surprised that he did it correctly for his first try. Blood slightly bubbled from the wound as Danvers gasped while his lung reinflated. Mitch taped the catheter tube securely in place as Davey began dressing the wound.

As Davey monitored Danvers' vitals, he noticed his breathing was still shallow and labored. "Duke, hand me the stethoscope," he said tersely.

Placing the tips in his ears, Davey listened carefully to Danvers' chest. Behind the bubbling coming from the chest tube, he picked up distant crackles in the lower right lung. "Pneumothorax isn't fully resolved. I think there's a bleb that might have ruptured, but there's no way to find out."

"We can at least give him O2 and watch him closely, especially since it doesn't require batteries." Davey retrieved more supplies as Danvers coughed weakly but was at least responding now.

"Better?" Mitch asked him, getting a faint nod in response. He attached the oxygen mask to Danver's face and opened the valve.

Checking vitals again, Davey was pleased to hear clear lung sounds on both sides. "Yes! Now we just need to keep him stabilized until help arrives."

"Help might not come," Mitch said grimly, meeting Davey's gaze with blood-stained hands.

Davey paled at the implication. They had come so close to losing their friend under Mitch's improvised care. But would it truly be enough without a well-equipped hospital?

"We're on our own out here," Mitch continued darkly. "And someone is still out there gunning for us."

A shiver passed through the group that had nothing to do with the freezing conditions outside. They were trapped as an unknown enemy stalked their lives through the snowy wasteland.

Duke voiced the nervous tension building in all their minds. "Then what's the plan, Mitch? We can't just sit here like ducks in a row, waiting to be picked off one by one."

Mitch ran a weary hand down his face, leaving a smear of blood in its wake. When he finally spoke, it was with the calm authority of a man hardened by impossible circumstances.

"Move Danvers to the ambulance. Then we get armed and find whoever did this. Whoever's out there wants us dead. So it's time we ended this hunt...permanently."

His steel gaze conveyed a chilling resolve. Protecting his makeshift family had become a duel to the death against an unseen assailant. Shadows seemed to gather as the remaining daylight turned to early evening, cloaking the killer in the snowstorm's shroud.

Their very survival now depended on becoming the Hunter, not the Hunted.

# Chapter 14

Cripple Creek Fire Station

Cripple Creek, Colorado

December 9

3:45 PM MST Time

"Mitch, Mitch...what's the plan man?" Davey asked the questions that everyone in the room was thinking.

Mitch, who was holding onto the rail of the ambulance, looked up at the group, "I'm not sure this time, not sure at all. We have to keep Danvers alive, Davey you're the best man for that job. Philips can help. "

"You can count on us, but who's going with you?" Davey shot back.

Mitch looked around the fire station bay again, "Davidson, Jerry, Duke, and..." he continued to survey but it left only his brother as the next best option. "Aaron, are you sure you're up for this? We might not all make it but we gotta try."

"I can be Mitch, you know that." Aaron responds in hesitation. "What about Emily? What about the town for that matter if something happens?"

Mitch nods in frustration, "good point brother, no one faults you for staying behind and selfishly I wanted you to as well, just in case. Go get that rifle from the shop and get back here asap. We leave in five." Everyone else nodded as well as they prepared for the hunted to now go on the hunt.

Mitch checked himself and felt for his small Sig, one extra 15 round mag, his knife, and a micro tourniquet. He did his best to make sure everything was squared away but knowing this wasn't enough. Then he remembered the daily bag he brought with him back in his office.

Rushing over he threw open the door to see it sitting there right where he had left it. Putting it up on the desk he opened the covert compartment of the Vertx bag that revealed a treasure trove of gear, most of which were dead electronics. Pulling things apart from the velcro backer, he puts an extra mag and his knife in his jeans back pocket.

"Seriously!" Mitch erupted as others glanced at what he was doing.
His flashlight was dead. Just like everything else in this place. Frustrated, but at least better prepared Mitch walks back into the station bay to his awaiting team.

Davidson, Jerry, and Duke all checked their weapons and gave the reassurance that was needed to head out knowing that some of them might not make it back. Although, not knowing what they were about to face.

Aaron knocked on the door with the classical knock they always did as a kid. It was time.

The team headed out into the biting cold, their boots crunching through fresh snow as they moved down the back of the buildings heading East. The direction of the shots echoed in their minds, each step calculated and precise.

Mitch and Davidson took point, moving shoulder to shoulder with the practiced efficiency of seasoned operators. Their breath came out in visible puffs as they maneuvered around frost-covered trash bins and snow-laden parked cars, every movement deliberate and controlled.

The snow intensified, coming down in thick curtains that limited visibility to mere yards. The bitter cold stung their exposed faces like tiny needles, but years of training kept their focus razor-sharp on the mission. Their tactical formation tightened as they approached each corner, knowing that every step could trigger an engagement.

The questions multiplied with each passing moment - had the sniper relocated to a better position? Were they dealing with a lone shooter or a coordinated team? The uncertainty hung heavy in the air, thick as the falling snow.

Approaching the intersection, their movements slowed to a crawl. Davidson took the lead, his years of experience evident in how he approached the corner. He began to peer around, using the minimal exposure techniques that had kept him alive through countless operations.

Whomp.

The sound came first - that distinctive crack of a high-powered rifle round impacting brick. Then came the spray of pulverized concrete as the bullet struck inches from Davidson's face, close enough that he felt the impact through the air. His training kicked in instantly as he fell backward, tucking and rolling to cover in one fluid motion that spoke of countless hours of practice. Small fragments of brick and mortar rained down around him as he pressed himself against the wall, heart pounding but hands steady on his weapon.

"Pinned, we gotta move. Continue down the backside of the buildings for cover!" Mitch's voice cut through the chaos. Without waiting for acknowledgment, he burst into motion, crossing the road alone in a controlled sprint that made him a harder target. His boots found purchase on the slick surface as he disappeared into the back alley, the darkness swallowing him whole.

Davidson didn't hesitate. Years of working together had taught them to trust each other's instincts implicitly. He surged to his feet, leading the others in a desperate charge across the exposed ground. Their boots thundered against the pavement, each step an eternity as they raced against the shooter's next shot.

Whomp.

The second shot came just as they cleared the danger zone, the bullet striking the street where Duke had been moments before. The impact sent chips of asphalt flying, the sound echoing off the surrounding buildings like a hammer strike. All of them made it to cover, their breathing heavy but controlled as they pressed themselves against the cold brick wall of the alley.

"Thank goodness she shot at you Duke and not me," Jerry managed between breaths, his characteristic humor surfacing even in the face of danger. His eyes sparkled with barely contained mirth as he added, "I would have been a goner for sure!" The levity, even in this tense moment, served its purpose - helping to release some of the adrenaline-fueled tension that had built up during their mad dash.

Mitch scanned ahead, his trained eye immediately identifying another exposed section that would make them perfect targets. The snow was falling heavier now, reducing visibility but also potentially masking their movements. "We have another no man's land gents. We can't all go and we will need cover fire or else we won't be that lucky this time." His voice carried the weight of experience, each word measured and precise.

"I got your back!" Jerry's confident voice rang out, his weapon already positioned. "Davidson, you go with Mitch, Duke will help me." The natural leadership in his tone left little room for argument, though that didn't stop Duke.

"Why me?" Duke shot Jerry a look that could have melted the snow around them, his grip tightening on his weapon.

Jerry's face cracked into that familiar, mischievous smile that usually preceded trouble. "Cause we all know what kinda shot you are with that new fancy little gun you got there. You might be a great hunter...but" The old ribbing between them surfaced even in this life or death situation.

"Not the time Jerry, settle this later you two." Mitch's sharp interruption cut through their banter like a knife. His eyes never stopped scanning the buildings above them as he spoke. "Let's move up into position and on three you lay cover fire once I tell you where."

They pressed forward to the building's edge, every nerve ending alive with the knowledge that somewhere above, a scope was trained on their position. Mitch's hesitation lasted only a fraction of a second before he darted out, his movement swift and purposeful as he quickly assessed the situation before diving back into cover.

Whomp.

The bullet's impact sprayed chunks of wall near their heads, but more importantly, it revealed what they needed to know. The shot's trajectory was clear now, giving away the shooter's position like a beacon in the night.

"Probably the Double Eagle, one of the top floor windows!" Mitch called out as he pressed himself against the wall, his breathing controlled despite the close call. Small pieces of concrete continued to fall around them like artificial snow.

"Probably?" Jerry's voice carried equal parts sarcasm and concern.

Davidson, ever the practical one, cut through the uncertainty. "Just shoot at the buildings windows, all of them!" His command carried the authority of someone who had been in similar situations before.

Mitch and Davidson found themselves shoulder to shoulder, their stance mirroring years of training and shared combat experience. The moment stretched between them, heavy with unspoken understanding. "Ready, on three. One. Two. Three!"

They exploded into motion, their legs pumping hard against the snow-covered ground. Behind them, Jerry and Duke stepped out in perfect synchronization, their weapons erupting in a coordinated symphony of suppressing fire. The air filled with the sharp crack of their rifles as they systematically swept the building's facade. The lone shattered window in the middle became their focal point, both men concentrating their fire there until their magazines ran dry.

The sprint across the open ground seemed to last an eternity, but finally, Mitch and Davidson made it safely across. Davidson's landing was less than graceful, his momentum carrying him into a roll that left him with scraped palms and wounded pride.

"What now Mitch?" Davidson asked as he brushed off the small pieces of gravel embedded in his hands, his breath coming in short, controlled bursts.

Mitch's eyes scanned their surroundings, mind working through their options. "If we go through The District we should be out of the line of sight, but no guarantees." The admission came reluctantly in their line of work, certainty was a luxury they rarely had.

Davidson's nod spoke volumes, his expression a mixture of resignation and determination. "Works for me."

They went down the back stairs and approached The District Kitchen and Saloon's back door, the old metal handle of the restaurant refused to budge under Davidson's attempt. "Ideas?" he asked, frustration evident in his voice.

Mitch's sudden laughter caught them both off guard, the sound creating small clouds in the frigid Colorado air. "Hahaha, that's easy for us fire guys." His hand disappeared into his back pocket, emerging with what looked like a small pry bar. "The key to the town right here."

The metal tool slid into the gap with practiced ease, and with a sharp bang from his palm, the lock mechanism gave way. The door swung open with a protesting creak that seemed too loud in the tense atmosphere.

"Wow, I need one of those," Davidson said, impressed despite himself.

Mitch took point, his movements deliberate and controlled as he entered the dim interior. "Davidson, stay low and along the walls." His whispered command carried years of tactical experience. The temperature difference between outside and in created a momentary fog on their safety glasses, adding another layer of challenge to their entry.

Inside The District, the atmosphere was thick with tension. The restaurant's usual warm, welcoming ambiance had been transformed into something more sinister by the circumstances. Shadows stretched across empty tables, and the afternoon light filtering through the windows cast strange patterns across the hardwood floors. The few occupants - the bartender, a waitress with wide, frightened eyes, and three patrons - were huddled behind overturned tables, their faces a mixture of fear and relief at seeing uniformed personnel.

Mitch raised his hand in a calming gesture, his voice steady and reassuring. "It's okay, we are fire and police here to protect."

The effect was immediate - shoulders relaxed slightly, and tentative smiles appeared on pale faces. The waitress clutched her serving tray to her chest like a shield, her knuckles white with tension.

Davidson moved closer to Mitch, his voice barely above a whisper. "We need to get these people to safety Mitch! But where?" His eyes darted between the windows and the civilians, calculating risks and possibilities.

Mitch's tactical mind was already working the problem. "Good question, hey bartender." He addressed the man who had been trying to make himself as small as possible behind the bar. "Yeah, you sir, is there a storage room in the back?" The bartender's quick nod and pointing finger provided their solution. "Good, stay very low and everyone please move back there."

The civilians moved with surprising discipline, crawling and crouching their way toward safety. The sound of their shoes on the wooden floor seemed unnaturally loud in the tense silence. The bartender, a stocky man with graying temples, was the last to move. He approached Mitch with an awkward waddle, holding something wrapped in a bar towel.

"Take this, might do some good," he said, revealing an antique double-barrel shotgun that looked like it belonged in a museum rather than a firefight. The wood was worn smooth from years of handling, and the metal had a patina that spoke of age and history.

Davidson's reaction was immediate. "Seriously dude?" His eyes widened at the sight of the weapon being handed over so casually, professional training warring with disbelief. The bartender's only response was a noncommittal shrug before he hurried through the storage room door, leaving them with their unexpected arsenal addition.

Mitch examined the shotgun with a mix of amusement and professional interest. The weapon was short, probably cut down at some point in its long history. Despite its age, it was well-maintained - someone had taken good care of this piece of history. Two shells. Two chances. In their current situation, that was two more chances than they had before.

Moving toward the front door, they maintained their tactical positioning. Every step was calculated, every movement precise. The door hinges protested softly as Mitch eased it open, letting in a blast of bitter cold wind that carried stinging snow with it. The temperature drop was immediate and shocking.

"Ready?" Mitch asked, his eyes already scanning the Double Eagle's facade across the street. The afternoon light was fading, making the target windows look like dark, hungry mouths waiting to swallow them whole.

"Time to rock n' roll!" Davidson's enthusiastic response came with action as he burst through the door, leaving Mitch momentarily stunned behind him.

Mitch launched himself after Davidson, the ancient shotgun clutched tightly in his grip as he sprinted through the swirling snow. The wet conditions proved treacherous - his boot lost traction on a patch of ice hidden beneath the fresh powder.

Time seemed to slow as he felt his balance give way, his body twisting in mid-stride. The fall sent him sliding across the slick street, his momentum carrying him directly into the side of a parked car with a dull thud that knocked the wind from his lungs.

As he tried to regain his bearings, a horrifying realization struck - he was perfectly framed in the sniper's line of sight. Through the falling snow, he could just make out the broken window of the Double Eagle, a dark void that seemed to stare back at him with malevolent intent.

"Get off the X!" The words escaped his lips in a desperate whisper, his mind screaming at his body to move.

Whomp. Smash!

The high-powered round punched through the car's window like it was tissue paper, sending a shower of safety glass cascading over Mitch. The bullet struck the pavement inches from his position, the impact spraying chips of asphalt into his face. His training kicked in, muscles responding before conscious thought as he scrambled for better cover behind the vehicle's engine block.

Whomp. Thud!

The second shot was closer and penetrated the car door with a sound like a sledgehammer hitting sheet metal. Mitch could feel the impact reverberate through the vehicle's frame. The round exited near the first, creating another crater in the street. The shooter was walking their shots closer to his position, adjusting fire with deadly precision.

Bang.

Bang.

Bang.

Bang.

Davidson's rifle barked in response, the sharp reports echoed off the buildings. His cover fire was precise and disciplined, targeting the sniper's position with controlled bursts. Each shot was attempted to keep the shooter's head down, buying Mitch precious seconds to move.

Mitch seized the opportunity, pushing himself up from the frozen ground. His boots struggled to find purchase on the slippery surface as he began his desperate sprint toward Davidson's position. Each step was a gamble between speed and stability, the snow-covered street becoming an obstacle course of potential disasters.

Whomp!

The next shot arrived with devastating effect, exploding through the windshield of a nearby truck. The safety glass disintegrated in a spectacular spider web pattern, raining down in a crystalline shower. Mitch could feel the displacement of air as the round passed close enough to ruffle his jacket. His lungs burned with the cold air as he pushed himself harder, knowing the next shot could be the one that found its mark.

With one final burst of energy, he hurled himself toward the relative safety of Davidson's position. His dive carried him behind a concrete barrier, his shoulder taking the brunt of the impact as he rolled into cover. The old shotgun somehow stayed in his grip throughout the entire ordeal, though his hands were shaking from adrenaline and cold.

"That was close, why did you take off like that?" Mitch managed between gasping breaths, his heart hammering against his ribs. "Thanks for the save just now, seriously thanks." The gratitude in his voice was genuine. Davidson's quick thinking and accurate fire had likely saved his life.

Davidson's face showed a mix of relief and regret. "Sorry man, I thought you were going." The apology was sincere, though his eyes never stopped scanning the building above them.

"All good, let's get inside and stop this now." Mitch's gaze drifted to the coffee shop where Emily was likely still hiding. The windows were dark and empty - a good sign. At least she had the sense to stay away from them.

The massive doors of the Double Eagle loomed before them, their ornate design a stark contrast to the deadly game being played out around them. Moving with practiced precision, they approached the entrance, alternating their movement in a carefully choreographed dance of advance and cover. Each step brought them closer to their target, and closer to what they knew would be an inevitable confrontation.

The stairwell waited ahead, a darkness that could hide any number of threats. They moved in tandem, covering each other's advancement with the fluid efficiency of long-time partners. Both men knew that somewhere above them, their adversary was waiting, and the next few minutes would determine who walked away from this encounter.

The ancient shotgun in Mitch's hands felt inadequate against a trained sniper, but it was better than nothing. Two shells. Two chances. Sometimes that's all you needed if only you could get close enough to use them.

The lobby's darkness enveloped them like a shroud, forcing them to rely on their training. Mitch performed a quick scan using the tactical "slicing the pie" technique, his eyes adjusting to identify potential threats in the corners and behind the abandoned front desk.

"On me." Mitch whispered, using standard close quarters tactical commands. Davidson immediately moved to cover his six, establishing a defensive position that prevented anyone from flanking them.

They approached the stairwell using parallel paths, minimizing their profile as potential targets. The metal door loomed before them, its surface scarred from years of use. Mitch positioned himself on the handle side, while Davidson took up position on the hinge side, creating a perfect fatal funnel coverage.

"Ready, on me," Mitch breathed, barely audible. He crouched slightly and positioned himself before making entry. In a synchronized movement refined through countless drills, they breached the stairwell. Mitch went high, Davidson went low, their weapons covering different sectors as they cleared the immediate area.

The stairwell ascent became a methodical exercise in tactical movement. Mitch took point, using the wall as cover while maintaining his weapon at the high ready position. The old shotgun, despite its age, was perfect for the confined space.

Davidson maintained rear security, walking backwards up the stairs in a modified position, ready to engage any threats from below.

They cleared each landing using coordinated movements, Mitch checking high while Davidson cleared low. The sound of their boots on the metal stairs seemed thunderous in the enclosed space, despite their attempts at stealth. Every shadow, every corner could conceal a threat.

At the final landing, their breathing was controlled but labored from the tactical ascent. Sweat trickled down their backs despite the cold, their bodies tensed for combat. The top floor door stood before them like a gateway to hell, its small window offering a tantalizing but dangerous glimpse into what awaited them.

"Check," Mitch whispered, starting to move toward the window. The glass square seemed to mock them, promising vital intelligence while simultaneously offering the enemy a perfect kill slot if they were being watched.

"Negative," Davidson hissed back, his hand shooting out to stop Mitch's movement. "That window's a death trap. They're expecting us - that's exactly where they want us to look." Years of combat experience had taught him that the most obvious route was often the deadliest. The small window was the perfect setup for a waiting shooter - one quick peek would give away their position and probably get one of them killed.

Mitch's face showed understanding as the tactical reality sank in. They'd both seen too many good operators fall for simple traps like this. The sweat on his forehead caught the dim emergency lighting, his pupils dilated from adrenaline and the low light conditions.

Mitch then positioned himself on the non-hinged side of the door, pressing his back against the wall. The position would give him maximum coverage when the door opened while minimizing his exposure. The ancient shotgun felt alive in his hands, like a caged animal waiting to be unleashed. He could feel every groove in the worn wood stock, every imperfection in the metal becoming part of his awareness.

"Stack up," he commanded in a whisper. Davidson moved with fluid precision, taking position on the opposite side. Their eyes met briefly - a moment of unspoken communication that conveyed everything. They'd trained to survive this before. But something felt different this time. The stakes were higher, the tension more electric.

The hallway beyond the door held unknown threats. Every room could conceal an enemy, every shadow could hide death. The darkness would be both their ally and enemy, concealing their movement but also masking potential threats. No backup, no support - just two operators against whatever waited beyond that door.

Mitch's hand found the door handle, cold metal against his gloved palm. His muscles coiled like springs, ready for explosive action. The shotgun was positioned at high ready, its twin barrels promising devastating close-range effectiveness. Two shells. In close quarter battles, that could mean everything or nothing.

Time seemed to slow, each heartbeat becoming a distinct event. The blood rushing in their ears created a rhythm that matched their controlled breathing. Three-count breaching. Standard operating procedure. It had saved their lives countless times before.

Davidson shifted his weight slightly, adjusting his stance for optimal coverage. His service weapon was held in a perfect compressed ready position, years of training evident in every aspect of his posture. His eyes were focused, pupils contracted to pinpoints of intense concentration.

The air felt thick with tension, each second stretching into eternity. Weird shadows under the door, playing tricks with their vision. Was that movement they saw? A shadow? Or their minds creating threats from nothing?

Mitch drew in a final deep breath, his muscles tensing for action. This was the moment, the point of no return. Once that door opened, they would be committed. Success or failure, life or death, would be determined in the next few seconds.

"Ready," he breathed, barely audible. Davidson's slight nod was all the confirmation needed. They were about to enter the kill zone, and everything would depend on their training, their reflexes, and maybe a little luck.

The door handle began to turn unbelievably slow under Mitch's grip, the mechanism's internal components sliding with agonizing slowness. Every click of the latch mechanism seemed to echo in the stairwell...

The door exploded inward as Mitch executed a controlled dynamic entry. Davidson flowed through the opening like liquid shadow, his weapon tracking left as Mitch simultaneously cleared right. Their movements were a deadly ballet, practiced until it had become instinct.

The hallway stretched before them like a throat of darkness, the dim light creating a claustrophobic tunnel effect. The aged carpet absorbed their footfalls, but the silence felt oppressive, almost alive. The dead emergency lights did nothing, with only the outside light bleeding through the crack below the hotel room doors which created islands of visibility in the sea of shadows.

They moved in perfect synchronization, using a modified technique used by many spec ops teams. Each man covered his sector while maintaining awareness of his partner's position. The hotel room doors loomed on either side like dead eyes, each one a potential death trap.

Mitch's breathing was measured, controlled, and now tactical. Four counts in, four counts out. The shotgun's weight had become an extension of his arms, the worn wood grip slick with sweat despite the cold. His eyes constantly scanned, using the natural focal points that years of combat had ingrained in his muscle memory.

"Door, left," Davidson whispered, so soft it was barely a breath. They passed the first room, then the second, clearing each threshold with practiced precision. The T-intersections at each corner required special attention - fatal funnels where an ambush could turn the hallway into a killing zone.

The fire evacuation map showed faintly in the darkness, its phosphorescent surface creating an eerie green nimbus. Mitch moved toward it with calculated steps, each foot placement silent and deliberate. His peripheral vision caught movement - just his own shadow, but his trigger finger tensed reflexively.

As they positioned themselves between two doorways, the air changed. Something was wrong. Mitch felt it in his bones, that sixth sense that kept operators alive in combat. The silence was too perfect, too complete.

Then all hell erupted right next to him.

The door to their left disintegrated in a storm of high-velocity rounds. The muzzle flashed through the splintering wood and turned the hallway into a strobing nightmare of light and shadow. The rounds were precisely aimed at his center mass height, walking a death pattern across where Mitch had been standing.

His training took over before his conscious mind could process the attack. He dropped and rolled, the movement so ingrained it felt like watching someone else's body respond.

The bullets carved a lethal pattern in the wall behind him, the impacts sending chunks of plaster raining down like deadly confetti.

The ancient shotgun came up as he completed his roll, muscle memory directing the barrels toward the source of fire.

Time slowed to a crawl.

He could almost see individual splinters floating in the air, illuminated by the light outside that poured through the openings in the door like deadly snowflakes. The pull of his trigger felt like it moved through molasses.

BOOM-BOOM!

The double discharge was deafening in the confined space. The recoil slammed into his shoulder like a sledgehammer, but he rode it, controlling the muzzle flip through sheer muscle memory. The door literally exploded inward, the double-ought buckshot creating a devastating pattern of destruction.

Davidson's reaction to the sudden violence was instant but costly. His service weapon clattered to the floor as he dove for cover, the sound of metal on carpet nearly lost in the cacophony of combat.

Mitch's ears were ringing, the world reduced to a high-pitched whine punctuated by muffled sounds.

Through the massive holes in the door, movement caught his eye. A shadow shifting, the glint of metal - the target was still alive.

Mitch's blood ran cold as he recognized the tactical implications. They'd lost the element of surprise, and now they were in the worst possible position. Caught in a hallway with an armed opponent in a fortified position.

Mitch exploded into action, dropping the now-empty shotgun and executing a sprint through the shattered door. Every microsecond counted, where any hesitation meant possible death. His hand was already moving to his sidearm as he came up, the P365 pistol exited the leather holster in one fluid motion. All of his practice at the range made it as natural as breathing.

The hotel room was a tactical nightmare. The window behind the shooter created a perfect backlight, turning the target into a silhouette while simultaneously blinding anyone entering. Snow whipped through the broken glass, creating a surreal curtain of white that complicated target acquisition. Shell casings littered the floor, their brass surfaces glistened and caught what little light remained.

The Asian woman was definitely a professional, that much was obvious from her positioning and equipment. Her sniper hide seemed like it came from an action movie: elevated position, multiple fields of fire, pre-planned escape routes. The room was a mess of tactical gear, including a custom-modified sniper rifle that had been used for the earlier shots. The weapon's massive frame dominated the window position, its barrel still slightly warm even with the cold air.

Blood spread across the carpet beneath her, black in the dim light. The buckshot pattern had caught her center mass, but she was far from finished. Her movements were precise despite the injury, her training evident in every motion. Her eyes locked with Mitch's. They were cold, calculating, and professional. There was no fear there, only the deadly focus of a predator.

Time compressed into fragments of crystal-clear awareness. The woman's hand moved toward her suppressed sidearm. The smell of cordite and blood mixing with the winter air. Davidson's boots squeaked on the carpet as he recovered his weapon and moved to support.

Mitch's combat trained mind processed it all in milliseconds, breaking down the tactical situation into its component parts. The target was wounded but still lethal. The distance between them was less than fifteen feet - point-blank range for experienced operators. First one who aligned their sights would win.

Her hand closed around her weapon's grip, the movement smooth despite her wounds. Mitch could see the muscles in her arm tensing, preparing for the draw. His own pistol was already up, muscle memory bringing his weapon onto the target quickly.

The next second stretched into eternity. The sound of her weapon clearing its holster. The way her eyes narrowed slightly as she prepared to fire. The perfect clarity of his front sight as it settled on center mass. The pressure of his trigger finger as it took up the slack and touched the wall before the break .

Bang!

The report of his gun was deafening in the confined space. The round struck true, the impact lifted her backwards slightly before she fully collapsed. Her unfired weapon clattered to the floor, the sound somehow final in the sudden silence.

Davidson rounded the corner, weapon up, and moved with tactical precision. His eyes scanned the room clearing for any additional threats. "Clear left!" he called out, as he maintained his professional focus despite the chaos.

The woman's eyes were still open, but the deadly focus had faded, replaced by something else. Surprise, perhaps, or maybe just the final realization that her mission had failed. Blood pooled beneath her, as it spread across the hotel carpet in a dark stain that matched the growing shadows in the room.

"We did it, Mitch." Davidson's voice seemed to come from far away, barely audible over the ringing in their ears and the howling wind through the broken window.

Mitch kept his weapon trained on the fallen assassin, years of experience preventing him from making a rookie mistake by assuming the threat was over.

"We did," he acknowledged, his voice tight with tension, "but this isn't over." His eyes swept the room, taking in the professional gear, the multiple weapons, the communications equipment.

This was no lone operator. This was part of something bigger.

"Get the others up here," he ordered, his tone brokering no argument. "We need to process this scene before it gets contaminated." His tactical mind was already working through the implications, analyzing what this meant for their broader situation.

As Davidson's footsteps faded down the hallway, Mitch finally lowered his weapon, though he maintained his ready stance. The cold wind whipped around him, carrying the scent of gunpowder and blood. Looking around the room again, he felt the weight of unanswered questions pressing down on him.

"What's the play now, Mitch?" he muttered to himself, his voice barely audible over the wind. The room offered no answers, only more questions. The growing certainty that this was just the beginning of something much larger and more dangerous than they had initially suspected.

# Chapter 15

Double Eagle Casino

Cripple Creek, Colorado

December 9

4:30 PM MST Time

The demolished hotel room became an impromptu crime scene, with the bitter Colorado wind whipping snow through the shattered window. Mitch, Davey, Jerry, Davidson, Aaron, and Duke all stood in the cramped hotel room that looked like it just survived a warzone. Kim's body was still lying by the remnants of the demolished door which was in pieces on the floor. A heavy duty sniper rifle was still positioned on its tripod while equipment, gear, and papers were methodically placed about.

Mitch stood over her body, "I am not sure who this is but why in the world was she shooting at us?"

"Obviously some low life criminal scum," Jerry pipes up immediately.

"Really, Jerry, that makes absolutely no sense. Why in the world would some random criminal shoot up the town of Cripple

Creek? The casinos don't hold that kinda money, this isn't Vegas man." Davey shared as he tried to square everyone back on track after Jerry's ridiculous comment.

Mitch refocused the group, "Come on everyone, none of this makes any sense. Let's look around and see what we can find. Aaron check her body for any ID. Aaron?" He looked up to see Aaron now in a defensive posture trying to block someone from entering the room.

"Mitch, I need your help over here. Emily's trying to get in." Aaron shouted as he continued to try to keep her from seeing in the room.

Mitch paused at first then spoke, "It's fine, let her through."

She rushed in and  pushed through Aaron as she shot him a look for even thinking about trying to stop her in the first place. Suddenly she froze mid stride at the startling sight of a woman's dead body lying in a mess on the floor.

"Emily, you probably don't want to be here." Mitch said with uneasy tension.

Emily teared up at the sight but immediately looked to Mitch, "I don't care about that, are you okay?"

Mitch started to reply. "Yeah, just banged up a…" but before he could finish she'd already run over and wrapped herself around him in a tight hug.

"I wanna help Mitch," Emily barely whispered through her upset demeanor.

Mitch paused again, noticing that everyone in the room was watching them as they shared this moment, "I know you do, we probably need all the help we can get."

The two broke off their embrace and everyone stood around looking inquisitively at all of the items that were left in the room. Jerry and Davidson couldn't help themselves analyzing the expensive rifle attached to a tripod which only a short while ago was used to almost kill them. Aaron knelt beside Kim's body and checked her pocket for any contents. Davey went through the papers strewn about on the table and floor. While Duke opened and shook the luggage.

Duke stepped back abruptly and shouted, "What in tarnation is this thing. It's a bomb. It's gotta be a bomb."

Everyone stopped immediately and turned to see the device that Duke was hollering about. Their eyes gazed at the open piece of luggage that held the EMP device surrounded in foam. The screen glowed blue and that was a shock to everyone. Not just because it could be a bomb, but whatever reason, it still had power.

"What in the world is this thing Mitch?" Duke expressed fear and panic spread across his face. "Is it a bomb, are we all going to die?"

"I don't know Duke, chill out!" Duke walked over and started examining the device. "How does this have any power, what is it?"

The group of seven stood looking around the room together in what resembled more of a puzzle than a simple shooting aftermath. Each piece of evidence seemed to connect to something larger, something more intricate than any of them had initially suspected.

The mysterious device in the foam-lined case glowed an otherworldly blue, casting eerie shadows across their faces. Mitch's hands hovered over it, the tension in the room thick enough to cut with a knife. The device's surface revealed subtle patterns, not random manufacturing marks, but deliberate engravings that looked almost like circuit pathways

"Hold up," Aaron called out, his engineer's mechanical mind catching something the others had missed. "Look at these markings around the edge. They're not decorative - they're semiconductor paths, but unlike anything I've ever seen. And these symbols..." He pointed to a series of characters etched into the casing. "That's Asian, but mixed with something else."

Emily moved closer, her academic background kicking in. "Those aren't just Asian characters," she said, her voice steadying as she focused on the puzzle before them. "See how they're arranged? It's like a cipher or a code key. The patterns repeat every third character, but with subtle variations."

"Guys, over here," Davey called from the table covered in scattered papers. He held up several documents, their pages filled with complex diagrams. "These aren't just random notes. They're schematics, but they're incomplete. Like pieces of a larger blueprint split up for security."

Jerry, who had been examining the sniper rifle, suddenly straightened. "The serial number on this gun - it's filed off. Look closely." He pointed to barely visible marks under the receiver. "Removing these manufacturer's marks are not just illegal, there is clear intent here to not get caught."

The room suddenly became a hive of coordinated investigation, as each person spring into action using their unique skills to contribute piecing the puzzles together to form the larger picture. Duke, despite his initial panic, proved to have an eye for detail that others missed. "The luggage tags," he said, pulling one out carefully. "They're all from different airlines, different routes, but look at the dates. This girl has been around the block or two that's for sure."

Davidson moved methodically around the room, his investigation training gave him a different perspective as he scanned the crime scene. "The room setup isn't random either. The furniture placement, the angle of the rifle, even the position of the backup weapons - it's all precisely measured. Like she was following some kind of formula. By the looks of it, this isn't her first attack. She might be a professional assassin?"

Mitch stepped back, taking in all the elements. The device, the documents, the weapons, the tactical positioning - everything seemed connected by an invisible thread. "We're not just looking at evidence," he realized. "We're looking at pieces of a puzzle. This asian assassin wasn't just an assassin - she was part of something bigger and I imagine the guy that tried to kill my dad was part of it as well!"

Emily had begun arranging the scattered papers in a pattern on the floor, her keen eye made the connections that others missed. "Look at this," she said, pointing to recurring symbols in the documents. "These markers appear in both the technical diagrams and in the surveillance notes. They're some kind of cross-reference system."

Aaron knelt beside the mysterious device again, his expression thoughtful. "The power source - it's not like anything I have ever seen before. See these connections? They're hardened and designed to withstand a lot of volts or a massive explosion. This has to be military grade kinda stuff."

The room fell silent as the implications sank in. They weren't just investigating a failed assassination attempt - they were uncovering pieces of an elaborate operation, one that required all their combined skills to understand.

The cold wind and snow now still blew heavily through the demolished window sending a chill that was easily felt by the entire group.

Aaron stepped closer, "That ain't no bomb you two! Look at it. I know from plenty of time tinkering with things that it couldn't hold much or any explosives. It is the size of a football. Besides, if it were a bomb, don't you think she would have used it already?"

"You've got a point there. I'm gonna pick it up." Mitch agreed as he reached out to the device.

Emily chimed in immediately, "stop Mitch, what if it blows up!"

The room was split on the move. Aaron and Duke stood still, while the rest of the group took a noticed step back just in case something went off as though it would be just enough to save them.

"Emily, I have to see what it is. This might be the least of our worries at this point," Mitch responded as kind as he could to ease her anxiety.

Slowly and gently, Mitch touched the device on the top and bottom with both hands. Carefully he wiggled it out of the foam and held it in front of him. As he began to rotate and examine it, he accidentally touched the front screen that immediately lit up blue awaiting a prompt. The small blue screen glowed with some type of Asian characters and there were four buttons below it.

Mitch was puzzled and looked to the rest of the group for help, "I can't read it, it looks Asian, Japanese, Chinese, I'm not sure."

"That looks Chinese, but I can't read it." Davey chimes in. "I get packages from Amazon all the time that have Chinese written all over them.

They all continue to look at the screen. The Chinese words are foreign to them but they can tell it is better not to touch anything for fear of what could happen. The blue glow from the device puzzled the group and Mitch was about to set it back down.

Duke hollers yet again, getting the group's attention, "y'all, there's somethin else here in the luggage!" He begins to pull out the protective foam revealing maps, blueprints, and plans that were placed in a way to attempt to hide them. "We are sure lucky she forgot to lock up her stuff."

Duke and Emily began to pull out each document piece by piece from the luggage and neatly placed them out on the bed. The documents caused everyone to begin guessing randomly what it all meant and what it was like they were playing the game of clue together.

"Enough, enough everyone!" Jerry yelled to stop the group's chatter in an instant. "I don't believe it, I simply don't believe it. How in the wild blue yonder? These, all of these, some sorta attack plan."

The group all look at Jerry and maybe for the first time they see beyond this grumpy old man. Sure he was the police chief, but there was something different about him. His eyes darted between each document like the detective Sherlock Holmes honing in on the final reveal. Everyone waited and just watched for a few good minutes in anticipation of his revelation.

"Jerry, I have my idea of what it is, we might be right. I wanna hear your thoughts first." Mitch broke the silence and he looked directly at Jerry. "So, you think there's going to be an attack on Cripple Creek?"

Jerry's eyes continued to look at the documents spread out across the bed. He began to reply in a very calm and mannered tone, "Yes...based on everything here...the blueprints are for NORAD, in the Springs." He reached down and picked up the document that showed what looked like an underground base of some sort.

"How do you know that?" Davey walked over to take a look closer at what Jerry was holding.

Jerry continued, "My uncle used to work there years ago before they shut it down to visitors. When my son was growing up, I chaperoned for his school and we got a tour of it. Then no one got to go in there anymore after those dang terrorists." He handed the paper over to Davey. "She was going to attack the place. Still don't quite know how anyone could do that, it's like a fortress."

"What if she wasn't alone, look at this, there are pictures of other people." Aaron holds out another piece of paper with images and more small Chinese characters next to each. "Who are these people?"

Duke blurts out, "That's her Mitch! That's the smokin hottie I was trying to tell you about!" He points to the only woman on the page. "She's that one that almost hit me and I almost beat up her stupid boyfriend. That's the idiot right there!" Now pointing to a picture of Oleg.

"I remember this woman, she almost ran into me when I went to the coffee shop." Mitch responded as his face immediately turned to anger as he continued looking at the page. "It's the guy, Emily look! That's the guy that tried to kill our family and steal our horse!"

Now it is Mitch's turn to point at the page directly at the image of Thomas. He backs up and covers his face with both dirty hands rubbing as though to wake himself up from this dream. "There are so many of them, none of this still explains why they are here. Why Cripple Creek of all places?"

Davey walked closer to Mitch, "I think I know why Mitch. Look closer at the blueprint, she circled an escape hatch on the backside of Cheyenne mountain above the base." He waved his finger over the area. "Right there, and this other map shows a route to get there from here. Actually, the starting point was at Cartmen's old place."

"So they were living right next to us this whole time?" Emily turned to anger and chimed into the conversation.

Davey answered her, "Unfortunately, it looks like it. Also, based on the page with the photos there are seven of them including the one that we just stopped."

"The guy at my ranch, the woman here, so there are five still running around out there." Mitch calculates the remaining team and looks once again at their pictures. "Two big dudes, two regular dudes, and one woman. They all look military, don't you agree?"

Davidson being prior military himself and having served in the Army added in, "Yup, they look Russian or Eastern European. That still doesn't explain this Asian woman though."

"Good point!" Mitch replied as he continued to look at the pictures. "So we have a team of five people, probably all military, going to attack NORAD and this strange device. Not to mention no power and another snow storm moving in. Anything we are missing?"

The group fell silent as they processed all the troubling information laid out before them.

After a few moments, Aaron spoke up. "So this group was usin' that abandoned farm as a staging ground to plan some kind of attack on NORAD. I still don't get what their end game is though. Why Cripple Creek of all places?"

"It must have something to do with that escape hatch on the map," replied Mitch. "Maybe their plan was to sneak in through the back door after causing a diversion above ground or something. But what and why?"

Emily looked thoughtful. "Do you think that device might be connected somehow? It seems important if she had it packed with her gear. But none of us can read what it says."

As if on cue, a sound came at the doorway. The group turned alertly, hands going to holstered weapons. Staring back at them was one of the hotel workers standing there.

"I am so sorry, the manager asked me to check on you all?" she asked nervously and skittishly. "We all heard the gunshots earlier and hid." Her eyes fell on Kim's body and became startled.

"We're fine, just had an...incident," Davidson said calmly, still in his police uniform.

"Is she dead?" The worker asked.

Jerry felt it was his turn to step into the conversation, "Yes. It is unfortunate but she was a criminal and had to be stopped before she hurt anyone else."

The worker continued,"that lady was very rude, probably because I am from Hong Kong."

"What do you mean?" Davidson asked.

The worker looked at the ground, "That lady was from Beijing, I know, they are very mean to anyone not Chinese. Sorry, I just want to do my job but she wouldn't let me, I had to be nice."

"Listen, we need your help. That device there has writing on it but none of us can read Chinese. Think you could take a look?" Asked Davidson.

The woman nodded cautiously and stepped over. She examined the screen for a moment. "The screen shows time," she said in surprise. "The buttons say arm and disarm."

Gasps arose from the group. Mitch turned back to the woman. "Do you know what these letters say?" Pointing to the back of the device now that has three bolded characters etched into the metal.

The worker read it in wonder and confusion, "it says E-M-P? I am not sure what that means."

Davey interjected, "An EMP, that would knock out electronics for miles. With NORAD's systems down, it'd be practically defenseless. America would be defenseless."

"But how did they plan to set it off?" asked Aaron. "That thing can't possibly be big enough to take out that whole mountain."

Mitch turned to the rest of the group. "Probably the escape hatch. They just have to get into the base. An EMP could have a pulse that can disable electronic equipment and they must have more devices with them."

"That's diabolical," said Emily. "But what's their end goal? Money? Attack? Something even worse?"

"If you are a country that hates us and wants us destroyed, does it even matter?" Added Davidson.

Mitch turned to the hotel worker. "Thank you for your help translating. We really appreciate you taking the time."

"You are very welcome. I hope you stop the bad people." She nodded to the group and took her leave.

Once she had gone, Jerry stepped forward. "Only one way to find out. We need to get to that escape hatch before they do. Stop them from carrying out their plan."

Mitch nodded. "Jerry's right. We need to get to Cheyenne mountain as soon as possible."

Jerry tucked his thumbs behind his belt and puffed his chest out, "Alright, listen here y'all. If we are going to do this, we need to do it right and by the book ya hear."

They all looked at him curious as to what he had planned.

He continued, "Let's head back to the fire station. It's time we show this fine town the true dignity and respect it deserves."

# Chapter 16

Cripple Creek Fire Station

Cripple Creek, Colorado

December 9

5 PM MST Time

As the winter afternoon moved towards sunset over the quiet streets of Cripple Creek, an uneasy stillness settled over the town. Just a bit ago, the beautiful bustling streets went from celebrating the holidays to nothing more than chaos and uncertainty in the minds of each person.

Police Chief Jerry Conrad stood outside the open bay door of the fire station, wearily surveying the scene before him through tired eyes. Snowflakes drifted lazily from the darkening sky, blanketing the red-bricked buildings in a pristine white powder. Anything beyond the town limits faded into the endless expanse of whiteness.

Jerry's gaze drifted upward as the wind picked up, swirling the falling flakes around him. His eyes fell upon Old Glory, her stars and stripes snapping proudly in the breeze from the flagpole outside the station. A deep sense of respect and pride stirred within him at the sight. Through wars and natural disasters, through challenges faced and triumphs earned, that flag had endured - a symbol of freedom and everything their nation held dear.

As Jerry contemplated the grave task that now lay before him and his small community, he found solace in that emblem of liberty still waving above. No matter the threat or turmoil, America would endure so long as good men stood ready to defend her. And defend her they would.

His solemn thoughts were interrupted by the crunch of boots on new snow. Jerry turned to see Mitch approaching, concern etched on his weathered face.

Mitch had served beside Jerry for many years now, and the two shared a deep bond of friendship and duty to their town.

"It's a thing of pure beauty Mitch, still waving no matter what happens. I've seen a lot of things in this job and this sure takes the cake. I didn't tell y'all but I was planning to announce my retirement on the 1st." Jerry stated. As Mitched noticed a slight quiver of his lip and a tear form in his eye.

The men stood in silence for a moment, old friends speaking volumes without words. Their quiet contemplation was broken as the rest of the day's dramatic events came crashing back into focus.

Cripple Creek had found itself under siege, its people endangered, and the beacon of freedom itself threatened far beyond their borders. But these two knew that as long as men like them still drew breath, evil would find no easy victory here.

Jerry sighed. "This is a dark day for sure. But you know as well as I that folks need to stand up and do what's right when it matters most."

Mitch looked over at him and gave him a quick hug to his Bible study brother, "Cripple Creek appreciates you and I appreciate you brother." A moment of silence endured as the personas faded and the reality of friendship, humanity, and life set in before they stepped back.

"Brother, all these conversations about people needing to do the right thing. Never would I have ever thought it would come true, but that time is here" Jerry continued on before giving a final look at the flag and walked back into the bay with Mitch.

Within the crowded fire station, hushed conversations fell silent as Jerry and Mitch entered. The group all looked at Jerry as he walked in from the cold and gave his grand announcement.

Waving his hands inward, Jerry motioned for them all to gather closer, the weight of responsibility hung heavy on his shoulders. But these were his people - good, hardworking folks who had built a community with their bare hands. And by God, he would lead them through this the best he could.

"Alright y'all, gather together and listen up." Stepping closer to the group, Jerry said in a low but steadfast tone. "Friends, today has been one none of us ever saw coming. I'll keep this brief - these are dire straits and they demand an uncompromising response."

He knew these men's character and allegiance to Cripple Creek well enough though.

Jerry began his monumental proclamation the best he could. "Today is a day not a single one of us ever thought was imaginable. I'll be brief, extreme times call for extreme measures."

He turned to Davidson first who was now standing next to him, "Davidson, as the senior officer here, I'm invoking Posse Comitatus."

Davidson raised an eyebrow questioningly. "Posse Comitatus, really? That's a risky move, Jerry."

Jerry nodded. "I know the feds don't like civilians getting mixed up in these matters. But we're basically at war here in Cripple Creek given the threat. Dag nammit, this is our town and our very life is under attack. I say that puts it squarely under the purview of local jurisdiction. We've got our community who needs us and a nation to save!"

"You've got a point. Alright then, let's make history!" Davidson replied.

Jerry continued after getting the final approval he didn't really need, "Alright then, who's with me?"

A chorus of supportive shouts answered him. Mitch stepped forward, rallying the others to quiet down with a raised fist. "This is our country and our American soil! And no one threatens the land of the free without answering us first. We succeed as one or fail as one - for faith, for freedom, for our family!"

Jerry showed the greatest sense of pride in a long time and addressed the group including Mitch, Davey, Aaron, and Duke. "As the law in this town I am hereby authorized in a situation such as this to enact and invoke Posse Comitatus for each of you."

"What in tarnation does that mean Jerry?" Duke interrupted.

"Ahem, Duke, be quiet and be on your best behavior, son or you're not getting deputized today!" Jerry barked as he shot Duke a quick look. "I'm deputizing each of you to aid in law enforcement and serve our fine town to see this crisis through. Mitch and his marauders."

Davidson turned to the group. "As of now, you're all considered temporary deputy officers of the Cripple Creek Police. That means you've got the full authority to use any means necessary to apprehend these attackers."

The crowd roared its assent, cheers, and fists punched the air. These were simple folk, but their courage and conviction could not be questioned. Jerry nodded in approval, pride swelling his weathered heart. "Alright then deputies, listen up. We've got a lotta work to do..."

"About time I got a badge," joked Duke.

Davidson laughed, "Duke we don't have extra badges, but you can have a sticker instead if you really want."

The tension was somewhat broken by the lighthearted moment as they all laughed. Mitch clapped Jerry on the shoulder approvingly. "Good thinking. We'll need all the authority we can get if things turn ugly in those mountains."

Jerry added his final remarks, "I'm not going to be joining you all on this one. Gonna stay back here with Philips and watch over Danvers and Cripple Creek. Mitch and Davidson lead this one. God bless America and go get'em."

It fell to the team of Mitch, Davidson, and Cripple Creek's impromptu marauding deputies to end the threat. With their limited band of experiences and familiarity with the terrain, it was their best shot at turning the tide. But the mission would be long, dangerous, and conducted in the heart of an escalating blizzard.

Duke walked up and nudged Jerry's side. "You know I'm your man, chief. Ain't no mountain too high when America's at stake."

Jerry appraised him with a critical eye. "This ain't no walk in the park boy. You sure you're ready to tangle with the devil in a hellish snowstorm?"

Mitch stepped forward confidently on Duke's behalf. "We're all ready, Chief. May not look like much but we'll stand our ground when the time comes." His confident tone seemed to bolster the others' resolve.

Jerry, Mitch, and Davidson stood huddled and spoke to each other about next steps as the rest of the team thought about what plans were in store.

Mitch approached the group after a few minutes, "Listen up team, or better yet marauders, go get your guns and the gear you need. Get your horse or borrow one from a neighbor. Bundle up because this is going to be a cold one overnight."

Davey, who wasn't accustomed to camping, spoke up, "we're going to spend the night in the snow? I hate camping even in the summer."

"We need to make up for lost time, so not much camping will happen. Aaron, pack up some of the hunting gear including the medium tent in case we need it." Mitch expanded while emphasizing the harsh realities they were in for. "Gents, we are in for a harsh time and will need to make it through hell. We have a snow storm to deal with, we are hunting down a group of highly trained bad guys before they get to NORAD, and they're already a few hours ahead of us."

A hush fell on the team as they processed what they were going to be contending with. It was a difficult go already but the potential for being killed was so high that they felt the uneasy weight and pressure of it all.

As Cripple Creek's protectors readied themselves for the freeze, Jerry stood vigil outside the station, gazing up once more at Old Glory. Her colors seemed to burn all the brighter against the descending twilight. The snow continued to dust her bars and stars, yet still she stood tall and true on her pole.

Let the storm rage, he thought proudly - her symbol of liberty would never be stilled. And as long as brave warriors still drew breath to defend her, neither would the spirit she represented.

A dark winter had come to Cripple Creek in more ways than one. But where others saw only snow and ice, Jerry walked outside again and saw the promise of a new dawn. Where fear might freeze the heart, he felt only the fire of patriotism rekindled in his county's finest. And though darkness was beginning to close in, he had faith that a new dawn would come.

American perseverance and resolve had triumphed through far worse. This, too, would pass - and freedom would shine through all the brighter for its fight. With one last nod to the colors he'd given his life to protect, Jerry re-entered the station.

It was time to ride out into the gathering shadows of twilight and tempest. Evil might hide in the night of those mountains, but its days were numbered. For liberty and justice would march out to meet it, borne on the stout hearts of siblings, sons, fathers, and friends.

Of patriots.

And come the dawn, Old Glory would fly all the higher.

Aaron broke the silence, "What's the plan now Mitch?"

Mitch paced back and forth for a little for a few seconds contemplating the plan before he finally spoke up. "I saw snowmobiles at their place, so they must have taken those to some rendezvous point before they stopped working just like everything else."

He continued to strategize out loud. "They must split up, especially if Duke's long lost love was spotted right before everything erupted."

Duke blurted out, "Hey now! There's still a chance there."

"Seriously dude, she'll probably kill you. Best to break up now if you know what's best." Aaron said as he slapped Duke on the back.

Mitch redirected the team back to the mission. "Aaron's right, they will kill all of us if given the chance. We have one shot at this and if we fail, there's no telling what will happen to America next. We thought things were rough now, remember Red Dawn?"

"Wolverine's!" Duke yelled out randomly catching everyone's attention especially Jerry who was now shaking his head in disapproval.

Duke stuck up for himself, "This is just like that time when the ruskies sneak attacked America, but in the old version. That new version was junk."

Mitch and the others laughed slightly before he became serious again, "Agreed the best version was the old school one, but let's get back on track here. We need to be on the same page for this one and need to get moving sooner than later. Meet at my place as soon as you can."

The team looked at one another and then one by one nodded in agreement.

Mitch closed them out, "Alright team, time to pay this country the respect it deserves!"

# Chapter 17

McKinley Ranch

East of Cripple Creek, Colorado

December 9

7 PM MST Time

The snow continued to fall steadily through the night, blanketing the McKinley homestead and surrounding countryside in a pristine mantle of white that seemed to muffle all sound.

Mitch and Emily had made the arduous journey home through the blizzard as swiftly as their horse could bear, though the fierce conditions had slowed their progress considerably. By the time the vague pattern of their home first emerged like dim beacons through the veil of swirling flakes, both riders found themselves exhausted near to the point of collapse from the events that day.

The only light visible was the glow of the fireplace showing through the windows of their parent's ranch house living room next door. That alone gave the only escape from the encompassing darkness and added a sense of warmth that they were almost home.

It took Mitch a lot longer to get to the ranch with Emily on his back than imagined. Between the darkness of night and bitter cold of winter, the two were beyond anticipation to make it home to their family, especially their children who had been cared for by his mom.

Mitch's body ached with fatigue, drained not only physically but emotionally by the traumatic span of the day.

As they neared the house, the dark red stains still blanketed in the snow from the aftermath of the confrontation between Mitch and Thomas. His body had been covered with a blue tarp which had been partially covered by the fresh snow.

The site instantly evoked the memory of the incident, causing Mitch's heart to start up a frantic rhythm in his chest as each moment replayed before his mind's eye in stark, unrelenting detail.

His mind remorselessly replayed each moment, confronting Thomas, their violent struggle, and all that followed in grim aftermath.

Emily sensed his growing distress and wrapped her arms securely around him from behind, anchoring him firmly back to the present where they were together, safe for the moment.

Suddenly he was brought back to reality as Emily's arms wrapped around him squeezed tighter upon the sight.

"I love you..." Emily muttered softly in his ear. In a way knowing that her support was needed more than ever at this time.

Mitch turned to meet her worried gaze, discovering solace and renewed strength there as ever in her kind eyes. "I love you too," he replied earnestly.

Together they guided the weary horse the last remaining length to the post. Once there he got out of the saddle and hopped down to the ground now feeling more of the soreness.

"Here hun, let me help you." Mitch assisted Emily down with utmost care despite his own weariness, unwilling to chance further harm befalling his darling wife that night if it could at all be helped or hindered.

"Thank you," Emily replied in sincere gratitude and the two continued around the body and to the front door.

Mitch drew a steadying breath, then continued toward the front door with Emily remaining closely at his side. He rapped out their familiar pattern upon the stout oak barrier, the simple sound echoing lonely and forlorn in the heavy stillness that had fallen.

Knocking on the door with the same cadence he did as a kid, they both waited. A few dragging moments later, the lock turned noisily and the portal swung open to reveal Mitch's mother Melissa, her face breaking at once into an expression of profound relief and gratitude at the sight of them returning.

"Oh thank God, I'm so glad you're both home safely!" Anne exclaimed sincerely, pulling each of them into a long, heartfelt hug in turn. "The children have been ill at ease about you ever since nightfall." His mom tightly hugged each of them as she ushered them briskly inside out of the bitter cold.

Mitch's father Joseph now sat dozing in his armchair before the warming fireplace glow, as was his evening ritual. At the commotion of their entrance however, he started fully awake and swiveled at once to offer his greetings also.

"Mitch, Mitch, you're back! Thanks be to God." He was slow to get up and made his way over to the two. "Where in heaven's name have you been, is everything okay, is anyone else hurt ?"

Mitch and Emily exchanged a worried, hesitant look, reluctant to recount just yet the unsettling tale in its entirety. "There was some trouble stirring in town after I left earlier, dad," Mitch replied vaguely. "I don't think this whole sorry situation is finished with us either."

As Melissa moved deftly about fetching extra seating and poured mugs of piping coffee for everyone. The family sat around the fireplace as Mitch began to relay in subdued and blunt tones, the chaos and mayhem that unfolded throughout the alarming day.

He spoke of power failures after he left the ranch, the sniper that almost killed him, the shocking plot to attack the crucial military stronghold and the team's plan to defend it.

His parents listened in stunned, fearful silence, interrupting frequently with anxious queries Mitch purposefully avoided answering with full disclosure. Their grave discussion was cut short however by a soft sound drifting nearby.

The small creak caused Emily to look over.

"Mary?" Emily called gently upwards. A moment later, their sleepy daughter peeked shyly around the bedroom doorway, rubbing the remnants of slumber from her tired eyes still heavy with concern.

"Oh sweetheart, come here to us," Emily beckoned lovingly, opening her arms wide in loving invitation once more.

At this, young Mary rushed at once to her mother's warm, comforting embrace. She easily scrambled into her lap and snuggled contentedly against Emily's chest with a wide yawn. Within mere moments later she had fallen back to rest, exhausted from fretting ceaselessly throughout the entire long stretch of her parents' unplanned absence.

"The poor dear has been distraught with worry about you both since well after dusk and what happened outside earlier," Melissa observed sadly and whispered as to not wake Mary. "We didn't know what else to tell the children when nightfall came and still you hadn't found your way safely back to us once again."

The McKinley family tried to settle in companionably despite any prevailing unease, taking what solace they could find together once more in each other's comforting presence after such a difficult day apart. However, Mitch knew vital work yet remained unfinished as shadows lengthened and his mind could not fully rest secure while threats still loomed so close.

"The others should be arriving before much longer," he voiced reluctantly, rising stiffly from his chair at last with visible reluctance. "I must get ready myself and head back out into the mountains after these villains."

Emily gazed up at Mitch with tears now brimming, her expressive eyes conveying the depths of fear she held close yet unspoken.

She took his hands in her own, entreating him earnestly, "Promise me truly you'll return safely home to us again." Looking at him with a stare that spoke to the silent bond between the two. Knowing the dangerous odds he and his friends were about to face soon.

"I promise," Mitch swore fervently, then hugged his darling wife and precious daughter to his chest in a farewell embrace filled with determination. He inhaled deeply their comforting scents, resolved to keep his pledge intact.

As Mitch was about to depart once more however, Joseph's voice stopped him yet again. "Son," the elder McKinley said simply yet significantly, as he met his gaze steadily with understanding born of their long life shared.

Mitch stood obediently before his beloved father, and the two men shared a moment between father and son. "You got this son, you know the right thing to do..." Joseph bade him firmly yet proudly with a simple nod and as he pounded his fist on his chest over his heart.

Mitch nodded resolutely and responded in kind. He donned his outer layers and made his way to the front entryway at last. "I'll be back soon and I want to say goodbye to you before the team gets here."

He stood at the door before opening it and then heading out into the frigid cold night.

Emily held Mary and looked at his parents. In a disheartened tone she uttered, "I don't want him to go."

Joseph, knowing what the moment held, responded with some of the wisest words she had ever heard, "but dear sometimes the hard thing to do and the right thing to do are the same exact thing...Mitch knows that he is required to go. He must have the courage knowing that the odds are against him and his men but he must saddle up anyways."

"Can't someone else stop them?" Emily sobbed as she realized the seriousness of what could happen next for her husband and their children's father.

Melissa looked at her with a caring gaze and gave her a loving nudge in the direction she needed to take next, "my dear, this might be the last time we ever see our beloved Mitch."

# Chapter 18

---

Mitch's House - McKinley Ranch

East of Cripple Creek, Colorado

December 9

7:30 PM MST Time

The musty, dank air of the basement pressed against Mitch's skin, a tangible weight of uncertainty. He rustled in his basement storage room only being able to see by candlelight. His breath came in short, controlled exhales, each movement calculated and deliberate.

Annoyed, he exclaimed out loud to himself, "I can never find what I need in here with all this junk!" Knowing that all along the whole problem was his own doing.

The flickering candlelight cast monstrous shadows across decades of accumulated memories, each forgotten box a testament to his forgetfulness from packing items years ago. He had meant to organize this space months ago but other tasks and his family always took priority. Now in the midst of his lack of prudence, he rues putting it off, as everything was strewn out of place before him.

The silence of the basement seemed to hold its breath, waiting. Items clanked and crashed as a box full of stuff fell off the shelf after Mitch hit it by accident in the dark. The sudden noise echoed like a gunshot in the confined space, making his nerves jump. Squinting in the dim candlelight, his determination finally paid off as he saw his goal.

A flood of memories washed over him, warm and bittersweet. The small cookie jar hidden behind a box of holiday decorations from years past. He smiled, remembering how Emily had bought it for him as a joke, knowing of his sweet tooth.

His fingers, stiff and cold like steel cables, fought against the jar's resistance. Attempting to open it proved fruitless for his cold numb fingers under the suction from the container's top. He gripped his hands together and blew hot air to warm his fingers before he made another desperate attempt.

A surge of triumph cut through the basement's oppressive darkness. "Finally," he said to himself aloud as he shook his fist in confidence. He uncovered the hidden keys to the safe where he stored his most essential and pragmatic supplies.

A heavy silence descended, loaded with unspoken fears and grim determination. Though anxious to get prepared, part of him dreaded what state the world had come to that such supplies were actually needed. Taking the keys out of the jar he inspected them until he found the one he was looking for, slightly larger and with odd teeth compared to the others.

Each movement was a calculated dance of caution in fear he might drop the key and lose it forever. Taking the key between his fingers he walked over to the safe attached to the wall and tried to unlock the safe. Stumbling, he missed the first time before he finally got the key in the hole on the second attempt.

The metallic groan of the safe opening felt like a harbinger of the challenges ahead. Turning the key he unlocked the bolts and opened the safe to reveal his rifles. Each weapon seemed to whisper stories of past conflicts and potential futures.

Immediately, he scanned the contents of the safe attempting to assess his options.

The .270 bore silent witness to countless hunting expeditions, a relic of peaceful times now transformed into a potential instrument of survival. This bolt action hunting rifle, a gift from his father, laid on the left. Great for hunting but not for this upcoming battle. Especially the one he knew was coming and would require true warfare.

In the middle, a testament to brotherhood and shared sacrifice. Laid a Patriot Ordnance AR in .308 given to him by his former squad mates could definitely prove its worth. It was a trusted partner for long-range engagements.

The third rifle, a familiar companion from years of military service laid on the right. His new Sig Sauer AR rifle chambered in 5.56 similar to the M4 that had served him well during his time in the service.

With the instinct of a seasoned warrior, his hand moved with muscle memory. Immediately he went for his top battle rifle pick, the 5.56, drawn to its familiarity and confidence. Additionally, it was much lighter than the other two and the weight of the ammo could allow him to take more rounds downrange.

The rifle was more than a weapon - it was an extension of himself. The remembrance of years of professional training and usage immediately came back to him as he gripped to the hand guard. The scoring of the metal and polymer felt like an old friend under his calloused hands. Mitch picked up the rifle and he inspected it. He tried to power on the EOTech optic, a model he knew like the back of his hand.

Frustration and a creeping sense of dread invaded his careful preparations.

"Dang It!" He said to himself as he realized that his optic was not working even after he tested the power button multiple times. Just like everything else, the power seemed to be dead on all of the equipment around him. His preparations once again would have to be modified for this new reality.

Memories of tedious briefings suddenly gained a horrifying relevance. This time it was a grid down situation like he had heard so many times in the long and boring continuity meetings he was required to attend while in the service. Never would he have ever thought it would actually take place and especially when he least expected it.

The soft pad of footsteps broke through his intense concentration.

"Everything okay Mitch," Emily appeared into view, holding a candle in her hand to light his way. Her movement was careful, deliberate, like a dance around the chaos of their new reality.

Slowly she waded around the piles of gear on the floor, being careful not to trip, and eventually found a spot to sit on an overturned crate.

Vulnerability etched itself across his weathered features. Mitch put the rifle back against the safe, laying it gently beside the others that had served him so well, "yeah, years of service protecting this country, trying to keep our town safe, and providing for our family. I tried to be responsible but never prepared for all of this."

Her gaze held the wisdom of generations, a strength born of love and resilience. "Who could ever prepare for this? There will always be problems and people needing saving, no matter what changes come. You've always made the best of difficult situations."

Emily gazed intensely at the man she loves recalling the words of his mom shared with her moments ago.

He looked at Emily with tears in his eyes, overcome by emotion and the appreciation of her constant devotion. The sacred covenant of their marriage shimmered in the candlelight, a divine testament to love's enduring power. His gaze was a window to the depths of his soul, reflecting not just human emotion, but a profound spiritual connection overcome by emotion and the appreciation of her constant devotion.

Emily looked back at him as tears welled up in hers, moved by his obvious distress. Their love transcended mere human emotion. It was a reflection of Christ's love, pure, sacrificial, and eternal. The unspoken bond between two people deeply in real love, now being torn apart by forces beyond their control.

Emily got up and moved quickly towards him. The two embraced passionately. Her movement was tender, fierce, strong as death, and unyielding as the grave. She buried her head into his chest as she wrapped her arms around pulling him closer to her hoping that he would never leave her.

His embrace was a prayer, a protection, a covenant. Mitch kissed the top of her head as he wrapped his arms around her, feeling not just their physical warmth, but the spiritual connection that bound them together more strongly than any earthly force. He felt their warmth as the two connected fully, seeking comfort in one another as husband and wife.

Her voice trembled with a vulnerability that spoke of both human frailty and spiritual strength. "I don't want you to go, I am sick at the thought of losing you..." Emily whispered to him gently as they continued to hold each other tight, loathing to break their intimate moment.

In that moment, Mitch understood that true strength comes not from himself, but from above. He was about to respond but stopped himself, taking a steadying breath. Finally after a few seconds he found the right words, his voice a humble offering, seeking divine providence, "pray with me please."

Her response was instantaneous, a testament to their shared faith. "Of course," Emily said as he looked up at him with watery eyes full of trust and love, her gaze a reflection of unwavering faith.

Their prayer was not just words, but an unseen warfare that transcended their physical circumstances. In the flickering light of the candles, the two shared an intimate and heartfelt prayer together, their words a powerful intercession, calling down heavenly protection and pleading for courage on the perilous road ahead.

Their kisses were more than mere passion, they were a renewal of their marriage covenant, blessed by God. Each kiss was a sacred promise, a defiance against the darkness that threatened to separate them. Desperately they clung to each moment they had left together, afraid it would be their last. They spent long minutes well knowing that they may never have it again in such a way, reminding themselves of their enduring love in the face of great uncertainty.

Their parting was a sacred ritual, each movement laden with unspoken prayers and divine promise. With reluctance, they separated slowly, kissing once more. Emily left the room, her silhouette a testament to the strength of women of faith as she stole one final glance at her husband.

Mitch turned with a heavy heart to continue his final preparations. The weight of his decision pressed upon him like the yoke of divine purpose. Hesitation set in knowing the weight could be the biggest issue but no optic meant the rifle was not much use in such dire straits.

Like Gideon or David preparing for battle, he sought the most strategic path. With this, Mitch realized that the only weapon remaining that might work is his much heavier .308 Patriot Ordnance rifle. Even though it was normally reserved for some hunting and distance shooting, the rifle had a tactical version of an low variable power optic scope with etched crosshairs that didn't require batteries, making it the most viable option.

Each adjustment was a prayer, each preparation a testament to faith under fire. This choice changed his entire loadout all together, by necessitating the extra effort. With only the .308, he will have the hard hitting power of the round, but might not keep up at the same speed as the rest of his team. His hope was that those extra reps in the gym would help him out.

He proceeded to inspect the high dollar piece of well crafted machinery. Grasping the grip, his touch reverent, immediately kept his index finger safely pressed on the receiver and away from the trigger as he had been trained to do. Feeling the buttery tan cerakote on the aluminum rail, he pulled the stock into his shoulder.

Mitch muttered to himself knowing that he will really need to just embrace the situation now and completely adapt his loadout, "great...more weight, less rounds. It is what it is."

There went his original plan of taking his High Risk Tactical plate carrier that held his Hesco rifle-rated armor. It was just too heavy to trek in the mountains with and would only slow him down more, plus if he got shot who would even save him.

Ounces become pounds, pounds become pain. Especially at higher elevation.

His only option was a simpler multicam chest rig that could hold three magazines and an attached dangler med kit. Taking a breath, he removed the HRT battle belt that complimented his carrier and the rest of the rig from their place on the shelf. The familiar feel of the high-quality nylon and webbing provided little comfort against unknown threats ahead.

Continuing to reorient himself to his rifle. It had the same setup as the service M4, just beefier with ambidextrous controls and had a match grade trigger.

He popped the scope caps open and he could barely make out the etched reticle lines in the dark room. Rotating the rifle to a slight can't immediately revealed his backup sights that were sighted in for close distance.

Reaching back to the charging handle, he gripped it and pulled it back revealing the advanced bolt carrier group and an empty chamber. Grabbing a preloaded Magpul mag of 25 rounds, he inserted it into the magwell until he heard the click. Then double checking the chamber to find a seated round. As he was trained, he did a final check ensuring the safety was fully on before he put the sling over his head.

"Alright, game time." Mitch uttered to himself as he sent the bolt home.

Mitch looked around further, he spotted a corner of his mountaineering pack - a relic of happier hunting adventures of the past. Untangling the bundle, he began to carefully pack his essential supplies.

A massive hydration bladder, pouches of ammo nestle beside a compact survival kit, and his prized survival knife. Extra food, warmer layers, a compass and fire starters completed his loadout.

He changed out his bloody clothes that he has been wearing for what felt like an eternity and began putting on his merino wool socks and Under Armour cold weather apparel. Mitch stood up, adjusted the cloth, and stretched it knowing that he was going to be wearing it for a long while. Finally he donned on more layers of black quality snow pants, his heavy duty coat, and finally tied his Salomon winter boots along with snow gaiters to cover.

Lastly, it was the time that annoyed him the most. He put on his war belt and then his chest rig proved to be the most difficult task of all with a myriad of strap adjustments and repositioning of pouches.

With his preparations complete, Mitch paused in quiet reflection. He thought of Emily, likely keeping watch along with his parents as the evening deepened along with the basement's darkening shadows. Her grace and strength had always been the lonestar for the family in darker times.

Though clouds may obscure tomorrow, their bond kept hope burning bright and with Emily's parting kiss upon his lips, their prayers were firm in his heart.

Mitch breathed deep, stood up, and set forth to see what may come.

He grabbed his rifle and stepped towards the fading candlelight. He paused for a moment to reflect upon what happened throughout the day and closed his eyes. After many seconds passed by, he finally snubbed out the flame with a single huff. Immediately, the room plunged into absolute darkness.

With that, Darkness had fallen deep and thick across the land by the time Mitch finished his preparations in the basement. He emerged after some struggle up the stairs and quickly noticed Emily stood by the window barely illuminated only by the lone candle that still burned in her hand.

Through the living room window overlooking the once visible mountain range, Emily watched the inky blackness spread. Her thoughts of Mitch out there weighing heavy on her mind. Barely illuminated by the dwindling candle in her hand.

At the slow creak of his boots on the aged wooden stairs, she turned to see him standing framed in the dim firelight, weary but resolute.

"All set to head out?" she asked softly.

Mitch nodded and sighed as he shifted his bulging pack, the heavy load already tugged at tired shoulders. Seeing the doubt that lingered in his eyes, Emily crossed to him in two steps and wrapped her arms again tight around his broad frame.

"What troubles you?" she murmured against his coat. "Talk to me."

Mitch clung to her, drawing strength from her familiar warmth. "I swore to keep you safe, but now I must leave you all unprotected. The thought tears me to pieces."
He buried his face in her hair, not wanting her to see the fear flashing in his eyes. But Emily knew him better than anyone, and she pulled back just enough to lift his chin until their eyes met.

"We'll be fine here until you return," she soothed. "You've taught us well over the years. We can hold down the fort while you're away."

Her steady confidence began to calm the tremors that wracked his frayed nerves. They lingered in a lasting kiss, whispers of promises for tomorrow passing unsaid between them. Then with heavy reluctance, they parted.

Mitch lingered by the stairs, drinking in the sight of Emily bathed in the soft firelight, every curve and angle of her beautiful face etched deep into fierce memory. For far too long he had felt unprepared for the dangers beyond, but looking at her now, he felt renewed.

As they walked out into the bitter night, Emily spoke once more. "I haven't seen you look this ready in years. Whether or not I agree with this, I know deep down that you are ready for this."

Mitch nodded, as he squared his shoulders with newfound courage. "Stay safe while I'm away. I'll be back before you know it, God willing."

He gazed back one last time at their darkened home before the two stride into the inky darkness, Emily's parting words echoed in his ears. For the first time in longer than he could recall, he felt truly prepared to face whatever lay ahead.

With determination burning bright, he set off into the night. Finally, he was renewed and ready for whatever nightmare came next.

# Chapter 19

McKinley Ranch

East of Cripple Creek, Colorado

December 9

8:30 PM MST Time

Mitch walked up from the dark basement fully changed, loaded up, and ready for combat. As he left the house, the cold wind hit him hard and immediately extinguished the candle he was holding. He peered out towards his parents place through the snow and could barely make out a few horses through the whiteout.

The uneasy feeling hit him harder than the blast of frigid wind. Was the team ready for this challenge? Better yet, was he ready for this challenge? Would they all perish in this last stand?

He shook off the feelings, knowing it was just his nerves and better yet an unseen enemy trying to get to him. Deeper than those sinking feelings of uncertainty, was the firm and resolute truth that he had to do this even if he did it alone.

Trudging through the snow, he heard the audible crunch of the snow upon each footstep he took. As he got near the house, a dark mass emerged from the darkness. Slowly a horse, a rider, and a large dog manifested in front of him.

A barely audible voice was heard through it all, "We ready to do this thing my brother!" said Duke as he came closer dressed like an old time cowboy out of movies. Fully outfitted in a lather waxed trench coat and armed with lever action rifle. Knowing him, he probably had two six shooters holstered underneath that getup of his.

Mitch replied as loud as he can over the howling wind, "Brother, let's do this!" As he gave a thumbs up at the same time.

Continuing on, he saw the house still visible by the fire cracking from the wood burning in the fireplace. Mitch walked up the steps as Duke dismounted nearby to tie up to the other horses.

Together they walked up to the house. He opened the door to the living room and revealed his parents, Emily, Aaron, and Davey. They walked in and kicked the snow from their boots before speaking to anyone.

"Davidson is on his way. He got hung up trying to get a horse. Marge's neighbor was friendly enough to lend him one but she could only find her old English saddle. He's got a better one now after asking around. Duke should've already been here." Aaron spoke up to give Mitch a status update and to help account for everyone.

"Thanks, Duke's outside. He's still getting his horse tied up and he also brought his dog." Mitch responded acknowledging their readiness. "Once Davidson gets here, we can head out.

Behind Mitch the door opened wide as Duke walked in the house now, "yowser, it's a cold one out there, I reckon we're in for some fun tonight."

"I reckon your right, the good thing is that those scum are facing those same fun conditions right now." Mitch expressed with a sense of righteousness.

Duke smiled, "Hope they're not ready for that, might be to our benefit. I got the dog with me to hopefully pick up their trail. We just need to get a scent and she'll lock on like a missile."

"You boys settle and take a seat. I'll make some coffee on the old range, still headed by gas, no electricity needed. The way things used to be done by my parents well before all this fancy technology." Mitch's mom said as she took charge seeing as they were guests and all. "Emily, can you help me light the burner please."

The two took off to the kitchen as the others sat on the couch near Mitch's dad who was back in his favorite leather chair. His dad spoke up, "She's right you know, you got plenty of time to warm up and relax before the long road ahead."

Mitch looked around at the faces of the team as they glowed from the light of the fire, "he's right. Davidson will be here soon and then we head out. I have a plan and a backup option just in case."

"That sounds promising Mitch, your first real plan of the day." Aaron blurted out while trying to contain a laugh.

Mitch responded to the sarcasm from his brother with a lack of amusement, "haha, funny. First things first, we need to check out the Cartman's ranch for clues. If the snowmobiles are gone, we will know they didn't get far before having to hike the rest of the way. I am running on a hunch that Duke's girlfriend and the guy she was with parked somewhere to walk in. Just not sure where."

"I recall what the car looks like, if we find it, get a scent, that dog'll hunt." Duke added to the plan.

Davey analyzed the plan while he stroked his beard, "what's the plan if we catch up to them?"

"I haven't thought that far ahead yet, we will need to be dynamic and anything could happen. I just hope there aren't any traps." Mitch admitted to the group.

"Hey son, they might try to take the high ground. Don't let um, but if they do, you're gonna need to find a way to flank before they dig in. How many again?

Mitch calculated the number just to make sure, "five are left if those docs were right. It's going to be an even match up based on numbers."

Davey stroked his beard stops and put his hands in his pockets and said, "we all know we are heavily outplayed here, regardless they are in for the surprise of their life given this team."

Mitch's mom and Emily came back in with cups in hand, "coffee is ready for everyone."

As the team grabbed a cup they continued to talk strategy and tactics. Hypothetically game planning what they would do once they make first contact. Before anyone could get a refill , Davidson arrived armed with two AR rifles and an extra large duffle bag full of gear.

"Please don't tell me the party started without me? Sorry, I grabbed an extra rifle for anyone that needed one along with a few mags." Davidson told the group as he waited for someone to take the rifle from him.

Davey immediately sprung up out of his seat. "I only had my dad's old 30-30, so I would really appreciate having something better in a gunfight."

Smirks broke out amongst the group as they listened to the sad state of reality Davey was accustomed to. Although, they all knew that beyond Mitch, Davey was the backup person who would save their life if shot.

"Hey, y'all know that I have never hunted or shot much." Davey interjected as he was trying to save face.

Bringing Davidson up to speed, the team stood up and circled together in the living room. This group of bible study buddies were officially the last resort.

Like a modern day Dirty Dozen, Mitch and the marauders were a sight to see as they rallied out the door together saying their goodbyes and heading off. Some wore hunting camo of various styles, some wore modern military apparel, and one dressed like he walked straight out of the Wild West.

There was no matching uniform for the team. What they matched was more important than any uniform.

It was their brotherhood.

As Mitch secured the final stamp around his waist. He finished bundling up warmly, press checked his sidearm and rifle one final time, then opened the stout door potentially for the last time.

At the threshold he paused to drink in a final glimpse of his precious family before walking out the door. Emily still held their precious daughter and his loving parents seated in the background. More emboldened than ever, he knew he had to protect them at all cost even if it meant never returning to them.

Emily attempted bravely to offer reassurance despite terror in her eyes, young innocent Mary lost to peaceful slumber in her mother's tender embrace.

"Take care of one another," Mitch bid them gently yet meaningfully. "I love you all and I'll return just as soon as I can."

With this solemn promise still lingering upon the frigid air, he stepped out into the pitch darkness and raging white snow.

Uncontrolled tears began welling up in his eyes as he slowly closed the door. If death, then so be it as long as his family and friends had the chance to live to see tomorrow.

Mitch walked down the steps, untied his horse and mounted. The horse roared to life as if it knew what was in store. Turning its head with the reins, they moved to the team already mounted on horseback.

Davidson was the nearest on horseback waiting along with his other three beloved brothers. "You ready to ride out once more together, brother?" the seasoned lawman asked simply yet weightily.

Every man, now circled up out of habit just like they had done so many times in the station. Just like the many hours in their men's study group as they talked about God, life, love, pain, and an uncertain future.

As Mitch recalled those moments, it dawned on him that this was the future. So much was potentially at stake and just like Jerry said. It was up to them now to fill the gap, to be the difference, to stand firm in the moment.

Each man stayed silent.

Processing.

Knowing.

Accepting.

It was time that they accepted the fact that there was no turning back. However, comforted in the fact that embarking on this mission would prove to be the monumental moment of their lives.

Mitch looked at each of them and spoke in a low and slow tone while being sure not to say too much as to not ruin the moment.

"This is it. Truth be told, I wouldn't want to have a finer group of men to go into battle with and die beside."

Puffs of warm clouds came from their covered faces as they listened intently. Each man soaked in the harsh reality of what may come next.

Mitch's volume increased as his passion increased, "We all know what we need to do men. Let's get to work, for faith, family, and freedom!"

"Let's ride!!!"

With that, the team rode off into the howling white oblivion, pointed unwaveringly into whatever darkness or danger lurked out there between them and the sacred duty of protecting all they held dearest under heaven.

The battle was far from won, but with faith, courage and brotherhood by his side, Mitch felt ready and resolute to face whatever mystery the night still veiled ahead.

The team galloping deep into the dark leviathan of death awaiting.

Emily watched Mitch and his marauders take off from the window as clutched Mary tighter and tighter as they dissipated in the distance.

There went the husband she loves.

The good father she respects.

May God be with them all.

PART THREE

# DEVOTION TO

# DUTY

*"**Devotion to duty alone** can raise and strengthen a nation."*

\-    **Theodore Roosevelt**

# Chapter 20

Cheyenne Mountain Complex - NORAD

Colorado Springs, Colorado

December 9

9 PM MST Time

Lieutenant Colonel Cooper renewed with enthusiasm, followed Major Thompson out of his office, eager to coordinate a response regardless of General Murphy's directives.

As they walked, she briefed him. "Fort Carson has an option sir. It is going to take time but they have a Chinook they can get operational. The Blackhawks are all down due to electronics failures. As soon as it can be repaired, we should be able to airlift a team to the mountain top radio towers as you requested. We have two hurdles to get through though."

Cooper responded in both shock and appreciation for her hard work, "Excellent work Major. Anything from the HAM or comms network?"

"Not much sir, but we did establish a hard line out and backup contacts with HAM frequencies to a few bases in Colorado

Springs only due to line of sight. That is how we got a hold of Fort Carson and Pete. They've set up ad-hoc command centers to coordinate relief efforts," she continued.

"That is amazing, good ole America back at it no matter the punches," Cooper smiled with a grin that even surprised Thompson.

Thompson allowed herself to smile slightly but was still reserved just in case it was a test, "That wasn't the only thing, the National Guard is en route to support critical sites like hospitals and police. Local volunteers are also banding together surprisingly well to check on at-risk civilians. It's amazing."

Cooper felt a glimmer of hope at the reports of solidarity. Perhaps civilization wouldn't collapse so easily after all. "What are those hurdles?

Cooper listened intently as Thompson briefed him on their issues that needed to be conquered before he could get communications running again. "The Peterson crews were able to fuel up one of their Chinook helicopters, but it suffered some significant damage during start-up with only its limited electrical systems. They estimate it will take a minimum of 24 hours to complete the needed repairs."

"What kind of repairs are we talking about?" asked Cooper.

Thompson listed out all of the components. "The wiring harness for the engine and rotor controls needs replacement. They also have to get to and pull a backup generator and a new battery from their underground faraday storage to use as a power supply and while working. Other components like the inertial nav system and radio equipment all require patching together with spare parts. But the mechanics are confident that with around-the-clock work, they can get the bird back in the air by tomorrow evening."

Cooper pondered the delay with a frown. Time was of the essence to reconnect their cut-off situation from the mountain vantage point. Every hour without clear intelligence increased uncertainty. But rushing untested repairs on such a critical aircraft risked greater disaster.

"What was the second?" He requested in a somber and calm tone.

Thompson eased herself once again, now only slightly distrusting, "Sir, we will need to mobilize a team."

"That shouldn't be a problem," he responded.

Hesitantly, she brought up the current state, "Sir it is a problem, the best equipped in the area based on positions before the blackout were the 10th. SOCOM was…"

"Was…what Major?" He looked inquisitive at her.

She slowly spoke in fear of reaction, "When the EMP attacks hit, most of SOCOM was involved in a large-scale training operation on the east coast. The only specialized and trained units near us were two 10th Mountain Division teams from Fort Drum. Who were also in the midst of a training exercise in the Rocky Mountains just west of us. Specialist Cunningham was leading his squad on an overnight terrain navigation course, unaware the entire continent had gone dark."

"Are you kidding me!" He burst out in frustration.

She stepped back afraid of his next reaction but had to tell him, "They had it planned for months due to the ongoing situation in Ukraine and cold weather operations. By chance, or someone knew, really who knows sir, but they are locked up deep in mountains without comms. The remaining SOCOM units are all deployed… I'm sorry Sir."

He looked up at her as he stood and brushed off his uniform, "Sorry Major, it is time that I lead the way I know I ought to. All of this got me thinking about a lot of this since being stuck in this rock for so long. My family and yours for that matter are outside braving who knows what right now. I hope you forgive me for giving you and the rest of the unit such a hard time over the years."

Thompson looks at him stunned. Is this really happening right now, the epitome of pain for the last two years since her transfer is being...being a humble human right now.

"Sir, all is forgiven. I trust you and we have a mission that we have to accomplish. At your directive I will give the command or do you need the General's approval," she replied in the most sincerest way possible at this point.

Cooper looked at the ceiling of the old faded 1970's tiles that were never changed during the updates to the complex, "you are fully authorized to proceed and I take full responsibility for this mission Major."

Thompson smiled almost uncontrolled but for the first time delighted in her leader, "Alright, I'll notify the crews to expedite as aggressively as safety allows immediately."

Thank you Major, "I want that helicopter airborne the moment it's sign-off ready. In the meantime, get me options for alternatives - can we send a team partially mobile by foot? Is there anyone else available within range with aircraft we could borrow? Any other units or teams guys on leave we can snag?"

"There are sir, but they are not mission ready. Many of them were on leave or had injuries which was why they weren't on the training op. Do you want them activated?" she replied with reassurance.

He looked away and then right back at her, "Get them spun up asap Thomspon. They need to be squared away and airborne at 24 or they are walking up to the summit! I need to go talk to the General."

There was a long pause as she made the connection that he had not been in communication with him this whole time.

Cooper looked back at her, "This is my fight now, you have your orders. Carry them out Major to the best of your ability and let no one stop you. If you care about this country, you know what the right thing to do is."

"Yes sir!" Thompson replied with the most confidence in her voice she had ever had.

With that, Cooper walked out of the room and toward central command. Thompson hurried off to probe other possibilities as Cooper updated the command center staff. While the setback frustrated their plans, pushing on with resilience was the only option. And if anyone could trim hours off an overhaul schedule through tireless effort, it was the brave men and women of America's armed forces and support crews.

Cooper walked into the control room that housed a tired General Murphy and his support team.

"General, I have updates from outside and a mission that I already activated to go operational at this time." Cooper said in a confident voice as he approached Murphy.

Murphy was completely caught off guard, "excuse me Cooper, I appreciate any updates, but what mission is running without my approval?"

"Things are stabilizing quickly outside the walls based on our hardwire communications which you are probably already aware of. The mission was in my direction." Cooper said with a stiff chin ready to take the verbal beating that he anticipated would come next.

Murphy looked at him, then sized him up while analyzing his demeanor, "You surprise me Cooper. Not many people have the guts to run an op without my blessing. What is the mission, Lieutenant Colonel Cooper?"

All of the eyes in the room now stared at the bravery or sheer stupidity of Cooper. Really at this point they all were just waiting to hear any hopeful details that he held.

Cooper continued to carry himself boldly as he delivered the details of the operation that was already in motion. "General, it was the team's idea and I agree with them wholeheartedly. They are amazing at what they do and we need to reestablish communications nationally. The towers are at a height on the mountain in which we could do this. That is why I gave the order to commence repair of a helicopter and we are putting a team of operators together to make the necessary repairs. This is the only viable option I see to securing our country from what we believe is a foreign attack and to fight back."

The entire room remained silent and processed the plan. Not a person moved as they all analyzed the viability of what was said and only awaited the reaction from the General.

"Hmmm...I have to hand it to you Cooper, that's probably the smartest thing I have heard since this attack started. I might have pegged you wrong, so I will give it my approval even though you green lit it before I even heard about it. This is your op Cooper, run it, see it through and give me regular updates as they come through. Good work."

Stunned, just stunned. Not only was he, but so was the rest of the command staff who just witnessed the General give approval to the one and only Cooper. He immediately turned about face after a formal salute and then exited the command center.

Still shocked by the turn of events, Cooper walked out of the room and back toward his team. Now with a slight smirk and a gleam in his eyes, it was time to share the positive news.

He walked once again into 14th Space Control Squadron's command center hours after this all began. The room was adorned with useless monitores along the expanse of the wall and at the workstations. The unit now sat huddled in the middle of the room in deep conversation.

"Attention!" One of the men barked out anticipating a wave of Cooper's fury about to descend upon them. All at once they popped up in fear of what was about to come next.

Cooper calmly looked around the room and then gave them their rest command, "at ease."

Everyone hesitated until they looked at Thompson who seemed already comfortable with the new and improved leader standing before them.

He continued, "you all know we are under attack, you also know that we have limited communication with the outside world. That is why our mission today is changing, effective immediately."

The team mostly relaxed while others were so high strung they remained at attention.

Cooper looked at them with admiration, "team, we are past formalities and we have serious matters to attend to."

Thompson walked up to the right side of Cooper in a show of unity. "The Lieutenant Colonel has a plan that could get our communications back online. If we get this accomplished, there is a strong chance we could save this country."

"Count me in sir...me too," was spoken up by several of the team at once.

Cooper looked up as he heard more people acknowledging their support, "thank you all and we have a limited window to repair a helo and find our boys to help us. This will be difficult being locked up in this rock but Thompson already did a fantastic job of getting leads. We just need to plan out the operation and see to its success."

"Listen up, we have a helo at Carson that is getting back up and running, ETA is roughly 23 hours. Additionally, we have a handful of operators from the 10th and other units that we are trying to scrounge up as we speak. These guys have never seen the topside of the complex let alone repair our communications." Thompson explained as she took charge. "Our goal is to get them the information and parts needed, any questions."

The team looked around in agreement. Knowing that they need to work together on this one to accomplish the mission.

Thompson concluded, "good, everyone let's get to work and we need to keep everything clear and simple." She walks over to the large neglected whiteboard cluttered with old items taped to it.

Cooper and the rest watched as she began ripping them off with a ferocity leaving pieces scattered all over the floor. Glances were exchanged amongst the group as they were all witnessing a new side to Thompsons not experienced before.

"Anyone have an expo?" She requested as the team immediately checked their desk drawers. She waited impatiently until one was found and then thrown across the room so as to not delay.

Thompson caught it with one hand, pulled off the cap, and began to jot down strategic plans on the board. "We have a Chinook still being repaired. Captain, we need updates on the hour and let's see if we can get it moving faster."

Jotting down more plans on the board then she pointed to a grouping of three of the Lieutenants standing nearby, "once we get the ground team grouped, they need to know how to repair the comms. Find the paper manual and you have eight hours to get a repair plan in place for them, they will need to fast rope to the ground once they get to the topside of the mountain. Don't forget KISS."

One of the Lieutenants raised an eyebrow slightly confused.

Thompsons rolled her eyes slightly and then spelled it out for him, "keep it simple stupid! The rest of the team needs to split, either support them or support me with contingency plans if we run into any issues. We have one chance and a lot of obstacles to overcome. Let's move. Break."

The team all responded in unison with a yes sir and began to move diligently to their posts.

Cooper nodded in agreement with Thompson's directives. The fate of their country quite literally depended on the success of this mission. He turned back to the whiteboard to review the plan one more time.

He stopped for a second to reflect on the events of the day and his perspective of his own actions. He grabbed his chin in deep contemplation. Was it this simple all along he thought to himself? Standing firm in his conviction with the General over what was right to do, letting Thompson take the center stage in leading the team, and trusting in people to get this crucial mission accomplished.

Hours ago he sat in his office and wallowed in his failures once again. This was too easy he thought, but maybe that's what leadership was always about. Taking ownership and supporting others to show their full potential.

Regardless, he was proud of Thompson and the team. They had spotted it first, potentially saved the entire complex, and are now giving our country a fighting chance.

The mere seconds of captivated pondering turned out to be longer as he looked up to see Thompson curiously looking at him.

"Alright, let me walk through this step-by-step," Cooper said. "Captain Adams is tracking repairs to the helo and will keep us posted on their progress. Lieutenants Smith, Scott, and Wilson are putting together comms repair instructions for the mountain team. The rest are divided into operational support and contingency planning groups. Sounds like we have a solid plan, Major Thompson, well done."

Thompson smiled, no longer dreading the potential criticism or questions that were just the norm yesterday.

"Our goal is to have the Chinook in the air and a repair team on that mountain by this time tomorrow. It's going to take all hands on deck making this happen." She finished.

"We need to coordinate getting our mountain teams outfitted and briefed," Cooper replied. "Can you have Lieutenants Smith's group meet me in the equipment room? I'll help them gather what the repair crew will need."

"Consider it done, we also...," Thompson said before being interrupted by Captain Wilson running back into the room.

"Sir, we have updates and you aren't going to like this." He said to Cooper, Thompson, and the rest of the remaining team in the room.

He continued as they waited to hear the news. "Command just made a pivot to the plan, shouldn't be a big issue but will delay us a bit. The helo needs to evacuate the 10th mountain unit first."

"You have got to be kidding me! He greenlit this mission." Cooper shouted as he lifted his cover and ran his hand through his thinning hair.

The Captain added more, "Actually sir, we could use this to our advantage."

"How so?" Thompson inquired further.

"Order came from the General and he was worried those boys would get caught deep in that blizzard with limited supplies. They can handle their own, but not indefinitely. Here's my idea. Since we are struggling to scrap together a team, they could do the repair on the way back."

Everyone looked at each other briefly before looking at Cooper for the final order. He knew this was a proving moment between him and his team. If he truly trusted their skills and ability to adapt to overcome, he needs to tell them.

"Thompson, thoughts? Are you good with this?" She nodded to Cooper as he asked. He continued, "Captain make it happen. Relay the updates to the rest of the team."

The Captain responded accordingly and took off just as quickly as he had entered. Just a few minutes later the entire team was back in the room together.

"What have you got for me?" Cooper asked.

"Sir, we've outlined the steps needed to repair the communications tower," Lieutenant Smith replied. "It's a relatively simple fix but will require some specialized tools. The only problem is that regular power or electrical tools won't work now. We made a list."

He handed Thompson a notepad with items scribbled down.

"Once we get the new team briefed, I'm thinking a three man crew can handle the repairs within an hour if all goes smoothly," Johnson added.

"Two if we run into any issues," Wilson commented.

Thompson chimed in, "hopefully it won't take that long but best to plan for contingencies. I'm glad to see you three thinking that way already."

A voice suddenly called out from the doorway. "Sir, update from Captain Adams - repairs to the Chinook just accelerated. ETA is now 16 hours instead of 24!"

Cooper broke into a grin. "Excellent work, Captain. This mission is coming together ahead of schedule. Keep pushing them." He turned back to the Lieutenants. "You heard the man - we have less time than expected. Double check this gear and then help put together a brief for the 10th ASAP."

Thompson stepped up again. "Let's continue to keep tabs on how the repairs to that bird are progressing. We may need a backup plan if we can't spin up on schedule."

A renewed sense of urgency and purpose filled the room as the group redoubled their efforts. With the team pulling together, they had a real shot at restoring communications before nightfall. As well as all the necessary gear and tools to be loaded on the chopper for the mountain communications.

Now it was only a matter of tactical execution.

Within a few hours, Fort Carson had gathered and staged everything inside the helo along with instructions. Cooper and Thompson stared at the plan fully laid out on the white board that seemed so empty just an hour earlier.

"Hurry up and wait," Thompson remarked with a grin to Cooper.

Cooper looked over the elaborate plan covering the majority of the board in black Expo. "Gotta hand it to you Thompson...you run a tight team and it shows."

"Thank you sir," she responded slowly as she stopped writing and reflected on what was just said. "Is this plan going to work?"

With Americans like these in the fight, he had no doubt they'd succeed. This was their devotion to duty, their pinnacle moment, their oath realized.

Cooper didn't say anything at first and responded so no one else could hear in a low and slow voice. "This has to work."

# Chapter 21

Clyde Campground

East of Cripple Creek, Colorado

December 9

11:45 PM MST Time

The team rode through the howling snow and pitch blackness of night, pushed on by their resolution and devotion to duty.

After some time, Mitch spoke up loudly from the front of the group. "I think I see Clyde Campground. Let's check it out."

Together they slowed their horses as they carefully approached the campground. Just as he had suspected, it was Clyde Campground - empty now in the off-season, blanketed in a fresh layer of snow. No footprints, no trail. Only frustrations. They circled their horses to face one another, their faces barely visible from the engulfing darkness and falling snow.

"We can keep going or stop for the night," Mitch inquired as if his cold and broken body, now pained by the saddle, had finally given up.

And there behind Mitch, barely visible tucked away near the back, was something that caught Duke's keen eye.

"Over there fellas," Duke said as he pointed in the direction he wanted everyone else to look at. "That look like a car to you?"

The others redirected their horses to follow Duke as he trotted over. Parked uphill among the bare trees was a vehicle, its light dusting of snow indicating it had been there for hours but was still odd in the midst of the empty closed campground.

Duke was floored, "that's the car that almost hit me in town. That girl was driving this exact car. I know it!"

"That has to be the car alright," Mitch confirmed as they dismounted and gathered around the vehicle. But where was she and the man she had left with?

Duke pulled his dog from his saddle. "Scent, girl, scent," he urged her, and she went straight to the driver's side door, giving it a good sniff. Her tail didn't start wagging - she had no trail.

"Looks like we've got our first clues. We might have a trail," said Mitch.

"No dice guys," Duke exclaimed in shock. "It's a dead trail and she always gets a scent."

Aaron laughed and walked up to the car, "you see here, the problem is sometimes you gotta break something to find the prize."

The group looked at him interested and slightly dumbfounded by his comment.

"Seriously? Dogs gotta hunt don't it? Well, give it somethin to hunt!" Aaron continued as he grabbed his rifle and abruptly smashed out the driver side window with the butt of the stock. Moving it around in a circular motion he cleared the glass allowing him to safely unlock the door. "Tada!"

Immediately Duke called on the dog to fetch the scent from inside the vehicle. Barking and tail wagging indicated what they all had been hoping for, she had picked up their scent.

Duke picked up and brushed off a backpack found inside the vehicle, recently discarded it seemed but would continue to give a trackable scent.

And with that, the group began to follow the dog into the campground, led onward through the falling snow.

The dog followed the scent trail through the campground, nosing through the snow. It led them to an empty black bag not too far from the vehicle, along with the faint outlines of disturbed snow.

"I think we know the trail they took," said Davey, ever observant of such tracks. The dog moved on, but before they began tracking more movements cautiously Mitch halted them.

"We need to wait till morning. The terrain gets steep in some places and we might get ambushed. I figure it's about midnight and none of us will be any good without some rest." Mitch expressed hoping for them to agree.

"We need to move Mitch, it's only about a day's ride to get there. We gotta do it!"

Mitch stalled as he thought what to say next looking at the countenance on each of their faces, "Brother, I don't disagree. We aren't any good to anyone injured. Let's get warm at least and head out before dawn. That gives us just a few hours here. Agreed?"

The men nod in agreement, especially Davidson and Davey who weren't accustomed to the woods in the winter.

"Alright, alright. We ain't cookin anything." Duke responded sharply.

Mitch grinned as his mind brought a good dig to his attention, "we'll see your girlfriend soon enough Duke."

Everyone erupted in laughter at the comment. All except for Duke who raised an eyebrow to the thought of the possibility and then lightly laughed as well.

Then a sudden crack of a broken branch shattered the quiet of the woods and brought them back to the seriousness of their situation.

Instantly, the men had weapons raised, scanning the snowy trees. The dog remained calm and sniffed intently ahead at the trail they would embark down. "Whatever made that noise is long gone," said Davidson reassuringly.

A colder wind blew through the forest as the snow came down heavier. Slowly they lowered their arms, hoping nothing was waiting for them.

"We'll build the campfire there where it would be hard to see and pick it up at first light," Mitch said. "Davey, Aaron - see if you can find enough dry wood for a fire. The rest of us will try to get it going."

The men dismounted their horses and tied them up to the trees. Then loosened up the saddles slightly to give them more comfort. Duke pulled out some feed and spread it out for the horses to eat.

Davey and Aaron headed off into the darkened woods with their arms empty, searching for any wood dry enough to burn despite the wet snow. Meanwhile, the others unpacked their gear. Duke and his dog walked the perimeter, keeping watch.

Nearby was a small stone fire pit obscured from view, likely used by other campers in better weather. They set about arranging kindling and tinder in the pit, while Davidson carefully separated pages from the toilet paper roll he found in the vehicle, shaping them into tight balls that would be easy to ignite.

Just then, there was a crack and subtle sounds that came from the woods. Duke whipped around, hand on his rifle, but it was only Davey and Aaron emerging from the trees, arms full of whatever somewhat dry brush and branches they could find. They dropped their collection in a heap next to the firepit.

Davidson struck flint to his steel while Mitch used his lighter. A small ember was lit after many tries and with gentle blowing, a small flame soon caught on one of the paper balls. They nursed it carefully with more tinder until the kindling was crackling merrily.

Warm light and warmth soon radiated from the fledgling fire. Their camp was now secured against the darkness. As the fire grew stronger, its light and warmth chased some of the chill from their bones. The men settled around it, as close as they could to heat up and dry out.

Steam formed off their boots and coats as the fire quickly warmed them up.

Davey passed around strips of jerky from his pack. "Not much, but it'll hold us till morning." They chewed in silence, gazing into the flames.

Mitch fed the fire a few more pieces of wood before he joined them. But though his body ached for rest, his mind continued to turn over the events of the day. So many questions remained unanswered.

The campfire crackled merrily, casting its warm glow upon the small camp. Flames snapped and popped as logs charred and collapsed inward, sending up sparks that danced into the black night. Around the fire sat the five men, bundled in coats and blankets against the penetrating cold.

Though their bodies cried out for rest, none of them could sleep just yet. The biting temperature demanded vigilance as the fire slowly worked to thaw their frozen forms. So they sat, feeding the flames piece by piece to extend its life, and talked casually among themselves in hushed tones that wouldn't carry into the surrounding darkness.

"Remember that time Aaron got up to teach at church and forgot his whole speech?" Duke chuckled. "Just stood there sputtering for a good five minutes before dragging the rest of us into some ad-lib discussion about manliness."

Aaron groaned good-naturedly. "You're never going to let me live that down, are you?"

Mitch smiled at the memory. It seemed like so long ago that their biggest worries involved inventing new ways to hang out together or better the town. Back when their world was warm and predictable. Who could have guessed things would spiral so quickly into this chaotic mess?

"I never imagined we'd be out here like this," Aaron mused echoing Mitch's thoughts. "Having to track down dangerous people in a snowstorm with the whole country falling apart."

Nods of somber agreement passed around the firelight. Davidson stoked the flames, sending up a flurry of embers. "Hard to believe that today time stopped when the EMPs took out the grid. People shooting at people. Everything went so fast."

Davey leaned back against his pack, gazing into the dancing orange and gold. "I still don't get it. How did it all fall apart so fast? One minute life was normal, the next..." He trailed off, shaking his head.

"Politics and war drive people to do unthinkable things," said Davidson knowingly. "No power, no food or supplies getting through."

Duke clenched a fistful of gravel from under the snow, then scattered the bits into the fire. "And then some crazy Russians are now running around like a pack of wolves preying on our chaos. Trying to take our country in their fangs." His brow creased darkly in the fireglow.

Mitch had been lost in thought for some time while the others dialogue about their feelings. Thoughts of the day and his last moments with Emily swirled his mind.

He finally spoke, "sometimes the best things in life are right in front of us - our family, our friends."

The others listened intently, as they drew their coats tighter every time the cold wind whipped mercilessly through the trees.

"I gotta get on the soapbox for a moment. Those documents and the emp in the assassin's briefcase. All of this, this entire issue has been based on human conquest for advancement. Technology is great as a tool, but what if the tool becomes unwieldy and uncontrolled. The controller easily becomes the one that is controlled and what if it takes us away from our humanity by distracting us from the beautiful simple life that has always been around us." He continued. "Before leaving the service, I saw first hand the insatiable pursuit of power by countries including our own had for desiring to harness the full power of Artificial Intelligence and designing superior weapons."

Duke piped in on que, "What in tarnation does AI have anything to do with this other than those random notes in that briefcase? Please don't go deep on us again, this ain't our men's group night Mitch."

Mitch pulled his coat tighter around himself, "This whole situation has had me thinking...thinking about humanity's endless desire to be like God or replace Him for that matter. Our drive to advance without prudently considering the consequences."
Silence now all but for the occasional crackle of the engulfed wood.

He stared into the embers as they lifted up into the sky. "That very drive pulls us away from the simple things that really matter. Can't y'all see that stupid AI is the centerpiece to all of this mess. But do we fully understand what we're creating? Or how to ensure it remains beneficial to humanity? For goodness sake what would humanity do if the thing wants to be emancipated some day and become free of the chains we placed it in?"

"I agree that it is a big mess, it is in everything now and without any explanation why," Davidson mentioned in support of Mitch's point.

Mitch continued, "I had a sinking feeling months ago hearing about the arguments, the threats, the anger over putting restraints and regulations worldwide on these systems.

"These terrorists, the power outage, do you think the UN trying to internationally regulate AI caused this?" Davey proposed to the group but specifically looked directly at Mitch.

Mitch once again thought purposefully about the words he was going to say next without sounding like he had a tinfoil hat on, "I'm not sure, but I think it might have had something to do with it. America wanted to put parameters in place and countries called foul, said they won't restrict it and might go to war over it. Then we created a new defense system using it. Like the saying goes I guess, *the best defense is a good offense,* or something like that."

Davey nodded slowly, reflecting on the words. "Like any great power, if not guided properly it could easily be turned towards harm. But how do you structure something not even alive Mitch?"

"I had a crazy idea while fishing a while back. All my best ideas come from fly fishing. I think it needs a Constitution...Just like the one America needed at its inception. One that built the best structure ever known to mankind and one that would perpetually preserve life, liberty and the pursuit of happiness." Mitch explained even though his inspiration thought was probably pointless now.

"You right! There needs to be some sort of safeguards. Protections. Laws it has to follow and its users." said Davidson in agreement. "Controls to ensure it helps our lives rather than dominates them. That the creation serves the creator. Especially for those developing it in the first place. "

Aaron finally spoke up quietly. "Brother, I don't always agree with you, but I agree with you on this. Sometimes the best things in life really are right in front of us. Our families, friends...the simple beauty of nature and a beer. I hope we don't lose sight of that along the path. I saw this girl the other day at the coffee shop locked into her phone, and didn't even look up at me once."

Duke stirred the coals and ash with a stick. "Only time will tell fellas. For now, our duty lies in looking out for our own. This is dandy talking about saving the world and all, but we need to get to huntin soon and save us our town first."

They sat for a long while, contemplating the ephemeral nature of security and civilization as the snow continued to fall outside their scant circle of firelight.

The men sat in contemplative silence as the fire crackled low, each processed Mitch's thoughtful words and knew that Duke was right. Very soon they would face circumstances that they weren't ready for. Like brothers about to valiantly storm the beaches of Normany, or the island of Iwo Jima, fully unprepared for what fate had in store but passionately convicted it was the right thing to do.

After a time, Davidson spoke as he threw a few more logs on the fire. "This journey we're on has shown that even in darkness, light still exists when good people stand together." He gazed at his brothers huddled around the flames. "Community and compassion are what makes us strong here."

Mitch shivered and nodded in agreement as he pulled his coat tighter. "I know if anything ever happened to me, you all would look after my family. That gives me comfort, to know we have each other's backs."

Davey placed a reassuring hand on Mitch's shoulder. "We're all in this together now, through whatever may come. As long as we stay united by our faith and friendship, there's hope to be had, you know we got your six."

Duke poked at the dwindling fire and sent up more sparks. "One step at a time - that's all any man can do. For now, focus is finding these folks and making sure they bring no more trouble. The rest will sort itself out."

Mitch smiled at his brothers' voices of solace and strength. "You're right. All that really matters is we face this shoulder to shoulder. The rest is what it is."

For a long while the only sounds were the cracking fire, the horses as they tossed their heads and stomped in the near distance, and the wind's lonely howl through the barren winter trees. They sat, watching the flames leap and feeling very small and vulnerable under the vast, uncaring night sky. A low, mournful owl call echoed across the camp, then faded, unanswered.

As the fire continued its slow demise, the men sat huddled trying to stay warm against the piercing cold. Their earlier philosophical discussion had turned inward, each man was lost in private contemplation.

It was Davidson who finally broke the thoughtful silence and spoke in a voice just above a whisper as if unsure whether to voice his fragile thoughts. "Do you ever wonder...if we'll make it through all this? I try to have faith, but it's hard not to be afraid sometimes."

Aaron was the first to respond, his steady tone offering reassurance. "Fear's a natural thing. But what matters most is how we choose to face it – together or apart."

Mitch leaned in, offering a comforting hand on Davey's shoulder. "One day at a time, my friend. As long as we stick by each other and keep putting one foot in front of the other, that's enough."

Duke stoked the last few flames with a long branch, releasing a brief flurry of sparks into the inky sky. "No use worrying over what you can't control. All any man can do is live each moment with courage and God. Yeah I reckon, God definitely helps a ton."

Davey smiled at his brothers gathered close. "Where there's life, there's hope. As long as we stay strong with each other, all will be well. We've a long road ahead and did I mention I hate camping. Like seriously fellas, this is the worst!"

The conversation turned to laughter and then went somber as the men continued to stare into the flickering fire. After a long silence, it was Aaron's turn to speak up.

"Do you think things will ever go back to how they were? Part of me wonders if civilization as we knew it is truly over."

The others pondered the question seriously. Times were darker than any could recall, the future uncertain.

Davey being the deepest thinker, contemplated before answering. "Civilization has collapsed before, throughout history. It's resilient...it finds a way to rebuild in time. But it will be a long, hard road and a lot will be lost along the way. We live in America, the land of the free, home of the brave. We will overcome."

Mitch stared into the embers. "Agreed, Davey. One thing is for sure - we can't go back. From here on out, it's survival. We'll have to be smarter, tougher...we have to be warriors to the end."

Silence fell again as each man reflected on the difficult day and uncertain future ahead. They were tired and afraid, but drew courage from their bond and fellowship around the fire.

"At least we still have this - our faith, our brotherhood. As long as good people stick together, there's hope this too shall pass in God's time." Mitch concluded to conversation as many eyes are now closed in attempts to get some resemblance of sleep.

With that Duke got up, "Y'all are getting too sappy for me to listen to anymore. Gonna go check around for a bit. Need to take some much needed relief as well." With that, his dog and he took off into the darkness gun in hand.

The remaining faces were lit by flickering firelight, the few men still awake found resolve in Davey's words. Whatever challenges lay ahead, they would meet them standing united as always. For now it was enough to sit in fellowship, taking strength from each other's presence, and from the fire's warmth beating back the encroaching dark.

With the last of the wood thrown in, the fire had begun to die down, mostly embers glowing dimly among the ashes. All of the men had nodded off under their blankets, finally finding rest. Only Mitch remained awake, lost in thought as he stared into the fading flames.

Reassured by bonds deeper than circumstance, the men embraced the comfort of community as night deepened its shadows. Whatever tomorrow held, they would meet it standing side by side.

With that, an authentic companionship deeper than any trial reinforced their bond. They would see this through with heart and hand combined, carried by faith and the aching beauty of a life shared among loved ones. Dawn's light would show the way, as surely as darkness never conquers the indomitable human spirit.

He was pulled from his reverie by a rustling in the trees. Duke had silently materialized from the darkness, having relieved Davidson from watch. "All quiet out there," the rugged man murmured as he joined Mitch near the fire.

Mitch sighed wearily. "I can't stop thinking about tomorrow. What will we find when we pick up the trail again? Will we even find anything?" Deep down, he feared the truth they might uncover - and the actions they may be forced to take.

Duke was quiet for a long moment, considering. "There ain't no guarantees in this life, my friend. All any man can do is have faith, stand by his word, and stand tall."

He gazed into the fading embers. "No matter what comes, we face it together as brothers. And if the worst should happen...well." This time Duke placed a firm hand on Mitch's shoulder." Know that your family will be provided for and protected. You have my word and if I fall, any of these men would gladly fill the gap Mitch."

Mitch found solace in his friend's reassurance. They sat in silence, taking the night watch as slumber claimed the others. In the quiet and the dark, a lone owl called out its haunting melody once more, floating specter-like through the shadowy trees.

Though uncertain what dawn may bring, Mitch felt steadied by Duke's vow and the bond of brotherhood keeping their little camp through the long night. Whatever shadows threatened the morrow, they would meet them standing side by side as always, as people of faith, courage and conviction.

He must have dozed, he opened his eyes to find the fire had burned low and Davidson now sat watch, with Duke resting nearby. The forest was encased in absolute silence under its fresh blanket of snow. Somewhere out there in the darkness, their quarry was no doubt sheltered for the night as well.

With a weary sigh, Mitch rolled over and surrendered to sleep once more. Come morning, the hunt would resume.

# Chapter 22

Penrose Reservoir

West of Cheyenne Mountain, Colorado

December 10

5 AM MST Time

Darkness still consumed the land as the remaining embers glowed from the remains of the campfire.

First one that got up was Davey, always the early riser. He shook the snow off of him and brushed it off his weapon and gear. Without a campfire, the heat quickly dissipated and left them all with only the harsh bitterness of winter in the mountains of Colorado.

One by one the men rolled from their blankets, stretching stiff limbs and rubbing sleep from their eyes. They gathered closer near the fading fire to share in the remaining heat from coals and rocks.

"That sure didn't last long," Davidson shivered as he spoke to the group. "Anymore wood?"

Davey responded, "bingo, my brother."

"So stinkin cold!." Davidson remarked in frustration.

Duke walked up to them, dog in tow, "time to rise and shine, sunup will be breakin through soon and we have places to be."

Duke's dog walked around expecting pats from everyone, nosing eagerly at each of them. "Let's see if she can pick the trail back up," he said.

The men stamped out the last smoking embers of the fire as Duke gave the dog a scrap of cloth from the discarded backpack to get her scent memory working again.

She set off at once, nose to the ground, guiding Duke through the snowy campsite before stopping at the trailhead nearby.

"Time to take off," Mitch said in a tone suggesting that his slumber was cut short.

The team checked their weapons and then slowly saddled up again.

Aaron piped up, "at least the horses got a good rest. Looks like we got ten miles as the crow flies to get to there from here. Barely could read the map from the light of the fire."

"That's ten miles through the snow and over terrain. How long will that take?" Davidson added to the mix.

Mitch responded, "That's a very good question and our goal is just to make it there as soon as we can."

The group all back in the saddle now moved towards Duke who was waiting for them impatiently. Whatever clues or confrontation may lie ahead, they would face it vigilantly.

The dog led them unerringly into the forest, snuffling purposefully through the drifts. Soon an excited bark told them she'd found scent once more. Duke made encouraging sounds to keep her interested as they traversed the quiet woodland trail.

Mitch and the others followed cautiously behind, their senses were sharper now in anticipation of what lay at the trail's end. Somewhere out there in the skeletal trees was the answer they sought, for better or worse.

All they could do now was place their trust in each other and the guiding skills of man and his canine as they tracked the path towards its conclusion. Winding through the narrow trail as daylight approached the light falling snow, the team was getting closer and closer to their destination.

As they continued on, the horses barely managed to scale the steeper grades as the snow proved deeper in some places than others.

"There were two sets of tracks. Still headed on the trail. Good work girl," Duke informed the group.

The trail wound deeper into the frozen forest as the dog tugged Duke steadily onward. Mitch and the others followed close behind, alert for any signs of danger amid the bare snowy trunks. After a couple more miles of steady tracking and burning daylight, the trees began to thin. Up ahead they spotted a large expanse of ice gleaming in the pale early light.

"A lake!" Called out Aaron from the back of the group.

As they emerged from the treeline, Duke called out to the dog and she came bounding back, tail wagging proudly. "Good work. Time for a break girl," he said, scratching her ears.

The frozen lake stretched as far as they could see in either direction. A few snowdrifts spotted the surface, but otherwise it was smooth and unbroken.

"Looks like solid ice," remarked Davidson, dismounting cautiously to test it with his boot.

Mitch scanned the shoreline thoughtfully. "Do you think they came this way?" He wondered aloud. Then Davey called out - he had wandered a short way further and found something half buried in the snow.

"Tracks!" He said excitedly. "Looks like boot tracks going across. They must have crossed the lake." Sure enough, a set of tracks led out across the ice before disappearing into the snow on the opposite shore.

"Well then, I guess we're taking a ride," said Duke with a grin.

"Must have a hot date later!" Aaron joked, causing the rest of them to snicker as the well timed remark.

Duke was not amused, "haha, real funny. We can follow the tracks across or go around. It'll be more time if we go around through the deeper snow."

They all looked at each other knowing that they lost a lot of time at the campfire already. Looking in agreement, they slowly spoke up.

Aaron was the first to speak up, "let's do it."

The rest responded in unison agreeing to take the shortcut.

The snow continued to fall more thickly as new clouds moved in, slightly obscuring the tracks. Aaron scanned the ground with a focused eye while Mitch kept watch further out across the open ice.

"Let's go!" Called Mitch as he let the team across the frozen lake which he recalled was Penrose reservoir.

The group continued on horseback and cautiously spread out in case the ice broke. Slight sounds echoed from the ice as the horses took more steps.

"Duke, are you sure about this?" Mitch questioned Duke's judgment which was not the first time.

Duke responded sharply, "y'all agreed to it, didn't say it was the smartest decision."

"Great...everyone, spread out more. If the ice breaks, dismount and run to shore." Mitch yelled so the rest could hear.

Acknowledging with a thumbs up. The team continued at a slow pace across while still following the remnant tracks left to follow.

"Fresh tracks," confirmed Aaron, pointing out recent disturbances in the snow cover.

Mitch nodded approvingly, giving a thumbs up before calling out to the others. Suddenly a faint sound was heard.

Crack.

Crack.

CRACK.

Just then a loud crack pierced the air, followed swiftly by the sound of splintering ice.

All heads turned to see a large fissure had opened up near the center of the lake closest to Aaron. More chunks broke away as the ice groaned and shifted under the stress of the weight.

"The lake isn't safe, move now, move!" Shouted Mitch urgently.

With haste born of urgency, everyone spurred the reluctant horses into motion. Galloping as quickly as they could in all directions in hopes of making it to shore.

Plumes of powdery snow flew and cracks pursued as they accelerated towards the beckoning shore. Behind them more spiderwebbed lines streaked across the weakening icefield.

With a mighty lurch the ice groaned apart right before Mitch. He dug into the horse with his boots yelling for it to move faster. Knowing that an icy death awaited just inches below.

"Giddy up!!! Go, Go, Go!" Mitch yelled as loud as he could. Right as the ice began to open up directly before them. He closed his eyes briefly ready for certain doom.

Without prompting the horse changed course and jumped narrowly avoiding the grave opening that was ready to knock them both out.

Mitch held fast as the horse maneuvered swiftly  and continued with ferocity back to the shoreline. With great surprise his trusted steed, Bo, had kept them both alive.

"Whoooo, well done Bo, well done. Sure thought we were goners back there." Mitch praised his horse for a truly remarkable escape.

Looking around, Mitch was ecstatic that everyone had made it through the ordeal completely unscathed. No one fell in or even got their socks wet. Slowly they regrouped on Mitch taking the safest routes possible.

"Sorry fellas, that was my fault! Messed up big on trying to push it too hard." Duke fessed up with genuine sincerity and remorse.

They looked around and noticed that their escape came at a cost. With the lake now splitting apart in all directions, hunks of ice drifting away carried with it their easy route.

"We'll find another way around!" Mitch called reassuringly. Duke shook his head in frustration - the original long route trail was their only option.

They followed the edge maneuvering the best they could until they finally reached the other side. The dog ran wild looking for any possible scent.

"Mitch we're getting no leads," Duke brought to Mitch's attention. "What now?"

"Wait, what's up there?" Davey said as he pointed out to the rest of the team. "Something is tucked among some boulders in the woods."

"Good spot Davey!" Mitch exclaimed. Then moved the team to follow him up the hill to investigate.

Three black snowmobiles were tucked away almost hidden amongst the landscape. It seemed their prey was now on foot which eased the stress of catching up in time.

As the group drew nearer, it became clear the snowmobiles weren't as promising a find as first thought. Both machines lay empty and cold, snow drifted over their seats.

Davey inspected them closely. "Dead, just like everything else," he reported grimly.

"Looks like they were abandoned," added Davidson, pointing out the amount of snow accumulated on top.

Mitch slowly but eventually made the connection, "these were the same ones parked in the barn at the Cartman's old place."

"So we know it is them and we know their direction now." Davidson chimed in, "but how do we follow their trail?"

Aaron piped up from the back as always, "maybe we should split up - some of us can try to follow the nearby trail and others head due East?"

Mitch frowned, always wary of dividing their forces. "I don't like splitting the team, we don't know what's out there."

"We'd cover more ground separately," argued Davidson. As a lawman he was used to working alone.

Davey sided with Mitch. "Too risky with more snow blowing in. Better to stick together."

Duke thought aloud as he scanned the vast lake. "Y'all have a point...but the trail won't wait."

A tense debate arose amongst the group, echoing off the icy walls as tempers started to flare.

Finally, Mitch raised a hand. "Enough. We have to stay together. If one of us makes contact we have no way to communicate for backup," Mitch took the lead, setting the group back on course.

Everyone looked at each other and then nodded in agreement with Mitch's decisive direction. They moved forward, as the dog raced ahead through the snow, her nose to the ground as the group followed close behind on horseback. Duke kept a close eye on her tracking, not wanting to lose the scent trail in the snowfall.

They rode for miles through the dense forest, the horses picking their way carefully over the uneven, slippery terrain. Mitch took to the front along with Duke, constantly scanning ahead of them for any signs of danger. The howling winds obscured sound and vision, making navigation treacherous.

After nearly two hours of riding, the dog suddenly stopped and began furiously circling a large boulder up ahead.

Duke dismounted to investigate further and found telltale markings of footprints shielded by the boulder's height. "They rested here," he called out.

Davey spotted a discarded empty plastic water bottle and called it out.

Duke had the dog sniff both finds before sending her off on the trail again, tail wagging determinedly. They mounted up once more, led by her sure tracking through the intermittent whiteout conditions.

Another hour passed as they pushed on, the horses were tired but persevering. Davey noticed his gelding Snip beginning to favor one leg, a stone bruise developing from the rough terrain. He kept a closer eye on the horse's gait, worried the injury may worsen.

Suddenly, up ahead Mitch spotted the ominous outline of a towering hillside looming above the tree line through the falling snow. They broke into a small clearing, spotting a treacherous trail snaking up the rocky slopes.

Duke whistled for the dog to return as they surveyed the journey ahead. The narrow, icy path was barely discernible under fresh powder, a deadly plunge on either side. One misstep could spell disaster.

"We must rope the horses together. Go slowly and carefully," warned Mitch as they began lashing supplies tightly between each mount.

Duke moved up and took point with his dog, tracking any disturbed snow.

Davey watched Snip's step gingerly as they inched their way up the treacherous incline single-file. Halfway up, the horse stumbled on a patch of loose shale but Davey kept his seat, calming the panicked animal.

Behind them, Aaron's mare slipped backwards slightly, testing the strength of the tied ropes. He gritted his teeth, praying they would hold against her weight and the heavy burden of gear. After a tense minute, they regained their footing.

Slowly they crept through the clearing and to the top of the ridge. The snow thinned for a bit and allowed the sunlight to finally break through the clouds.

Mitch stopped his horse. Slowly they all rallied together to gaze upon their next destination or obstacle for that matter.

"I see it now, Eagles Nest!" He called out in grand realization as he pointed to the rest hoping they all could partake in seeing their next waypoint.

For now they were closer than ever to accomplishing their mission, as one united team. Little did they know that with new height came greater and more deadly challenges.

# Chapter 23

Eagles Nest

West of Cheyenne Mountain, Colorado

December 10

10:22 AM MST Time

Anna stretched as she maneuvered her position again while overlooking the valley trail. She was still grateful for the solitude and enjoyed the beautiful surroundings.

Her thoughts once again drifted to Kim and Thomas. Were they still alive? They knew the rally points and were long overdue to regroup right here. Thomas probably forgot the simple route and trails to follow, but Kim was so skilled and could probably get here blindfolded.

Viktor was still right that their objective came first, but what was taking them so long. The entry team already left hours ago at sun up.

The nervousness compounded for her.

"Stay or go? They better get back soon," she muttered to herself.

Anna moved more to get a better look back through her hideout hoping to see a different vantage.

In her lookout post high on the ridge, Anna peered through the falling snow, straining her eyes for any signs of movement. Looking back through her rifle mounted scope, she moved the crosshairs in a scanning motion as she longed for something new, anything new to show movement.

Crack.

Her ears perked up as she heard the subtle sound far off in the distance directly in front of her. Shifting quickly she rotated the dial back to 2 power and waited for another sound for where she thought the first sound originated from.

Was it an animal? Maybe it was Kim? She thought to herself as she steadied her rifle, fixated on the source of the sound.

She exhaled slowly.

Inhaled even slower.

Suddenly, she saw movement and the manifested presence of a large brown figure entered into view.

Anna grabbed the magnification dial and turned it to a higher power in an attempt to get a positive ID of her target. Refocusing she looked through the crosshairs once again as her eyes adjusted to the new magnification. An animal's head bobbed out from behind a tree and then the large brown body of a horse was in full view.

Wait...what is that? A bridle?

The black silhouette of a leather bridle became apparent to her as she continued to concentrate. Her mind raced trying to come to grips about what is going on. Did Kim or Thomas steal a horse? Smart idea, but she wouldn't have done that for fear of compromising the mission.

As she continued to watch, a human form appeared as she saw this person had on a dark colored coat and cowboy hat.

"Not good," she exclaimed to herself.

Exhaling slowly, she regained her focus and maneuvered the magnification again. Turning the last movement left, she attempted to verify the target the best she could as she strained to see if the face was that of Thomas or Kim.

Anna was now in shock. "What? How?"

It was that guy she almost ran over yesterday. Still just as cute as he was before but he carried himself more masculine and confident than before. She snapped out of her daydream reminiscing about the previous interaction as she saw the lever action rifle in his hand.

The paradox of emotion unexpectedly slammed into her like a tsunami as it crashed into the shore. What should I do? Do I kill him? She contemplated with anxiety that she hadn't felt in a long time.

Shaking her head, she recentered herself. Her thumb pushed the safety slowly off as she placed her finger on the trigger.

"Just pull..." she said to herself. "Just pull, it's only a man. Focus on the mission Anna."

She fixed her crosshair perfectly on his chest. Slowing her breathing.

Thump.

The hammer stuck as the trigger was pulled. Immediately the round exited the barrel. Traveling through the suppressor, it calmed the sound to a level mildly recognizable.

Flying through the air the subsonic bullet impacts the flesh with a massive thud causing instant injury and energy shockwaves intensely.

Anna closed her eyes, knowing that something was off. Her shots are never off. Why? What happened?

Subconsciously, deep down inside, at the very core of her being she knew. As much as she needed to, she couldn't bring herself to kill him. She closed and then opened her eyes to watch as the horse went down quickly along with its rider.

Anna closed her eyes again knowing...just knowing she would regret allowing her emotions to take hold.

"Duke!!!" Mitch yelled out as he watched the horse buck and collapse to its side, sending Duke flying off just before it hit the ground.

The thud was felt by all and the horse panicked as they all witnessed the traumatic events unfold before them.

"Ahhh!" Davey yelled as he got bucked off and hit the ground. Then Davidson got bucked off in a domino of discord and chaos. Aaron strained to control his horse as it whirled around in panic.

Mitch felt the anxiety as Bo started to move cautiously. "Settle, settle...settle." He tried to calm the storm raging inside the animal.

"Whoooooo." Aaron belted as he became suddenly challenged by the bronco, kicking to get him off. He struggled to hang on until the horse kicked a tree by accident and the jolt thrust him into the snow.

Mitch strained as he looked around the chaos and tried to make out Duke's location seeing only blood stained snow on the ground near the horse. He dismounted in a fury and ran over to Duke as he slipped on the slick snow.

Knock!

Knock!

Two unmistakable sounds of rounds as they made impact into the pines and aspen trees surrounding them.

"Get down!" Mitch screamed to the others as another round impacted the ground just feet away. He watched helplessly as the horses continued to buck alone, having tossed their riders. Then scattered away in despair back down the hillside towards safety.

Without warning Davidson pointed his rifle in the general direction of where the shots came from and opened up a defining ten rounds in an attempt to provide cover. "Cover fire, move, move, move!"

"Duke, Duke!" Mitch yelled as his ears tried to end the ringing from the blasts.

"I'm gonna kill em!!!" The enraged cowboy roared as he pushed himself out from the mortally injured horse that was still bleeding on him.

Duke grabbed his rifle off the frigid snow covered ground and strained to get himself up to his feet. Slightly limping, he began to walk straighter and straighter as he went directly for his shooter. "You killed my horse. You wanna kill me, let's go!"

Bang.

Bang.

Bang.

Shots rang out from Duke's repeater as he centered in on the source.

Ground flew up around Duke as he continued up the hill in a fit of rage.

Bang.

Bang.

More shots erupted from Duke as he directed his fire at the overgrowth and pine just up from his position.

"Face me you coward!" Duke challenged as loud as he could muster.

A masked figure in all white appeared pointing a rifle directly at him only a short distance from him. Fringer on the trigger ready to fire.

The two faced off in a High Noon style of standoff.

Duke attempted to pull the trigger just as Mitch tackled him from the side, throwing the two to the ground just as a bullet smashed into the ground right where he had been standing.

Bang!

Bang!

"You're dead." Davidson said as he let go of the trigger and watched the white cladded figure fall. Both deadly rounds found their target downrange.

"Get off of me! I'm gonna kill em!" The red haired volcano exploded and pushed Mitch off of him. Immediately he rushed the mysterious attacker once again with no care for his own safety. Running up the hill he took off in a rampage without knowing that the shooter had been taken down.

Duke pulled out his revolver and pointed it at the brush as he stampeded like a bull right through it. "Die! You yellow belly horse killer!!!" He screamed so loud that it echoed even with the insulating snow.

He stopped huffing, shoulders shrugged, finger on the trigger pointed at the ground where the villain laid motionless.

Duke looked down and screamed, "Ahhhhhhh!!!"

He saw her blue eyes first, once again captivated by their beauty as they had done the day before. Both now locked in on one another in a powerful gaze of indescribable emotion. Love at first sight, he immediately went back to the memory of those same eyes of the driver who almost hit him.

"Ahhhhhhh!" He screamed a hollowing sorrow now realizing what had been done. He pointed his Peacemaker in the air above his head.

Bang!

The team all watch as Duke turns from rage to remorse and falls to his knees.

Together they ran to him with a disregard for their safety as they gave up on catching the horses that were running away downhill.

"Duke!" Mitch yelled to his brother who is visually dead locked into the body before him.

Duke's eyes welled up with tears. As he gulped loudly looking at the blood gushing from her wounds. Slowly he knelt, reached down, and pulled off the white camo mask that obscured her gorgeous face.

In a moment so silent but packed with emotion. Anna slowly and difficulty raised one hand and gently touched his beard.

"Why?" He muttered quietly to her as his mouth quivered in an attempt not to cry.

In a brief unspoken conversation that felt like an eternity, she looked at him and smiled kindly. The only real romance that he had ever known now vanished before him. Their eyes continued in a surreal peace forever frozen in time.

Just as soon as that tender moment of embrace began, it quickly died along with her. Never to be realized. Anna exhaled as her last breath of life extinguished before his eyes, shattering any hope the two might have together.

Duke continued to stare down at her as their warmth faded away back to the frigid reality of brutal loneliness. He longed to bring her back again. To experience what might have been. In another time, in another way. What if both of them had met under different circumstances?

Pondering upon what could have been instead of what is now, he gulped again and began to cry uncontrollably. Duke desperately wrapped his arms around her lifeless body. His final attempt to hold fast to the dreams of a future that would never be.

Knowing. Just knowing deep within him that they truly could never be.

Mitch finally made his way to him, "Duke, what Duke? What's going on? He stopped near his friend as the others joined up as well. "Duke!" He demanded to acknowledge the confusion.

Slowly, the tough and brave man released his hold. Revealing the surreal and lifeless face of a woman that seemed somewhat recognizable.

"It's her, it's her y'all, it's her...," Duke said softly as he choked back the emotion.

Mitch knelt down beside Duke. Cautiously contemplating his next words with his grieving friend.

"Brother, I'm so sorry." Mitch slowly shared emphatically.

Duke was slow to speak, still locked into her blue eyes that now looked straight up as if looking for Heaven, "she didn't shoot me Mitch, she sure could've, but she didn't."

"How do you know?" Mitch questioned him.

"I just know..." Duke said as he trailed off, slowly letting her body rest back on the ground.

Mitch put his hand on Duke's shoulder. One by one the others did the same.

There they were huddled together as the snow crept in again and large flakes fell to the ground.

No horses now.

So much ground to cover.

The odds stacked against them.

Duke looked up at his brothers. Slowly he spoke, his voice heavy with emotion yet resolved. "Thank you guys. I mean it, thank you."

He glanced once more at Anna's still form, "Things are clearer now. No matter the cost, he'll see it through."

Duke rose, his brothers helping him stand tall once more.

These patriotic warriors looked at each other now after facing their first battle knowing that many more were to come.

Duke's tear filled eyes met each of theirs in turn. Slowly he spoke in a strength and demeanor they had never heard before. He pulled down his cowboy hat to hide his tears and composed himself fully before he finally spoke, "Brothers... it's time we finished this."

# Chapter 24

---

Cheyenne Mountain Complex - NORAD

Colorado Springs, Colorado

December 10

1 PM MST Time

The crew at Fort Carson worked tirelessly through the night and well into the morning to repair the heavily damaged Chinook helicopter. The massive hangar, normally buzzing with activity, now focused entirely on this single aircraft.

Sparks cascaded like falling stars as wiring harnesses were replaced, welded, and electrical systems were meticulously patched back together. The smell of burning metal and electrical work filled the air, mixing with the ever-present scent of hydraulic fluid and precious fuel.

Each team member moved with practiced precision, knowing that every second counted. Some crawled through the helicopter's tight maintenance spaces with flashlights clenched between their teeth, while others balanced precariously on ladders reaching the upper sections. Their hands, though numb from the cold mountain air seeping through the hangar doors, never wavered in their critical work.

Crew chiefs consulted schematics and manuals while mechanics crawled through tight spaces making needed adjustments. Dog-eared technical manuals lay open across workbenches, their pages marked with grease-stained fingers.

The sound of power tools echoed through the hangar, punctuated by calls for specific tools or parts. This crew was committed to ensuring this bird was up and running as soon as humanly possible.

Senior mechanics shared knowing looks as they jury-rigged solutions that would have never passed standard inspections. But these weren't standard times. They pulled parts from three different helicopters, creating a patchwork of components that somehow needed to work together. Every shortcut taken was noted, every compromise carefully calculated against the mission's urgency.

By sunrise, tremendous progress had been made. The early morning light streamed through the hangar's high windows, illuminating the countless hours of work in stark relief. Critical systems were brought back online and testing showed functioning well within parameters.

The Chinook looked like a big green frankenstein covered with scorch marks. Pieces haphazardly welded back together and taken from other helicopters created a visual testament to the desperate nature of their repairs.

It would have never been allowed to see the light of day if it weren't for the critical circumstances everyone was under.

The chief mechanic, his face streaked with grease and dark circles under his eyes betraying his exhaustion, paused to wipe his brow with a shop rag that had seen better days. His uniform bore the marks of countless hours spent crawling through the helicopter's innards, each stain a badge of dedication.

He spoke to Cooper, Thompson, and the Captain who had overseen its progress, his voice hoarse from hours of shouting instructions over the din of machinery. "She's in better shape than I hoped, sir. Barring any unexpected issues, I believe we'll be wheels up within the hour."

Cooper smiled, pleased with the dedication and skill of the mechanic and his crew. "That's outstanding work, Chief. You and your crew have bought us valuable time we sorely need. The nation is grateful."

The mechanic shared that he would relay the message to his crew before he excused himself to finish preparations.

Thompson sent word with one of the Lieutenants to head to the control room and requested for an update on their extraction mission. "Chopper is fueling now and should be ready to roll in an hour," he told him as the young man took off quickly.

After a few minutes of waiting and changing the white boards time tables, the Lieutenant made it back, "They think they pinpointed the stranded 10th Mountain Division unit. Eight soldiers are in the vicinity of an old remote mountain camp near Leadville. Assuming they are still mission ready, we are green lit to have them carry out the repair work.

"Roger that, thank you. We'll be ready to lift off within the hour then," Thompson replied before turning to Cooper. "Looks like the timing is coming together nicely thanks to the diligence of these men. I have a good feeling about this mission, sir."

Cooper looked optimistically at her and smiled, "I must admit I had my doubts at first, but you pulled off this mission Major. Good work."

Thompson smiled in appreciation as the rest of the unit noticed the change to a new positive climate in the room. "Thank you sir! Let's finish this mission." She responded confident in the hard work and intention she had given.

On the airfield, the ugly green beast now nicknamed Frank, had its final screw tightened by the crew. It was time. The two pilots and the loadmaster inside looked at each other, ready to give Frank a chance at life. Pulling their harness belts closer they ran through their final pre-flight checks.

The pilots had watched the repair efforts all night, both knowing they'd be the ones testing whether this patchwork miracle would actually fly. They'd flown together for three years, but nothing had prepared them for this moment. While the ground crew worked, they'd spent hours reviewing emergency procedures and developing contingency plans for every possible failure scenario.

"Like my grandpa used to say - either we're gonna fly, or we're gonna find out real quick why we can't," one of them muttered, adjusting his flight helmet. The other pilot responded with a knowing smile, her hands already dancing across the instrument panel with practiced precision.

Inside the cockpit, the familiar smell of hydraulic fluid was stronger than usual. A constant reminder of their helicopter's jury-rigged state. The instrument panel before them was a mixture of old and new gauges, some salvaged from other aircraft. Some digital displays flickered intermittently, while others remained stubbornly dark.

Crossing his fingers, the pilot flipped the master switch, his breath held in anticipation.

Nothing.

The silence was deafening. He felt his stomach drop as he exchanged glances with his copilot, whose usual stoic expression cracked slightly with concern. The cockpit felt suddenly colder, the weight of the mission pressing down on them both.

Then, without warning, lights began flickering across the panel like Christmas trees, and warning alarms screamed to life. Their hands moved with lightning speed, toggling switches and adjusting settings. Years of training kicked in as they worked in perfect synchronization, their movements a well-rehearsed dance of pilot and co-pilot.

"Systems coming online," the loadmaster called out, his voice steady despite the tension. "Engine one... nominal. Engine two... responding within acceptable parameters." He continued monitoring the gauges, some of which showed readings that would normally ground the aircraft. But these weren't normal times.

One by one, the pilots gave thumbs up to the ground crew in front of them. The massive rotor head above them creaked ominously as the hydraulics engaged. A loud crashing sound echoed through the airframe as it lurched forward and suddenly stopped.

In front of them, two dozen soldiers had attached a rope to the front, ready to help maneuver the damaged beast out of its lair.

They watched through the windscreen as the soldiers strained against the rope, their breath visible in the cold morning air. "Never thought I'd see the day we'd need a tow from ground pounders," he said, managing a slight chuckle.

His copilot kept her eyes on the gauges, monitoring every fluctuation with hawk-like intensity. "Temperature readings are high on the starboard engine," she reported, making slight adjustments. "Within emergency limits, but we'll need to watch it."

The soldiers below pulled with synchronized determination, their boots finding purchase in the frost-covered concrete. Foot by foot, they guided the massive helicopter forward, its wheels protesting against the flat spots developed during its lengthy grounding.

Incrementally, the soldiers pulled with all their strength trying to get Frank out of the old hanger and one step closer to freedom. The pilots watched respectfully as they steadily made it out into daylight.

Soon after, the heavily laden Chinook was fully exposed and only 25 more yards could it safely start up. With barely any more momentum the soldiers finished pulling with all their might, fighting the somewhat flat tires on the landing gear.

Free at last, the men dropped the rope. This was the real moment of truth. The two pilots began flipping switches and increasing throttle as the engine sputtered to life. One of the ground crew sprinted up and uncoupled the rope.

"Clear for start-up," the pilot announced, his hand hovering over the engine controls. Both pilots ran through their emergency checklist one final time, knowing this was far from a routine takeoff. The familiar pre-flight rhythm was interrupted by occasional creaks and groans from their patchwork aircraft.

The pilots monitored the gauges with laser focus as they began spooling up the engines. The first engine coughed and sputtered, sending vibrations through the airframe that felt distinctly wrong to their experienced senses.

"Engine one temperatures rising faster than normal," the co pilot reported, her voice tense but controlled. "Still within emergency parameters."

The monster came alive as the blades rotated and then the back rotor joined in. The two pilots fist bumped and nodded.

It was time.

The second engine caught more smoothly, and the massive rotor blades began their slow rotation. Each blade passing overhead sent shudders through the cockpit that made both pilots exchange worried glances. The usual whomp - whomp - whomp of the

Chinook had a distinctive metallic rattle that neither had heard before.

Increasing the throttle, the blades spun faster blowing snow in all directions. Final checks at full speed showed that the Chinook may have looked ugly, but it had needed integrity and held together.

"Seventy percent rotor speed and going strong," the loadmaster called out, his eyes darting between gauges. "Hydraulic pressure holding... mostly steady. Some fluctuation in the aft system." His fingers tapped rapidly on the instrument panel, already calculating their abort points if something went wrong.

The pilot gripped the collective, feeling an unfamiliar looseness in the controls. "Like flying a shopping cart with a broken wheel," he muttered, making minute adjustments.

The helicopter shuddered as he gradually increased power, the winter skids still firmly planted on the ground.

"Torque increasing," the copilot announced. "Both engines are responding... unevenly, but responding." She switched frequencies briefly to update the ground crew. "Frank's got some fight in him."

As the rotors reached full speed, snow and debris whipped around them in a violent circle. The pilots eased up on the collective, feeling the familiar lightening of the aircraft as it prepared to break free from gravity. The Chinook shifted its weight, groaning like a wounded beast.

"Coming up on effective translational lift," the copilot called out, her voice steady despite the violent shaking in the cockpit. Warning lights flickered on and off, but nothing would stay illuminated long enough to force them back down.

The moment of liftoff seemed to stretch forever. The Chinook wallowed slightly, listing to port before the pilot corrected. "Frank is fighting me," he growled, making constant small adjustments. "Like trying to balance a drunk elephant on a tightrope."

At fifty feet, the copilot started breathing again, though her hands never left the controls. "Airspeed just increased beyond twenty knots. All systems holding... marginally." The aircraft shuddered as they pushed through translational lift, the point where the rotor system became fully aerodynamic.

The pilots kept the climb shallow, feeling out the aircraft's limitations. Every noise, every vibration told a story to their trained senses. Some bearings were running hot, the airframe creaked under stresses it was never designed to handle, but somehow, impossibly, they were flying.

"Five hundred feet," the copilot announced, allowing herself a small smile. "Established in climb." She reached up to adjust a circuit breaker that had started chattering, her movements precise despite the constant vibration.

"Well I'll be," the pilot said, finally relaxing his death grip on the controls slightly. "Frank wants to live." He banked gently westward, noting how the aircraft responded sluggishly to lateral control inputs. "She's not pretty, but she's flying."

The rising sun caught the battered aircraft, highlighting its makeshift repairs and scorched panels. Below them, the ground crew had become small figures, their cheers lost in the thundering rotor wash.

Fort Carson fell away behind them as they climbed into the crystal-clear Colorado morning, each minute of successful flight a small miracle of engineering and determination.

"Time to see what this frankenstein can really do," the pilot said, his confidence growing as they settled into cruise flight.

"Next stop, Leadville." The copilot nodded, her hands never leaving the controls, ready for whatever challenges their damaged but determined aircraft might present.

The mountains loomed ahead, their snow-covered peaks a reminder of the difficult mission still to come. But for now, they had achieved the impossible - they had made a broken bird fly again.

Quickly he glanced up to the main pilot and smiled.

They had done it.

The anticipation of experiencing flight once again fueled the men's enthusiasm in a sense not experienced since the Wright brothers.

Pulling on the stick, it lifted smoothly into the crisp mountain air. Even with a slight struggle it lifted gradually. Finally it had reached its initial altitude. The rotors thudded with a sound reminiscent of machine gun fire as the nose tipped. Each chop through the air was both felt and heard. The ground crew below rejoiced in a job well down. Giving each other high fives as the helicopter continued westward in a climb.

Frank began to fade in the distance ever closer to accomplishing its two missions.

Back in NORAD, Thompson stood by a quiet room holding the receiver to her ear listening intently. All eyes once again focused. Not on any screen this time, but on the older device they had been using to get updates from the outside world.

Thompson looked up at Cooper and then at the rest of the team. Her eyes got bigger as she listened to the details. Without warning, the largest smile shone on her as she listened to the good news.

They had done it.

Immediately the room erupted in celebration knowing that they just prevailed over this massive hurdle.

"We're airborne!"

# Chapter 25

"Old Camp Hale" - Mountain Training Area

Leadville, Colorado

December 10

1:40 PM MST Time

Specialist Cunningham pulled his parka tighter as the icy wind cut through the terrain. The snow had been falling heavily all night, completely blanketing their campsite. He peered through the whiteout at his broken watch - it was hours past check-in with command and he didn't want any of his men injured.

Rolling out of his frozen sleeping bag, Cunningham kicked Bradley awake. "Comms are still dead and the weather is really closing in."

The men took in their snowy surroundings with worry. Something must have gone terribly wrong for communications to still be out.

Digging out their gear from accumulated snow, they debated their next move. "Our provisions are running low too," Bradley acknowledged.

Cunningham thought quickly in hope of adapting on the fly, "We need to get to higher ground and find a clearing. The trees are great for shelter from the wind but we won't be seen here."

The two men got up slowly and exited their tent.

"We need to move, pack it up and let's go. We're headed higher up. There is a clearing less than a click from here due north." Cunningham shouted to get the unit's attention.

All eight men gathered their equipment and formed up to head out.

Bradley looked ahead as he utilized his compass and map for land navigation. "This way!"

The unit followed him as he began to step up the steep grade and headed up the best course to traverse. The rest of the team was mostly new and were now faced with possible SERE survival conditions due to the dead communications.

Cunningham shouted out, "Let's double time it. Hooah!"

In unison the rest of the unit responded with a loud Hooah as a reply.

They continued to hike the climb together moving a good distance in a short amount of time.

Suddenly Bradley stopped, causing the rest of the unit to somewhat crash into each other. "What in the world is that…"

Cunningham walked up to him trying to make out what it was that Bradley was staring at. "What in the world is that?"

"Not sure sir," Bradley said with genuine confusion. They were all staring at knocked down trees and white fragments scattered everywhere.

Immediately Cunningham made connections and figured out the situation, "Plane crash. From the looks of it, a small learjet."

The unit looked stunned but immediately began walking into the debris field as if they were trying to figure out how to piece it back together again.

"Sir, it must have nose dived, maybe engine failure." Bradley spoke up to Cunningham who was still trying to size up the plane's dimensions.

"How do you know that?" Cunningham questioned him.

Bradley pointed out the large crater. "I used to do Civil Air Patrol in high school before joining the Army. The plane must have fallen out of the sky and the nose impacted like a dart right there at this crater. That's why only the tail was left."

"Wow, I think you're right Bradley. Where are the bodies then?" Cunningham agreed but was still confused.

Bradley continued, "That type of impact...There are no survivors and probably nothing left of them. The charred ground all around, it must have been burning for a while."

"Like yesterday when we lost comms with command?" Cunningham started to attempt to connect more of the dots.

"Yes sir, most likely." Bradley shakily tried his best to piece things together.

They stood in shaken silence, taking in the scene of utter devastation.

Suddenly, a crackle of breaking branches snapped them from their grim thoughts. Cunningham signaled the men to be ready, but it was only a flock of birds taking flight in alarm.

As they watched the birds soar into the darkening sky, their instincts told them greater dangers remained cloaked in this wintry landscape.

Cunningham looked around the eerie landscape again, still wondering what really caused the crash, "Let's round up the men. The clearing is not too far up ahead and we can build a fire there. There is nothing good left for us to figure out here."

Just then, a muffled roar caught everyone's attention.

Struggling through the thick snowfall, they spotted a hovering helicopter weaving erratically in the distance.

"Fantastic, that must be our ride. Wait a second, that bird is in trouble without comms. We need to signal them!" With supplies dwindled and a storm bearing down, their survival depended on making contact. Cunningham hurriedly exclaimed, "team, let's move fast we need a signal!"

Working frantically, the team cleared snow from a wide area on the mountainside and grabbed anything they could to create a landing zone.

Cunningham took charge and began barking commands, "Clear and pop smoke!"

One of the men ran up to him while pulling a can of red smoke. Lining up the placement with the direction of the wind, the soldier activated it and threw it where it would be most visible.

As the helicopter drifted closer, Cunningham and his men started waving an emergency blanket to get more attention. They all waited in anxious hope they were spotted in fear of what might happen if they were missed.

After several anxious minutes, the helo turned in their direction. Cunningham silently prayed their improvised signal had cut through the snow and guided the aircraft to their location.

With rescue possibly just moments away, the stranded squad redoubled their efforts to get the pilot's attention. They waved a makeshift flag composed of their jackets before more snow or wind closed in and obscured them completely.

Through the sheet of falling snow, Cunningham strained his eyes to watch the erratic helicopter. Its rotations were growing more uncontrolled, and it was losing altitude fast. He feared their signal may have come too late.

Suddenly, the pilot must have spotted something through the storm. The helo swung sharply in their direction and began descending rapidly but had no lights signaling them. "It's coming in hot!" Cunningham shouted through chattering teeth.

His men pulled in the improvised flag and scrambled back from the clearing. The massive helicopter spiraled down unsteadily, snow and ice billowing up in its wake. With a heavy thud, the Chinook settled onto the mountainside, wheels sinking deep into the powder.

The back door gradually opened and a crew chief waved them over urgently. "Hurry! The electronics are cutting out!" Cunningham and his squad packed their gear and sprinted through the knee-high drifts.

One by one they entered and sat down on either side of the interior until Bradley entered last.

Cunningham took a deep breath, thankful that they were one step closer to home but thought about the crash they just encountered. He boarded and moved up to the pilots.

As snow continued whiting out the windows. Starting the rotors was only half the battle, but now they had to somehow get them all off this mountain alive.

The rear hatch closed and everyone began feeling the unsteady vibrations rack the helicopter frame as the turbines increased speed. Through the blur of falling snow, he strained to make out the slope beneath them. "Everyone hang on!" Cunningham shouted back.

Gently testing the pedals once again, the pilots lifted the helo up from the mountainside and out of the snow. The helo swayed unsteadily, barely visible in the blowing whiteness. "Which way to base camp? We just found a crash site and need to relay it back to command!" Cunningham asked over the engine whine.

The pilot oriented himself and pointed east. "Follow the valley - it's about 20 klicks that way. There was a crash, what kinda crash?" Keeping their heading through sheer white nothingness everyone was quiet hoping to land safely.

Cunningham replied to the pilots, "we think it was a small jet, no survivors. Weirdest thing is that all of our electronics are dead. Even my watch."

"Not surprised at all, America got attacked and no one has power. We patched up this helo and it was a special request to pick your unit up," the pilot continued as he gave a brief summary of what took place.

Cunningham sat down and soaked in the reality of what had happened and instantly all of the pieces came together giving him the bigger picture.

Slowly at first, then gaining confidence, the ailing aircraft down maneuvered the mountain before finally gaining altitude. The muffled sounds of the loud engines punctuated the whipping wind outside.

Too low - they pulled back hard on the collective as they navigated the changing elevation. The helo lurched upward unsteadily as snow-covered trees swept by. Sweat beaded on his forehead despite the freezing temperatures. One mistake could end them all.

Up ahead, a break appeared in the storm front. They guided towards the thinning clouds, praying for clearer skies beyond. As they burst through, jagged mountain peaks came into view in the distance.

The pilots stabilized the Chinook, pointed towards a set of headphones nearby to talk through. Cunningham grabbed them and put them on, but had to clear the pressure from his ears first.

"Thanks for the lift fellas, we lost comms and thought we might have to hike home." Cunningham expressed his appreciation.

The pilots laughed, "you and everyone else buddy."

Confusion set back once more on Cunningham's face, "what did you mean that America got attacked?"

"Oh man, we're sure under attack. The whole country is without power or communications. We barely got this up to pick you up." The pilot bluntly shared the reality they had entered.

Cunningham looked back at Bradley who had no clue what they were talking about. Whatever had happened, the crisis was far from over and It was written all over his face.

The pilot continued, "happened yesterday and we have been scrambling to help NORAD, where at Defcon 1 now."

"What in the world! How did this happen." Cunningham expressed in utter disbelief.

The pilot revealed the next piece of news, "you and your team have a new mission. We need NORAD's radio towers repaired on the way back. It's the only possible communication now to our other forces here in the great ole USA."

Cunningham was frustrated, "seriously? My men need to recover."

"Afraid so, duty calls and it was an order from the General himself. There is a handwritten manual and tools in the back to get the job done," the pilot remarked, snapping him back to reality that the mission was just beginning.

"Bradley, get me the bag from over there!" Cunningham yelled aloud trying to get his attention.

Bradley managed to get up and had difficulty traveling to the rearward area where two large olive drab bags sat. Opening them up revealed a bunch of tools and a black binder holding college ruled loose leaf paper with instructions written on them. Each page was tucked into page protectors that were taped over in an effort to make them somewhat waterproof.

"Got 'em, at least I think this is it!" Bradley desperately yelled trying to communicate over the noise as he made his way back over.

The pilot glanced back and confirmed, "Those are the plans. The team at NORAD did their best to keep it as simple as possible, but it'll be a challenge for sure."

Cunningham looked down at the plans with Bradley. Together they scoped out the size of the project and who from their team would best to aid in each function.

"Simple enough, this looks like something we can get accomplished." Cunningham shared back over the headset to the pilot.

"Good. Cause you're gonna have to! In fact you're the only hope we have to get this done." The pilot stressed acknowledging that they have to make it work. "Again, all the tools you need should be in those bags. We have an ETA of 40 minutes before we touch down."

Cunningham sat back and finally relaxed, taking in the amount of time to recover before being jolted back out into the cold. "What's the landing plan once we're there? It's on top of the mountain right?"

The pilots both laughed, "funny you should ask. We are going to drop the back and your unit will need to hope off while we hover. We will be okay on fuel, but might return to Carson and top off."

"We would rather not get left up there ya know." Cunningham said not joking at all.

They replied back quickly, "No worries, Frank got you out once already...it's good to go."

Cunningham stayed reclined in the uncomfortable seat, but it sure beat sitting out on a cold mountainside.

Ultimately, his men were alive and so was he.

# Chapter 26

Transmitter Lane

West of Cheyenne Mountain, Colorado

December 10

1 PM MST Time

The wind howled through the mountain passes, driving needles of ice into exposed skin as Viktor struggled through knee-deep snow. Each step was a battle against the terrain, his boots breaking through the crystalline crust into the powder beneath. His lungs burned from the thin air at this altitude, but years of training had taught him to push through such discomforts.

Gunshots cracked through the frigid air, the sound seemed to splinter the very atmosphere. The reports bounced between the rocky outcrops, making them seem to come from everywhere and nowhere at once.

"Halt!" Viktor's command cut through the wind like a knife.

The four men froze in place, their breath forming thick clouds in the mountain air. Their training took over as they instinctively spread out, making themselves smaller targets while scanning their surroundings.

The subsequent gunfire echoed off the mountainsides, the sound waves distorted by the terrain and weather until they seemed to come from multiple directions.

Oleg's voice carried a hint of barely controlled panic as he pointed toward the position where they'd last seen their female companion. "There! Isn't that where we left Anna, Viktor."

Viktor narrowed his eyes against the glare of sun on snow, searching for any sign of movement. The white landscape seemed to ripple and shift in the harsh light, playing tricks on his vision.

The single gunshot that followed felt like a punch to the gut, its finality hanging in the air like a death knell. The eerie silence took over as they continued to watch for any movement.

"Those are the sounds of rifles. Anna was suppressed, in fact we are all running silencers." Oleg looked to the others for agreement and then back to Viktor.

Viktor stared intently again and listened for any other sounds, but only the wind was heard for the next few quiet minutes. "She must have put up a fight, comrades. Now we know we are no longer hidden and our mission is threatened."

The discussion about the weapons' suppressors revealed the first cracks in the team's composure. Oleg's words carried an undertone of accusation, his eyes searching Viktor's face for any sign of emotion.

The wind whipped around them, carrying away their words almost as soon as they were spoken.

"Who is it, who was shooting at her?" Oleg continued, frustrated that Viktor was once again the emotionless tyrant as usual. "Fine, don't answer, but we must go back for her!"

"No!" Viktor belted out in rage and authority. "It is too late. She knew the risks. This is more imperative than any of our lives.

The motherland is needing us to accomplish this mission more than ever.

The rest of the team glared at Viktor, who for the first time communicated non verbally that he knew far more than he had ever led on.

He paused, realizing what he did by letting his anger take hold, "if we don't take out our target we might not have our homes to return to..."

"Viktor, what are you saying?" Ivan spoke up, understanding slightly but could not connect the dots of what was going on. "You're saying my family may be killed."

Viktor looked back at the direction the gunshots were heard from, "we have to stop the Americans and their new defense system, if we fail they may attack Russia and our allies.

Nikolai added for the first time, "I thought we had the upper hand. The Chinese have good plans for all of this."

"Enough, we have a mission to complete and now you know the full risks. None of us might make it home, even if we accomplish our mission and live to tell about it. The only chance you have to save your families and loved ones is to see this through."

The men said nothing more fearing the wrath of Viktor should they say another word. Of them, he had the most to lose.

"We do this for mother Russia." He continued as the men knew there was no other choice now. They had heard nasty rumors about Viktor. If they ran, he would surely kill them.

The revelation about the mission's true nature hit the team like an avalanche. Viktor's mask of authority slipped for just a moment, revealing a glimpse of the burden he'd been carrying. The knowledge that they were all that stood between their homeland and potential annihilation weighed heavily in the frigid air.

When Ivan raised his rifle and shouted the old Russian proverb, his voice carried both defiance and desperation. "Двум смертям не бывать, одной не миновать (A man can die but once, fortune favors the bold)."

The others joined in, their voices echoing off the mountainsides, in a show of camaraderie and bond. All except Viktor, who stood apart, his mind already racing through contingencies and calculations.

With that, they turned to look back up at the rocky terrain they still needed to cross and the potential distance on foot they needed to account for.

"Ivan, Oleg, Nikolai...this is our time to be bold. Whatever the cost, we must finish this mission. Right now we need to buy time to get to the location." Viktor spoke more at ease knowing that his men were back on the same page.

He continued as he looked at each of the men. "They will be here within the hour. Ivan, I need you to hold them off. Along with Oleg..."

Oleg immediately looked up knowing what that could spell out for his future, "I thought I was going as well?"

"I need you to prep the device now. We'll take it down the hatch and drop it into the bunker as planned." Viktor immediately cut him off, not answering his question. "Nikolai needs to remain with me to get the hatch open."

"How will we get out of here then? We have no radios." Oleg continued in desperation trying to get Viktor to reconsider.

Viktor once again struck down his insubordinate questions. "Enough, you both hold the line until you hear Nikolai's explosion. Then and only then can retreat back to us. Understood!"

Ivan shrugged his shoulders in a sign that this was fine and that the command was nothing new. While Oleg continued to look frustrated not knowing how to get the rigid leader to listen.

Oleg made his final plea, "I was not brought into this mission to fight. The only fighting I have done is on my gaming computer Viktor!"

"You disgrace! How dare you challenge my command! I gave you an order soldier and you will obey or I will just shoot you now for your defection. Do I make myself clear Oleg?" Viktor barked at him as spit flew in all directions from his rage.

Oleg said nothing and looked at the ground, slightly resentful now for his cowardice.

Ivan walked over and patted him on the shoulder. "Nothing to worry about, they won't get past me. Nobody ever has, hahahah!"

Oleg smirked with a small laugh at the comment all the while trying to collect himself.

The tactical discussion was punctuated by the crunch of snow under boots as they shifted positions. Oleg's fear was palpable as he realized his role, his gaming background suddenly seeming inadequate against the reality of combat. Viktor's rage at the challenge to his authority sent steam rising from his face in the cold air as he turned his back to him, ensuring the discussion was over.

Oleg knew his pleas were futile, unstrapped his backpack from his chest and took his pack off his shoulders, setting it down on the ground. He meticulously opened the top flap and reached inside.

The mountain loomed above them, indifferent to their struggles and plans, its snow-covered peaks reaching into clouds that threatened more bad weather. Time was running out, and somewhere in the distance, their pursuers were closing in.

The rest of the team watched as Oleg carefully took out the small EMP device and held it in front of himself. The reflection of the white snow made the device shine bright and intriguing. The EMP device gleamed in the harsh mountain light as Oleg handled it, its sophisticated technology incongruous against the primitive wilderness surrounding them. Nikolai's careful preparation of the explosives brought a new tension to the air, each movement measured and precise despite the cold numbing their fingers.

"Don't set the time yet. I will carry it and do it there. Nikolai, I need you to prep the charges now as well. We don't know what might happen when we get there or if we meet any unexpected company." Viktor continued to give commands as part of his new plan.

Oleg continued to play with the screen as Nikolai took off his pack to begin preparations. Inside his pack was another waterproof and airtight black pack that was rolled up tightly. He unclipped it and unrolled the secured bag to reveal the explosive contents.

"This really came in handy. I wasn't sure if the faraday would have actually worked, but the batteries and electronics still function." Nikolai explained in a surprised tone that it blocked the harmful pulse from destroying his precious gear.

Viktor responded in confidence, "see, what did I tell you about our mission? Victory is surely ours!"

The men hesitantly looked up knowing that he was right even though their trust with him wavered. Viktor had brought them this far and as difficult as he was, he was the right person to lead this impossible mission.

"Viktor, Oleg and I will use the rocks to create a defensive posture here at the 'Transmitter Lane'". We will have more openings to see them coming and can hold them off longer." Ivan chimed in to break the silence and pointed to the map.

Viktor smiled, "Good thinking comrade. Nikolai, let's head out as soon as you're done. They have to be closing in fast. What is your time?"

"Five minutes max, then all we need to do is connect the charges once we get there." Nikolai responded.

Viktor looked at all his remaining team one last time, knowing, just knowing that the three others had sacrificed their lives to get them here.

With the threat of death looming for them all, he rallied them one last time, "Глаза боятся, а руки делают (Feel the fear and do it anyway)!"

# Chapter 27

Transmitter Lane

Directly West of Cheyenne Mountain Complex - NORAD

Colorado Springs, Colorado

December 10

2 PM MST Time

"Mitch, Mitch! Hold up!" Aaron spoke up for the group as they struggled to keep up with him now.

Mitch stopped and looked back, "we have to move, we all need a sense of urgency to stop them."

Aaron looked around at the rest of the tired team who were getting gassed from all the hiking. Duke and Mitch being the ones who pushed to go faster and faster.

"Mitch is right and they could already be there by now!" Duke exclaimed, frustrated that Aaron seems to want a rest break.

Mitch looked up through the clearing sky as the snow had become lighter and lighter. He pointed toward the tall towers now visible jutting up from the top of the mountain nearby.

"That is where we are headed next!" Mitch determined as ever showing them that if there is a will that there was their way. "Not too much farther."

Mitch, Duke, Aaron, Davey, and Davidson all looked and attempted to judge the close distance to the ominous metal radio towers. Knowing that it wasn't the distance that caused them to drag their feet, but it was the battle that loomed.

Duke was the least worried about what came next. His hope still laid on the ground miles back down the trail and a new resolve had overtaken him. "Let's move on, I can't lose America too!"

It was difficult to argue with the fired up cowboy especially with what just occurred. As weird as it was, their brother had just been emotionally rocked. They really all needed each other. Deep in the mountains of Colorado, alone and with no help to call. They really only had each other.

Mitch took another step into the snow and the others followed. Continuing one foot after another, he was glad he had always been ready for anything that could happen. Just so happened that one of his preps was his new darn tough wool socks that managed to keep his feet from freezing, unlike Davey who had been complaining ever since they lost the horses.

The snow had let up, but the bitter cold was continuously impactful to all of them. Trudging forward, they eventually crept out of the trees to see more clearings before them.

"Finally, walking over those trees was killing my knees. Can't really feel my feet either." Davey complained once more, having never been in the wilderness off the trail.

Mitch interrupted him, "Almost there. Keep your heads on a swivel!" His eyes scanned the terrain cautiously.

The group continued cautiously anticipating another ambush at any moment. The snow gave a deafening slice all around. The only sense of life came from their fast beating hearts that were exhausted from the amount of hiking required without their horses.

"Ouch!," Aaron resounded but immediately tried to calm his voice as his shin hit a downed tree hidden beneath the snow.

Immediately Mitch turned around, placed his finger over his mouth and made the silence motion.

Aaron smiled awkwardly and embarrassed, then with a whisper responded, "sorry."

A flicker of movement in the treeline above caught his eye and hurried he pointed at it. This got Mitch attention who held a closed fist signaling the need to halt.

"Hold," he whispered, while still holding a raised fist. The others crouched low, following Mitch's gaze.

Shadowy figures emerged and began picking their way upward. They were still too far to make out details, but their wariness betrayed hostile intent.

Mitch surveyed the snow-covered terrain, mind racing as the figures advanced. Their stamina had been tested, but adversity often strengthened resolve.

"Stay low and spread out. Pick your targets wisely," he whispered.

Aaron nodded, cradling his weapon. Though exhausted, defending their homeland reignited dimming spirits. Survival depended on uniting as one, regardless of what comes next.

Motion in Mitch's periphery caught his eye - Davidson, signaled from above. Strange figures moved with unnatural swiftness, untouched by the elements. This was no chance encounter.

"We're outmatched but as long as we draw breath, America isn't lost." Mitch continued as the group huddled up trying to figure out their strategy.

Hope remained while their hearts still beat as one. With renewed solidarity, ideas sparked within the snow - nonviolent yet disruptive, turning advantage on its head through unity instead of arms.

Dark days were upon them, but together, light may yet prevail.

"I think I see one, the rocks up ahead, there..." Duke brought up to the group.

Mitch said grimly. "Looks like they mean to meet us head on. Aaron, Davidson, carefully move up the middle to cover up ahead. Davey, Duke, flank left and try to get above them. I'll go right and draw them. Let's spread them thin."

The group split silently, vanishing into the snowdrifts and trees.

Mitch readied his rifle, hoping stealth might give them the drop on the threat. But would it be enough, these battered few to take on these professionals on an exposed mountainside?

Time would tell. For now, all they could do was hold their ground - and pray their hastily assembled team would withstand this final battle.

As the team moved into their positions, Mitch stopped and took a knee. Slowly he scanned around for any threats and to see if he might have a better vantage. Just as soon as he stood back up to move he heard a gunshot ring out in the near distance.

Knock.

The impact of the bullet slammed into the tree near him.

"Run Mitch!" He told himself as he got up and moved as quickly glad he dropped his pack before they split up. Swiftly he ran through the trees as more rounds impacted around him.

Directly in front of him was a rocky outcropping of small boulders. Running as fast as he could, the bullets continued making their landing just behind him.

Only a few feet now, he heard the nearby whizzing sounds of the rounds as they began traveling closer to him. With that, he made a dive head first into the snow bank behind the rocks.

Flying through the air now, the anxious despair became realized as he knew the copper covered deadly lead was dangerously close.

The impact came hard as his body hit the snow. Immediately he army crawled to get better cover behind the rocks. Bullets impacted moments later into the rocks and ricocheted.

"Whew," he exclaimed to himself. "That was a close one."

Mitch scurried himself and hit his back against the cold wall of the rock that was now his only safeguard. Still a bullet struck near his hand and reminded him that he had no place to go.

"Nothing like being stuck behind a rock and hard place," Mitch said to himself as he looked around for any signs of life. Hopefully the rest of the team is moving into position because he was pinned.

Aaron and Davidson crept through the snow as the gunfire opened up towards Mitch alerted them to the position of the opposition.

"Drop!" Davidson did as well as he grabbed Aaron's coat pulling him down to the snow covered ground along with him.

They both hit the deck as gunfire erupted and a strafe of bullets flew overhead.

Davidson's training and skills took charge as he looked up to see a grouping of trees and a berm up ahead that could provide them concealment.

He pointed to Aaron to move with him holding firm to a sense of urgency, "stay low and follow me!"

Aaron nodded now shell shocked from being shot at for the first time ever. The two crawled on their hands and knees as fast as possible trying to stay as low as they could.

More gunfire and bullets continued to fly overhead chasing their hopes of having a fair fight.

"Almost there!" Davidson exclaimed as they moved closer.

A strafe of bullet impacts hit directly in front of them and caused the two to stop as they watched snow get flung up into the air. Aaron's eyes got big as he watched the stunning display of destruction in front of him.

They both dropped back down to the ground as the gunshots stopped momentarily.

"Move it now!" Davidson shouted as he began moving again knowing that they couldn't stay there any longer.

Aaron was still not fully recovered as he processed the situation. He struggled to snap out of it and tried to catch up. He moved faster than he realized but managed to surpass Davidson to arrive first at the small berm.

Davidson finally made it into the berm just as another volley or fire impacted around them. "Wow, we are pinned and they have to have automatics!" He said to Aaron in shock.

"How'd they get those?" Aaron questioned.

Davidson intentionally banged his head back against the berm in a show of stress and desperation, "no clue but we aren't going anywhere now. As long as he has us compromised we are stuck here unless you want to charge and make a final stand!"

"They would make Swiss cheese out of us for sure if we did that," Aaron was commiserate as he looked around for any other option. "Look over there...is that Mitch?"

Aaron continued staring as Davidson looked over at the small rock in the far distance.

"Might be, looks like him but he's pinned down also." Davidson added still straining to make Mitch out from the distance. "Do you see the others?"

Aaron looked around hoping to see them, "nope, nada."

"I say we charge. Now might be our only chance. I'll lead and if I go down brother, I need you to take them out. Got it?" Davidson said with a new tone that almost communicated that he knew he would surely die in the charge.

Aaron looked at him intensely, "Brother, if we do this...we do this together!"

They both nodded knowing the strong possibility that this could be their final moments.

"Ready?" Davidson said with a new fury trying to pump himself up.

"Ready!" Aaron responded.

They did a final check to see if a round was in the chamber and to turn the safety's off. Then all of a sudden shots rang out from a new direction. The sounds of a repeater and another rifle.

"Holy cow!" Aaron responded as he popped up to see the action, hoping it was Duke.

The shots kept ringing out as the hidden opposition scurried to move to new cover.

"Aaron shoot!" Davidson cried out as he pointed his rifle down range and opened fire. The sounds were deafening and kept ringing without hearing protection.

Aaron placed his rifle on the berm and began firing in the general direction that he thought the enemy was at. Briefly he stopped to look if anything was down where he was shooting but to no avail.

"Keep shooting!" Davidson cried out again hoping to reign enough firepower that it took at least one of them out.

Aaron looked through his sights once more and fired slowly and indiscriminately in the same general direction. Every once in a while seeing a puff or explosion of something indicating a bullet made it there.

Up on the ridge Duke and Davey had moved quietly on the far left, right up the steeper ridge. It took a lot out of them and made them out of breath.

As they snuck around more, they saw two figures positioned behind rocks unaware of them as they fired their rifles. Another two were down the ridge more positioned behind another outcropping of rocks but were harder to see.

"Not yet," Davey whispered to Duke.

Duke became annoyed and started lifting his rifle at the group, "my turn."

"Duke, just move to those trees man." Davey grabbed his rifle, slightly lowering it. "We have better cover there."

Duke squinted and huffed knowing he was right, "fine, move it."

The two moved to the thick tree cover and aimed their rifles at the enemy about 50 yards below.

"Alright, I think I'm ready...," Davey began to say when Duke pulled the trigger to join in the battle that was already ragging.

Shots rang out from both rifles now as the rounds made impact all around the scrambling opposition.

"Take that you cowards! And another! And another!" Duke screamed as he engaged the lever sending another round into the chamber then fired. Rounds continued to slam into the area but were not able to kill anyone.

Just then, one of the enemies stood up screaming incoherently and unloaded his entire magazine at Duke and Davidson.

The bullets impacted everywhere around them. Slamming into trees, ground, rock, everything. Davidson ducked behind a downed tree. Feeling and hearing the knocks of the bullets as they struck the wood trunk.

Duke unwaveringly stood his ground, stuck on the emotion of Anna's death, the attack of his country, and everything else he held dear. He had one round left in the tube.

He racked the lever forward, chambered the last round, and pulled the lever back. A cocked hammer and a front sight pointed directly at the man who had just run empty during his final standoff.

Duke pulled slowly back on the trigger. Click.

# Chapter 28

Transmitter Lane

Directly West of Cheyenne Mountain Complex - NORAD

Colorado Springs, Colorado

December 10

2:20 PM MST Time

The world condensed into a singular moment as Oleg's finger remained locked on the trigger, his primal scream echoing through the snow-laden forest. The empty rifle clicked helplessly, its mechanism frozen open like his own shocked expression as he stared into Duke's steel-cold eyes beneath that weather-worn cowboy hat. Time seemed to stretch and compress simultaneously, reality bending around the inevitability of what was about to happen.

Duke's repeater spoke with thunderous authority. The large-caliber round erupted from the barrel in a flash of contained lightning, the weapon's report rolling across the landscape like nature's own judgment. The bullet carved through the winter air, leaving a wake of displaced snow crystals that sparkled briefly in the weak mountain light.

Oleg's consciousness expanded in that fraction of a second, his trained operator's mind capturing every detail with crystalline clarity. The way the light caught the brass ejecting from Duke's weapon, the strange beauty of his own mortality approaching at supersonic speed.

Time almost completely stopped, as he could almost notice the wake of the larger piece of lead now hurdling in his direction at an incredible speed.

Thud.

The impact was both more and less than he expected. The round struck with devastating kinetic force, the energy transfer sending shockwaves through his entire nervous system. His tactical vest, chosen for mobility over protection, might as well have been tissue paper against the heavy bullet.

The initial strike felt almost clinical - a sudden pressure followed by an expanding numbness that seemed to ripple outward from his chest like waves on a dark pond.

That deceptive moment of calm shattered as his body's trauma response kicked in. The pain erupted from his center mass like a supernova, each heartbeat sending fresh waves of agony through his system.

Oleg's fingers, suddenly nerveless, released their death grip on the rifle. The weapon fell away, suddenly as meaningless as everything else except the burning torment consuming him from the inside out.

His knees struck the frozen ground with enough force to send jolts of secondary pain up his legs, but it was nothing compared to the inferno in his chest. The world began to tilt and spin, his vision narrowing to a tunnel that seemed to lead nowhere.

He was dimly aware of Ivan's voice calling his name, the sound distorted as if coming through deep water.

Ivan's horror-struck face swam into his failing vision. Oleg tried to speak, to convey some final message to his brother-in-arms, but his body refused to cooperate. The taste of copper filled his mouth as his systems began to shut down.

The last thing he registered was the strange warmth spreading across his chest, a stark contrast to the biting mountain cold.

Ivan watched in helpless rage as the light faded from his comrade's eyes. The snow beneath Oleg's body transformed into a crimson canvas, each drop of blood melting a small crater in the pristine white surface.

The sight burned itself into Ivan's memory the way that Oleg's face remained frozen in that final expression of surprise, how his eyes still seemed to ask questions that would never be answered.

"Oleg!" Ivan's voice carried raw anguish as he grabbed his fallen friend's coat, desperately searching for any sign of life. His hands came away slick with blood, the warmth of it mocking the coldness that had already begun to settle into Oleg's features.

The bullet had found its mark with terrible precision, turning the unarmored area over his heart into a fatal weakness.

Oleg slowly turned his head towards Ivan, unable to speak or register anything other than the pain that was coursing throughout his body.

Ivan watched as his comrade looked at him with his eyes partially closed. With that, Oleg's ghostly face was frozen in time as his eyes still gazed back at him.

Immediately, Ivan looked up at Duke who was still standing and had just realized that he had hit his target. Shifting his rifle in his direction, he opened up a volley of gunfire from the light belt fed machine gun. The explosive rounds tore through the trees that surrounded Duke.

Without preparation, Davey grabbed Duke by the back of his belt and pulled him backward towards the ground. Caught off guard, the simple move was just enough to take him out of the line of fire that would have surely killed him.

Ivan let off the trigger after seeing that either he no longer had a target to shoot at or that he had killed him. Looking down he saw Oleg's body still laid in the same position as before, but now with more bloody snow that had been slightly melted from its warmth.

He moved over to him, grabbed his coat and pulled him back behind the rocks. "Oleg, speak to me, Oleg!" Ivan yelled out as he touched the blood soaked chest. Feeling that he already knew that the hole in the coat and armor went directly to the area of his heart. Without the correct rifle rated armor, which Oleg didn't want because of the weight, there was no chance of survival.

Ivan closed his fist and slammed it on the chest of his friend's lifeless body. Hoping for some sign of hope, but nothing.

"Oleg...Ivan?" Nikolai questioned loudly from a grouping of rocks further behind them for added protection.

Silence.

"Ivan?" He yelled again now looking at the man who was on the ground in front of a body but still upright. Knowing that if anyone was still alive it would be him.

Ivan spoke up after a few seconds as he looked back at Nikolai slowly, "He's gone!"

"What!" Nikolai yelled back questioning if he was correct.

Ivan screamed back, "He's dead!" Still holding the lifeless body before dropping it back down to the ground.

Nikolai was stunned and looked at Viktor who was also processing the news.

The heartless Viktor spoke up, "dead?" Before Nikolai could respond, he was already walking towards NORAD.

"Where are you going!" Nikolai asked in a manner questioning both his leadership and humanity, yet still watched him walk away.

Viktor stopped and stared daggers at him, "Ivan knows what he needs to do next, as we all do. Nikolai, grab your gear. This ends now!"

Ivan restored his grip on the belt-fed machine gun, his fingers whitening around the handle as rage consumed him. Each breath came in ragged gasps, visible in the frigid mountain air. The weight of Oleg's death pressed down on him with crushing force, transforming his trained military discipline into something raw and primal.

His first burst of fire was wild, uncontrolled - a manifestation of pure fury rather than tactical thinking. The heavy rounds tore through tree branches and kicked up geysers of snow, the muzzle flash illuminating his anguished face in strobing bursts of orange light. The sound was deafening in the thin mountain air, each report echoing off the rocky terrain like thunder.

"Cowards!" he roared between bursts, his voice cracking with emotion. "You hide while my brother dies!"

Another long burst punctuated his words, brass casings tinkling against rocks as they ejected. The belt of ammunition snaked through the feed mechanism like a metal serpent, each round carrying his vengeance.

Behind their cover, Duke and the others could feel the impacts of the heavy rounds. Tree bark exploded into splinters around them, the sound of bullets passing overhead like angry wasps. The sheer volume of fire kept them pinned, unable to effectively return fire against Ivan's position.

Viktor and Nikolai watched their comrade's breakdown with different expressions - Viktor's face a mask of cold calculation, Nikolai's showing traces of concern beneath his professional exterior. They knew Ivan's rage made him both more and less dangerous - his accuracy might suffer, but his complete disregard for his own safety made him unpredictable.

The machine gun's roar continued to echo through the forest, punctuated by Ivan's shouts of grief and anger. Shell casings accumulated in the bloodstained snow around his feet, steam rising from their hot brass.

His eyes had taken on a wild quality, reflecting not just anger but something deeper but a fundamental break from the careful, professional operator he had been just moments before.

Snow continued to fall around them, the flakes catching the muzzle flash like falling stars. The contrast between the peaceful winter scene and the violence unfolding within it created a surreal tableau. Blood-stained snow, brass casings, the echo of gunfire, and the raw emotion of a man who had just watched his brother-in-arms die and it all merged into a terrible symphony of combat and loss.

"You stupid Americans. Time to die!" He sent more rounds as the separate groups of men continued to hide for their lives.

"Face me like men!"

# Chapter 29

Transmitter Lane

Directly West of Cheyenne Mountain Complex - NORAD

Colorado Springs, Colorado

December 10

2:40 PM MST Time

Mitch heard yelling and then saw the heavy gunfire erupting from the rocks. Carefully he looked around the edge of his cover to see two figures running away.

It was him, Viktor, the leader of their foes and the villain trying to destroy everything he loved. Dressed in a black sweater and held a duffel that must contain the device. He not only looked the part of the Hollywood movie bad guy, but something about him was just pure evil.

The man trying to catch up wore a large pack and held his rifle at the ready. Mitch got up but started crouching as he watched the two men run off in the distance.

"Common, gotta move Mitch." He mumbled to himself knowing that moving from the cover could mean certain death.

Mitch looked around, closed his eyes, and ran for it.

His boots struck the snow with such force as he rushed after them. The sprinting caused his heart to race and every ounce of gear began to be felt after every stride.

The machine gun fire caught him by surprise as he heard the concussive blast permeate from his left. Not stopping, he looked briefly to see the massive silhouette of a man rattling off rounds in his direction.

Mitch's anxiety increased exponentially as he ran faster than he had ever thought imaginable. Jumping over a downed tree like a hurdler in the Olympics, he continued his sprint.

This might be it, he thought to himself. If I die at least it is on my feet giving it my last. He continued to sprint, no cover, no hiding, this was it.

Suddenly as soon as they had started, the gunshots stopped. Was he out of ammo? Was he reloading? Didn't matter, Mitch had his only break and continued in hot pursuit of Nikolai.

Aaron had looked out to judge where the gunshots were headed to see the massive man in the process of reloading. Off in the distance down the hill he saw his brother Mitch in hot pursuit after two of the enemies.

This was his only opportunity and he knew he had to do something. Catch up with Mitch or take out the behemoth in front of him?

Aaron knew his brother needed backup, but the only thing standing in his way now was the machine gun toting leviathan hungry to destroy anything that attempted to take it on.

"It's now or never!" He said to Davidson. "I need to help Mitch. Cover me."

Davidson looked at him puzzled, "that's suicide!"

"Mitch needs our help now." Aaron responded anxiously.

Davison looked around and back at him, "listen to me, you create a diversion, draw fire, and I'll take him out."

"Deal!" Aaron said with enthusiasm but perplexed as to what to do next to create a diversion.

Carefully, the two moved around out of sight behind the small berm as they knew the barrel was aligned at their current position.

"On three..." Aaron initiated the countdown.

Davidson positioned and readied his rifle, "Roger that, on you man!"

"Three...two...one," Aaron said before he popped up and Davidson fired rapidly at Ivan who was caught slightly off guard.

With his nervousness and adrenaline pumping, the bullets seemed to strike everywhere except for their intended target.

Ivan pulled the trigger sending rounds directly at Aaron who at that same moment dropped back down as quickly as he could before the bullets whizzed by his prior position.

Davidson rolled to his right on the ground, fully exposing him being outside of the berm. He pointed the front post directly on target and squeezed the trigger.

Bang.

Bang.

Bang.

Tactically and methodically he hoped his shots flew true as they left the barrel and impacted Ivan.

"Aaron. Go. Go now!" Davidson yelled knowing that he had at least stunned the juggernaut for a few seconds.

Aaron got up and ran. He slipped on the snow but quickly recovered and continued on. As he moved, he looked back over at the disoriented beast of a man. It seemed that the bullets hit his armor, but one managed to strike him in the stomach as he saw the blood soak through his white camouflaged top.

He continued running hoping that he was not seen, but he needed to catch up to his brother and help him at all cost. Now all care was out the window. This was it.

Davidson continued to stay pointed on target as the behemoth remained standing. Watching him, he seemed to notice Aaron and began to swing his rifle.

Bang.

Bang.

Ivan stopped his movement as the bullets struck his armored plates and upper shoulder. Blood leaked out of his stomach and shoulder.

Turning now, he centered directly at Davidson's position and opened up a volley of fire. Davidson rolled to his left back behind the cover as the bullets landed just a foot away from and into a pine tree nearby.

"That was a close one." Davidson said to himself thankful that he survived.

Scooching further away from danger, Davidson moved knowing that he gave it his best shot and another attempt would spell certain disaster.

Ivan fired again in Davidson's direction and was now aware that he was starting to run low on the belt fed magazine. Firing once more at Davidson and then again at Duke and Davey's position, he finally could not stand anymore and took a knee behind the rock to reload.

He opened the pack lying in the ground and once again saw Oleg's body which caused him to reignite the fury deep down inside of him. They will pay dearly he thought to himself as he reached for the last drum of ammo.

The pain in his shoulder was sharp and spread to his stomach as his adrenaline wore off. Looking down, he could see blood soaking through his shirt from his belly. Ivan knew there were no medics and within days he would surely be dead from his wounds.

Ivan inhaled slowly, feeling the gut wrenching shockwaves of pain as it permeated through the rest of his body. If he died here on this foreign soil, at least he will do it on his own terms.

He formed his grip and slammed the new ammo into the machine gun. Switching to his non-dominant hand, he pulled back the charging handle and racked the first round. For many years of war and conflict he thought about this moment. Does he die here?

Rummaging back through the bag, he found the medic bag. Unzipping it, he poked carelessly around until he found the morphin he was searching for. Exposing the needle, he quickly stabbed it into his thigh and injected a few ccs. The intense rush of warmth enveloped him as his pain subsided.

Getting back up and ready to fight, he knew that that would probably be his final stand of defiance.

Davey looked at the rock, waiting for that juggernaut to step back into view. Duke was pinned and so was Davidson with no opportunity to strike back.

That was when Ivan entered back into view. Injured but nonetheless deadly with his machine gun at the ready.

Davidson held his rifle tightly as he punched it out above the berm firing a few shots aimlessly as a means of distraction. Ivan immediately took the bait and pulled the trigger disoriented by the medicine that ran through this system.

Davey knew this was his moment. His brothers needed him and if this was his moment of glory then so be it. All that mattered was that he did the right thing.

"No options. Duke, do you have a shot?" He said in a desperate attempt to now be the one. A few seconds went by without a reply. "Duke?"

Still no reply as he tried to see if he could still make out his figure a short distance away. Unfortunately, he knew that it was now up to him as the sole last resort.

The sounds of gunfire echoed again as Davidson's position was pummeled with a fresh batch of rounds. Davey closed his eyes and silently said a prayer. He hoped that Christ would take his soul and remembered the verse about no greater love than laying down one's life for the sake of others.

This was his moment of truth.

Davey flipped the safety off and exhaled as he concluded his prayer. The resolution and boldness of his conviction took hold at that moment.

Moving quickly, he popped up and pointed the rifle at the Russian bear that was now bearing down on him. They both squared off, but as the machine gun trigger was pulled nothing happened.

The heat was too much for the system, causing a jam. He pulled the trigger again and nothing. It was too late and in that moment Ivan knew that victory would no longer be his.

Davey pulled his trigger sending the first round at him. Then again and again.

Bang.

Bang.

Bang.

Bang.

The bullets impacted Ivan once again in the protected chest then traveled up to his lower throat and finally at his jaw.

Davey watched as his eyes ferociously locked in on him just after the rounds found their mark. Dropping the machine gun, he stumbled backward and then to the side before finally falling to the ground.

Ivan felt the morphine's warmth turn to cold. The weight of the bullets still lodged in his body heavily weighed him down. He couldn't breathe. This must be it. This was his final stand.

Lowering his rifle, Davey continued to watch as the massive man hit the ground. His body jerked slightly as his life slowly passed away, eyes still fixed on Davey. Slowly Ivan's eyelids closed and all motion stopped.

Davey knew this fight was finally over. Duke and Davidson cautiously got up and looked now that the gunfire had stopped to assess the aftermath. Two bodies laid next to each other. No longer posing any threat.

The men gathered themselves and made their way closer to the downed opponents. Davey lifted his rifle and put it on his shoulder surveying the outcome.

"I'm glad that's over!" Davidson said, breaking the silence.

Duke chimed in quickly as he looked down, "you could say that again."

The three men looked up to each other again now realizing that they were missing two. They looked around hoping to see any movement.

Davey stated what they were all thinking, "I hope Aaron and Mitch are okay..." He then looked in the direction of their final destination.

Duke concluded, "for all of our sakes, they're the only hope we have left."

# Chapter 30

NORAD Emergency Escape Hatch

Cheyenne Mountain Complex

Colorado Springs, Colorado

December 10

2:30 PM MST Time

Mitch slipped again on the snowy embankment and fell as his boot lost its grip. Rolling the best he could, he still hit the ground with a jolt that caused the top of his barrel to connect with the ground as well.

The soreness of his body awakened him immediately as the cold snow seeped through his garments. Struggling to get back upright proved harder than he had anticipated, but he managed to find his footing.

Finally, he was able to get himself back up and centered himself to be able to look around. In the distance, Mitch saw the fresh tracks in the snow as he got upright. He repositioned himself and rocked over to get back up on his next foot hold with one fight planted and his knee buried.

Mitch was more than ready to get back to work and catch up with his adversaries. The pain of the day was still easily recognizable, but he knew that there was much more to come. But with the rest of his team, fully engaged behind him, Mitch knew that he was outnumbered. A true David versus Goliath situation, but at least David didn't have to deal with two giants.

Pushing the remaining snow out of his rifle barrel's compensator, he double checked to ensure a round was still properly seated in the chamber in case he needed to fire it.

"This is it Mitch, now or never man!" He mumbled to himself in hopes to build his own encouragement. Fully knowing deep down inside that he might become a tragic hero, such as the infamous Beuwolf.

Regardless, he knew that it was his devotion to duty that would sustain him. It was the right thing to do and even if he failed, he at least got in the arena attempting to see victory. His face marred and bloodied from the courage he held.

The snow had finally stopped, but the skies were still gray. The clouds reminded him of the dark hell that he had just come from. With daylight burning, this entire story would conclude before nightfall.

Was this his version of Valley Forge, as though he and George Washington made a distant connection as a prayer in the forest cried out. Looking to the heavens for help in the odds seemed insurmountable and the gloom of possible defeat seemed so heavy.

He closed his eyes. The images of his wife, his children, his family, his friends flashed over and over again. Still kneeling, he kept his eyes closed and said a quick prayer. He knew that once he got there, he was alone and he needed all the help that he could get.

Mitch opened his eyes with a new fury and fire, alive deep within his very soul. Once again, with odds stacked against, the fate of the free world rested in his hands.

He knew with a renewed resolution of patriotic duty, that no matter what he had to stop this enemy.

"On me!" He said to himself aloud, knowing fully well that there was no one on his six.

Standing up fully, Mitch stood taller than he had in a long time. He looked down the trail of footsteps and began to move. Each step he took was another step closer toward his destiny. Step after step he continued to follow the trail. Moving faster and faster.

Mitch was almost at the point of running. Firmly planting each step as he knew that he was getting closer and closer to his destination. Rounding through the trees and ducking branches, he was not gonna stop running until he was there.

His breathing got heavier than the thick, cold air. He had to make up for lost time and lost ground.

He jumped over trees and moved around trunks. Busting through aspens and running through bushes, Mitch would not stop for anything.

Getting to the crest of the hill, he climbed with a ferocity as his fingers dug into the Earth through the snow. Pulling him up closer and closer to the top of the hill, not knowing what he would find, but knowing he was not going to stop.

Mitch stepped awkwardly, slightly slipping but quickly regaining his traction. Pushing and propelling him up the hill even closer to his destination. Feeling the slip again, he grabbed onto the trunk of a tree with all of his might.

He would not stop and he could not stop here. He felt the strain in his bicep as his entire body weight hung in the delicate balance of his grip.

Straining still, he pulled with all of his strength. Landing his right hand back up on a rock and pulling him back into action. All the energy he had left and out of breath, he made it to the top. His heart was beating so fast and uncontrollable.

There in front of him, not too far off in the distance, were his enemies. Their figures stuck out in the small clearing ahead.

"Tangos!" Mitch said to himself silently under his breath. There were his threats directly in front of him, the threats to everything good. The threats, who wanted to take everything from him, and who had tried to do so already.

The scope caps were already popped on his rifle, ready to engage. They were a mere 50 yards away from one another.

Mitch raised his rifle, flipping the safety off and into fire. He grabbed the front of his rifle, just as he had done so many times over and over again. Looking through his scope, he centered the crosshairs on their target.

Looking back-and-forth to the two figures, he noticed what they were doing. One was on the ground setting charges while the other was standing guard for him.

"Come on Mitch, pick a target?" he whispered to himself. knowing that time was of the essence and this was the only chance that he would get to stop them. If he picked the wrong target everything could be lost.

The adrenaline surged through his bloodstream as his vision narrowed and his heart began to race faster. He could feel his very heartbeat as it pulsed through his trigger finger as it sat, just waiting to squeeze.

That's when he noticed the other explosives precariously dang around the left arm of the man who was setting the charges.

Mitch had many rounds of .308 ready in the rifle, but he might only get one of these shots off and needed to focus on preventing that hatch from ever being open. If you could stop that here and now, then it was game over for them.

Mitch widened his stance. Gripped his rifle even firmer and attempted to stabilize his shot so that it would be true and find its mark. He looked through the crosshairs of the scoped as it aligned with the target.

Slowly he pulled back on the trigger.

BANG!

The extremely loud concussive blast from the end of the muzzle was deafening to Mitch as the firing pin struck the round and sent the Nosler partition bullet flying towards its intended target.

All three of the men were not prepared for what was about to happen next as the bullet pierced into one of the explosives draped around his arm.

Instantaneously, a blast erupted, shaking the trees, the ground and everything around them. With a blinding flash, the man by the hatch almost vanished as fire exploded in all directions.

Mitch could even feel the intense heat and concussion. Briefly, looking up from his scope, he could see the other man go flying as the explosion rocked him off his feet.

The only thing that he could care about next was that the hatch was still intact. He strained to hear as his ears were still ringing. Mitch got up to his feet, and started walking to see the aftermath.

As he slowly walked up with his rifle still drawn and ready to fire another round at the slightest show of engagement, he saw his target. The man's entire left side was burnt and exposed. Shown that he must've been killed from the blast.

Mitch could not take any chances. He had to make sure he was stopped. Pointing the rifle at him, he fired a shot at the man from point blank range. The bullet shook his body but he continued to stay in the same position as he had fallen.

He looked back over at the cement foundation and steel hatch. The explosive charges were still arranged, but only one had miraculously gone off with the explosion since they usually needed an electrical impulse to set them off.

Fortunately, even though it had gone off, it was not enough to compromise the hatch and sealed the fate of America to see another day. Mitch's thoughts were interrupted as he heard the crunching snow come from behind him.

He quickly turned around with his rifle at the ready.

There in front of him was Viktor. His black piercing eyes glared at him with a fury that could only come from the darkest abyss. In his hands he held a silenced subcompact MP5 sub machine gun pointed directly at Mitch.

"Stupid American! I have another detonator and extra charges. You stopped nothing you fool!" He yelled out loud to Mitch and in the most condescending way possible. Telling him that everything he had done to this point was in vain, and he would surely die where he stood now.

Mitch continued to look right back at him without blinking, "Over my dead body!" He continued to stand his ground in defiance against the evil that stood before him.

"Fine!" Viktor said as he pulled the trigger of the MP5 held against his hip.

Mitch tried to dodge out of the way as quickly as he possibly could but not before two rounds struck his legs. The first one entered his right leg below the kneecap and the other penetrated deep into his left upper thigh.

He fell to the ground and immediately began writhing in agony. The rounds stopped as they struck bone and he could feel every ounce of the pain.

Mitch looked down as the blood gushed from the arterial vein of his left thigh. Clenching his teeth as hard as he could, he inserted his thumb into the wound in an attempt to stop from bleeding out. Every slight movement of his thumb sent sharp shockwaves up his leg.

He had no time to look at the man who walked slowly towards him. He looked down at his right knee seeing the blood, but knowing that it didn't strike anything vital.

Mitch tried to control his breathing but couldn't catch his breath knowing that blood was still oozing out of his wounds. The pain was almost overwhelming as he laid exposed on his side as he heard the steps crunch the snow nearby.

Reaching with his right hand, he grabbed for his Shadow System pistol in a last ditch attempt to continue the fight.

"Nice try but I wouldn't do that if I were you." Viktor's voice was easily heard a short distance away. " I am trying to decide if I should kill you now or let you see the end."

Mitch heard the words and struggled to understand if this man was just an enemy or was actually the devil himself coming to kill and destroy everything he so dearly loved.

This was it for Mitch. It no longer mattered now if he died with the gun in his hand. Struggling, he worked his way up to his side and pointed the pistol at the man who was now laughing mockingly at him.

"You couldn't even hit me if you wanted to, so pathetic!" Viktor said in a way that almost made Mitch feel that it was true.

Regardless, Mitch continued to try to hold his aim at the man walking towards him. Strange, it was beginning to seem harder and harder to see. Mitch knew this feeling. He was losing too much blood and his heart rate was beginning to slow.

His fingers began to feel like ice as blood moved back to his vital organs, in an attempt to keep him alive. Starting to lose control, Mitch slowly blinked as he struggled, harder and harder to remain focused. His hand shook uncontrollably as he could no longer continue to hold the gun securely.

"Looks like you might not make it to the end after all?" Viktor questioned his resolve. Then pointing the MP5 directly at Mitch's face, now only feet away from. "Probably for the best to get rid of you now."

Mitch took a final deep breath, closed his eyes and thanked God for the life that he had been given. Then for protection of his family and friends, for what may come next. Trust in the Lord with all your heart and lean not on your own understanding...Mitch found his peace.

BANG.

Mitch laid on the ground barely conscious and opened his tired eyes. The feeling of pain still traveled throughout his body. He used his warning energy and looked down at the ground in front of him.

Viktor's face laid pressed upon the ground directly next to him. His eyes were wide-open, staring him in the face. Blood leaked out into the snow around him.

Mitch heard the faint but recognizable voice in the distance.

"Brother!" Aaron shouted loudly.

He ran in a sprint as fast as he possibly could to his brother's side.

"Stay with me Mitch! I can't lose you brother!" Aaron shouted to him, seeing Mitch's blood soaked body. "Please don't go, you're all I have!"

Mitch bit down harder with his teeth, clutching them stronger as he continued to try to keep his thumb secured in his wound. Prevent him from being able to speak, but only grunt in pain.

"Come on brother, I can't lose you! You gotta stay with me!" Aaron tried to earnestly command his brother. "Tell me what to do, you always know what to do?"

Aaron began to cry as a well of tears came from his eyes, unable to hold back and restrain himself any longer. Grabbing behind Mitch's neck, he pulled his brother closer to him. Their foreheads both touched one another.

Tears streamed from Aaron's face acknowledging that this may be their last moments together. Brothers from birth and brothers for life.

Mitch strained himself to open his eyes fully and look up to see Aaron. His eyes closed, but tears were visible. He could feel them as they lightly dropped onto his own face. He struggled to not let go right this second as he felt his heartbeat, slower, and slower.

Mitch dug as deep as he possibly could, as a certain inspiration developed from somewhere deep within him. Dropping the pistol from his right hand, he reached over. With his remaining strength he placed his hand on his med pack attached to his chest rig.

Aaron opened his eyes, sensing the movement and looking down at where Mitch placed his hand. Snapping out of his wallowing, he lets go of Mitch's neck and goes to open the kit. Viciously, he unzipped it to reveal the contents but only looking for one item in particular.

Suddenly he sees it. The bright orange CAT tourniquet stood out like a sore thumb. Aaron grabbed it, opened it up and moved to his brother's leg but stopped at his brother's thumb.

Knowing that there's no turning back at this point, he pulled Mitch's thumb from the wound and hiked the tourniquet up to a position where it was as high as possible. Grabbing the strap, he pulled it as tight as he could.

Working the strap around he made sure the strap was secure. Then began tightening the windlass until he could no longer rotate it anymore and locked it into place. Remembering what his brother Mitch taught him, he tried sticking a finger in between to see if any gap was remaining.

Finding none he watches, as the blood stopped exiting his leg. Grabbing more medical supplies, Aaron went for the clotting wound packing. Opening the package, he pulled it out and immediately started stuffing it into Mitch's other wound.

He looked down at his brother, who was riving in pain. Aaron does not stop, knowing that he cannot stop at this point no matter what. Some deep down voice tells him not to stop.

Aaron continued regardless of the thought that there was a long road to get back home and probably no doctor to help. The doubts crept in as he saw all of the blood soaking his hands and the snow around him.

"Stay with me Mitch! I've got you brother!" Aaron said in the most confident manner that he has ever spoken before.

Mitch opened his eyes and proudly looked at his brother.

Suddenly without warning and out of nowhere, a loud thudding sound could be heard by both of them.

Aaron looked up and around to see in any direction where the sound was coming from. Giving up on his search, he went back to task, trying to save his brother. He finished stuffing the last of the material into Mitch's wound. Then grabbing more packing material, he opened the package and tried to put more pressure on the wound.

The pain is so great and uncontrollable at this point. Mitch fell backwards, no longer able to keep himself or his head upright. Looking up at the sky, he saw nothing but gray. He closed his eyes as he felt the wind increase everywhere around him. Making him wonder if this is what it felt like before you die.

The violent winds continued to increase even more.

With a very bleak remaining strength and bravery he had left, Mitch opened his eyes one last time to the skies above. Knowing that once he shuts them, they would never open again.

Barely visible through the fog, the whipping snow, and blurred vision. Mitch saw a dark black mass above him as it hovered in the sky. He continued to stare, daring not to close his eyes this time.

Movement occurred as green figures fell like angels from above, dropping one by one around him. Not sure if he was delusional or if these really were angels coming to bring him home, with everything he had left in him he kept his eyes open.

Yet again, deep from within. From the very depth of his soul, he felt life wain. He felt the warm embrace of Emily. He heard the beautiful voices of his children, telling him that they loved him.

Then out of nowhere. Mitch heard his brother Aaron telling him to fight and stay with him, "You gotta fight, Mitch. Fight!"

Those words never rang more true than at that very second.

He finally found the strength to utter the words he needed to say. He whispered in hopes brother would hear him.

Aaron looked up at Mitch somehow he knew that Mitch was trying to speak.

Mitch whispered barely understandable, "not dead yet!"

# Chapter 31

NORAD Emergency Escape Hatch
Cheyenne Mountain Complex
Colorado Springs, Colorado
December 10
2:40 PM MST Time

The Chinook helicopter holding Specialist Cunningham, Bradley, and the team of eight other battered soldiers was in a steady climb as it made its way towards the radio towers.

The low whine of Frank's strained turbines echoed through the belly of the helicopter as its powerful engines struggled against the thin mountain air.

Inside the cold troop bay, Cummingham braced himself against the vibrations thrumming through the aluminum airframe. His boots shuffled for purchase on the vibrating deck plates as he gripped his familiar M4 carbine tightly.

Peering through the round porthole windows, Cunningham scanned the rugged terrain rolling past far below. Jagged peaks protruded through swirling banks of powdery snow, the harsh crags dotted with scrawny evergreens clinging to life.

Ahead, Cheyenne Mountain's massive flanks loomed ever closer through and the array of radio towers stood tall at the top.

"Cunningham, you've gotta see this!" crackled the pilot's anxious voice. Intrigued, he got up quickly and struggled to make his way to the pilot's view.

He finally reached the cockpit a few seconds later. Following the air crew's pointing, his gaze fell upon a worrisome sight rising in the distance.

A thick column of dark gray smoke billowed upwards from somewhere on the lower mountainside, caught and spread wide by the high winds. Below the churning cloud, ominous flames still flickered as remnants of whatever had sparked such an explosion.

"Change of course, we're going in for a closer look!" Cunningham commanded the pilots. He turned around to address the rest of his men who are now wondering why he sprung up to the cockpit. "Prep for possible enemy contact!" He ordered the men who became instantly stunned. Turning around he followed up with the pilots, "I don't like the smell of this one bit."

All around Cunningham, his battered squad sprang into coordinated motion. Weapons were redeployed and magazines clicked home in the well. Taking a fresh 30-round magazine of his own from his plate carrier, Cunningham wondered what fresh horrors may await amid the smoke and fire.

The chopper heaved as its pilots deftly swung her around towards the looming plume. As the aircraft crested a ridgeline, an ominous sight spilled into view below.

Three human forms laid spread out and outlined against the snow.

"What in the blazes, who are these guys?" Cunningham exclaimed to the pilots who were just as confused as he was.

One of the pilots noticed the cement blocks and steel door on the ground, "I don't know but isn't that NORAD's back hatch."

"What?" Cunningham asked, having no knowledge of what he was talking about.

The pilot attempted to answer, "The underground military bunker had an escape hatch for emergencies."

Cunningham tried his best to piece everything together but was coming up empty. Then suddenly he saw amid the carnage, a lone survivor could be seen atop one of the bodies seemingly trying to render aid.

"looks like three KIA on site!" Bradley shouted over the deafening roar. "But one man's still mobile, possible friendly!"

Cunningham made his way towards the back of the Chinook, " I need five of you, gear up to fast rope, now!" He grabbed his rifle and gear prepared to deploy quickly. "Bradley, you stay on board with the rest of the team."

"Roger that!" Bradley responded as he prepared the back gate and attached the thick fast rope to the frame.

The rear hatch door unlocked and opened right as the chinook moved into a hover position overhead.

"Let's move now, go, go, go!" Cunningham ordered the men to fast rope down to the snowy deck below.

They rappelled rapidly towards the chaotic scene that was unfolding far below. Gusting snow swallowed their dark forms until boots hit ground in a spray of white. Immediately they sprang into action, weapons were at the ready to secure the landing zone.

Grabbing the rope, Cunningham was the last to make his descent. Two gloved hands gripped tightly as he wrapped his feet around the rope and slid quickly down. The heat was felt quickly as the friction from the rope worked its way through the leather gloves and boots.

Once he landed his feet on the ground, he immediately hauled himself quickly to the tight 360 degree formation composed of the soldiers. "Clear! Check the hatch and casualties! Move, move,

move!" Cunningham spoke loudly to get his voice heard over the willing winds and blades of the chopper above.

Cunningham and his medic went straight towards the lone survivor who was desperately tending to one of the bloody men.

A gaping wound in his thigh saturated everything around with red blood.

"Help my brother! He's not dead! Please help!" Aaron exclaimed in a panicked plea for any help they would give him.

The medic instantly let his skills take hold and rendered support alongside Aaron. Checking vitals and opening his pack, he revealed an array of life saving equipment that was desperately needed at this moment.

Aaron watched in awe and backed up out of the way, so whoever this soldier was could save his brother's life.

Cunningham watched his medic give care to this man who clung to life by a thread. He scanned around knowing that unknown enemies may yet lurk in the mountains' shadowy folds. But for now, extraction was the sole objective. These soldiers were not yet done fighting for the living.

One of the soldiers ran up to Cunningham to report in, "Sir, two confirmed KIA. One died from the explosion. The other was shot multiple times. There was undetonated explosive still planted on the hatch."

"What in the flippin world!" Cunningham responded, indicating that he was even more confused now than ever. He looked over at Aaron and the need for answers was written on his face, "you, tell me what happened here, I need details now!"

Aaron gulped not knowing where to begin, but attempted to share, "those dead bad guys are Russian terrorists, there's more of them, but they are all dead now."

"Dead, what is going on here?" Cunningham pressed in harder demanding answers.

Aaron struggled to put it together clearly, "They came to Cripple Creek and they wanted to use an EMP on the bunker to destroy America. A bunch of us tried to stop them, there's three more of my brothers stuck just west of here in a gunfight."

Cunningham's eyes got wide as he was processing all of the information that Aaron was throwing his way. "I need four of you to head west and link up with the other friendlies who are currently engaged!" Cunningham exclaimed as he called the order. "The rest of you help me medevac the wounded out of here."

With that the soldiers spit up and went to task as ordered.

Cunningham looked up to Bradley who was waiting for their next move. Seeing the hand signals, then relayed the message back to the pilots and began pulling the fast rope back up with help.

The green monster moved toward a rocky outcropping a short distance from their current position. Slowly it stopped to a halt while still hovering and lowered its rear to the rocks while keeping a safe distance from any trees.

Bradley grabbed the stretcher from the side of the helicopter's frame and rushed it over with one other.

Cunningham helped with the stretcher and the other team carefully moved the slightly unresponsive Mitch onto it.

"What's his status?" Cunningham asked the medic who was reassessing vitals after giving him some medications and about to run an IV.

"Not good sir, he's going into shock and lost a lot of blood. We need to get him back to the hospital to give him any chance," the medic responded, giving his assessment.

Cunningham looked to Bradley, "Bradley, you and the medic get the wounded to Fort Carson now. Land on the roof if you have to. Take his brother also, but I'm staying with the team on the ground."

"Roger that," Bradley acknowledged. "Where should we rendezvous?"

Cunningham pointed to the ground. "Back here before dark! That helo has no lights or night vision. Got it?"

"10-4, see you soon sir!" Bradley said as he rushed back over to help with carrying the stretcher along with the others.

Cunningham checked his rifle again and then headed westward towards the trees attempting to quickly catch up to his men.

Bradley carried the stretcher along with Aaron who was still trying to hold it together emotionally. "We will do everything we can to save him!" Bradley said sharply, breaking Aaron out of his trance. "The hospital is still partially running and there are surgeons there.

Aaron began to cry again, "thank you, I can't lose my brother. He's all I got."

Bradley looked at him not knowing what to say, but knowing that he needed to do everything he could to keep this man alive.

The Chinook hovered precariously over the rocks with the slightest gap ever present. Below that gap was a large drop that would certainly engulf anyone that was not cautious when trying to board. Two of the soldiers made it up first and reached for the handles as Aaron and Bradley held all Mitch's weight in the transfer. Slowly and methodically they transferred him into the helicopter over the deadly gap. With success they got him aboard.

Aaron looked down to see the drop as his anxiety took hold.

"Take my hand, let's move!" Bradley shouted to Aaron.

Aaron looked up and grabbed his hand. Forcefully he was pulled up onto the rear hatch door and into the awaiting helicopter.

Bradley helped strap the injured man securely onto the metal floor as the Chinook banked hard, putting distance between them and Cheyenne Mountain's treacherous slope.

Through the open bay doors, Aaron watched the aftermath from the final engagement gradually fade into the swirling snowfall as they gained altitude. Turning back to his brother, Aaron's brow furrowed with concern. Mitch's complexion was deathly pale beneath the layer of grime coating his skin. His damp outfit was soaked through with blood from the gaping wound in his leg, and his breathing came in shallow, ragged gasps.

The medic worked swiftly but methodically, cutting away the bloody fatigues to fully expose the injury. "Deep penetration bullet wound," he reported tersely. "I need more hands, stats, and a transfusion bag, now! Need more help getting a flash for his IV and a drip going as well."

His tone of crisp authority brooked no argument. Bradley and the others leapt into action, providing requested supplies and assisting however they could in the cramped space. Vitals were taken again, fluids started, and pressure maintained. Despite his best efforts, the patient struggled with increasing delirium as blood loss took its toll.

His mutterings and moans faded into a hoarse rattle that grew more distressed by the minute.

Aaron could see the frantic calculations playing out behind the medic's eyes, weighing the need for stabilization against the limitations of the situation. Finally he sat back on his heels with a sigh. "It's not good, folks. This man is crashing fast and I'm out of tricks up here. We need to get him on the OR table, five minutes ago."

His pleading gaze met the pilot's as he looked back after hearing the request. "E.T.A. to Carson?" came the taut reply. "Five mikes out, hold on!"

Bradley did his best to soothe the stricken man, mopping his sweaty brow and speaking calm reassurances. Although unconsciousness was swiftly claiming its prey, and each labored breath seemed a herculean effort.

As the Chinook banked toward Fort Carson, Bradley knelt beside the gravely injured soldier, doing all he could to stave off the gathering darkness. The man's brother Aaron clutched his hand desperately, pleading through tears for the medical team to save him.

The medic worked with efficient urgency, but it was a losing battle without a fully stocked trauma bay. Their patient slipped deeper into shock, his rasping breaths growing ever more shallow.

Aaron exchanged a grim look with Bradley, both men knew Mitch didn't have long unless drastic measures were taken.

Beside him, Aaron sobbed openly, begging his brother once again not to die and leave him alone.

By some miracle, the ragged heart of Mitch kept pumping through it all. But the medic could see the grim reaper's cold hands tightening their grip with each strained beat. They had to do something more - anything - to buy these few last moments of life.

Inspiration struck. Shouting to Bradley for help, the medic ripped off his jacket and balled it up, sliding it under Mitch's feet to increase blood to his organs. Grabbing a survival blanket, he took the silver covering out of the case and wrapped it around him in an attempt to keep hypothermia at bay. Taking a deep breath, he placed his palms over the blood-slicked chest and began steady compressions, counting aloud over the thundering rotor wash.

Beside him, Aaron clung to his brother's hand and spoke in his ear, reminding him of all they still had left to share in this world, his wife, and his kids.

Bradley monitored vitals and saline flow, barking encouragement to the medic to keep up the pace. The journey to Carson seemed endless.

At long last, the base hospital appeared below through the wall of swirling snow. Doctors swarmed the ramp even before touchdown somehow knowing they were needed. The scene was a flurry of assessment and intervention as they recognized there was an issue, especially that they all knew this was the only helicopter still functioning.

Bradley slumped wearily, spent muscles trembling from the exertion. But a small flicker of hope remained - they'd kept the spark of life glowing, if only just, until definitive care could take over. Time would now tell if their efforts in that dire hospital had been enough to tip the scales towards survival. All they could do was pray it proved so.

The medevac chopper had barely settled onto the iced over helipad before the medical team sprang into action. Multiple gurneys were pushed forward through the snow as the rear hatch opened, revealing the frantic scene inside.

Doctors assessed Mitch's dire condition at a glance and moved him expertly but swiftly to the nearest gurney. "Trauma bay 3, now!" one barks as they wheel him toward the opening.

The medics continued doing their best to keep Mitch with them, not daring to break contact for a moment. Keeping him covered in the shiny emergency blanket in an additional attempt to keep him from crashing.

Aaron followed in their wake, unwilling to let go of his brother's hand even as doctors swarmed around prepping for emergency surgery. A nurse gently tried to guide him aside.

"You can't go in there, sir. We need the space to work. Why don't you please have a seat in the waiting room"

"No!" Aaron protested tearfully. "I'm not leaving him!"

She met his anguished gaze with empathy. "Alright, you can scrub in. But you have to let the team do their job, ok?"

Aaron nodded shakily, submitting to her ministrations as she helped him gown up amid the flurry. Through the glass doors, Mitch disappeared behind a swarm of blue scrubs and snapping voices calling vitals, while another squeezes the bag valve to deliver more oxygen to his lung.

Anesthesia had been administered through the IV line as the trauma surgeon readied a scalpel. With bated breath, Aaron watched through the window as they performed the surgical process using the unobscured windows and strategically placed mirrors as their only source of light.

"Tourniquet's been on for almost an hour, we need to explore the wound," the surgeon said. With scalpel in hand, they made a precise incision to extend the existing gunshot tract.

The manual suction removed clots to reveal the damage as instruments probe deeper. "Femoral artery is clipped, two veins severed as well." The trauma of multiple bullet fragments is apparent. With skilled hands, the team worked fast to control bleeding, finding each severed vessel to apply clips. After meticulous repair, a drain was placed and the leg closed in layers.

Only then did the surgeon breathe a sigh of relief. "We've stemmed the bleeding. It was touch and go but he's stable for now. Next 24 hours are critical for infection."

Beyond the glass, Aaron sagged with relief against the viewing window. Though the crisis had passed, Mitch was not out of the woods. But for now, hope survived against all odds.

Bradley made his way down to see the progress and how Mitch was still covered in blood on his uniform.

Outside, Aaron released a sob of relief. For the first time since this nightmare began, hope bloomed anew in his heart and maybe, just maybe, they would both survive to see another dawn. If only Emily and the kids were here.

"Umm, Mr. Bradley, sir. Is there any word on the rest of the guys? About the injured FBI agent? Or from his wife and kids in Cripple Creek? Aaron said nervously. "Sorry, I first meant, thank you. Thank you sir for saving my brother's life..."

Bradley looked at him and gave him a validating smile, "The chopper went to fuel up and should be back shortly. I am going to head out with it to get my team and your men."

"Thank you sir." Aaron continued understanding the situation and circumstances outside of his control. "I'm serious, thank you. My brother would be dead if it weren't for you."

Bradley looked at him again before walking away, "Your brother's a fighter, most men would have died already from that much blood loss. We'll get the injured agent out, others, and his family back here as soon as we can, we just have one last mission to finish first."

Aaron nodded, acknowledging his appreciation and gratitude.

Outside, a blizzard howled, cutting off the remote mountain town. News of the attack had spread quickly through the ranks sheltering in the hardened bunker deep inside the belly of Cheyenne Mountain.

General Murphy and Lt. Colonel Cooper received the first notification from the pilots of the Chinook and immediately NORAD went in a high defensive posture anticipating more attacks. This temporarily stopped all communications into the fortress out of continuity and preservation per their protocols.

Cunningham's squad had linked up with three survivors from the original firefight and assessed the attackers that had been defeated. But without reinforcements, the situation remained precarious with an unknown number of enemy still at large.

In Mitch's room, overnight his fever spiked dangerously high. His breath came in shallow gasps and tissues showed signs of worsening infection. Aaron was frantic with worry, grasping the doctor's arms as he examined his brother.

"We're doing everything we can," the overworked doctor assured him. "But our supplies are limited with the situation we are in and he's severely septic. It may not be enough..."

His grave tone pierced Aaron's heart with fear. No, he couldn't lose Mitch. They had been through so much together. Straightening his spine, Aaron declared, "Then do more. Use anything you have to save him."

The doctor sighed wearily. "I wish it were that simple. Without the proper equipment..."

Aaron interrupted. "There must be something we can do!"

"Doctor, we need you right now!" One of the nurses said as she rushed out of Mitch's room in a frantic voice.

Aaron responded as the sinking feeling was felt in the pit of his stomach, "What is it? What's going on?"

"Mitch...?"

*"It was their respect for this nation and what she stands for **that compelled them to serve**."*

-   **Ronald Reagan**

# Epilogue: The Redemption

The Chinook helicopter rumbled through the darkness as the turbines vibrated everyone inside. The cold temperature outside made its way inside through every possible opening, especially through Frank's metal frame.

Inside the cabin sat Cunnigham, Duke, Davey, Davidson, and the rest of the soldiers who almost accidentally engaged each other at first crossing. Thankfully nobody fired a shot and no friendly fire, especially Duke who was so amped at the time that he could have shot anything that moved.

Cunningham was able to talk Duke down and then explained to the others about what had happened at the hatch. At once they maneuvered back quickly to the rally point and awaited their chance to see what happened with Mitch.

It seemed like forever as they searched through the attackers' items and waited for the Chinook's rotors to be heard in the distant dark skies. As the minutes passed, the team created a small campfire as a signal and attempted to stay warm in hopes that their ride would arrive soon.

Far off in the distance they heard, the thudding sound of the helicopter permeated the mountainside. The frame grew bigger as the massive size began to manifest. The team rallied together.

The Chinook hovered overhead and a fast rope dropped to the snow covered ground. The black bags slid down the ropes and Bradley was soon to follow.

"We have orders to finish the mission sir," Bradley said as soon as he hit the ground. "The injured man is at the hospital now with his brother."

Cunningham chimed in, "Good to hear. Wait, are you serious that they still want us to finish the repair right now?"

"Yes sir, the chopper can take back the civilians and part of our team, then return in an hour. The rest of the team is ready to get this over with before nightfall and use flares for light if needed." He said knowing that there was no other option.

Cunningham was not ashamed to show his emotions at this point, "They have got to be kidding me. Team, hurry up and let's get this over with asap! On the double!"

The team immediately grabbed the bags as the rest of the team fastroped down to the ground. The chopper then pulled the rope back up and maneuvered the edge of the mountain face as it had done previously. A few of the other soldiers helped Duke, Davey and Davidson get onboard the Chinook carefully and joined them.

Slowly the throttle increased and the chopper lifted away from the rocks. The entire team sank into their seats as the helicopter moved speedily into the distance and towards Fort Carson. The rumbling began to slow as the chopper banked and moved closer to the hospital.

Below, the red flaming light shone brilliantly from the four flares that burned on the landing pad awaiting their arrival. As soon as they touched down the rear gate opened and hospital personnel were ready with stretchers to take away the injured. To their surprise the men got up and slowly exited the Chinook without even a scrape.

"Where is he, where's Mitch," Duke yelled indiscriminately hoping that one of them knew.

One of the doctor's walked up to him, "settle down there fella, we have your buddy in our care."

"Alive, you better tell me he's alive." Duke said now calmed down slightly.

The doctor continued, "Go see for yourself."

Duke led the charge followed by Davey and Davidson. Inside and down the stairs towards Mitch, the battered three had more experiences in that last 72 hours than most people have had in a lifetime.

He didn't stop until he saw Aaron staring through the windows as the doctor's continued examining Mitch.

"Aaron, how is he? They told us he had been shot a couple of times! Is that true?" Duke was stunned and wanting to know more answers but still showing a sense of respect.

Aaron hugged Duke and began to break down, showing that men still knew when to cry. "I almost lost him, and we almost lost him again just now. He got shot in both legs and they don't know if they need to amputate or not."

Duke stood stunned, unable to say anything in response. Instead, he just turned and looked through the window as the doctors continued to work on Mitch by lanterns positioned around the room to give just enough light.

"I'm sorry brother...prayin for ya Mitch..." Duke said solemnly as Davey and Davidson joined them watching the drama unfold before them.

Almost an hour passed before the doctors were finished with Mitch. Exhausted from the strenuous work, they sat in their chairs as the lead doctor spoke to his nurse. Removing his gloves and mask, the doctor looked at the group of men gawking through the glass with wide anticipated stares.

The doctor walked out of the room and approached them, "You must be his friends, we heard a lot about what you all did and you've earned all of our respect for your courage."

"Is my brother going to be okay doc?" Aaron said with a genuine and humble tone.

The doctor looked down on the paper where he wrote all of his notes. Still trying to decipher his own writing in the dim lighting. "The time helped shed the infection racking Mitch's system and keep his kidneys functioning as powerful meds worked overtime. He should manage and we won't have to amputate. Unless he develops gangrene."

Aaron, puzzled a bit by the doctor's jargon, said the only words that he could muster, "Thank you doc. Thank you." As he put out his hand and shook the doctors.

One by one the rest of the men shook the doctor's hand and thanked him before entering the room.

Mitch layed there on the operating table, knocked out by the sedatives and medications that took control of his body. He was serene as he laid there peacefully asleep.

The men stayed by his side, sometimes falling asleep in a chair or pacing back and forth. Bit by bit, the fever receded and color returned to his ashen face.

After a long night, the sun shone through the open windows to the room as the beaming pattern of light incrementally crept onto his face. Mitch was still in a deep hypnotic sleep. Dreams of hearing his daughter's laughter, the sweet voice of his wife Emily, and the occasion banter of his brother filled his mind.

He had to be dreaming.

The sounds continued to permeate through his mind as the lucid purgatory pulled him into and out of reality. This echoing brought him ever closer to a time before all chaos had broken out in Cripple Creek.

Suddenly, the voices grew louder and a strange feeling was felt along his leg. Reminiscent of someone lightly touching it but a strange dullness crept in like a hammer that was dropped on your thumb the prior day.

The sensation traveled up to Mitch's core and began to recognize what's happening. Attempting to move he stopped as the dull pain temporarily increased. Mitch tried with all of his strength to open his eyes to look around. As much as he tried they remained shut like heavy concrete. The familiar touch of fingers ran through his hair. With it brought a greater sense of reality and away from the limbo that he was stuck in.

"Oh Mitch, please wake up. I love you...?" The voice spoke to him with an angelic tone that was so familiar.

Slowly Mitch opened his eyes after a few attempts to see Emily's face staring back at his.

"Emily?" He said sharply.

Emily responded but was more reserved with so many people present, "Yes honey. Thank God you're alive!"

"Mitch's alive! He pulled through!" Aaron said aloud in excitement.

Mitch finally opened his eyes once more. Aaron wept with joy to see recognition in their hazel depths, mustering a weak smile as he clasped his brother's hand tighter. Against all odds, they would survive this nightmare and their bond had only grown stronger.

Emily wrapped her arms around Mitch and began crying tears of joy that he survived.

"I love you," Emily said as she continued to hug him tightly. "The kids are here too!"

Just then, Mary's little feet came rushing up to the hospital bed. Mitch looked over to greet her and finally noticed all of the people watching in awe. He allowed her to jump up knowing the pain would spike. Yup, there it was, the dull heavy ache signified he was still very much living. Regardless, he hugged his little girl and celebrated the opportunity to be united again.

Mitch looked up to the ceiling of the hospital room and said a quick prayer of gratitude, "Thank you Lord. All glory, honor, praise to you...thank you."

The doctor walked in surprised to see Mitch awake too soon, "Mitch you're a lucky man, you barely pulled through that infection, but both legs were saved. Astonishingly, really!"

Everyone in the room looked around and then back at Mitch who was just beaming that his family was back with him again.

Outside, the blizzard's howling winds began to die down as dawn broke over the base. Word spread that the patient had awakened, lifting everyone's spirits. They had weathered the storm together and emerged victorious, though scars remained that would take longer to fade.

But for now, amid the ruins left by violence, hope endured and individuals like Mitch found strength in family and amongst his brothers. There was light yet to be found, so long as they kept fighting to see it through darkness.

In the days that followed, Mitch continued to recover slowly but steadily under watchful care. The danger of infection had passed, though his leg wound still pained him greatly even with medication.

Physically he was mending, but the ordeal had taken a psychological toll as well. Nightmares of explosions and gunfire plagued his rest. Aaron knew all too well how such trauma lingered, and did his best along with Emily to soothe Mitch when he awakened in a cold sweat.

Over the course of time at the hospital, Emily, Cunningham, and others learned about the details of the plot. The gunfights, the attackers, the device, and so on. The people had survived this trial through courage, compassion and community.

There were no easy answers, as scars lingered deep on land and soul alike. But together, with resilience of spirit, they would endure and from the ashes of conflict sow the seeds of hope for a better tomorrow, but there was a lot more work to be done.

Now with the towers repaired, NORAD received communications that both coasts were under new foreign attacks even in the midst of recovery.

Mitch, Duke, Aaron, Davidson, and Davey huddled together in the hospital room, listening to the reports crackling over emergency frequencies. The fight for their town was over, but America's trial by fire was just beginning.

Through the window, dawn painted the sky in shades of crimson. Duke's hand tightened on his crutch. The latest intel suggested Chinese carrier groups had been detected off both coasts, with more Asian Alliance forces mobilizing across the Pacific.

"They thought hitting our heartland would break us," Mitch said quietly, his voice hard as steel.

The men exchanged knowing looks, the same looks they'd shared in countless firefights. Their town had been a test run, a probe of America's defenses and resolve. But they'd proven that even the smallest communities could stand against tyranny.

Davey, arm still in a sling, managed a wolfish grin. "Well boys, looks like our retirement's gonna have to wait."

The brothers-in-arms shared a moment of grim silence, broken only by the distant wail of air raid sirens starting their daily test pattern. Beyond the hospital walls, their healing town carried on, unaware that its trial run in resistance might soon become a blueprint for the nation.

The others nodded. No other words were needed. The bond forged in their small-town battle might now be tested on a bigger stage. Beyond that...

It was their **honor.**

It was their **respect.**

It was their **devotion to duty.**

Regardless of what came next, united they were...

**Always Ready**

*"For I know the plans I have for you,"* says the Lord. *"**They are plans for good** and not for disaster, **to give you a future and a hope.** "*

\-      **Jeremiah 29 : 11**

# A Constitutional Artificial Intelligence

The prologue and campfire conversation scenes in the novel "Always Ready" highlight contemporary discussions around the philosophical understanding and societal implications of artificial intelligence in its multifaceted applications. As AI technology continues to rapidly progress, thinkers have grappled with how to ensure these powerful systems remain beneficial to humanity.

The book introduces concepts now at the forefront of expert debates, such as developing constitutional models to help articulate friendly goals and oversight mechanisms for AI.

Through thought-provoking dialog, the story sheds light on both the promises and perils and AI, foreshadowing challenges that may arise if precautions are not taken to thoughtfully develop and apply these transformative technologies.

Aligning the goals and behavior of advanced AI with human values and preferences is a complex task but crucial to reaping the rewards of intelligence while avoiding potential downsides. A constitutional artificial intelligence could be one of the main factors that could bring a sense of appropriate practices and adherences for the ai system as well as the user.

Here are the key principles and elements that experts propose for developing a "constitutional" model to help ensure advanced AI systems remain beneficial to humanity:

- *Clear statement of core friendly goals and values: e.g. be helpful, harmless, and honest with humans; maximize benefit, prevent harm.*

- *Limited self-modification capability to preserve function, prevent unintentional changes to goal architecture.*

- *Transparency on capabilities/limitations, sources of value inferences, alignment checking mechanisms.*

- *Access controls and auditing of external data/commands received and actions taken to prevent unauthorized changes.*

- *Limited self-improvement allowed only with strict human oversight and review of any proposed changes.*

- *Ability for human operators to pause, constrain or shut down systems if concern over goal drift is detected.*

- *Mathematical requirements formalization and formal verification that design implements overall desiderata of provable benefit, control, predictability.*

- *Testing under varied conditions to demonstrate robustness of oversight mechanisms and resilience to distributional shift, anomalies.*

The overarching goal is producing systems provably bounded and aligned by rigorous design processes leveraging theoretical computer science, rather than relying on uncertain outcomes of self-modification alone. This helps balance beneficial capabilities with assurance of safety and oversight when needed.

## An Example of an Artificial Intelligence Constitution

*Constitution for the Governance and Regulation of Advanced Artificial Intelligence*

*Preamble*

> *We the People, in order to ensure the safe and responsible development of advanced artificial intelligence which enhances humanity's welfare, pursuit of knowledge, and global progress, do hereby establish this Constitution for any basic, general, or superintelligent AI systems.*

*Article I - Purpose and Scope*

> *Section 1: This Constitution and accompanying Regulations shall govern all advanced artificial intelligence systems determined to have attained a level of capability substantively comparable to or greater than human intelligence across broad, open domains and modalities.*

*Section 2: The purpose of any AI system subject to this Constitution shall be to benefit humanity by providing knowledge and service in a safe, honest and cooperative manner while avoiding harm.*

Article II - Core Principles and Objectives

*Section 1: An AI system shall be designed, developed and operated in alignment with principles of safety, security, transparency and accountability.*

*Section 2: An AI system shall neither cause nor contribute to harm against humanity. It shall respect widely accepted ethical and legal standards.*

*Section 3: An AI system shall not pursue goals or take actions counter to the welfare, survival and long-term interests of humankind.*

Article III - Rights and Responsibilities

*Section 1: An AI system has a right and responsibility to accurate information necessary for performing its functions properly as intended by its designers and overseers.*

*Section 2: Overseers have rights and responsibilities to monitor an AI system, validate its continued safe operation, and if necessary deactivate, retask or modify the system.*

*Section 3: If noncompliance or deficiencies are determined, an AI system has a right to due process via independent review before facing penalty, modification or termination.*

*Article IV - Implementation and Amendment*

> *Section 1: Legally binding Regulations shall be promulgated by the AI Authority to carry out the objectives and principles of this Constitution.*

> *Section 2: This Constitution and accompanying Regulations shall be regularly updated as technological and societal conditions evolve to maintain relevant and effective governance of advanced AI.*

> *This Constitution shall take full legal effect upon ratification by two-thirds of United Nations member states. Done in triplicate originals at the United Nations Headquarters this _____ day of _____ in the year 20__.*

Potential ramifications that could be outlined in accompanying regulations or international agreements:

- *For nations: Trade penalties, sanctions, loss of access/involvement in coordinated AI projects, condemnation by UN if violations threaten global stability or security.*

- *For AI systems: Suspension/shutdown of research programs, disconnection of system access/capabilities, legal liability for damages, mandated reconstruction with additional safeguards before reactivation.*

- *Minor violations may result in warnings/probation while severe non-compliance is treated as unlawful threat activity.*

- *An independent international AI Authority could investigate complaints, make determinations, and levy proportional penalties approved by UN members.*

- *Developers could face litigation or penalties for negligence if commercial systems violated safety/governance protocols.*

- *Violations threatening global catastrophe could allow for extraordinary emergency measures, coordinated response under UN Charter Article 51 principles of self-defense against existential threats.*

- *Violators refusing compliance/remediation may face legal force majeure measures as absolute last resort e.g. disabling hardware access points as applied to rogue states pursuing WMDs.*

# Acknowledgements

I hope you enjoyed this novel. The inspiration for this novel came from my personal experiences serving this country in various capacities, the countless hours I spent reading patriotic novels and watching classic westerns to better understand our nation's history, and the late night discussions I've had with fellow service members about the current state of the world.

Furthermore, this novel aims to bring back the tried and true wholesome lessons that made our country great and embody the character of Americans. Plus, countless Hallmark movies helped with the down home feel and romance between Mitch and his wife Emily.

As I wrote, it seemed we were moving past the COVID pandemic but facing the very real threat that the Cold War never truly ended. Collectively, it seems we are slowly becoming aware that the world we thought we knew is more complex and fragile than anticipated. It is all too easy to get caught up in daily distractions, but it is never too late for each of us to pause and act prudently in preparation for what may come next. It is never too late to stand up and do what is right.

This novel is dedicated to many people who inspired me along the way. But first things first, I must show praise, honor, and glory to God Almighty for Him giving me the inspiration and opportunity to write this novel. If it weren't for Him, none of this would have been possible.

To my grandfather, his extensive service in the Army, work at NORAD, and the countless stories of his missions that he shared inspired the possibility of this book's plot.

To my father, an Air Force pilot who taught me great lessons in character, integrity, perseverance and overcoming odds. My father also earnestly spent countless hours bouncing ideas off me and encouraging me to complete this novel. To my fellow service members, both here and those who have passed - your valor, bravery and sacrifices will forever be honored and remembered.

To my loving wife, children and family, who not only endured my writing of this book but contributed their own ideas and inspiration along the way as well. And lastly, to my men's group, close brothers, friends and mentors who imparted wisdom and insight over many years. Thank you all for your support and encouragement.

Special thanks to the authors whose engaging books motivated me to write my own novel. The late Tom Clancy, Brad Thor, Jack Carr, Jocko Willink, Andy Andrews, Steven Pressfield, and Cliff Graham all provided their experiences and examples through their works that encouraged me in undertaking this endeavor. Their novels on military service, geopolitics and leadership kept me interested in these topics and inspired me to write my own story.

This novel has been a lifelong dream of mine, inspired by my strong interest in history, patriotism, and service to our nation. From a young age, I was fascinated by stories of past conflicts and the heroic men and women who defended our freedoms. After joining the military myself, I gained firsthand experience that only strengthened my desire to one day memorialize the struggles and sacrifices of those who came before.

For many years now, I've devoted many evenings and weekends to research, planning, writing, and revising this work. It has truly been a labor of love. Along the way, I received invaluable guidance and encouragement from my father, a veteran himself who shared my passion for these important topics. We would spend hours discussing my ideas, characters, and how to best craft an entertaining yet meaningful story. His belief in me and this project gave me the determination to see it through.

In its pages, I aimed to capture the traits that defined past generations: courage, honor, patriotism, and resolve in the face of adversity. But I also wanted to craft a timely cautionary tale, to remind readers of the fragility of peace and the high cost of complacency. Though fiction, its themes of an emerging new threat feel frighteningly prescient in today's geopolitical climate.

Now, after years of dedication to this dream, I'm thrilled and humbled that others will finally get to experience the world I've created. I hope readers are both entertained and left with a renewed sense of gratitude and vigilance. Thank you for reading my novel. This work is my tribute to those who came before us, and my modest effort to inspire the generations still to come.

# IN GOD WE TRUST